HAPPY JACK AND THE SCARY-ASS BOOK OF DOOM

Shadows Over Earth-That-Was: Volume One

Rich Partain

The characters and events portrayed in this book are fictitious. Any similarity to real persons, living or dead, is coincidental and not intended by the author.

ISBN-13: 9798865966425

Cover design by: Rich Partain
Library of Congress Control Number: 2018675309
Printed in the United States of America

For Bryant Cox, my friend. You taught me so much about laughter, friendship, kindness and loyalty. You were far better than you thought you were. In fact, you were the best. You are missed.

CONTENTS

PREFACE

This book is absolutely filthy. I'm not kidding. It is filled with adult language and adult humor. There are *at least* two F bombs per page. I haven't bothered to count the dick jokes, the "your mom" jokes, or any of the other various and sundry vulgarities within. If you are the sort that is easily offended, I can pretty much guarantee this is not the book (or soon-to-be series) for you.

There is violence and bloodshed but far less of that than of the aforementioned lewdness. There are also religious deities/ beings that are discussed in a non-traditional way that some might feel is disrespectful. I believe them to have been treated lovingly and thoughtfully with a lightly irreverent touch, but your mileage may vary.

With all of that said, if you love to laugh and think that profanity is the spice of language and are willing to fully embrace that this work of adventure/sci-fi/fantasy fiction you hold is intended to be, above all, an intentionally ridiculous COMEDY and not to be taken seriously, then come on in. The water's fine. Let 'er rip, tater chip.

After all, your mom thought it was *fucking hilarious.*

Happy Jack

and the
Scary-Ass Book of Doom

Shadows Over Earth-That-Was: Vol. 1

Rich Partain

CHAPTER ONE

Sunset is one of my favorite times. Okay ... yeah, maybe it's a cliché. Back in the 20th and 21st centuries, it was a running joke that people with any depth or airs of romance about them liked "long walks on the beach", "sunsets", and "drinking piña coladas and getting caught in the rain." And finding humor in mutual attempted adultery, or so the old song goes. I never quite got that part. Just another example of shitty people doing shitty things to each other to me, but whatever. I'm an odd duck, I suppose, hardwired for loyalty. My people are my people, and my word is something I will go to extreme lengths not to break.

It was the 1970s, though, which according to my extensive research, was a very unique decade. While I kind of like all of the aforementioned cheesy pastimes and am, in a general sense, a romantic about quite a few things in life ... old books, ancient beer styles, Scotch whisky, and good music chief among them ... this particular sunset on this particular afternoon had less to do with blonde bombshells in crocheted bikinis and guys in ball-hugging, cut-off jean shorts (What? Don't look at me like that. I don't make this shit up. Who in their right mind could? Look it up.) and more to do with the way the pink and purple clouds parted to reveal the dusty husk of old Earth, setting it ablaze with color and light. The right atmosphere is everything. There's a very dark pun in there somewhere, considering my current location.

The sun set gorgeously over the blue-green waters of the tiny faux harbor beyond my window and the pastoral walking park below with its Henry Moore-inspired sculpture garden, turning everything into an autumnal burst of burnt gold and orange hues … also reminding me of the 70s, now that I think of it. Jesus, the personal appliances of those days. I shudder from time to time and experience an odd, unearned nostalgia as I have mainly only seen the artifacts of that era in digital format and the odd antique coffee table book. I was born some 400-plus years after the last lawn dart was thrown. Freaking savages, those folks. Snazzy dressers, though. Anyway, I digress.

I was enjoying the beauty of the aforementioned natural phenomenon juxtaposed with the sad reminder of humankind's hubris and self-destructive bent from one of my favorite places on all of the orbitals: a giant, overstuffed armchair on the second-floor balcony of my shop, Happy Jack's Emporium of Cool Shit.

Ok, that's not its real name. That's just how I think of it in my head. Because my shit is indeed cool. And my regulars, rarified birds and lovers of cool shit all, would heartily agree with me. Its full name is Happy Jack's Emporium of Needful Things and Enchanting Curiosities. But that's quite the mouthful, honestly, and to be fair, everything after "Emporium" is in much smaller script on the ancient-looking pub sign outside, which sports the colorful bas-relief of a drunken 18th-century sailor in his Cracker Jacks fighting a bear in a cocktail gown. Don't fucking ask. You wouldn't like the answer. Let's just say it's something of a family crest.

Most people simply refer to my place as Happy Jack's or The Emporium. It's a smallish, three-story warehouse of super cool shit – one part antique store, one part music store, one part beer and whisky bar, and one part book store and comic shop. What an odd combination of things, one might say, if one were into things that suck and unable to fathom the awesomeness of such a nostalgia-laden adult wonderland. What can I say? I am not wealthy by any stretch of the imagination. I'm a working stiff just like most of you and barely skate by on my bills each month, but both my chosen vocation and side hustle have offered me the chance to surround myself with the things I love in life while occupying a not-too-shabby piece of real estate. Another fantastic bonus is that having these cool things in such a cool place draws cool people to me like moths to the proverbial flame. They also like to be surrounded by these things among like-minded, cool-ass folk like myself. Because that's my real stock in trade. People.

No, you fuckwits. Not in a human trafficking sort of way. Ewww. Those people need to be killed. In fact, between you and me, I might've killed one or two myself. I'm mostly a pacifist in my daily life, but you know what? Some people just need to die. Slavers are pretty high on that list for me. Along with people who prey on kids and those that talk nonstop during movies and television shows.

I mean to say I know a lot of people who know a lot of interesting and useful things. And, as G.I. Joe used to say in the cartoons, knowing is half the battle. The other half is a willingness to hand out and/or take a beating, usually. They never really came out and said that part, but it was understood.

Jesus, maybe I need a sed patch to give me a bit of focus here. There's just a lot to tell. Sunset. Me. Big-ass chair. I had an honest-to-ancient-gods actual book on my lap giving off that wonderful old book smell that digital still has yet to pull off, although some of the fancier e-readers these days actually pump a synthesized approximation of that scent at you continuously as you read. (Or the scent of baking cinnamon rolls, if you prefer.) For a scholar of the 20th and 21st centuries like myself, however, sometimes only the real thing will do.

In my right hand, I held a tumbler of very fine Scotch whisky with a few tiny pebbles of ice. At my feet, purely for shits and giggles, I had programmed a portion of the chromatocast pane in front of me to display a small Victorian-era fireplace with a burning log inside. Not big enough to interfere with the view, but just enough to make me chuckle at my own silliness. It was a fine afternoon slash soon-to-be evening after a long day of hawking pop culture artifacts and bullshitting with my regulars, and it was time to relax. Which, as you might expect, was exactly when my business partner yelled upstairs, her husky baritone snapping me immediately from my peaceful - albeit smug and just a touch self-indulgent - reverie.

"Guy down here looking for Jack," Mary Ann bellowed loudly. I sighed heavily and imagined I saw the tiny frozen orbs floating lazily in my Scotch vibrate at the throaty timbre of her beastly summons.

"No one here by that name!" I shouted back, allowing my head to loll back on the chair in exasperation.

"Hey!" she replied with a hint of playful venom in her tone. "That's not very professional." I barely heard a murmured apology to our guest as I sighed even louder and put my book on the ornate faux mahogany table beside the chair. We have a lot of faux everything these days.

"Fucksticks," I grumbled. I swirled my Scotch gently in my upturned hand as a wizard might ponder his orb and groaned upward out of my chair to stand and stretch. I ambled down the wrought-iron spiral staircase and weaved through the low shelves of vinyl LPs, books and carnival sideshow exhibits toward the bar at the Emporium's entrance. As I did so, I surreptitiously patted the left side of my hooded jacket to make sure my Narcoject pistol was nestled safely in its shoulder rig. I'm not paranoid or anything, but strangers are an unknown, and it wouldn't be the first time an old grudge came calling.

Not that I'd likely need the pistol with Mary Ann behind the bar. If the guy looked at me sideways, she'd turn him into a fleshy douchebag pretzel surprise using his tongue as a Christmas bow before I could even draw the thing, my subtly jacked reflexes aside. Sigh. I love her. She's my BFF, and she's a badass.

"Aaaannd you could've called me on your smartwatch or phone instead of yelling upstairs like an absolute barbarian. Also, not very professional," I groused, taking a sip of whisky as I glared mock menacingly at the gigantic greenish-gray woman behind the bar, who was now grinning through large, blunt mandibular tusks as she absently but professionally polished a beer glass.

My business partner, the lovely, talented and absurdly muscular Ms. Mary Ann Maguire is an orc, by the way. She wasn't born as such, of course. Nor were any of the elves, dwarves, halflings, vampires, werewolves or any other of the various cybernatural "species" of the New Earth Orbital System – NEOS for short – born any way other than as regular old human beings.

As members of a rather small yet infinitely fascinating minority of citizens in our pseudo-transhuman society, cybernaturals have elected to become something other than human through an amalgam of genetic modification and cybernetic enhancements. Not only can we choose to change our primary and secondary gender traits if we wish, but we can literally become characters out of the myths of the Old World if we so choose. Or reasonable, non-magical facsimiles. It's not supernatural, it's super-science. But to the senses – and in some cases the lizard hind-brain with its predator/prey hardwiring, it plays the same.

It's not a cheap process, nor is it a painless one, but it is a pretty natural and organic one when all things are said and done. We've grown out of the antiquated notion that other people's bodies are any of our business, luckily, and we are pretty happy to let everyone work toward making their physical reality match their mental and emotional one, whatever that may be. Be a man, be a woman, be a wholly non-binary human with characteristics of each, be a part-time, seven-foot-tall she-wolf with a furry cock and balls.

In the old days on Earth-That-Was, all of that stuff would've been politicized and polarizing, but it's amazing how an apocalyptic event that wiped out billions of people and drove the remaining few humans to the skies makes folks not sweat the small stuff so much.

No one cares much these days what's in your pants, if

anything. As long as you don't attempt to show it to them or touch them with it without their consent. And, you know, as long as you don't go murdering folks at the full moon and eating them. We still frown upon such things. Even if they've signed waivers and would like to be eaten. Don't act shocked. I've seen it. (I try not to kink shame, but what the actual fuck? Don't you Rule 34 me, either.) Otherwise, it's literally live and let live in our post-biological determinism society. Which is fine with me. I love and respect everyone ... until they give me reason not to. Just don't be a giant douchebag and we'll get along fine.

Back to Mary Ann Maguire, though. I'm pretty sure she doesn't have an Irish bone in her body, the name notwithstanding. Honestly, she probably picked it because of the greenish skin and red hair that came with the upgrade. Or Orc-grade, if you're feeling cute. For all I know, she was a skinny, teenaged Asian boy who weighed 90 pounds soaking wet before transitioning. Sometimes she gives me indications that she might've been a young black woman. Or someone's abuela. I don't know. Or care, really. She is my people, and she's exactly who she wants to be these days, living her best life. Many of her people, her adopted/chosen tribe, live on Avalon, one of the other orbitals that was crafted by the mega-rich, uber-powerful, super-nerdy Powers That Be to resemble a medieval European/Tolkien-esque Middle Earth. (Sigh. This is what happens when the Geeks inherit the Earth. Or what's left of it. Better them than the fascist, robber-baron shitbags, though, I suppose.)

Like the other cybernaturals, they've also been known to haunt the cobblestone streets of neo-Victorian/Edwardian New Arcadia and are often found here in the glittering razor chrome corporate sprawl of Elysia, too. I heard there was a small contingent of them on Canaan, the now-defunct ninth orbital that was shared by the most ultra-religious of the settlers. No one knows what happened to them exactly, but a giant floating city-state full of fundamentalists of every stripe ended up pretty much as you might imagine. I've visited the ruins once or twice for work, but save for the odd tribe of half-feral squatters, and maybe a cannibal cultist or two, there's no one there that'd be likely to know. Sometimes, in my more cynical moments, I wonder if that was the plan all along ... let the extremists take each other out. But, hey ... I might have trust issues. Among many, many others. I like to think it's part of my charm.

High tech exists on all the orbitals including Avalon, it's just well-hidden on many of the other eight surviving ones. And if you take tech there, it has to be camouflaged. People living their best lives in a more primitive fantasy state of delusion - cosplaying their days away - don't like to be reminded overmuch of reality, and NEOS has kindly and somewhat absurdly crafted laws to that effect. Like Trekkies showing up to a 21st century Ren-Faire and pretending to be time travelers, it's frowned upon ... and upheld by some uncomfortably stringent laws.

Anything goes in Elysia, though, which is a huge part of why I make it my home. The other places are fun to visit, but I really don't want to spend the rest of my life disguising my sonic toothbrush as a furry stick or sneaking into the wine cellar to watch old films on a vid unit hidden in a dusty barrel. Or keeping my business journal on a parchment with a goddamned inky quill. Fuck all that. To each their own, though. Live and let live, you weird motherfuckers. I won't judge you. Much. Out loud, anyway.

Mary Ann inclined her gigantic cranium toward our guest, who cut quite a fine figure in his trench coat and fedora, looking like he just stepped out of a neo-noir vid serial. Not to be rude, but nattily dressed or no, he looked like it was his first time in human skin ... all low-key discomfort and twitchy tics. I toyed with the idea that under his long coat he might be three sheep standing on each other's shoulders or two gap-toothed, patch-kneed kids from an Eric Powell comic trying to sneak in where they didn't belong, but I immediately discarded the idea as ludicrous, amusing as it might be.

“Daniel Davidson at your service, sir,” I announced with a bit more pomp than might strictly be warranted. “Proprietor of this quality establishment. How can I be of service? Please forgive my rudeness, but I was not expecting custom this late in the day as we are technically closed. Care for a Scotch? It’s Talisker 18 year, the Pride of New Arcadia.” I pointed my tumbler at him and waggled my eyebrows upward to indicate that the experience was damnably near impropriety and might be considered at least a misdemeanor on half of the orbitals.

“Um, I don’t ... I was told to ask for Jack? As in Happy Jack?” The man fumbled over himself as he stretched his neck and shot his cuffs, all jaundiced skin and gigantic eyes, the latter unpleasantly magnified by his thick, round spectacles. “And, no thank you.” Strange accent. Maybe a hint of Germany or Austria? Subtle, though. Barely enough to notice.

“It’s sort of an inside joke and a password all in one,” I grinned amiably, as if I didn’t have to explain this at least three times a week. “I’m the proverbial jack of all trades. Master of at least one or two, but I don’t like to brag. But, hey, nothing wrong with tooting your own horn a bit when talking shop to a potential client. Right, Mary Ann?”

The jolly green giantess grinned toothily. “I call him Double D. Because ... boobs.” She continued polishing the glass in her hand innocently.

I narrowed my eyes at her and sighed. “ANYWAY, charmingly juvenile banter aside, I’m the guy you’re looking for, Mister ...” I trailed off.

“Archer,” he said, smiling and showcasing a plethora of crooked-ass teeth that would make an Ozark hillbilly run for his Bible and maybe a blunderbuss. “Miles Archer. I have a job for you ... if you are so inclined.”

I raised an eyebrow. Miles Archer was Sam Spade’s murdered partner in the Maltese Falcon, an absolute classic of mid-20th century noir starring Humphrey Bogart and Mary Astor. Not to mention the great Peter Lorre. Which meant his name was either assumed or a waaay too on-the-nose, against astronomical odds coincidence, given his wardrobe and the fact he was standing in a veritable shrine to pop culture detritus of the past, chatting up a guy who could be the Indiana Jones of digging up said artifacts. (Come on ... Raiders of the Lost Ark? Sigh. Forget it.)

He raised an eyebrow back in a subtle mocking fashion. Ok. So, he knew I knew. And I knew that he knew I knew. *So*, I thought ... *fine*. Let's play the fucking game and see where it goes.

"Well, Mister ... *Archer*," I drawled for emphasis, because letting him know I knew he knew I knew was somehow very important to me at the moment. "Tell me more. I might be interested. Or I might just go finish this Scotch and read my book. I'm not going to lie ... it's kind of a toss-up at this point. So, sell me. Give me the elevator pitch and make me give a shit. Make it worth my while." I sipped my Scotch aggressively. Or indifferently. Or with aggressive indifference. I gestured Archer toward a dimly lit booth in the window across from the bar where we then sat, with me facing the door out of longstanding habit and painful lessons learned.

"Elevator pitch? I don't know what that is," he huffed with mild indignation, making a steeple of his fingers as he leaned slightly toward me and placed his elbows on the wood-grained tabletop. He paused for dramatic emphasis, as if to let the banality of my comments fade into pregnant silence, and then began.

"I am seeking a book. I have been told you are something of a historian as well as something of a ... finder of lost things? Someone who can take care of himself and get the job done? And who might appreciate the idea of ... uncovering knowledge that has been lost to mankind for quite some time?" He seemed to phrase everything as a question. "Someone who is, shall we say, like a two-fisted adventurer of old?" He chuckled, pleased with himself. He'd practiced this in front of a mirror, the silly git. And he was pouring it on thick. Of course, flattery from strangers (or exotic dancers) immediately raises red flags with me.

"Well, I do have two fists," I offered, sipping my Scotch. "Not a huge fan of using them unless I have to, but point taken. Tell me more about this book. Wait. It's not the goddamned Necronomicon, is it? Or De Vermis Mysteriis? Tell me this has nothing to do with the Illuminati or the Hidden Masters of Hollow Earth, because I am NOT falling for that shit again. Worst summer of my life. I have scars, and the rash lasted WEEKS. There's the door, pal."

He didn't seem to take offense, which meant I was either out of practice, charmingly and amusingly impertinent, or he was seriously in need of help. Or backed by someone that would either make it worth his while to reel me in or punish him mightily if he didn't. I wasn't sure which.

"Heh. Charming, really." (Told you. Nyah.) He smiled another insincere smile that looked like a picket fence with a board or two missing. "No, Mr. Davidson, I don't seek either of those venerated and eldritch tomes, but something a little less infamous ... perhaps of no less value, though? Are you familiar with the hierarchy of Heaven in the Christian faith? Of seraphim, cherubim and archangels, et cetera?"

"A bit. I have read of such things. Out of an academic interest, of course ... not as a devotee or practitioner, you understand," I replied, wondering where the hell he was going with the religious angle. As far as I knew, most of those folks only cared about one book, and copies of it are still pretty easy to find. Maybe a signed edition?

"Have you ever heard of the Archangel Raziel?" He practically whispered the name, reverential and maybe even with a hint of fear but also barely contained excitement. "In Jewish mysticism and some sects of the Christian faith, he is the Archangel of Mysteries, who holds the keys to the universe and of Creation. It is said he stood at the right hand of Jehovah and recorded the secrets of Creation in a book – in

Angelic script - which he passed on to Adam and Eve after their expulsion from Eden to help them find their way back to God and the garden. The other angels took issue with this and attacked him, seizing the book and casting it into the sea. God Himself retrieved it and returned it to Adam and Eve, refusing to punish Raziel."

He paused to remove his spectacles and wiped them on a hopefully as-yet-unused handkerchief he pulled from his pocket as he took a breath and cleared his throat. I took the opportunity to aim my now empty glass at Mary Ann and look pitiful. She grabbed a bottle of golden-amber liquid off the top shelf, dropped a few small ice spheres in a fresh glass and poured me a double. She sauntered over to the table and replaced my glass, turning saucily on her heel and departing with a rude gesture over her shoulder. Sigh. She-Orcs, amirite? High fives and knowing guffaws all around. Twice as salty as He-Orcs and They-Orcs. At least they are better than Were-Orcs. Nah, I'm kidding. That's not a real thing. I don't think, anyway. Fuck if I know. More things in Heaven and Low Earth Orbit, Horatio. Archer watched her go with a clinical detachment and resumed his story.

"Supposedly, the book was passed down to the prophet and patriarch Enoch, who added his own wisdom. And to Noah, who used the knowledge within to craft the ark and save human and animal kind from God's wrath ... again. And then to King Solomon, the mighty ruler and occultist, who added his wealth of forbidden, mystic knowledge: summoning rituals, arcane spells and incantations."

"From there, little is known of the path it took. It is rumored to have fallen into the hands of the Knights Templar, the warrior priests who once resided on the site of Solomon's temple fortress, and then to a Gnostic sect in France, who were supposedly burned for heresy. The rest of its journey is rife with lurid and fantastic embellishments: secret Papal vaults, thieves, pirates, assassins, buried treasure, revolutionaries, the rise and fall of empires, and narrowly dodged apocalyptic events. All conjecture and the stuff of pulp ... what were they called? Magazines? Yes. Very, ah, crazy stuff as one might say."

"I mean, no crazier than the gods and angels stuff, if you ask me," I said good-naturedly, gently rolling my glass between my palms. "But I get your point. So, this is the prize? This book. Written by an angel. You think it's real? And you want *me* to get it for you?"

"Oh, Mr. Davidson," he chuckled drily. "I *know* it's real. Beyond a shadow of a doubt. And my employers will pay you a *very* handsome fee to obtain it and deliver it into my hands."

"You KNOW? As in you've SEEN it? Held it in your hands? Rubbed the gold leaf and leather with your own grubby hands and smelled the heavenly ink?" My skepticism rolled off of me in waves, but the strange, dapper gent took no offense or notice. He merely smiled again – which increased his creep factor by 10 at the least – and opened his arms in a vaguely cruciform gesture.

"I have not seen it, nor do I need to, Mr. Davidson. I have *faith*." He rested his hands palm down on the table as if he had just played an Ace of Spades to my two of hearts and dialed down his creep-tastic toothy smile into a very smug grin. A very punch-able grin, if I am being honest. But I am nothing if not a man of infinite patience and restraint. Occasionally. Sometimes. When the situation requires it. Mostly.

"You're kidding, I hope," I groused and took a sip of the slightly chilled nectar. "Because I can't plan and execute a halfway professional endeavor of any sort based on *faith,* Mr. Archer. I need FACTS. Maps, photos, old diaries, manifests, bills of lading, a harbormaster's ledger, records of some sort, videos ... maybe even sworn testimony from a reliable source? I'll even settle for the ravings of a lunatic scrawled in blood and/or feces on the walls of an asylum in a pinch, but I need a little something more than your fervent belief that this mythological artifact does indeed exist."

"And you shall have it," he grinned again. "I did not say I operate on faith *alone*. We have eyewitness testimony and ..."

The fucker actually paused for dramatic effect. “A map.”

Archer reached into the left breast pocket of his trench coat, causing me to tense ever so slightly and switch my glass to my left hand again in case I had to chuck it into his face and pull my Narcoject to send him off to dreamland for a few hours. He took it slow, though, obviously realizing that sudden moves were a giant faux pas during business transactions with pseudo mercenary detectives and pop culture collectors of dubious repute. Is that what I am? Am I a mercenary? I had a moment of quick reflection and soul searching but came up blank. Oh, well. Why put a label on awesomeness?

Besides. I seem to vaguely remember selling my soul for a pristine 21st Century box set of Lamb of God CDs from the back of a black market oxcart on Avalon a few years back, so searching it was a fool’s errand. The entire discography, too. They were hidden in an actual LOG. It was kind of cute. Anywho ... Archer pulled out a rolled document bound in red ribbon and pushed it across the table toward me.

I reached toward it and pulled up short. “That’s not ... tell me that’s not human skin.”

“It’s not human skin,” he grinned.

“It looks like human skin,” I stated matter-of-factly. “I have skin, and I’m human. I know what it looks like. I might’ve even seen it on and off other people. I’m practically an expert.”

“It IS human skin,” he practically purred and raised his eyebrows slightly in an approximation of innuendo.

“You just said it wasn’t!” I took a sip of Scotch and gave him the stink eye.

“You told me to tell you that,” he sighed. “So, I did. But that was a lie, so I am coming clean.” He brushed imaginary dust off his left sleeve with the back of his hand.

“Fuck. I suppose I deserved that. FINE. But this is gross as hell.” I untied the ribbon and stretched out the human parchment, which appeared to be tattooed with a rather intricate – and beautiful - map. It was drawn in the style of an old European woodcut, with a colorful compass rose and everything. Of course, as the cartography represented one of the orbitals, it was obviously an homage.

"Canaan. FUCK." Of course it was Canaan. It would have to be Canaan. If I had a nattily dressed pianist sidekick stationed nearby, I'd turn to him knowingly and groan "Why'd it have to be Canaan, Sam?" And he'd commiserate in a world weary way, saying something like "Fuck if I know, boss." But I don't. More's the pity. Maybe I'll put out an ad.

"You say 'fuck' a lot," Archer offered matter-of-factly and without obvious judgment.

"I do. I *really* fucking do," I said. "Especially when it looks like I might have to visit defunct orbitals and possibly dodge religious nutbag Children-of-the-Corn cannibals for a payday."

"Oh, but what a payday it will be if you are successful, Mr. Davidson!" He grinned again and looked down, peering over his spectacles and ratcheting up the creep factor up to playground pedo levels. "We are prepared to offer you an operating budget of 50,000 credits to get you started, an additional 5,000 credits per week for the duration of the assignment, and a final sum of 250,000 credits upon the successful return of the book into our safekeeping. This amount is non-negotiable. You may take it or leave it, but we will not haggle."

I exhaled slowly and deliberately. It wasn't a bad payday at all. Not like retirement fuck-you-guys, go live on a fake beach somewhere money, but it was respectable. Like pay the rent for a few years respectable. I was intrigued. I certainly didn't like this guy or trust him as far as I could launch him with a trebuchet bought from Wish.com (They have existed continuously since the early 2000s and are still going strong. Where else would the perverts of an ultra-modern society purchase their dildo bongs and fisting sporks?), but his story checked quite a few boxes on my mental list of fun shit to do when not sitting in overstuffed armchairs reading ancient horror novels and sipping tasty beverages. I am a sucker for books, obviously, and rare, legendary items ... especially religious artifacts.

Again, not that I am a believer, but objects that have been held with such reverence by so many - especially those that might contain forbidden or esoteric knowledge – they fascinate me to no end. The simple fact that he came here with this offer let me know he knew more about me than I am comfortable with, and I doubt he's a good guesser. But, damn his googly eyes, he dangled just the right bait in front of me and tossed in a gigantic pile of credits to sweeten the deal. I probably would have taken a job like this sheerly for fun, but my clients never need to know that about me. I have a reputation and a very cool and comfortable if not opulent lifestyle to maintain.

"So, no haggling. Ok. I can respect that, I suppose. One more question ... who else is after it? Any big corporations with massive resources going to try and bump me off in a dark alley while I am book hunting? Do I need a black ops team as backup?"

"You have a black ops team on call?" He looked slightly impressed.

"Not as such," I allowed. "But I can put together a pretty close approximation on short notice." He could take that as an implied threat if he liked, but it was a simple statement of truth.

"I do not think that will be necessary," he said. "I do not believe there are other interested parties in play, but I could be wrong. I certainly would not go unarmed, were I in your place."

"Well, duh," I said, in a snarky but not malicious way. "It's Canaan. Going unarmed would be like rubbing myself down with barbecue sauce and jumping into a dog fighting pit."

"You are so very colorful, Mr. Davidson." His smile didn't reach the corner of his eyes. "If you are half as competent as you are pithy and droll, we shall have our prize in no time."

"Not going to tell me who WE are, are you?" I offered.

"No," he stated simply. "That is information that you do not require to succeed, and I believe we are paying you enough that discretion on both our parts is within the bounds of our contract as it were."

"Fine." I was used to working with middlemen. "I had to ask, though."

We concluded our business with few more words and he handed me a credstick, which I touched to my smartwatch to upload to my bank account. 50,000 credits as promised, along with a digital contact card. Archer smiled and said his goodbyes and slouched creepily out of my shop. I scanned and digitized the map with my watch as well and backed it up to cloud storage so that I didn't have to worry about losing it in the course of my adventures, and then I set about making a travel plan and checklist for my loadout on a holographic touchscreen the watch projected in front of me. Mary Ann finished her duties behind the bar, poured herself a glass of clear liquor of some kind and made her way over to the booth, squeezing her muscular bulk into the seat across from me in a feat just short of miraculous.

"I don't like him, D," she said in a low, husky voice. Not sultry, mind you, more of a subtle warning growl. "I don't like you going to Canaan, either. And I HATE religious nuts."

"You and I are of one mind on this, as usual," I said, sipping my Scotch. "But it's a hell of a payday, and I may get to gander at the source code of Creation if the stories are true."

"I highly doubt that," she said with a grimace. "You don't buy into that crap any more than I do."

"Not really," I said. "But there's often a touch of truth at the heart of most myths, however fantastical and fuckwitted. I mean, look at us, for instance. I'm sitting here drinking with and chatting up a horrifying creature out of high fantasy as she Mother Hens me." I grinned.

"I am NOT Mother Henning you, you douche," she cocked her middle finger with her thumb and flicked me on the arm hard enough to leave a welt through my hoodie. "I'm your friend and your business partner and I have a vested interest in you being in one piece, you ass. And I'm horrifyingly HOT." She grinned and licked an oversized incisor as a wolf might before pouncing on her prey.

"As your colleague in this oh-so-professional endeavor, I can neither confirm nor deny this lest I get a visit from HR in the morning," I warned solemnly.

"I'm HR," she grinned.

"That's what worries me," I chuckled. "You're grumpy as fuck in the morning and would likely turn me into pulp before throwing a pink slip onto ... or into ... my remains."

"Touché," she smiled and took a sip of her drink, the ice cubes clinking against her fangs.

"Besides," I said, "If I get into trouble, I'll call you or one of the gang to assist. You can certainly manage the place for a few weeks without me. Feel free to call in help if you get in the weeds."

"I knew you were hooked," she said, shaking her head. "I knew it from the way you looked like a kid opening Christmas presents when Mr. Creeper started talking about spooky-ass books. Your face actually lit up. You, my friend, are predictable AF - as the kids say - when it comes to treasure hunts. It's like he knew your True Name and summoned you from a floor-drawn pentacle surrounded by bottles of Scotch and old metal music. This is the sort of thing you'd do for a lark without any payday whatsoever, isn't it?"

She knows me way too well. Good thing she's on my side.

I grinned and winked at her in an exaggerated fashion. "Maaaybe. Anyway, I'm in for a penny, a pound or 30 pieces of silver." I tossed back my drink. "Let's shut this place down for the night. I have packing to do."

CHAPTER TWO

Ah, packing. I do enjoy a good loadout. There is something totally Zen about standing in front of a giant, well-lit armored safe and picking out the toys you might need for a given excursion. I would imagine it is akin to the feeling a well-heeled lady or gent or non-binary folk get when they are shopping at a high-end tailor or dressmaker and money is no object. I mean, I already own all this stuff, so it's a little different, but it is still a really cool feeling.

The next morning, after hitting the old treadmill (A.K.A. dreadmill) for an hour or so in my little apartment in the Emporium's basement, I scarfed down a protein bar and protein shake and showered up. I wrapped myself in an oversized towel and went shopping as it were. Next to my bedroom, I have a little rec room with a vintage billiard table, a pinball machine and a stand-up multicade filled with thousands of classic video games from the 20th and 21st centuries. Because I am a giant nerd, obviously. There is also a refurbished ancient CD jukebox filled with my favorites, which includes a lot of classic metal but also some jazz, blues, classic R&B – I love the Stax sound – and even some gothic-ass classic country.

One of my favorite features of the room, however, are two vintage soda machines, Coke and Pepsi, naturally ... both veterans of the soda wars of the mid-1980s. While they light up and are fully functional, I've added a few mods. They've been retrofitted to function with mechanical guts that are half the depth of the old machines, and a quick swipe of my smartwatch in the right spot causes both to swing outward like cabinet doors, exposing my armory. The left cabinet behind the Coke machine houses my special wardrobe, with reinforced and armored clothing to fit the quirky time period of each orbital. Victorian/Edwardian dress for New Arcadia, barbaric bullshit for Avalon, and on down the line. A huge part of my stock in trade is blending in, and even if stealth wasn't paramount, well, abiding by the dumbass NEOS laws makes my life much easier. While I have no doubt I would enjoy all the time for reading and sketching and working out that a stint in prison might allow, the limited choices of victuals, refreshments and sexual partners would no doubt thoroughly harsh my mellow. Along with the fact that consent or lack thereof isn't a huge deal behind bars.

The right side hidden by the Pepsi machine is strictly weaponry, also period specific ... or tooled to look like it, anyway. Sword cane and a Webley repro, chambered in an absolutely absurd size to please (or threaten) the neo-Anglos; blades of all shapes and sizes if I have to visit Avalon, Nirvana, Tian or Valhalla; and lots of guns for everywhere else. Including varieties of Narcoject pistols for several of the genre-specific geeklands. My favorite is probably the 10-shot pepperbox Derringer Narcoject with its spring loaded forearm holster. Makes me feel like a riverboat gambler.

I *am* willing to kill if it is absolutely necessary to protect my own life, but I prefer not to. I may be a mercenary sonofabitch, but I'm not an asshole. The Narcoject line, with its needle-thin spines laced with an unholy amalgam of spider and blowfish toxins that will pierce even the toughest hides and many armors as well, will reliably put the toughest brutes to sleep for hours. Long enough for me to do my business and GTFO, usually. If not, there's always the old double tap, but that usually unlocks the floodgates of bodily function and causes a huge, reeking mess. Anyway, I'm a bit of a gearhead but not quite a collector when it comes to weaponry. Strictly functional, pragmatic and useful. A few sniper rifles, a CQB rifle or two, a couple of shotguns, and a smattering of pistols.

So, I knew this mission would start out in Canaan – thanks to the handy-dandy gross-as-fuck fleshmap - but I had no idea where it would end up. My luck being what it is, I would have to visit three or four orbitals and the ruins of Old Earth to grab this bitch of a book, so I did not pack light. Am I prescient? No, but it is always my policy to hope for the best and expect (and pack) for the worst. I threw a bunch of my kits in transit cases and dressed for casual non-period specific battle: black hoodie and stretchy jeans over light Second Skyn nano-armor, lightweight and waterproof crew-style steel-toe shoes, classic Wayfarer HUD specs, Narcoject pistol in my left shoulder rig, my 15-round .40-caliber Colt Heathen in a SOB (small-of-back) holster. Throwing knife in my left forearm sheath, stiletto in my right calf rig. Multi-tool with a tiny cutting laser on my hip. Small sling bag with some zip-tie restraints and various sundries. Slouchy beanie for style and warmth. I double-checked my smartwatch for the map, and I was just about ready to go. I stole a peek in the mirror. I looked like the Unabomber, for fuck's sake. Oh, well.

For shits and giggles, I snagged and bagged one of my favorite sniper rifles, the Excalibur SR-2500, a modern take on the workhorse Knight's Armament SR-25 used by spec ops teams around the world in the latter half of the 20th century and well into the 21st. Why fuck with perfection? It is chambered in 7.62×51mm NATO. With integral next-gen suppression allowing it to be comfortably used without ear protection, a 25-round magazine and an effective range over 1,000 meters, it is one of my favorite tack drivers. Extremely versatile, too. As it's only about six inches longer than your average combat rifle, it fulfils the role of a sniper rifle well, but it is still useful in damned close quarters or on the run. It has a low profile night-vision scope that brings things in pretty close and also has an infrared laser that pairs with my HUD specs, popping up a floating targeting reticle in my line of sight. It's pretty sexy as far as weapons go. I'm not saying I'd actually make out with it, but after a few too many drinks, who knows?

I say that for purely for dramatic effect, by the way. Getting drunk is not something I actually do, although my taste for Scotch and well-crafted beers might hint otherwise. I am not physically capable of getting drunk these days, as aside from a few other tasteful and not-too-invasive cybernetic body mods, I have an in-line esophageal filter that can handle just about every toxin known to humankind, including ethanol. I don't really miss it, as my state of being and/or perceptions being altered has never been something of which I am a huge fan. Bit of a control freak, I guess? Or maybe it's just that hangovers suck and I really hate the feeling that I may have done or said something incredibly stupid or hurtful while in my cups, as they say. At any rate, I do love my adult beverages, but strictly for the taste and inherent ritual.

I added a couple of spare mags for the Excalibur, although I hoped neither the rifle nor the spare ammo would be needed. Like I said, I'm not a huge fan of needless killing. It is almost always a "me or them" situation. But, if it comes down to that, it's gonna be me, kids. I'm a big fan of being alive, and I kind of take it personally when others take issue with that. If they are trying to kill me, fuck 'em and let the gods sort 'em out. Finally, last but not least, I grabbed a gargantuan, safety orange, ruggedized case branded with biohazard symbols. Can't forget my boys.

I stacked my loadout onto a small cart, slung the rifle bag on my shoulder and headed to the garage. I stopped to key in my personal code on the reinforced door's keypad, touched it with my watch for authentication, and then stepped in. The lights automatically snapped on, revealing my baby in all of its somewhat tacky glory ... cue spotlight, drumroll please ... ladies and gents, I give you the Shaggin' Wagon: my glorious orbital-hopping hover van. At home in the skies, on the streets of Elysia, or even the water if it comes to it. Said streets are not very crowded, luckily, as the NEOS public transit system is spectacular, and personal vehicles require all manner of licensure and the jumping through of many hoops, not to mention a pretty hefty cost besides. Fortunately for me and my innate sense of style, my job requires transportation with decent storage, and although it took me several years of grinding and filling out paperwork, the noble steed became mine. Oh, yes. I like to think we have enjoyed a mutually beneficial relationship.

Custom built, like all personal vehicles these days as production models are a thing of the past, the Shaggin' Wagon is an absolute beast, a giant slab of gleaming, metallic menace. The name is ironic, by the way: a throwback to the boxy, wheeled beasts of the 1970s it is modeled after and not a nod to any proclivity on my part for actually having sex inside. Not that, um, that hasn't happened. On occasion.

The Shaggin' Wagon – or SW for short – is a 2473 Honda Kustom HoverVan. Aside from the downward and back-facing vents of the circular gravlifts that fill her wheel wells, it greatly resembles the classic mid 1970s Gerring Streaker from which her inspiration comes. Gerring, Inc. was a company out of Elkhart, Indiana, that heavily modified and customized Dodge panel vans. This particular model is slightly more elongated than the classic, giving me about four more feet of interior. Like the original, it has a somewhat gothic, nautical-inspired theme (think Captain Nemo meets H.P. Lovecraft) that includes faux-wood paneled walls and floors, brass and copper appointments, a comfortable memory foam bunk bed that drops down from the driver's side wall on chains, a large memory foam rear bench that folds down into another bed, and faux-brass porthole windows at the upper rear of the body. It has lockers for small arms and storage, comfy captain's chair style seating, and plenty of other amenities, including a small bar, micro-kitchenette, a micro-mini restroom, and a food replicator. Fully computerized, ruggedized and lightly armored, it's my kitschy home away from home while on jobs.

The chromatocast paint job can be changed with a simple button push to matte or glossy versions of just about any color on the visible spectrum or to preprogrammed themes.

Hidden cameras along the body even allow the exterior to mimic its surroundings if need be, providing wonderful visual and digital camouflage, stopping just short of actual invisibility. With my music and media collection downloaded to the onboard server and a bang-up autopilot, it's a fantastic way to travel. Especially for an outgoing introvert like myself who loves people but also needs frequent breaks from being surrounded by them.

Currently, the SW is sporting one of my favorite exterior themes, a totally on-brand version of Frank Frazetta's Death Dealer, brandishing his well-worn ax as he sits atop his devilish mount on a pile of skulls. I also have a theme that has Tolkien's wizard Gandalf fighting a Balrog of Morgoth on the bridge in the Mines of Moria. It's pretty choice. Under the hood, the fusion drive nets me an airspeed of about 300 knots in low orbit or atmo and 50 knots in the water, half that if fully submerged. And it never needs refueling, obviously. Just a pit-stop for some new reactive material every 18-24 months, depending on how hard and how often I've travelled. The gravlifts give me full vertical takeoff and landing, and an additional large, flat grav buffer underneath helps cushion the ride if I am actually going over land.

In summation, imagine me slapping the roof like the proverbial used car salesman and telling you how much sheer awesomeness it can fit inside. It was neither cheap nor easy to obtain and outfit, but it has been totally worth every credit spent and every hour filling out paperwork. For two years, the Shaggin' Wagon has taken me everywhere I need to go in the lap of luxury and the pinnacle of style. As far as my rather Spartan, stoic and modest notions of those concepts go, anyway.

Fully packed and ready to head out, I walked up the side ramp and sealed it behind me. I plopped down in the pilot's seat and voice dialed Mary Ann for a quick video chat.

"UGH. WHAT THE FUCK DO YOU WANT AT THIS HOUR, D?" the sleepy giantess' growl issued from the cockpit speakers as her blanketed bulk appeared onscreen in night-vision green from her apartment bedroom.

"Potty mouth," I replied, drily. "Do you kiss your mother with that cesspool?"

"I kiss YOUR mother with this cesspool. I WILL reach through this phone and throttle you, you smug, cheerful, morning-person sonofabitch."

"I resent that. I am NOT a morning person. It's not even morning, you gorgeous, giant green sloth," I cheerily replied. "It's noon, and I'm headed out. Popping over to Canaan to look for this fucking book and get us a big ol' payday. Wanted to call and give you smooches and ask you to double check my tracking chip and the Shaggin' Wagon's before we get too far out."

"'K. Lemme look. Smooches to you too, I fucking guess. With morning breath. You are so lucky to have me." She rolled over with her back to me and grabbed her hand terminal from her other nightstand. "Yup. Two blips in your garage. I'll check in on you periodically. You do the same. You strapped to the gills? Are you sure you don't need to call in backup? Canaan is mondo ooky-spay, and I don't want you to end up getting eaten and shat out by feral cannibals. It's just not dignified. Not to mention I'd have to find another business partner and BFF, and I generally don't like people. And the audition process SUCKS."

"Doesn't stop you from plowing and/or getting plowed by them with an alarming frequency, though, you gigantic, emerald slut," I remarked, good-naturedly. "But, yes, I am heavily armed. And I have the boys with me."

"Do NOT slut-shame me, Daniel," she warned with a voice that had risen a whole octave. "Firstly, it's called being sexually liberated. I am a grown-ass orc woman, and I do whatever or whomever I want. Secondly, you are a hypocrite. You did not seem to mind when you were on the receiving end of my singular talents." If there had been an old-school curlicue phone cord, she would have twirled it around her finger. As it was, she just bounced her bushy eyebrows lasciviously.

"Thirdly, you are a turd. And a homely one at that"

"Jesus. You're never going to let that go, are you? That's ancient history, Maguire. We were young and drunk and too foolish to see what an historically bad romantic pairing we were. We work much better as friends. And I needed the money. College didn't pay for itself, you know. Plus, I kinda felt sorry for you."

"We were not drunk, just mildly uninhibited, and romance had little to do with it. It was pure animal lust. And availability. Had there actually been an *attractive* partner nearby for me to ... but, it WAS kind of cute how you did that thing with your ..."

"Silence, fiend. I am hanging up on you now. Try not to bone the entire orbital while I am gone."

"No promises, Tiger. Mama has needs. Mrrrrrow."

"Gross. Whatevs. Just don't use the shop. Love you, miss you, mean it. Out."

She blew a raspberry at the camera and hung up. Sigh. Orc women. Of course, she's probably sighing and lamenting human men. It's the least we deserve.

Good-byes said and safety measures engaged, I raised the garage door, fired up the fusion drive and headed toward the nearby port. I dialed up some classic driving music, Fu Manchu's "King of the Road", and put the pedal to the proverbial metal.

CHAPTER THREE

Ten minutes later, I was checking in with the Harbourmaster at Orbital Flight Control, stating my business, my destination, flight plan, expected length of stay, etc. There are no rules against visiting Canaan, mind you. It's just not generally considered a smart idea. So, this trip at least, I had nothing to hide. Boxes checked, digital signatures transmitted, I was waved on and my journey began in earnest.

The trip from Elysia to Canaan is not a quick one. Elysia is in roughly geostationary orbit over the city once known as Eureka, California. Canaan, or what is left of it, is above what once was Montgomery, Alabama. So, with the Shaggin' Wagon operating at top speed, the trip takes roughly 6.25 hours. I engaged the autopilot and popped back to the food replicator to whip up some lunch. I programmed in one of my favorite meals ... a personal Chicago-style deep dish pizza with pepperoni, Italian sausage, black olives and mushrooms along with a West Coast IPA. Boring fuck that I am, it's a mostly healthy version with cauliflower crust, turkey sausage and turkey pepperoni. Sigh. I know. What can I say? The full flavor version is more fun, but hypertension and heart disease run in my family. Fuck off. Modern medicine can only do so much when your lifestyle choices are shit. Thirty seconds later, my meal appeared. I took it back to the table next to the kitchenette and called up a video on the media wall. Much happiness ensued.

In the meantime, it occurs to me that I may not have fully described the orbitals and our modern society in a fashion that does not leave you with questions galore. I have no idea what the world will be like when you are reading this, or if humans will still be around at all.

Maybe our orbitals have crashed and fallen into the sea. For all I know, you are a tiny grey humanoid with giant almond-shaped eyes seeking to learn what our society was like in the 2400s … an alien sociologist picking through our Preservation Vault on Luna in the year 4000. If that is the case, allow me to apologize that you've stumbled upon my foul-mouthed adventure stories in an attempt to understand our culture. Hopefully your people have a sense of humor. Maybe you're a future human and are curious about what happened after we trashed our home planet and took to the skies. At any rate, let us enjoy a brief interlude of exposition for your edification and, hopefully, entertainment.

About 300 years ago, the scientists on Earth-That-Was decided we needed an escape plan. After centuries of sci-fi adventures and speculative fiction about colonizing and terraforming other planets and star-systems aside, we as a species decided that YES, we do need to do something as we have shit the bed climatologically speaking.

However, as exciting and interesting as those stories were, the fact was that it took a tremendous amount of resources to launch people across the solar system, much less the galaxy. And, if we were successful at doing that, our colonists would end up in a place with no breathable atmosphere, natural resources ranging from slim to none, AND they would be waaaay too far away from the one planet that does have all the things we need to support life to do much about it. So, the plan for NEOS was born. The New Earth Orbital System would be a way for us to escape the increasingly inhospitable surface of our planet without having to travel too far or to a planet or moon that was downright inhospitable and incompatible with human life.

The polar ice caps melted as predicted, bringing the sea levels up 200-plus feet. Strip mining, relentless deforestation and wildfires led to inhospitable CO2 levels and raging, unpredictable storms on the surface. Our population decimated by wars, pandemics and various other shitty human-caused problems, the remaining folks - approximately 5 million of them at the time - constructed giant city-sized platforms in low-Earth orbit and then gently dropped them down to just inside the troposphere, taking advantage of the proximity to all of the resources we need AND our planet's still mostly-intact atmosphere, which conveniently protects us from micro-meteors and being baked to a crisp by good ol' Sol.

Each orbital holds approximately a half million folks, a number that is pretty strictly adhered to for sustainability's sake, and measures about 15 miles in diameter for a habitable surface of about 180 square miles, or about the size of San Jose, California, back in our surface-dwelling days. Buildings near the edge are smaller in size and grow taller as one goes inward. Each orbital has 51 sub floors that mostly contain the anti-grav engines, power conversion plants, and other support machinery as well as hangar bays.

Technically, "orbital" is a misnomer as the orbitals themselves - as I mentioned - are not high enough to be in *actual* orbit anymore as that would negate the protection the remains of our atmosphere offers. They are only about five miles up. I guess the Powers That Be thought orbital sounded cooler than Big-Ass Floating Domed Cities? NEOS does have more of a ring than NEBAFDCS to be sure. I'm not even sure how one would pronounce that.

Through some sort of magic bullet technology that is way too difficult for my tiny brain to understand, the orbitals manage to generate enough power to keep their high-tech, anti-gravity systems running and keep these giant structures aloft that, frankly, have no business floating around the sky. I do know that the giant domes overhead and the orbital rims are covered with transparent solar panels and studded with wind turbines. The undersides as well. Practically every bit of running water on the orbitals, from creeks and rivers to the actual water pipes themselves have turbines in them.

An incredible amount of power is needed to keep the orbitals afloat and run our cities and towns. Well, the high-tech ones, anyway.

The orbitals tend to change altitude slightly in a rough approximation of the seasons. We basically terraformed these huge metal discs with all of the actual dirt and plant life and water we could reasonably pack in and spent the better part of a decade making them look like old Earth. Some of the orbitals even have entire buildings that were moved over piece by piece. Usually beloved or sacred structures, but also some ugly-ass, low-key skyscrapers. Avalon inherited some of Europe's cooler castles, as did New Arcadia. Tian has some wicked cool temples, including the entirety of Angkor Wat. Ditto Nirvana. A'aru actually scored the Great Pyramid of Giza, which sits near its center. I figure they probably worked some mojo and shaved some weight off, though. The surface of Earth is still used for mining and any number of harvesting operations, but no one actually calls it home anymore. I make periodic trips there to scour the ruins of settlements that remained above sea level for pop culture artifacts, but I have to wear an EVA suit whenever I leave my vehicle.

There are nine orbitals in all, including the miraculously still-floating, busted-ass hulk of Canaan. The largest of them is Elysia, the cyberpunk madhouse I call home. It is in a semi-geosynchronous "orbit" centered above the Pacific Northwest and Northern California. As I have said, anything goes there: misfit central, high-tech wonderland with coffin hotels, high-end brothels, black clinics, and all the cybernetic mods one could ever want. Not to mention the weird-ass flotsam and jetsam from the other orbitals. Canaan, or what is left of it, floats over what was formerly known as the Bible Belt: basically the American south.

New Arcadia, home to all things Anglophile, is perennially stuck between the Elizabethan and Edwardian eras of English culture with a touch of steampunk thrown in for good measure. It hovers roughly over the Isle of Man in the Irish

Sea. Avalon, the Medieval/Tolkien-esque fantasy world full of orcs, goblins, paladins and hobbits, generally can be found over Munich, Germany. Tian floats over the general vicinity of old Hong Kong and is a giant mishmash of feudal Japanese, ancient Chinese, and Indonesian cultures with a smattering of Polynesia. Valhalla, as one might assume, is a Scandinavian/Viking wonderland that hangs around in the skies over Umea, Sweden. Nirvana is home to the ancient cultures of India and Pakistan and spends its time over Katmandu, Nepal. A'aru, named after the idealized Egyptian afterlife, is the home of pre-colonial African, Egyptian, and Middle Eastern cultures. It hovers near north central Africa, specifically Aozou in Chad. Aztlán is home to a society steeped in pre-Columbian Mesoamerican traditions. It is located above Bogota, Columbia.

As you might guess, the more agrarian orbitals with their pastoral settings act as our breadbaskets. Elysia and parts of A'aru and Nirvana tend to pump out all the technological innovations that make the rest work. There's tons of trade between the orbitals, and some well-to-do folks even have homes on several of them. And that's it. There have been rumors for centuries of a secret tenth orbital, but I have little information other than the speculation of conspiracy theorists as to whether or not it is real. There's even a little cult of folks who believe the tenth orbital was built by aliens, and that we used their advanced tech to build ours. I mean, nine IS an odd number. Sure, there were nine ringwraiths, and nine members of Slipknot. But 10 is such a nice, round, even number. Anyway. Maybe someday someone will pay me enough money to find out.

If you're at all interested about me, your cheerful, mercenary protagonist, well, I hardly know where to start. I'm just your average guy ... average height, average weight, dirty-blond hair, grey-blue eyes. Almost 50 years of age, which in the 20th and 21st centuries would have been well into middle age, but these days science and medicine have come so far that 150 years of age is well within reach for most people. 50 is the new

30, as they say. I work hard to stay fit, but I'm hardly an action hero. If I dehydrate and starve myself for a week or so, you might see an ab or two. I'm a bit of a smartass, which should come as no shock whatsoever to anyone who has been paying attention. I have an incredibly wild and varied background, which lends to my reputation as a jack of all trades. I have been an investigative reporter, an officer of the law, a computer and network troubleshooter, a day laborer, a security specialist, a bartender, a cook, a bar manager, and a semi-professional musician.

I have studied four martial arts, but I am no master of any of them. I am a decent marksman, aided by kickass gear, which elevates me to mere competence. I am a passable swordsman. My life has been one of constant change, but I would not trade any of it for the world. My past makes me who I am. I am like a far less erudite version of Samuel Langhorne Clemens, that amazing Renaissance man better known by his pen name of Mark Twain. I'm not half as quotable or cool, but I've at least held as many jobs as that clever, mustachioed bastard.

In short, I can hold my own in a fistfight or a gunfight, I'm well read, and I have enough life experience to help me figure out a puzzle or two. I have a few fun cybernetic mods, including jacked reflexes, micro-thin subdermal interfaces in my palms that connect to my smart guns, and my toxin filter, but I draw the line at anything more. I'm still 99% human, and I intend to stay that way. I know folks who have tipped the balance in favor of full machination, and they make me sad. They have skills that are off the charts and that make me look like an absolute newb at anything and everything, but they have lost something essential that I am not sure I can quantify. I am still a hugely flawed human being with appetites and passions, but I would not have it any other way. I cry at movies and when hearing music that elevates the human (or transhuman) condition.

I love my tunes, I love my stories, I love my food and drink. I love my people and will fight for them to the death if need be. Including my jolly green giantess of a platonic (except for that ONE weekend that she manages to bring up constantly to fuck with me) life and work partner. And many more treasured souls you will meet in time. I love animals, books, movies, and life itself. I am highly opinionated but egalitarian. I respect your beliefs, no matter how odd. Until you try to curtail my freedoms based upon your own beliefs, in which case we have a big problem. Money is just a means to an end, but it enables me to live a lifestyle that would hardly be realistic without it. I have a strict moral code, it just may not jibe with yours. Live and let live is my general motto. Love is love. But fuck with me or mine, and I will make you regret it deeply. My loyalty is non-negotiable. And I will put you in the ground and think nothing of it.

Anyway, enough about me. And that last bit was kind of dark. The remainder of the flight to Canaan was rather boring. I forced myself through a few sets of sit-ups and pushups. I read up on the Gnostics and the Templars. I pored over plans and blueprints of Canaan. I took a nap. And before I knew it, my proximity alarms were ringing out. I had bumped them up to a few miles so that I could cut power to the running lights and prevent warning what fucked-up denizens remained on the orbital (or any other visitors) of my impending arrival. I scanned the cloud cover outside and waited for the orbital wreck to emerge.

CHAPTER FOUR

The gigantic bulk of Canaan filled the cockpit window, parting the haze as I approached, her dome glittering with reflected starlight. From a distance, the orbital still looked completely intact and functional, and indeed, except for the decimated population and tons of bombed/burned out buildings, it largely was. All of the mechanics and processes required to keep the orbitals afloat are autonomic and self-sustaining, and they have held up for the decade or so since Canaan's collapse. I don't know how long they will hold up, but I hope I am not here when they finally give out. I spotted a docking port slightly to starboard and nudged the Wagon in that direction. Within minutes, I touched down gently on the platform and engaged the system remotely that would convey the hovervan into and through the sally port/airlock. And to whatever we would find on the other side. Fuck, I hoped it wasn't cannibals.

With a hiss of pressurization and the blinking of an incredibly dusty green light, we were all systems go. I moved the SW forward at a snail's pace while I double-checked the maps I had of the orbital. Luckily, I was only a few miles from my destination. Although I really did not want to abandon the Wagon and cover the rest of the distance on foot, I decided it would probably be stealthier to do so. The airlock cycled, and I crept forward into a large docking bay roughly the size of an airplane hangar.

The place looked absolutely trashed. The caged lights above and on the walls blinked periodically in no particular pattern, illuminating large shipping containers, smaller tarp-covered pallets, and a few busted shuttles that looked like they had been rendered incapable of flight by small arms fire and explosives. Rust colored puddles and splatters were strewn about the deck seemingly randomly, the sad remnants of the lifeblood of both man and machine, no doubt. I had zero inclination to investigate further. This was definitely not one of the docking bays I had entered on previous visits, but considering how many there are and how few trips I have made here, the odds were never in favor of that happening. Not to mention previous visits had involved Muslim and Jewish sectors across the orbital and not the Evangelical Christian neighborhood that was my current destination.

I pulled the hovervan between a large shipping container and an exterior wall to at least partially hide it from view if anyone were to enter the hangar while I was roaming about topside, then I punched in the code to change the exterior to chameleon mode. I tossed some ration bars and a water or two in my small sling bag and removed the Excalibur from its bag as well, tossing the spare mags in with my snacks. I slung them both over my shoulders, the straps crisscrossing my chest, and grabbed the orange case with the biohazard symbols. I let down the ramp at the side of the van and stepped down onto the deck below. I gave the room another quick visual scan for movement or potential threats and set the case down on its side, popping the latches and opening the lid to reveal the contents.

Two matte black hover drones sat comfortably surrounded by protective foam inlays. The smaller of the two was roughly the size of your average quad-lift camera drone and bore the tiny stenciled legend HD/S-2112 "Electric Eye." The larger of the two was about 50% bigger than its little brother. It had twin drum magazines mounted on top giving the appearance of a figure 8 or infinity symbol and bore the name HD/K-5150 "Hellion." I swiped my smartwatch over them and punched in an authorization code on the holo display it projected in front of me, which caused a number of clicks and whirs to issue forth from the drones as they woke their sleepy electronic asses up and quietly rose out of their case to hover a couple of feet overhead and to my left. I removed a tiny charging box from the larger transit case and popped out two black tactical earbuds and placed them in my ears. They allowed me to not only communicate with the drones but also enhanced my hearing and allowed me to hear what the drones pick up through their internal mics if need be. They also electronically dampened any loud noises such as gunfire or sonic attacks from sound weapons. Neat stuff.

"Standard overwatch pattern, boys. Butch, 50-meter perimeter alarm. Sundance, non-lethal loads for now." I watched as they quietly chirped acknowledgement and spread out above and behind me with Butch, the smaller drone, off to my left and Sundance, my Hellion, floating off to the right, the tiny green running light below indicating he would be utilizing non-lethal Narcoject rounds unless I specifically told him to switch over to armor-piercing jacketed ammo.

I slid the case back into the van, locked the van up tight and started walking slowly toward the back wall of the bay and the lift to the surface. Upon arriving, the lift definitely looked like it had seen better days, so I opted for the stealthy approach and took the stairs to the upper deck. The boys followed after and slowly rose through the central shaft a floor or two above me, scanning for potential threats as I plodded along, floor by floor, sidestepping old grease and bloodstains the whole way.

At around flight 10, I had begun to regret not taking the lift, despite the potential dangers. By the time I hit flight 25, I was downright pissed at myself. My calves and quads also seemed to be annoyed with me. Luckily, by the time I hit the top of flight 35, there seemed to be natural light above, and my HUD specs dialed down the low-light filter to nearly nothing. Flight 40 seemed to be the last, and I huffed slightly – partly from exhaustion and partially in indignation and triumph – as I reached the top and stood in what seemed to be a small, glass-walled lobby looking out over the empty streets of a small town.

My drones waited patiently beside the exterior door, scanning the street and maybe laughing silently to themselves in binary at my human frailty. I am sure I imagined that as they don't really have the capacity for such, but I probably deserve it. I gave myself a moment to catch my breath and then eased open the door and stepped outside on what appeared to be a concrete sidewalk on the main street of your stereotypical, garden-variety, small town U.S.A of the early-to-mid 20th century. It was roughly 8:45 PM local time, so the streetlights that were still intact were lit, decorating the streets and sidewalks with sporadic cones of yellowish light.

The air smelled clean enough, if a bit stale with hints of smoke and something vaguely vegetal. The street was completely deserted. The buildings behind me that made up the facade I had just exited all seemed to be 1-2 stories in height with similar buildings across the street. That tracked. On most orbitals, the buildings tend to get taller toward the central spindle. The central district usually houses all sorts of administrative, executive, governmental, and legislative entities as well as the maintenance, engineering, power and utility buildings and services that surround the spindle.

Of course, this is Canaan, so there will likely be a church on just about every corner, too. The buildings themselves were mostly brick fronted with some primarily wooden structures mixed in. Lots of big glass windows. The oxidized green patina of the streetlamps was a nice touch, as were the boxy blue mailboxes with the rounded tops. An honest-to-gods striped barber pole could be seen nearby, and most of the shop signs were painted, wooden affairs with upward lights, the sole neon embellishments I could see limited to open signs in a few street-facing windows. All switched off, of course. Nothing here had been open for business for quite some time.

Most of the doors looked intact and locked up tight, but a few were ajar, a few were obviously broken or forced, and some had been boarded up. A business here or there was tagged with spray paint, emblazoned with the charming invectives of "infidel" or "heretic" or some unmentionable slur or symbol of hate. Loose papers caught gusts of wind and traveled the streets and sidewalks like tumbleweeds. I picked up a couple as I passed, neither the recruitment tracts nor the hateful propaganda much of a surprise. One corner store looked like it had been firebombed, a little bodega probably owned by someone with the wrong invisible sky daddy for someone else's tastes, I guess.

Although it occurred to me to stay under the cover of overhead awnings and out of sight from at least one direction, I opted to walk in the street itself to give me a chance to react to potential threats from either side equally. Chances are that Butch's perimeter alarm would warn me of danger long before my own human senses could. I heard the quiet hum of their quadlifts overhead, offering a pleasant sense of security. The place was creepy, no lie. Except for the obvious damages the citizens had inflicted here, the street showed little sign of wear and tear and could have been abandoned weeks ago as opposed to a decade. I suppose we can credit the resilience of the orbital's surface air scrubbers for that. Surprisingly little dust anywhere, which pleased my inner neat freak and inner antiquarian, both of whom loved to see things well preserved. It did little for the rest of me, though, the myriad facets of which found it unsettling to the max. Of course, the juxtaposition of the "perfect" town with symbols of hate and evidence of violence, however far in the past, didn't help at all.

I turned at the next opportunity and headed inward, or spindle-ward, walking past general stores and appliance shops, a newspaper office, a mechanic's garage, a bike shop, a café, a small clothier and a billiard parlor among other commercial ventures. There seemed to be residences or offices above them … probably both. There was even a little marble-clad Masonic Lodge. Green benches proliferated, as well as green mesh garbage bins. I passed underneath a traffic light that had long since fallen down on the job and what appeared to be a small red trolley underneath, emptied of passengers and forever frozen in the act of traversing this little intersection. I felt an odd pang of sadness for it. It was all very quaint and not the slightest bit haunting at all, certainly nothing like walking through a ghost town typifying the failed American dream. Or maybe the idyllic Christian nationalist dream. Whatever. It was just a bunch of buildings. There was no need to wax metaphorical.

My smartwatch beeped and projected an image of the fleshmap with three green icons on it; a delta for me, pointed in the direction I was facing; and little B and S circled dots for the flying good bois overhead. Faint lines showed the buildings I had passed and the road itself. A red X glowed faintly ahead, in what looked like it might be the outline of a town square. Sure enough, I looked ahead and saw the road ending in a T, branching hard right and left. A brick and wrought-iron fence and the overgrown remnants of some box hedges framed what looked like a courthouse or municipal building of some sort, with tons of brick and arched windows with some Georgian columns out front and a tiny clock tower perched on top like a little hat. The image of a dunce cap came to mind, but I disregarded it. I shouldn't generalize. I don't want to be that guy. Even if I am surrounded by the evidence of such widespread duncery. The X looked to be beyond the courthouse itself on the far side of the square. As I neared the courthouse and veered right, I saw what could only be a steeple emerge from behind the clock tower. Well, shit. Of course. It looked like I was going to church. Well, halle-fuckin-lujah. Praise be to whomever!

And that's what I did. The boys and I made our way around the square, passing more empty storefronts – an ol' timey soda fountain, a shoe repair place, a donut shop, a holy-shit-are-you-serious vacuum repair shop, a Christian E-bookstore (I have many, many questions.), and a boxing gym – and I finally reached the church itself. It was nothing special, just a white, clapboard, small-town church, painted white with black shutters and black diamond panes on the smaller windows.

A few larger stained glass windows bisected the building's length and flanked the double front doors, which were covered with a small black awning. A larger, round stained glass window depicting what looked to be the fall of Lucifer sat higher on the front wall, likely shining its array of pretty colors on a balcony or maybe choir seating.

The steeple was black roofed and reached a few stories into the sky, topped by a small golden cross and louvered windows on each of the four sides, which likely concealed bells or loudspeakers that broadcast an approximation of such. There was a small, brick paved courtyard to the right of the vestibule that contained a few black wrought iron benches and a couple of picnic tables. From the outside, it looked like it might've held a congregation of about 100 or so, just a neighborhood enclave with maybe a fellowship hall and rectory at the back. Small transom windows below the siding indicated that there was a basement. Probably where the super-cool youth pastor used to work his magic, winning hearts and minds through ping pong or video games and the strategic use of whatever slang his younger congregants used. At any rate, I walked past the church and made the block, checking it out from as many angles as possible. I whispered a command to Butch, and the little surveillance drone zipped to a higher altitude to give me a better idea of the layout.

"Scan for life signs and feed the image to my HUD," I told him. The church showed up on thermal as a giant cold block from both the side and above with no telltale red silhouettes. I called him back and the three of us headed toward a door at the rear left of the church. I figured it was always safer to avoid the grand entrance if at all possible, considering I had little idea of what I was walking into.

I reached out and turned the antiquated brass knob of the windowed door, the smoked or spray-painted glass of which less than useless to me. It was unlocked, so I gently pushed the door open at a snail's pace to avoid creaky hinges giving away my presence. The door open, I stepped inside what looked to be a mud room of sorts with a small wooden bench and a coatrack with shelves. There were no boots or jackets present, which was not surprising in the least. I moved on into a small, disheveled kitchenette that didn't look like it had gone unused for terribly long ... certainly not since the disaster. Dirty dishes in the sink, the odd cabinet open. The FEEL of a room that had recently been occupied. And something else. The windows over the sink were also painted black, and the walls had been treated with what looked like emergency blankets. Thermal blankets. SHIT, I thought to myself. The sort of thing that would fool a thermal imaging device like Butch's camera. I guessed the window paint had thermal properties as well. Above me, the boys hummed quietly.

"Butch," I whispered. "Take point. Feed to my left optic, 40 percent opacity."

Immediately, the little drone zipped stealthily forward and the left eye of my HUD specs sprouted the translucent feed from Butch's down-facing forward camera with a near 180-degree panorama of the room ahead overlaid over my own view of the room. It's always disconcerting at first, but once you get used to it, your brain does a decent job of parsing the disparate images. You don't want to try and run through a maze full-tilt while you're doing it, though.

I crept forward through the kitchen and Butch moved into what looked like a small sitting room. I figured I was in a small rectory addition behind the church proper. The antique-looking settee and chairs had definitely seen better days, and the coffee and end tables were scuffed to hell and back, pardon the pun. Foil-wrapped walls, spray-painted with such classy bon mots as "DEATH TO THE UNBELIEVERS" and "EAT OF MY FLESH BECOME ONE WITH GOD" and "BABYLON'S WHORES." Fucking religious nutbag cannibals. Not unexpected, obviously, but certainly not an awesome development. I walked gingerly to avoid bottles and cans thrown down indiscriminately. I mean, just once I'd like to visit a place like this and have it be pristine, well maintained and decorated tastefully. Oh, well. Cannibals are assholes, and their taste in decorating (and hygiene) leaves much to be desired.

Butch rounded the corner and moved through a small room that looked like an open closet with a door at the other end. There were still a few choir robes hanging there, so I guessed that was the purpose of the room. When he passed through the other side and through the open door, the room beyond widened out into what looked like the sanctuary itself, with a high vaulted ceiling overhead, maybe 12 double rows of wooden pews or so and what appeared to be a balcony in back. The stained glass windows had all been covered with thermal foil, but small holes here and there allowed shafts of party colored twilight to pierce the gloom of the sanctuary. Kind of creepy, kind of cool. Most interesting and most worrisome, though, was the small group of Mad Max looking motherfuckers gathered around the overturned pulpit, which was occupied by the sprawled form of a man who was most likely a fellow traveler like myself.

Seven unwholesome forms crowded around him dressed in a mixture of what looked like the remains of former Sunday suits coupled with random bondage gear ... studded codpieces over ripped trousers, harnesses over bare chests or tattered, stained button-ups, gimp masks or heavily pierced or scarified faces smeared with fresh blood. They all seemed to be holding blades of some sort, from fillet knives and cleavers to hunting Bowies and tactical folders.

They had opened the unfortunate seeker from crotch to throat - making him look like the splayed open subject of an autopsy – and were currently digging around inside with blades and bloodied hands, bringing bits of his organs and flesh to their greedy, gore-soaked mouths with a frenzy bordering on religious fervor. I felt my gorge rise and quickly tamped it down through sheer will. Butch hovered quietly near the back of the stage platform, slowly panning his electronic eyes around the room to ensure all the threats present had been identified and tagged for his brother and myself. I crept quietly through the robe storage area and whispered to Sundance as stealthily as I could.

"Sundance, seven subjects tagged. Put 'em to sleep. Start at left with Subject One."

The larger drone and I entered the sanctuary at the same time, the barrels of his Narcoject launcher spinning softly over my head. I had my own Narcoject out and raised. As ordered, Sundance began firing immediately as he cleared the overhang of the door. Butch had tagged the cannibals numerically from left to right, the red digits lighting up in my left optic over each of their heads. My smartgun's target reticle had popped into my visuals as soon as my hand had touched its grip and now rested over the throat of Subject Seven. I figured we'd start at opposite ends and meet in the middle. As they were occupied wholly by their extremely unsavory meal, it was pretty much shooting fish in a barrel for the both of us. The breathy, metallic coughs of our shots overlapped into a barely audible symphony of whispered *thwips* as the cannibals fell to the floor one by one, Narcoject spines sticking out of their exposed flesh like acupuncture needles.

"These are the ugliest fucking pincushions I have seen in a while, boys," I said to the drones overhead. They hummed quietly, which I took as agreement. "Any more of you hungry, nasty fuckers around here ready for naptime? A little nappy-nap?" I walked slowly across the stage, holding my Narcoject in a Weaver stance, moving the barrel slowly left to right and sweeping the room as I walked. No one answered. I kept the sleek, neon blue pistol at the ready as I walked over to the sleeping bodies around the pulpit and nudged them roughly with my foot one by one, checking that they were down for the count. I walked closer to their victim and holstered my weapon as I surveyed the damage, unstrapping the Excalibur from my back and leaning it on a nearby pew to free myself up for a closer look.

He was a black man of roughly middle age, I guessed. Short-cropped hair, black-rimmed specs, a light olive track suit or flight suit made of some neoprene-like material with ribbed, black racing stripes on the arms and legs, now doused liberally with blood and chunks of offal. He was a handsome fellow in life and in death, probably a treasure or curio hunter like myself or maybe just a thrill seeker. Probably a hit with the ladies. Or dudes. Or whomever. Maybe a smuggler or petty criminal or a mercenary motherfucker, also like me. It didn't matter now. He didn't deserve to go out like that. As far as I am concerned, no one does. I gently moved his specs up with my free hand and closed his eyes. I moved the glasses back down and rested my hand on his shoulder.

"I am sorry, brother," I mumbled. "You deserved better." I gave his shoulder a gentle pat and turned to face the dozing cannibals fanned out before me.

I knelt over them, retrieving all the Narcoject spines and placing them in a puncture-resistant bag in my pocket that I kept for just such occasions. Little bitches are too expensive to leave behind if I have time. After that was done, still kneeling, I weighed my options as far as the cannibals were concerned. They'd no longer be a danger to me unless I planned on sticking around more than four hours or so. I tried very hard to view them as human beings with a right to continued life and the pursuit of their particular brand of happiness or at least survival, no matter how twisted I might find it. Then I looked at the pulpit and its sad occupant. I reached down and took the filet knife out of the gore-crusted fist of the nearest cannibal.

"Know what? Fuck you guys," I whispered in a low voice. "An eye for an eye."

I slit all seven of their throats, crouch-walking from one to another, watching as their last breaths faded and their resting hearts pumped the last of their lifeblood onto the floor around us. I parked the filet knife between the ribs of Subject Number One when I was finished, lodging it right above a silvery O-ring held in place by riveted straps. I wiped my hands, back and front, on the remains of his gray suitcoat and thumped him on the left side of his chest with the flat of my palm in a neighborly fashion.

"The pleasure was all mine, Deacon," I smiled. "Thanks for the invite, but I think I'll keep searching for my forever home."

Despite my rather glib and snarky comment to the cannibal's corpse, killing him and his fellow cultists didn't exactly fill me with pride or a feeling of accomplishment. Death is still death, and rarely should the death of a human being be celebrated. Don't get me wrong, I wouldn't lose any sleep over taking these particular societal outliers off the game board as it would likely save innocent lives in the long run. It's not like they could have been rehabilitated or that the damage to the mind and/or soul (if you believe in such) that results from living as a feral, killing machine and consumer of human flesh for a decade could have been undone by some advanced psychotherapy. We've come a long way, but not quite that far. So, yeah. I put down a handful of frenzied, rabid animals that were a danger to others. Still, they were human once, and a part of me felt that loss and was somewhat uncomfortable with being the instrument of their destruction, however necessary and possibly just. I felt far more empathy for the lone traveler that they had victimized, though. It is what it is.

I stood and stretched. I retrieved the Excalibur and consulted my smartwatch and the map projection. From the look of it, I was standing very near my objective, but the lack of obvious hiding places in the room led me to believe it might be below me somewhere, possibly in a basement or cellar. I walked down the center aisle toward the front of the building and caught a glimpse of railings off to my left that indicated a stairwell leading down. I walked in that direction and my drones followed, the quiet hum of their gravlifts keeping me company. When we reached the stairs, I told Butch to take point again and check out the room or rooms below. Sundance and I followed.

CHAPTER FIVE

I crept down the stairs as quietly as I could, Narcoject again drawn, mindful of the Excalibur's stock and barrel in the narrow passageway. The grimy pink carpet on the stairs had molded and rotted through in many places, and again, drink containers and old, empty food cans were strewn about. Pictures lined the walls, cracked glass partially obscuring photos of church outings: picnics, baptisms and the like. The stairwell itself was not illuminated, but I could see the glow of a light source shining dimly through the gloom below that seemed to be coming from an open doorway or archway to the right.

Butch floated into the room below before I made it halfway down and fed the images to my optics. The basement looked like a giant storage area, filled with brown cardboard boxes that had been ripped open and pilfered for anything of value. Gray plastic tables held more boxes and detritus of all kinds: old lamps, stacks of clothing, older electronic devices. In its day, the church had probably gathered up disused items from its congregants to give to the poor or some such charitable pursuits, the artifacts of which spread out before me like an ocean of sadness and obsolescence ... like someone had thrown a pipe bomb in a lost and found. Beyond that forgotten sea of rubbish, however, a figure moved in the flickering light.

I had just made it to the bottom of the stairs and the beginning of the piles of discarded treasures – which I thought to myself might have to be sorted through more thoroughly after investigating any possible threats – and I whispered a command to Butch to hang back once the shadowy figure showed up in my feed. Sundance hovered over my left shoulder as I crept down the aisle to catch up with the smaller drone. As I moved closer, it became apparent that the flickering light came from hundreds of candles that covered nearly every flat surface of the basement. The golden-orange hues revealed cinderblock walls that had been covered with a neutral beige once upon a time before someone decided to scrawl strange, alien-looking characters and symbols on every square inch of it in red and black paint, probably with a finger or two.

Bookshelves lined every other bit of wall space, jam packed with hardbacks and paperbacks of various sizes and colors. A gray plastic table with metal legs sat in the center of the space, covered with tall, disheveled stacks of books in danger of toppling at any moment, loose papers strewn hither and yon, and even more candles. Pacing back and forth behind the table was a man in a tattered priest's raiment with a giant salt-and-pepper beard that would do any self-respecting mad prophet proud. His skin was sallow and pasty white, his eyes dark and sunken hollows behind wire-rimmed spectacles, his hair a crazed rat's nest of fine, white needles protruding in every direction. His Roman collar hung loose, and he sipped liberally from an open wine bottle as he muttered loudly to himself in the self-assured way of the truly mad.

I parked my target reticle over his chest as I approached. He didn't seem as frenzied as the assholes upstairs, but he wasn't exactly a model of the well-adjusted modern man upon first glance, either. About three meters out, I cleared my throat softly. The priest/prophet/homeless dude looked up with a visible jerk, almost dropping his wine bottle. I half expected him to throw it at me, but his expression changed quickly from surprise to welcoming. He put his hands on his hips, one still holding the wine bottle, and spoke.

"Oh. Hello. I was wondering when you'd show up." His voice was raspy with disuse, but no less friendly for it, as if we were college roommates reunited after many years apart and maybe he had experienced a battle with throat cancer in the interim.

"Um, hey?" I offered dumbly. "How's it going?"

He laughed then, the sound somewhere between a bark and a slightly unhinged chortle.

"Oh, it is definitely going, my friend! I feared I would never, EVER make strides ... never see progress, but the Fall, you see, it brought with it that which we all crave. Namely, TIME. Clarity of purpose, the discarding of all the chaff ... the winnowing, the separation of ... " He trailed off. "I was expecting you, of course."

"Little ol' me? I'm flattered," I said. "Was that your welcoming committee upstairs? They are all, um, dead by the way."

He smiled, his grin half gleeful and half death rictus.

"No matter. They were Philistines, wicked and depraved. And my jailers." He raised his right leg somewhat and shook it from side to side with a rattle, showing off a manacle and chain that ran to a cinderblock at his filthy, bare feet. He glanced about as if afraid of being overheard and whispered "They ate of human flesh. They performed vile acts upon the dead. I will *not* mourn their passing."

"Well, it's a good goddamned thing," I said cheerily, holstering the Narcoject. I raised my arms to the side, palms open in what I hoped was a universal symbol for *Let's fucking chill, shall we?*

"So, hey, before we go too far down the road of all things biblical, my name is Daniel. I am looking for a book. Hoping you might be able to help me with that?"

"I have many books," he said sagely, stating the obvious and taking a swig of his wine. "This humble basement notwithstanding, I have gathered many of the more important tomes left on the orbital over the last 20 years or so. Many of them came from the far corners of old Earth That Was. Some from the private collections of the rich, some from ancient castles and monasteries, some from the depths of the Vatican archives. I even have a signed copy of the Necronomicon here ... somewhere. Not the original, naturally. Just a copy. Still. Ghastly thing." He glanced around the piles as if expecting it to jump out and attack him.

"I'm looking for The Book of Raziel," I said. "No idea what it looks like. Probably written in Enochian script? Language of the angels or creation, supposedly. Was given a map to this place inked on human skin by a really shady dude that wants it something fierce. Be glad to pay you for your trouble, or, um, give you a ride to some place nicer with fewer cannibals. Or both. Maybe throw in a case of wine if you're down, Father ..."

"Hah!" he barked a laugh. "It's Father Bishop. Elias Bishop. Yes. I know. A priest named Bishop. It sounds like a joke. I have heard more than one made at my expense. I am afraid you are too late, my friend. It was indeed here. But it is long gone." He pointed with the neck of his wine bottle to a dusty old pulpit in the corner. "It sat there, in a place of reverence. I studied it for ages before the Fall. It had come to me along with a random lot of old tomes. Came from an estate in old Ontario, I think? The rest of the books were nothing special, but this ... oh. You could FEEL its power just by holding it in your hands. The strange symbols almost seemed to vibrate on the pages and crawl around when you weren't looking directly at them. What you see here are my feeble attempts to remember the cryptic phrases within ..." He gestured vaguely to the walls around us.

"Wow. Ok. How accurate do you think these are?" I asked. "You mind if I give them a quick scan?"

"No, go right ahead. I honestly have no idea. My memory isn't what it used to be, but I think they are mostly pretty close. They seem to sing to me when I get close." He walked over to the nearest wall and ran his dirty hands over the symbols, tracing a few with his fingertips, mumbling under his breath.

I told Butch to make a circuit of the room and scan the images as closely as possible, taking note of the cardinal directions of each wall. Sometimes that matters with the mystical bullshit. The priest watched him as he went, seemingly mildly amused.

"Any idea what happened to the book itself?" I asked. "Who might've taken it and where? When it disappeared?"

"Oh, absolutely! Just before the Fall ... I guess it was maybe a month or two ... there was a purge of, um, items deemed unholy by the Elders of Canaan. They sent their jackbooted thugs door to door, sniffing out anything deemed apocryphal or offensive to any of the fundamentalist sects that make up the Council and the populous of the orbital at large. They made off with it. I tried to stop them, but ..." The priest grew almost sheepish. "I am a man of peace, and not much in the way of physical means. Funny ... they left the copy of the Necronomicon, which is undoubtedly and objectively far more evil. Maybe not *quite* as dangerous ..." He trailed off.

"Okay ... gonna put a pin in that. Where do you think they might've taken it? Do you think they burned it or destroyed it?" I thought back to Archer's fantastical tale. "Or tried to?"

"No," he grimaced. "I highly doubt it. While their sort have never been shy about burning books, I believe even such as they could sense its value. And power. More likely they carried it off to a central repository near the spindle."

"Any idea where that might be located?"

"I could probably pick it out on a map," he said.

"Huh. How about this?" I punched up my smartwatch's projection display and pulled up one of the maps of the orbital I had loaded prior to the trip, zooming in on the spindle and the central administration district that surrounded it.

"Hmmm. AH. There." He pointed to a large building adjacent to the orbital governmental complex. "That's the central library. I went there for research some times. They have many sublevels that are, or were, not open to the general public. The book is likely there. I will warn you, however, there were rumors that the Powers That Be shipped the more valuable contents to other orbitals near the end, fearing another Library of Alexandria type event. Some of the admins likely used it as an excuse to flee themselves before the fighting began in earnest, taking a shipment off orbital and simply never coming back."

"I mean, not a bad idea, really. You can hardly blame them,"

I said. "Except it's usually the rare air breathing motherfuckers who start everything and leave others to fight their battles."

"Well, there is that," he sighed and took a swig of wine before offering me the bottle.

"Nah. I'm good," I said. "I try not to drink things offered to me by religious types. Still not quite over the Jonestown thing, I guess. Or Heaven's Gate. No offense to present company, Padre, as you seem a pretty decent sort for a mad prophet guy locked away in a basement."

He smiled and winked. "Oh, yes. I might be a bit barmy at that. But not in a dangerous way, I don't think?"

"That's what they all say until everyone drinks the Kool-Aid," I offered, not unkindly.

"Touché, my son. More for me, anyway." He drained the bottle, belched lightly and tossed the dead soldier onto his cot nearby.

"Alright, so I have some travelling to do, preacher man. What can I do for you? I can certainly get that chain and cinderblock off you and spare some rations if you're hungry. If you want, you can tag along to the library and I'll get you the fuck off of this hunk of junk."

"You say 'fuck' a lot," he noted.

"So I have been told."

"Hmm. I AM rather tired of these environs," he noted, scratching his chin. "Would it be possible for me to bring some of my books?"

"Tell you what," I said. "Pack your desert island playlist in a suitcase or something portable. We'll stash it nearby on the route back to my ride. Everything goes smoothly, we'll pick it up on the return trip. Shit hits the fan, we skip it and I get you a library card when we get back to Elysia. Sound good?"

"That is ... acceptable," he murmured. "Honestly, I would do nearly anything to be back among normal people again." He made a pained expression, and it really brought home the depths of his sorrow and loneliness. "Maybe someday I could even have a flock again? My own little parish somewhere? Visit the sick, carry meals to the shut-ins … maybe even give a eulogy or two …"

"No need to give me a handy or anything, my dude," I said, failing miserably at lightening the mood. "I'm glad to have you, and it's nothing I wouldn't do for anyone in your situation. You seem like a decent fellow, if a bit barmy. There's probably going to be some long hours of therapy and re-patriation type stuff in your near future, but once you pass some psych screenings, they'll probably let you pursue any vocation you want, within reason."

"That sounds nice," he offered. "I could probably use a bit of therapy at that. Honestly, I've always enjoyed sharing and connecting to someone on that level. It will be refreshing after what I have been through these past years."

"Fucking legit, my man," I said. "We need to get a move on, though, so pack anything you can't live without and let's get the hell out of this basement."

About 3 minutes of solid work with my multi-tool's cutting laser had the priest free of his chain. He then spent the next few minutes rummaging through piles of clothes and packing them in a small overnight bag from one of the donation piles. He took another 10 minutes choosing his favorite books from the tables and shelves and packed them in a plastic bag and put that in another tote, this one emblazoned with the bright, cheery, round face of a popular anime character. I should probably know her name, but I am not as well versed in modern pop culture as I am the culture of centuries past. It's a failing of mine. Anyway, I say this only to remark that her slightly unsettling smile and wink made me feel I was simultaneously being mocked and judged. Which is probably more indicative of my own insecurities than any malevolence or ill intent on her part. He finished up by digging an old set of sneakers out of a donation pile and squeezing them onto his filthy, bare feet without bothering to put on socks. I took a moment to have the boys label the priest as a friendly, and we were on our way.

CHAPTER SIX

We made our way back up the stairs and through the sanctuary, Butch again on point and Sundance hovering a few paces behind us. Upon reaching the makeshift altar and the grisly scene that surrounded it, the priest spent a few heartbeats gazing silently at the ring of corpses I had left behind. He touched the victimized traveler on the shoulder and murmured a few words under his breath ... some sort of last rites, I would presume. He then spat in the general direction of the cannibals and made the sign of the cross at them while whispering something else. Complicated man, our Padre.

The four of us slinked back out through the rectory and to the town square. Well, two of us slinked. The other two hovered, gravlifts humming quietly. I walked over to one of the colorful post office boxes on the corner and beckoned the priest over. A quick zip of burning light from my multi-tool cut the lock out and I opened the box. A small pile of envelopes spilled out. I still can't believe these guys reverted to snail mail, but I guess the Christians were taking their Mayberry cosplay as seriously as the rest of the orbitals do. I took the bag of clothes and the tote of books from Bishop, placed them in the mailbox, and shut the door. He let out a forlorn sigh as I did so.

"We'll come back for them, Father," I assured him quietly. "Unless we're forced to tear out of here with our hair on fire in a bullet storm." He made a face of reluctant resignation, and we moved on.

"So," I began, keeping my voice down so it didn't carry. "What's the quickest way to the spindle without attracting attention? Any old transit systems still online? Maintenance trolleys below decks or something? We could go snag my van and try to find a docking bay spindle-side if need be. I'm sure they had some sort of sally ports for the Grand Poohbahs and their toadies. Think I saw some on the blueprints, but they weren't labeled as such for security reasons, I'm sure. Might be locked up tight, though. What do you think?"

"The Elders had a private, mostly secret subway transit system that had seven equidistant lines running from the spindle to the outer rim," he said. "I believe there is a station fairly close. That might still be functional."

"How do you know about it if it was mostly secret?" I asked.

"Most of the clergy received a private tour of Canaan upon arrival," he shrugged. "Partly to impress us with the magnificence of our leaders, I would suppose, and partly to prepare us for emergency situations. And, naturally, to point out the borders and boundaries between the sects, places that were considered religiously neutral, and other salient things one had to know when living among so many fundamentalists and extremists."

"You don't strike me as either one," I said. "How did you end up here?"

"It's easy to be a holy man on a mountain," he grimaced. "Plus, where better to try and bring others back to some semblance of sanity and the actual spirit of my beliefs?"

"OH. You're a crusader, are you?"

"Nothing so heroic or, um, zealous," he grinned. "Just a simple shepherd trying to steer as much of the flock back to decency as possible, largely by example. More Mister Rogers than King Richard."

"You know Mister Rogers? That's pretty ancient stuff, man. Not quite as ancient as Richard I, but not exactly showing up in history books, either. You get my point."

"All true men of God should know Fred Rogers," he said, seriously. "He was the best of all of us. Did more to spread the spirit of holiness and all that is kind and good than any Emperor or Pope, in my opinion. A flawed and imperfect man, but an avatar of the Light nonetheless."

"True that, brother. Can't argue with that in the least," I smiled. "Which way we headed?"

"There's an alleyway a few blocks down that street and to our left. Should be a locked security door that looks like a small loading dock. Hiding in plain sight as it were."

"Ok, then. Let's go." If this were a movie, I would've started whistling "It's a Beautiful Day in the Neighborhood" as we set off on out journey, but it's not and I can't whistle, anyway. I'm not proud. It's a congenital trait, probably genetic. I can roll my tongue, though, and there's this neat trick where I make my right ring finger look boneless and it looks cool when I spin it around in a circle. Fuck off. People who whistle in public are annoying as hell, anyway. Seven Dwarves sounding motherfuckers.

We walked quietly down the street, not quite in the center, but again steering clear of the sidewalks.

"Good thing you were never promoted," I grinned evilly as I scanned the shopfronts for threats. "Bishop Bishop sounds preeetty goofy."

"Fuck off, my son," he admonished in a serious tone, but I think I heard a trace of a grin behind it.

"Potty mouth," I replied. Pretty sure I heard him stifle an actual chuckle at that.

We approached the alleyway that held the station's hidden entrance without fanfare or further fuckery. I sent Butch down the alley first to give it a once-over and scan the door for traps, hopefully getting me a rundown on any locking mechanisms he could spot. That done, we crept over to join him. In a convincing bit of cosplay, the alley smelled like an actual alley, despite a decade of not being pissed, puked or lived in. I couldn't believe they'd have had vagrants or partiers here back in the day, so I'm not quite sure what the source of the stink might've been. I suppose cannibal cultists might piss here for nostalgia's sake. I don't know. Oh, well. Alleys gonna alley.

Butch identified a cross-shaped section of brick on the left-hand side of the small, walk-up loading dock's rollup door that might hold a keypad or some similar contraption. I felt around and pressed bricks gently until the bricks slid upward to reveal a tiny alcove with a numeric keypad inside, a thumbprint scanner and a digital readout perched above it.

"Butch, see if you can get in through the scanner. Work some magic, buddy," I said to the little drone hovering above. I moved out of the way, and the drone dutifully zipped down to join me. He jockeyed for position a bit, lining up his forward facing camera array with the thumbprint scanner, and shot a wedge-shaped beam of green light into it. The beam turned clockwise and counterclockwise in turn once, twice, and then a third time. The numbers "01234" appeared on the digital readout, and the corrugated metal door began rolling into a metal box awning above.

"You gotta be shitting me. That's quite possibly the worst passkey ever. Next to five zeros, anyway. I could've guessed that. Anyone could've guessed that." I shook my head.

"But, you didn't," the priest said sagely.

"Touché," I allowed.

The door clinked and cranked quietly upward to reveal a small lit hallway, a line of caged safety lights flickering randomly overhead creating a mild strobe effect. Butch zipped in and up. The priest and I followed, me slightly behind and to the left, with Sundance acting as rear guard. I drew my Narcoject as we went. The hallway terminated in what appeared to be an elevator door with no buttons. I guessed they were not needed as the doors whooshed open with a slight whine as we approached a meter out.

"Hard to not feel like we're expected," I noted. "All automated systems I'm sure, but still a little creepy."

"Which reminds me," the priest said. "When I mentioned I had been expecting you, I simply meant someone LIKE you SOME day. Not you specifically today. I didn't mean to seem creepy. Well … okay. Maybe a little."

"Oh, it worked," I offered. "With the candlelight, the beard, the clinking of chains, and all the weird shit written on the walls ... you greeting me like that was just the icing on the creep-cake. You kind of have friendly eyes, though, and your vibe is pretty positive. You nailed the ambiance, but you might wanna work on the rest of that shit for next time. Maybe rub some kohl or ash all around your eyes to make them appear more sunken? More maniacal laughter? TOTALLY get you a Narcoject spine in the throat."

"Noted," he said with a grin bordering on unhinged. "Anything else? Should I be writing this down?"

"Oooh, that's it. Keep the weird smile. Babies will cry and dogs will probably turn tail and run from you."

"I hope not. I like dogs."

"Of course you do."

We stepped into the elevator, our hushed and witty banter dropping off as the doors whooshed closed and we began descending. The silence lasted perhaps a half minute before the asshole priest piped up.

"Into Tartarus," the priest said cryptically. "Abandon all hope ye who enter here and the like."

"Stifle that shit, Father," I growled. "I was kidding about wanting you creepier. You're at an 11. I need you at like a seven, tops. Anything over an 8 and you're no longer affably eccentric. You will be officially harshing my goddamned mellow."

"Point taken, my son," he began humming softly to himself.

"If that's Bach's Toccata and Fugue in D Minor, I will beat you."

He snorted, and his pitch and tone changed.

I rolled my eyes dramatically and glanced up at Butch for guidance.

"How do I end up with these yahoos, boy? The universe knows I hate escort missions and religion, and then it plops this fucking guy in my lap. Heavy sigh."

"Was that a gaming reference?" the priest asked.

"Yeah. You play?"

"I dabbled in some of the retro stuff in my youth. Grim Fandango, Assassin's Creed Black Flag ..." he trailed off, his eyes glinting in reverie.

"No shit? Grim Fandango? Haven't thought about that one in a while. Glottis is my spirit animal. Black Flag was THE FUCKING BEST. The travel mechanics?"

"Ah, but I do love a good sea shanty," he sighed wistfully.

"Girl, same," I said. "That's it. When you get out of re-pat, I'm taking you to this pirate-themed restaurant I know. They serve the most amazing chimichurri steak nachos in a little schooner. Little kitschy, but the food, service and drink selection are on point. And the music is choice. Pretty sure they have the whole ACIV:BF soundtrack on loop."

"Bless you, my son. It's a date," he said, and the bearded sonofabitch winked at me.

"If I don't kill you first," I shrugged.

"Fair," he shrugged back.

There was a tiny moment of almost anti-gravity as the elevator reached the bottom of the shaft (I assumed), and my stomach lurched as the doors slid open. I had my Narcoject aimed at the space between the doors before they even moved, but the dimly lit space beyond was empty.

We stepped out into what looked to be a small, rather elegant private subway station. The walls and ceiling were tiled in pristine white porcelain, and a giant mural of Christ on the cross greeted us to our right, bloody and barbaric. These guys were definitely the hellfire and brimstone types, I thought to myself. The wall to our left helpfully and redundantly displayed a giant red arrow pointing toward the tracks, as if there were any other direction to go from here. Perched on the tracks sat a tiny, bullet-like train car with bulbous windows studding its length and a larger, more angular viewing window ballooning up from the back of the car. No lights appeared to be on inside from our vantage point. The appointments on the shiny, white car appeared to be gold and very Ecclesiastical in nature at a glance, all knot-work and crosses, thorny crowns and whatnot. In fact, the vehicle bore a striking resemblance to the old armored "popemobiles" of the late 20th century. I doubted that was by accident. I vaguely wondered if all the other cars had their own individual religious motif ... mosques and minarets, yarmulkes and menorahs and the like.

We walked slowly toward the car, the priest ambling along - as was his way - with me a pace or two behind, scanning the periphery for threats. When we reached the train car, I expected the double doors to open of their own accord as we approached. Alas, it seemed our automated welcome was worn out. I felt around the door and found what appeared to be a small, round indentation the size of a small coin with an elaborate inlay inside. It appeared to be a mechanical lock of some sort.

"Shit. Butch can pick a garden variety lock, as can I, but this looks to be very intricate and very, VERY custom," I told the priest. "I wouldn't even begin to know how to crack something like this. Thoughts? Prayers? Any sort of Deus ex Machina would be welcome right about now. Think maybe you can turn on your weird-ass charm and creep the thing open? Go all mad prophet on it? Call down some lightning?"

"Well, um, NO to most of that," he said. "I do have this, though. It might help." He reached under his open Roman collar and pulled on a plain silver chain around his neck, pulling out what appeared to be a gold signet ring. He held it up and I could see that the raised insignia was a pretty close match for what I had spotted inside the lock.

"Padre," I began. "What is THAT?"

"It's an Elder Ring," he said simply. "All of the orbital leaders wore one. I took it from the hand of a corpse that my captors had, um, violated and ingested some years ago. I thought it might come in handy one day."

"Well, why didn't you list that among our assets in the first place?" I exclaimed, rolling my eyes.

"Is that *from* something? Should I know what ..." He looked at me quizzically, obviously confused.

"Ugh. The Princess Bride. 1987. Only one of the best movies of all time, you Philistine," I groaned. "Whatever. Gimme." I switched the Narcoject to my left hand and reached toward the priest with my right.

He pulled the necklace off and removed the ring, placing it in my outstretched palm. I took a deep breath, lined up the insignia on the ring with the ring-shaped hole on the train car, and inserted it.

Popemobile 2 (Electric Boogaloo!) came to life. Light bars blinked on inside, mechanical wheezes and clicks issued forth from under its body, and the double doors opened with a hydraulic whine. I heard the slightly tinny sound of an old hymn playing through speakers inside. I wasn't sure, but it might've been "Nearer My God to Thee." Not sure if that was supposed to be comforting or ominous. Considering our location, the latter was probably more appropriate.

"Butch, zip on in there and give it a once over, little guy." I turned to the priest as the little drone followed my order and hovered inside, cameras and scanners whirring lightly as he went to work.

"Alright, my man," I said. "All aboard the train to Damascus, or whatever biblical allusion works best for you. You're probably much better at that stuff than I am." An affirmative chirp and an accompanying message on my HUD told me Butch deemed it safe for entry, so I waved the priest in and followed. Sundance sauntered in – as was his way - as the doors began to close.

There were five rows of three white plastic seats each to the left of the car with a small aisle to the right. A few steps at the back of the car led up to what I guessed was the viewing platform for the grand poohbah. There were several rather large canopy windows inset into the roof as well that weren't visible from outside. No idea what the poohbah and his entourage might have found noteworthy to look at out of the roof of a subway car, but I guessed we'd find out. Bishop and

I chose seats about midway. I unslung my rifle and sat down, taking up an entire row with my back to the car's exterior wall and my legs stretching out to fill the adjacent seats. Bishop sat in the middle seat in the row behind me, his hands comfortably resting on his thighs.

The tinny music was silenced with an official sounding beep, and an automated voice that came across as slightly sluggish came through the speakers.

"Welcome, Elders and esteemed guests. Please take your seats and prepare for departure. Our current destination is the Central Administration District: E.T.A. ten minutes. If you wish to stop at another station, please press the corresponding number on the keypad in front of you as we approach. Thank you, and have a pleasant journey spindleside and a blessed day." The hymn resumed playing softly.

A small virtual keypad with the numbers one through five lit up on the back of each seat in front of me, and a holographic projection of the train's line appeared on the outcropping that arched over the front of the car and a door that I assumed led to an automated cockpit. The line showed five station blocks with only two lit up in green: five, which appeared to be ours; and one, which was placed right next to an icon representing the spindle. The virtual buttons were similarly colored, green LEDs illuminating five and one and red light emanating from two, three, and four.

"Good thing we weren't planning on making any stops," I deadpanned. The priest grunted and ignored me as he continued looking around the car. The interior was much more Spartan than the tarnished decadence of the outside, but I supposed anything was interesting after being trapped in a basement for a decade.

The car began creeping forward with a slight jolt. The ride smoothed out almost immediately after that. You have to give it to the orbital builders, man. They made stuff to last. I glanced up as a splash of color and light appeared through the windows over our heads, as did Bishop. What we saw there,

I have to say, was perhaps not an actual miracle, but it was pretty fucking spiffy nonetheless.

The tiles that lined the tunnel roof had switched to bright sky blue and had grown both smaller and infinitely more numerous. More splashes of color began popping up and forming pictures of clouds, a sun, and winged angels playing trumpets. The clever bastards had used the smaller tiles like pixels and stretched the artwork out so that the speed of the train car would make the pictures appear normal sized to the passengers ... a physical, 2D, 8-bit animation in forced perspective. The images began showing a time-lapsed construction of Canaan in low orbit, sped up to keep things engaging. I figured there was probably a soundtrack or narration of some sort that accompanied the show, but I had no idea how to turn it on. Or any desire to, really. The speeding tiles were fascinating enough. They were now showing a conclave of some sort that featured a bunch of clerical types in different robes and hats chatting amiably and seriously, probably discussing how they were going to make this little Fundamentalist (*coughs* *Fascist!*) Utopia work. As my interest began to wander, I pondered what trickery the dead builders would pull off to show another story or even the same one on the ride outward from the spindle as this one would be garbage in reverse. Maybe the tiles were small LED screens or something. I figured I'd find out soon enough on the ride back.

Bishop seemed pretty enthralled, so I took the opportunity to have my smartwatch project the close-up map of the administration district in front of me for planning purposes. The library was marked from when the priest had pointed it out to me earlier, and it looked as if the streets leading to and from it were many. Of course, that was before the Fall. There was really no way of telling how many obstacles we would find there now, or what shape the building itself would be in. I cut off the display with a sigh and lolled my head back, letting the pretty colors and pixelated animation outside lull me a bit while I zoned out. I didn't nap as such as that would be tactically moronic, even with the boys watching out for me from on high, but I let my mind wander for a bit. I *mostly* trusted the priest – inasmuch as I trust anyone - and was even starting to like him a bit, but he was still a stranger (and a strange one at that), and I was most definitely in a strange land.

I rested the Narcoject pistol in my lap but left my hand lazily draped across its grip. I reached out and gripped the forestock of the Excalibur where it was propped against the wall and let my arm dangle. I daydreamed about pulling the .40-caliber Colt Heathen from the holster at the small of my back and putting a round or two through the nearest speaker, but I decided it was not in me to commit random firearm-based vandalism just to silence the relatively inoffensive hymns played by the train car. Had it started belching late 20th /early 21st century bro country or hick hop at me, though, I could envision emptying an entire magazine into the speaker and maybe taking out its friends, too. And stabbing the remains repeatedly with my stiletto. And maybe pissing on what was left.

The dulcet tones of the train car's automated conductor woke me from my violent reverie.

"Now approaching Station One: Central Administration District. Please gather your belongings and prepare to exit the car. Please wait for the car to reach a full stop before standing. Enjoy your visit spindleside. Please respect others and do not violate any of the tenets or commandments of your particular faith while here. Remember: your god is watching you. Have a BLESSED day!"

I could hear the exclamation point. The robo-conductor was definitely more exuberant now. The car gradually slowed to a halt, and the tiles paving the tunnel above us resumed their larger format and stark whiteness. I stood with a soft grunt, and the priest stood with an even deeper one.

"How are ya now, dad?" I grinned at the priest.

"Are you quoting pop culture things again?" he asked, scrunching his eyebrows together. "You realize they are largely wasted on me. Although I did get the gaming one. That was fun." He made the universal downward curving, pursed-lip look for *Meh. I'll allow it.*

"It's mostly for my benefit and amusement," I allowed, grinning bigger. "As are most things I do. But, hey, every once in a while I strike gold. You're gonna get some pirate nachos out of it sometime soon, so don't bitch too much. Couple of months in re-pat following a week-long shower, maybe a successful meeting with the job service after we detangle your beard with a flame thrower, and we'll be singing shanties over a couple of pints, Padre. Just you wait and see."

"Point taken," he allowed. "I'd kill for a pint. I mean, not really. Thou shalt not and all that. But, I might think about maiming someone for a pitcher. Seriously."

"Speaking of which, are you hungry or thirsty?" I had completely spaced on offering the poor asshole a ration bar, which I quickly rectified. I holstered the Narcoject and dug into my sling bag, grabbing a small water bottle for each of us and a ration bar. "It's not chimichurri beef, but it'll tide you over until we can get back to the van and I can replicate something up for ya. Sorry for the delay. My manners are shit."

We stepped out into another dimly lit private station, munching on some protein-laden, vanilla crème bullshit bars and sipping water. Yet another large red arrow facing the tracks, and still another gruesome mural from Christian mythology: this one depicting the fall of Sodom and/or Gomorrah, I guessed. It was an ancient-looking city with comets, fireballs and other miscellaneous holy missiles taking out buildings, citizens, pets and livestock alike; smoke, flames, blood and tears everywhere. Holy baby jeebus these fucking guys were a laugh a minute. Even dead they manage to depress and annoy me in equal measure.

"Standard overwatch pattern, kids," I said to the drones, and they fanned out above us. We took a minute to finish our snacks, then I unslung the Excalibur and rested it on my shoulder. I felt I might need some bigger firepower spindleward. The priest and I walked toward the street, pausing to throw our empty bottles and wrappers in a trash bin beside a slotted bench. Old habits die hard, I guess. I find it hard to litter even in a post-apocalyptic wasteland. There was this advertisement in the 1970s of a crying Native American, and, I dunno. It hit me kind of hard, even watching it as an adult some 500 years later. Maybe if more folks had felt the same back then, we'd still be down there on Earth That Was. The fact that we are where we are just magnifies the sadness of that one single, solitary tear.

There wasn't an elevator at this station, only a ramp leading up a few stories to street level. As we hiked upward, something occurred to me.

"So, Padre," I began. "And I'm sorry if this is an uncomfortable question, but what did YOU eat this past decade whilst in the midst of cannibal central? You seemed pretty vehemently opposed to those guys and their unsavory practices."

"Doesn't bother me," he huffed, slightly out of breath with the exertion. I guessed that he hadn't done a ton of cardio while chained to a cinderblock. "There was a tiny replicator in the fellowship hall that I was allowed to use. I could've probably taken it to the basement at some point, but I liked the change of scenery. I just picked up my cinderblock and walked on up. Supervised, of course."

"Wait," I said and stopped walking, reaching out to grab him lightly by the arm. "You had functioning replicators that made actual, nutritious, delicious food? Why the FUCK is Canaan covered up with psycho cannibal cultists, then? I mean, seriously. What the actual hell?"

"Human flesh is a sacrament to them, some psychotic and twisted version of communion, only with less Latin and fewer 'And also with yous,'" he spat. "They don't subsist on humans alone. There aren't enough visitors or squatters to survive this long. It's not sustainable. It's just an occasional treat that brings them closer to their idea of God. If they go too long without some hapless stranger wandering in from the skies, they'll just eat the least healthy among them. Or just carve off tiny pieces of each other that will mostly heal eventually. They didn't start out like that, but a few months in, things devolved pretty quickly in the absence of authority of any sort. Secret desires and darker impulses welled to the surface, and they twisted the Word of God to serve their own ends. Not that that hasn't happened since prehistory ..."

"Gah. Alright. You can fucking stop right there. Sociology lesson is over for the day." I patted him on the shoulder and gave him a gentle push toward the street. "Sorry I fucking asked. Glad you didn't have to, you know, though."

"Me, too." He went silent but kept walking.

We approached the top of the ramp and a set of industrial gray double doors with safety yellow chevrons on them appeared out of the gloom. A hologram appeared to the right of the threshold as we neared, a stylized, anime-looking angel misting into existence over what looked to be a flower pot, his sword held high.

"GO WITH GOD." He spoke in all caps, leaving us no choice in the matter.

"Fuuuuuuck off," I fired back, my voice ululating a bit in a sing-songy way. Bishop snickered.

I pushed the right-hand door and nothing happened. In a moment of inspiration, I pulled the ring out of my pocket, slid it on my left pinkie and tried again. This time, the doors both opened automatically with a soft whoosh. I placed it back in my pocket. We stepped out into the dark streets of Canaan again. I pulled up my smartwatch map to see how far we had to go.

"Only a few blocks," I said. Then, like an absolute dumbass: "We've gotten fairly lucky on our little trip thus far, my man."

The sniper round hit the brick façade inches from my face, throwing jagged splinters of rock into my specs just as Butch's proximity alert buzzed in my ears and pinged my HUD.

CHAPTER SEVEN

I strong-armed the priest back through the door with my left arm while shouldering the Excalibur upward and down to a firing position.

"DOWN," I shouted. "Take cover! Sundance, Butch, engage!"

The smaller of the drones zipped out and up, soaring 50 meters or so in the air to get a better picture of the situation. Sundance veered right and up as well, no doubt zeroing in on the source of the shot.

I crouched down on the right side of the exit, my back against the wall. Bishop was on the other side, some five feet away from the doorway. I peeked around and almost caught a bullet for my trouble, but it scraped up ferrocrete 20 feet or so down the ramp and ricocheted off into the station. Felt the wind from it, though. Whoever the sniper was, it wasn't their first rodeo. If they were wired and had any sort of machine assist, though, we'd probably already be dead. Viva la naturale. I sprang across to the other side and landed in a crouch facing the door. If I were more tacticool, I probably would have rolled, but it is what it is. That shit is harder than it looks. Hell on the knees.

Butch fed me an overview of the surrounding streetscape. He was picking up five mild heat signatures from a building across the way, probably at least on the fourth floor or higher from the angle of these shots. Whoever these guys were, they had some sort of thermal masking, but not quite good enough to fool Butch completely. I leaned ever so slightly into the opening to my right and aimed the Excalibur one handed ... too cumbersome and front heavy to successfully make any sort of shot like this, but enough to get close. The target reticle on my right lens lit up as my barrel and scope drifted past a fifth floor window with a dark shape visible inside. I fired a shot, which wasn't even close, but it definitely made the shape flinch and back up. It was enough to delay the sniper, though, and it was enough for Sundance to hop on for a little piggyback action. The Hellion drone had already been en route, but it picked up speed as it swooped down to the fifth floor window. I could hear a tiny whir from above as Sundance switched to armor-piercing rounds to fire above the subject's head and shatter the window, then switch back to sleeper spines. Good boy, I thought. We need someone alive to question. A series of quick *thwips* were barely audible from my position, so close after the sound of breaking glass that they could've almost been an echo.

"Stay here," I told the priest. As I bolted for the building across the street, I heard his voice ring out behind me.

"No worries! Not going anywhere!"

There were no shots from above as I hauled ass across the street. Maybe Sundance had taken the sniper out and his compatriots had yet to pick up his slack. Maybe I just got lucky. I ran into the brick-lined entryway of the building where the sniper and his fire team were located, shouldering the glass door open and stumbling into a small lobby. Brass mailboxes lined the wall to my left, and a stairway lead upward past a brass and crystal chandelier that was just a bit too big and gaudy for the space. Other than a trash can filled to bursting with garbage that had long ago lost its pungence, there was little else remarkable about the room. I slung the rifle across my back again and pulled my Colt Heathen from its SOB holster and moved it to my left hand. I then unholstered the Narcoject. Dual-wielding pistols never quite works the way it does in action movies, but I had no plans to dive into the air firing both while ironically soothing classical music played counterpoint to my badassery as things blew up into orange fireballs behind me. It was just nice to have lethal and non-lethal weapons at my disposal. To fire one at a time, like a civilized merc. Of course, electronics do help with the off-hand accuracy. And, honestly, having been a drummer for most of my life, I am somewhat functionally ambidextrous. Can't write with my left, but can get the job done with a blade almost as well as with my right. As far as firearms go, I might even be slightly better with my left.

About three steps into the climb upward, it occurred to me that I might not be the target. If I wasn't, and if these guys had any brains whatsoever, they'd try to separate us.

"Sundance," I said quietly as I climbed the stairs as stealthily and quickly as possible, guns pointed into the dim stairwell above. "Disengage. Guard the friendly."

I looked across the stairwell and out of the window that faced the priest's hiding place and saw Sundance floating downward and toward the open double doors where Bishop was hopefully still crouched.

"Open a channel," I told the drone as I continued my climb, passing the third floor. "Padre ... you good? I am sending my Hellion to watch over you. His name is Sundance. He can't communicate with you per se, but I will leave this channel open. Let me know if you need help. Sundance, put anyone who isn't the priest the hell to sleep."

My stupid calves began to burn a bit as I approached the fifth floor landing, probably an indicator that I don't do enough incline work on the ol' dreadmill. What can I say? I'm a work in progress. The door to the rooms beyond was cracked, and I nudged it open with my left foot. I poked my head in and checked both directions, the barrel of the Heathen peeking out as well, and then proceeded toward where I thought the sniper's nest might be.

The hallway itself was neater than the cannibal's church had been, a well-worn runner with a fleur-de-lis pattern bisecting its length. Some of the doors I passed were open, some shut. I peeked in the open ones but saw very little in the way of paramilitary douchebags, merely small studio apartments in various degrees of disarray. I had Butch feed my optics the most current thermal view of the rooms beyond. I approached the door of apartment 514, which looked to be the correct hidey-hole for sharpshooting assholes. Five tagged shapes outlined in red seemed pretty still inside. Three of them had tiny zzzs above them, signifying they had been knocked cold by Narcoject spines. I toyed with the idea of kicking the door in and surprising the denizens of 514, but honestly, these doors look pretty solid and that can sometimes not work out the way you want it to. So I opted for the more humorous approach. I placed my back to the wall to the right of the door and knocked gently on it at about thigh-level with the butt of the Heathen.

"Candygram!" I said in a loud, cheerful voice, yanking my hand back away from the door as I did so.

The thin, metal sheath on the wooden door bloomed outward with the impact of a shotgun blast in the general vicinity of where my head would have been had I been an absolute moron straight out of the treasure hunting merc academy (And, no, that's not a real thing. Although ... maybe I could start one as my retirement plan?) who was standing in front of an apartment full of armed assholes who presumably wanted him dead. Splinters, jagged chunks of metal and red-hot buckshot flew across the hall in a fast-moving cloud of debris.

"Jehovah's Witness?" I yelled this time. Another blast from the shotgun – a little lower this time - drowned out the rest of my witty repartee, which, for your information included "Do you have a moment to talk about our Lord and Savior?"

I spun to my left and kicked the remainder of the door open, firing the Heathen as I did so, catching the gunman in the lower right abdomen. His white BDUs blossomed blood and the shotgun veered to his right away from me as he stifled a scream and stumbled back a step. Gunshots do not typically knock people across rooms in real life, by the way. That's strictly old-school action movie bullshit.

"I've been trying to contact you about your vehicle's

extended warranty!" I shouted as I took the opportunity to fire a Narcoject spine into his throat before he could recover himself. Despite the nearly instantaneous nature of the toxin, the bastard actually kept his feet, woozily swaying to and fro. He must've have some constitutional enhancements to manage even that. I closed the distance between us in a second and clocked him across the temple pretty damned hard with the side of the Heathen. Not hard enough to crack his skull, but enough to finish the job the sleeper spine started.

As he fell, I spun on my heels to take in the rest of the room, double-checking the corners and behind the door. Had anyone been there, I would've most likely been shot in the back already. Which was a bit sloppy on my part, perhaps, but the shotgun-wielding threat directly in my line of sight was definitely numero uno. And Butch had tagged the rest of these guys as sleepers, minus one. What I did see upon turning was a white-clad leg sticking out from under the small single bed, a crumpled white form caught half in and half out of the small bathroom to my left, and beyond the guy I had just shot, the sleeping form of the sniper, still cradling his rifle and crumpled under the window Sundance had shot out. That was four. I checked Butch's overlay again. It looked like a straggler had made it into the bathroom and was being very, very still.

I crept past the sleeping forms strewn about the apartment and stepped over the guy in the bathroom's doorway. As I passed, I noticed Narcoject spines sticking out of them in random places. It looked like Sundance had nailed the guy under the bed in the ankle as he tried to crawl to safety. Nice. As silently as I could, I approached the bathtub, where I could plainly make out the standing silhouette of a hooded person holding a gun aimed upward toward the ceiling in a two-hand grip through the floral patterned shower curtain, beautifully backlit and as tempting a target as ever I had seen.

I lowered the Narcoject and pointed it at the silhouette's crotch. *THWIP*.

"GAAAAAAHHHHHHH," the man screamed, for it was

indeed a man. A man with newly pierced junk. I decided he would henceforth be known as Prince Albert.

He flailed for just a second and tried to bring his gun to bear before his legs gave out. He managed to grab on to the shower curtain and take it down with him as he fell.

I hit Butch up for a further threat assessment as I looked upon the poor prince's sleeping form, wrapped around the crumpled plastic curtain like a napkin ring, and the little drone gave me an all clear. I also gave the priest an all clear and asked him to join me along with his flying escort.

I walked back into the room proper, holstering both of my pistols. I pulled a set of zip tie handcuffs from my sling bag and dragged the sniper until he was sitting upright against the wall between the two windows. I also raided his thigh holster and mag pouch while I was at it, pocketing the semi-auto and two spare mags. I gave him a thorough pat-down, practically making it to third base. Then I zip-tied his hands in front of him and snapped an ammonia and tetrodotoxin antidote ampoule under his nose. As he stirred, I kissed him lightly on the forehead underneath his dark widow's peak and slapped the ever-loving shit out of him. I really put my hips into it, too. It was definitely going to leave a mark.

"Hola, shithead!" I barked merrily. "Wake the fuck up and smell what I have cooking! Which is, at the very least, a major ass whooping if you don't tell me what I want to know. At worst, you're going to experience all manner of unpleasantness ranging from the downright medieval to the positively biblical. Sooo, what's it gonna be, sport?" I thumped his patrician nose with my middle finger for emphasis. He flinched back and blinked his eyes rapidly.

"Torture me if you want, Davidson," he snarled at me in a vaguely British sounding accent. "I will never tell you what you want to know."

"Tell me who sent you and why," I said simply.

"Oh. Well, actually I don't mind telling you that," he surprised me by saying. "That's the message we came to deliver, if we were unsuccessful at killing you."

"Huh," I replied. "Why not just deliver the message and NOT try to kill me? I'm a pretty reasonable guy." I raised my empty hands to the side, palms skyward, and shrugged. "I mean, you're all still alive. Even Prince Albert, but honestly, he's going to be hating life for a few days."

"Who? Never mind. They told me you were something of a comedian. We don't have time for your funny stuff. You have to abandon this quest for the Book of Raziel. The people, the THINGS that want it will remake reality with it or worse. It will be like handing a nuclear bomb to a group of sociopathic terrorists with a death wish."

"Ok, man. Your horrible similes aside, I have two notes: One, there's always time for funny stuff. Two, I don't believe any of that superstitious, supernatural bullshit, so it will literally be JUST like me handing a book to some dudes who paid me a lot of money to get said book for them. I have no doubt they are creeps, or at least their middleman is, but I can't conceive of a reality where they can do anything with that book other than look at the pretty pictures and/or bore themselves to tears trying to translate it over the next decade or so. Also, what can I call you? Dude or man seems, I dunno. You don't have to give me your real name as I don't really give a shit. How about we use code names? You can call me Bronco."

"My name is Jonas Sallow."

"That is a really shitty code name, bud," I said. "Makes you sound like a B-movie detective. How about I call you 'Nightstar'? Oooh, that sounds mysterious and cool. Just rolls off the tongue. *Niiightstar*." I waved my hands mysteriously and coolly.

"It's not a code name. It's my real name," he frowned at me.

"Why did you tell me that? I told you I didn't give a shit. You are a lousy listener, JONAS." I grinned at him as I reached over and plucked the Narcoject spine from the side of his neck. I pulled out my little bag of used spines and placed it inside. "And yes, I recycle because I care."

"I am NOT calling you Bronco," he said with disgust. "Besides, I already said your name. I obviously know your name. You KNOW I know your name."

The priest and my Hellion chose this moment to walk in and hover in respectively.

"He asked you to call him Bronco?" Bishop smiled with delight. "I know that one! Groundhog Day! Um, nineteen ninety ... four?"

"Wow! So close. 1993. Thanks for playing, though! You win a brand new set of steak knives."

"Cool," he gushed.

"Fuck. There are two of you," Sallow said, crestfallen.

"I resent that," I said. "I'm goddamned hilarious, and he's mildly barmy. We're definitely not the same. Seems a stand-up guy, though."

"Thank you, Daniel," the priest said solemnly, looking like he was about to happy cry.

"Ah ah ah," I admonished the priest gently, waving my index finger from side to side. "We're using code names now, Padre. Or should I call you *The Cardinal*?" I made the *dunh dunh DAAAH* sound.

"Is this the torture you were talking about?" Sallow asked, rolling his eyes. "Because you can go ahead and shoot me now."

"Whatever, Nightstar," I said. "If that IS your real name." I gave him my hardest stare.

"Are you sure you're not the crazy one?" Nightstar asked. "I have genuine concerns."

"That's just mean," I replied. "All of my personalities are perfectly sane. Ok. Enough chitty-chat. Back to business. Who do you work for? Actually, wait. Put a pin in that. Do you have a med kit? Your friend with the shotgun is probably bleeding out."

"Lucas is our medic. It's probably under there with him." Nightstar nodded his head toward the bed.

"K." I walked over and pulled on the legs sticking out from under the bed. I also nicked the spine from his ankle. Out popped another goon in white BDUs, face down and sleeping peacefully. He had a med pouch beside him that ran around his torso on a strap. I pulled out my multi-tool and cut through it, freeing the pack. I briefly toyed with using my stiletto, but I figured keeping that a secret from Nightstar might come in handy during future encounters, if I let the guy live. I was leaning that way, but the day was young.

I ripped open the pack and found a foam gun. I gave the long nozzle a once-over with an alcohol wipe and then duck walked over to shotgun guy. I ripped his BDU jacket away from the wound and lifted his shirt. It looked like the bullet missed everything vital. I felt around the back and found a decent-sized exit wound. I crammed the nozzle of the foam gun into the wound and pulled the trigger, filling it with medical foam until it began fluffing out onto his stomach. I gently rolled him over on his side and repeated the procedure for the entry wound, and then rolled him onto his back. I tossed the gun back down into the med pack, wiped my bloody hand off on his white outfit, and returned to my half-assed interrogation of Nightstar.

"Ok, pal. That'll keep him stable until you can get him somewhere. Which I guess also lets the cat out of the bag that I'm not planning on killing all of you. And I really don't care overmuch for torture, either, so there's no real stick here to hold over your head. The carrot is, I'll let you get back to your transport so you can get him med-evac'ed the fuck out of here. I guess the stick is, well, I'll shoot you in one or both legs and leave you all here to your fate? Nothing arterial, mind. Just enough to make it an absolute bitch for you to get out of here. These guys will be out for another four hours or more, so ... sounds pretty awful to me, crawling across the neighborhood and down forty floors to a docking bay. I guess you could take the quick way down, though. Anyway ... Where were we? Oh, yeah. Who sent you to kill me and why?"

He sighed. "We work for an organization dedicated to stopping the Angelic Host from traveling to our plane and destroying what is left of humanity and remaking reality to suit them. We're called The Order of Solomon's Temple, but you have probably known us by ..."

"Shut the fuck up," I said, interrupting and incredulous. "You're telling me you're Templars. Ok, let's put aside the fact that you're maybe the tenth bunch of whackos I've run across calling themselves that ..."

"Those others were but pale imitations borrowing our name to suit their own purposes," Nightstar said, indignantly. "We are descended from the actual Templars, and we have kept the faith for over 1200 years."

"Ok, there's the other part right there. I thought you guys were buddy-buddy with God and Jesus. Why would you not be on the side of the angels?"

"Well, if you'll remember your history, Mother Church put us all to the stake, and we're still a little bitter. That aside, it goes far deeper than a simple grudge and delves into the reasons we were eradicated in the first place. As you probably know from the history books, King Philip IV of France and Pope Clement V feared our power and desired our vast wealth and resources for themselves. They branded us heretics and Satanists, and went about rounding us up and killing us almost to the man. The truth is far more complex, though."

"It usually is," I noted. "History written by the victors and all. And often centuries after the actual events and jotted down by people who weren't actually witness to any of it. The Christian Bible is a perfect example."

"Point taken, and if I may say so, you seem a lot less insane now, by the way."

"Oh, that's mostly for effect and my own amusement. I enjoy fucking with people. Now you have my full attention, though, so I shall keep my snark and playfully unhinged banter to a minimum, good sir."

"Thank you," he said. "Anyway, so, the real reason for the papal genocide is that we discovered the Truth."

"Said every heretic, like, EVER," I remarked. "And don't

think the capital T was lost on me. But, please ... go on."

"Touché. Jacques de Molay, the last Grandmaster of our Order, accidentally witnessed a meeting between representatives of the Pope and one of these angelic beings ... who, by the way, are rather horrifying to look upon. It is my understanding that they can present the illusion of appearing like your average medieval drawing of an angel when needs must ... Caucasian, flowing blonde locks, pristine gossamer robes and fluffy white dove's wings ... but they are far closer to the Revelator's descriptions of them: nightmarish beings of many eyes, flaming hoops, many heads, legs like pillars of flame, sparrow wings sprouting from all parts of their amorphous bodies."

He shifted uncomfortably but continued. "In short, they look like what they actually are: alien beings from another dimension ... Lovecraftian horrors ... you know Lovecraft?" I nodded.

"Good. He was a bit of a shit, but he knew things, and his ideas of cosmic horror are closer to the truth than almost anyone has ever guessed. The Host have an agenda we can only guess at, but that is, to the best of our reckoning, 100% antithetical to our survival as a species. Keep in mind, they are not supernatural beings, but are instead so alien to us and possess a tech tree and methodologies so beyond our understanding that their science appears as magic to us. So, as a skeptic, you may not believe in the mystical and supernature, but I assume you have seen enough to believe in superscience? Our technologies would have appeared to be nothing short of miraculous to the people of the Middle Ages or even the Renaissance. Indeed, we believe many of the miracles outlined in the Bible were the result of Angelic intervention or the use of their tech."

I stared at him, arms crossed, deep in thought. Bishop had plopped down on the bed some time ago as he listened to our discussion, but he now stood and wrung his hands.

"Are you saying the Church is IN on this? That they have

been covering up the truth of this relationship and that all of the Biblical ... I mean, ALL of it is a lie?" The priest began to pace around the small room, avoiding the sleeping forms of the Templars scattered about but keeping his eyes on Nightstar.

"No, not all of it. And not all of the Church is to blame, either," Nightstar said in almost a consoling tone. "We believe those that have historically allied themselves with the angels are a large faction, but we don't know how many. At times, they have included Popes and large portions of the Council of Cardinals. Their power within the Church seems to have waxed and waned many times throughout history. And the vast majority of Christians are perfectly ignorant of this, and innocent of any wrongdoing. Likewise the Clergy. There are indeed parts of the Bible that can be taken quite literally but that tell a different story altogether when you know the origins and nature of the beings we have long considered to be gods and demigods. Lucifer's rebellion, Christ's virgin birth and resurrection ... "

"Are you saying God and Jesus are ALIENS?" The priest looked apoplectic.

"We think Jesus was a half-alien at the very least," Nightstar said. "Possibly created as a bridge between our two species. But, yes. The entity we think of as Jehovah is most likely an interdimensional alien being. The concept of the Trinity may have come about as a result of the hive mind or split consciousness shared by God and his half-human Son. The Holy Spirit could very well be a sentient, cloud-based neural network that shares that consciousness and can infect or inhabit organic networks – human brains – in a form of parasitism."

"Ok. First of all, this is all absolutely batshit," I said, waving at him in a halting gesture with both hands to slow his roll. "If I buy any of it, though, what makes you so sure they are out to get us? They've basically been leaving us alone for thousands of years, right? Or gently shaping our history without causing too much harm ... or anything so openly apocalyptic. This is End Times/Revelation/Ragnarok type stuff you are hinting at. Why do they want to take us off the board now? It's not like we have much of a planet left now for them to take."

"We don't know exactly," he said. "Maybe it is because of the damage we HAVE done to the earth they hoped to inherit? Maybe this has all been in the stars since John the Elder of Patmos accidentally ate the wrong berries or fungi and side-slipped his consciousness onto their otherworldly wavelength? Perhaps since they existed before us, they have always resented our creation or evolution, however intentional or unintentional or intelligently designed it may or may not have been? And they've been biding their time until the stars were right or the planets aligned to make it all possible? It's all conjecture as far as motive goes." He breathed out a long sigh and rolled his head back to stare at the ceiling, exhausted by this long discussion, the horrific ideas within, or both.

"I know, man. This is all really heavy," I sympathized. "But I need to know something relatively concrete here, because you're asking me to ... what, exactly? I mean, you were going to kill me to prevent me from finding the book. You fucked that up, so what's next?"

"We wanted to prevent you from obtaining the book at all costs, yes," he said. "Some of us did, anyway. Others wanted to let you find the book and then take it from you before you could deliver it to the Host. Or the Outsiders as we sometimes call them as it sounds less like an honorific."

"Stay gold, Ponyboy," I croaked. "Which camp were you in? You know what, never mind. It doesn't matter. What was the deciding factor?"

"You're not going to like this." He looked pained.

"Go ahead. Hit me."

He sighed again. "We flipped a coin and let fate decide." He had the decency to look embarrassed.

"You ..." I began. "You flipped a fucking coin."

"We were at a stalemate," he explained. "Deadlocked at 50/50 for days on end, and time was of the essence. If we were going to take action, we needed to do it now or else go further down the path to ensure the book fell into our hands after you ... stumbled and fumbled into successfully finding it."

"Ouch," I said, wounded. "That stings a bit. I'm pretty good at what I do. Some would say I'm one of the best." I rolled my shoulders and stretched my neck. I might've even clenched my fists and bowed up a bit.

"Oh, you're pretty good," he offered, raising his zip-tied wrists toward me in resignation. "It's not that. It's just that there are a lot of factors involved, and one of your chief skillsets seems to be, well, being lucky."

"I'll take that, I suppose," I grinned. "But one man's luck is another man's clever planning, perfect load-out, and effortless execution that is so next-level that it is indistinguishable from luck."

Both the Templar and the priest looked at me doubtfully. Doubtful to the extreme. Is there a word for light years beyond doubtful?

"Fuck off, the both of you," I said. "I swear, I will pick him up and beat you WITH him." I nodded toward the priest as I made narrowed-eye contact with Nightstar. "Anyway, so again, now what? I just let you go and you promise not to hunt me down and ambush me again, and I take your word on it? If our entire reality is at stake, why would you dare to do that?"

"I'm not sure you'd trust me even if I gave you my word," he said. "And we will most definitely try and stop you again."

"Huh. Ok. So, what if I agreed to hand over the book to you once it's found?"

"You'd do that? You'd betray a client? I thought you, um, had a code?" He looked doubtful again.

"Well, I do, and it's not my favorite thing ever, but let's just say I have a morality clause in my contract that makes it null and void if I find out you're planning to unmake reality," I said. "I mean, in the long run, that's basically like cheating me out of my pay. Can't spend it on cool shit if I ... and said cool shit ... no longer exist."

"That's valid," he said. "Solid reasoning."

"Stop sucking up. So, I could just contact them and tell them I'm off the job," I offered. "The biggest problem with that is, though, that they could just hire someone else. And if that person succeeds, well, we're still screwed. So I still need to find the book. But, you don't trust me to do that and not fulfill my contract as I could be lying to you to keep you - and your crosshairs - off my back. So, we have trust issues, basically, and I'm still not sure this is not all complete and total horseshit. I mean, again, let's say I buy all of this. How does the book work if it's not magic?"

"We believe the language within is quite literally the source code of, well, if not Creation itself, then at the very least it is a set of verbal and visual commands that were used to modify existing conditions in this dimension to make them suitable for life and to jumpstart human evolution."

"So, if I'm following, you're saying that Alien Jehovah said, in Enochian or Angelic speech or whatever, voice commands to the ethereal computer behind reality itself ... in effect 'Let there be light,' and conditions changed to allow us to develop? A bolt of lightning hit the proverbial primal stew and a little cluster of cells became a fishy proto-human or whatever that developed tiny little legs and walked out onto a beach and ordered a Mai Tai and started paying taxes?"

"Um, basically," he shrugged. "We're not sure about the particulars of the early stuff, but that sounds about right."

"And you know all of this how? From one dude overhearing a conversation between some churchmen and an angel? They must've been deep in their cups to be pondering all of this stuff."

"No, that was just the impetus for us to cast off the veil of ignorance we had been operating under," he said. "We found out the rest over many more centuries of research and successful intelligence operations. The survivors among us and their descendants, anyway. The Book of Raziel is not the only forbidden tome out there, after all. And the Host are not a monoculture. They are mostly united, but there have always been outliers and rebels and turncoats among them; some of whom had no more desire for this reality to be destroyed or remade than we do."

"That tracks," I said. "Ok. I'm now a solid 80/20 on your story."

"The 80 is believing me?"

"No," I grimaced. "It's the 20. But that's enough for me to think maybe handing this book over to Archer and his pals is not worth the gamble. And that maybe you're not so bad, despite having tried to kill me a short while ago."

"Well, to be fair, it was kind of a warning shot," he said. "Had I truly wanted you dead, you'd have never seen it coming."

"So, you were in the camp that didn't want me dead?"

"Not exactly. I was on the fence."

"That's fair. I'm on the fence about myself most days, too. So, here we are. Still at an impasse. I don't particularly want to kill you, but I can't have you dogging me from orbital to orbital taking pot shots at me until you decide to take me off the board for good," I said. "And you can't let me go after the book, knowing I might disregard your bullshit and honor my contract, giving it to the Outsiders ... which is an unoriginal and shit name by the way. And, FUCK. Now I want a Mai Tai."

We sat in silence for a few moments, pondering the situation.

"He could just come with us," the priest said.

"What?" Both Nightstar and I said in stereo.

"You said it yourself, Daniel," Bishop said sagely, as was his way. "We can't have him behind us or lying in wait for us. The situation is too dire for you NOT to believe him, or to risk killing him and his team. He can't trust us to deliver the book. So, he comes with us, helps us get the book, and by that time, maybe you'll have both figured out where you stand and come up with a way to get us out of this situation. Plus, you know, keep your friends close and your enemies closer. They'll be a lot less inclined to blow us up if he's with us and they believe we're working with him and not against them. And you won't be working against each other as you both need the book found. After that, well, that's another bridge entirely."

We stared at the priest.

"That ... actually makes a lot of sense," I said.

"Are you SURE he's the crazy one?" Nightstar asked.

"I mean, not entirely?" I shrugged. "He likes beer, nachos and pirate shanties and has seen Groundhog Day, so I'll give him the benefit of the doubt."

"Huh. I love a good sea shanty," Nightstar said.

I sighed. "Well, fuck. I guess we're doing this then."

CHAPTER EIGHT

I pulled out my multi-tool and cut Nightstar's bonds. I then collected all of my Narcoject spines, and we spent the next few minutes reviving the fire team (except for Shotgun Boy), including a very pissed and sulky Prince Albert.

"Sorry about your dick and stuff, my man," I offered my apology to the man I'd skewered. "I mean, I didn't know whether or not you'd be into it, and I got carried away. You're going to have to pick a better safeword than 'GAAAAAAH' next time. And maybe not, you know, be actively trying to kill me."

He stalked out of the room. The Templar team was regrouping in the room next door to discuss the tentative plans Nightstar and I had made. The priest and I sat side by side on the bed and listened as raised voices and shouts came through the wall and down the hall. Butch and Sundance hovered quietly nearby. I thought to myself that I really needed to look into upgrading their operating systems to include the full-on AI package. Would be nice for them to be able to tell me what they thought of all this. The three of us have seen some shit together.

After about 20 minutes of deliberation, Nightstar walked back into the room, alternately massaging his forehead and rubbing the stubble on his cheek in thought.

"Well, they're not happy about it, but they at least see the sense in our plan, such as it is," he said. "They are going to take Willis, the man you shot, back to our transport and home to The Order for medical attention. We'll proceed to ... where are we going?"

"Super-secret section of the Canaan Administrative Library," I said. "Or whatever the fuck the proper name is.

According to Bishop here ... oh. Yeah. Father Elias Bishop, humble steward of the faith and fellow lover of sea shanties. Up until recently, a basement gimp for a cannibal cult. Padre, meet Nightstar."

"PLEASE stop calling me that," Nightstar said.

"FINE. Father Bishop, meet Jonas Sallow, Templar Knight, which I can't even say with a straight face." I rolled my eyes.

"Thank you, Davidson," Sallow said, extending his hand to Bishop.

"It's Bronco," I began.

"NOPE," Sallow replied. "So, a priest named Bishop?"

"I know," Bishop said. "Just let it go."

"Do you mean the Bishop Bishop thing or the Bronco thing?" Sallow looked genuinely confused.

"Yes," the priest replied with a huff. "You're almost as exhausting as he is."

"The feeling is mutual," Sallow said. A thought occurred to him and he made a show of patting himself down. "Did you take my sidearm?"

"Oh, yeah," I reached into my hoodie pocket and drew out the pistol and spare magazines. "I was going to let the priest use it, but now that's you're along, we probably have a better survivability rate with your finger on the trigger."

I handed the firearm and mags back to him with my left hand. As I did so, I spoke to him softly and matter-of-factly.

"Sallow?" He looked up as he took the pistol. I drew my Heathen from its SOB holster with near blinding speed, my jacked reflexes maxing out as I touched the tip of the barrel between his eyes before he could even blink in surprise. The Heathen was hammerless, otherwise I would have cocked it for dramatic effect.

"I can trust you right? I mean, mostly. As much as any shitty human can trust another. Not to stab me or my friend here in the back?"

He became very still, eyes slightly crossed as he looked at the Heathen. "Yes, Davidson. You have my word. Until we have the book, and even then, we will discuss the matter like adults and decide upon a course of action."

"Good," I said, calmly, still aiming the pistol at his face. "Because if you fuck me over or hurt the priest, I will hunt down and execute everyone you've ever met. Even in passing. And their pets."

I slowly lowered the pistol and placed it back snugly into its holster.

"You're bluffing, right? Like with the torture?"

"I mean, yes," I said amiably. "I love animals and would never think of killing one. Unless, you know, I was on a desert island and starving. As for the rest, I guess you'll just have to fuck around and find out. I'd say the odds are a strong 80/20."

"The 80 is the chance you're bluffing. Right?"

I smiled and clapped him on the arm. "Whatever helps you sleep at night, pal. Maybe I'll flip a coin first."

I ambled out of the room without another word and began sauntering downstairs, as was my way after delivering a threat and coolly walking away like a badass. As I did so, I heard Sallow mumble something to the priest about me being a sociopath. I grinned even bigger and giggled. Which, to be fair, is probably what a sociopath would do.

I informed the boys to mark Sallow and his team as friendlies in their targeting systems. "Unless, of course, you have a setting for 'frenemies'?" I inquired of the drones. They did not. Maybe that comes with the upgrade package.

I waited by the door of the building. The priest came out first, followed by Sallow, his sniper rifle slung across his back. I dialed up the map on my smartwatch and projected it for them to see. Our destination was about five blocks away. I sent the drones up for overwatch duty and we began walking toward the library.

The buildings that surrounded us were fairly tall, but they were certainly dwarfed by the enormity of the spindle, which looked to be about a half-mile inward from us. The mass of the narrow, conical spindle shot up dome-ward to the tune of roughly 2,700 feet, not counting the 200 meter communications spire on top ... if I remember my spindle data correctly. All of the spires are the same size and are home to over 150 floors of administrative offices, public works and services, and premium rental office space.

Each spindle is a gleaming metal and glass tower that is roughly modeled after the famous Burj Khalifa tower in Dubai, filtered through their own design aesthetic of course ... kind of like a McDonald's burger joint on Earth That Was that had been forced to dress up as a Tudor cottage with half-timber appointments and peaked gables in a fancy neighborhood that required such. Despite each having its own distinctive look ranging from fairy tale castle to Arabesque fortress ... each one was basically a gigantic, razor-sharp, glinting spear tip stabbing toward the heavens. Here on Canaan, the spindle looked like someone had smashed a mosque and a gothic cathedral together, slapped a bunch of windows on it, and stretched it skyward until it ended in a needle-pointed minaret.

More skyscrapers - or domescrapers I suppose one could more accurately say – surround the spindle, but they get shorter as one travels outward. The next block drops to about 100 floors max, and the next 50. On the block we stood on, the buildings looked to be roughly 25 stories or so in height, the shiny façades far more modern than the Mayberry-esque outer rim neighborhood where I had found the priest. The streets were wider, but still mostly empty. A delivery van or two sat here and there, hunched low on its gravlifts, doors open. Otherwise, there was very little sign that the central district had ever been occupied.

Overturned ferrocrete barriers here and there bore signs of scorch marks and cracks presumably caused by small arms fire. Many of the street level windows likewise sported cracks or appeared smoked in color, but none appeared to be completely broken, which stood to reason given how tough the glass tended to be spindleward. Like many cities on the old Earth That Was, power and wealth tended to congregate in certain areas on the orbitals, usually near the center. The Powers That Be love to have a vantage point that allows them to look down upon others and survey all their mighty works, etc. Some things never change.

Our stroll, heavily armed as it was, remained uneventful except for some general gawping at the surroundings. The priest's head remained on a swivel, turning to and fro constantly, taking it all in. I had to keep reminding myself that his world view had been extremely limited over the last decade. The Artist Formerly Known as Nightstar, A.K.A. Bullshit Templar Knight Jonas Sallow, walked purposefully with a decidedly military bearing, his eyes taking in everything, his right hand never straying far from his thigh holster. I had my Excalibur at port arms, likewise scanning the streets and alleyways for potential threats while Butch and Sundance did their drone thing overhead.

We reached the library, a massive tower that looked much like the surrounding buildings with very little in the way of character or architecturally interesting appointments. Even the name "Canaan Central Library System – Administrative Branch" was bolted on the side of the building in bland, blocky letters. The one concession to color seemed to be two ferrocrete lions perched on small outcroppings on either side of the shallow steps that lead up to the entrance. And by color, I mean coolness, because even the rough-hewn, stylized lions were a boring-ass slate color that matched the rest of the building.

Our little dysfunctional fellowship marched up the stairs toward the mirrored glass double doors. I took point and pushed open the right door, quietly telling Butch to zip inside and get me a decent map of the main room and a threat assessment. Sallow pushed open the left hand door, and we all stepped inside. The interior lights illuminated as we entered, obviously on a motion-detection system that was still in perfect working order. I am not being hyperbolic in the least when I say the view left our jaws hanging wide.

CHAPTER NINE

What the exterior of the building lacked in color and interest, the interior of the library made up for in the biggest, best way possible. Stacks upon stacks of dark, wooden bookshelves stretched off into the sparsely and indirectly lit lobby as far as the eye could see, broken up only by reading tables or ornately decorated plinths containing marble busts, warmly lit globes, or 3D models of the orbitals. The floor appeared to be genuine Italian marble tiles or a close facsimile, divided into alternating black and gold squares. A gorgeous faux-mahogany (I assumed) circulation desk the size of a city bus sat square in the middle of the room. Spiral staircases that looked to be wrought iron led to mezzanines and balconies above us, surrounding the giant open space on all four sides, covered in even more bookshelves and buttressed by black marble columns. Frosted orange sconces and art-deco inspired bar lights carved beautiful cones of opulence from the darkness everywhere we looked.

The ceiling of the room looked to be at least ten stories above us, and - from what I could make out in the relative gloom above – it appeared to be covered by a holographic image of a stormy sky, smoky cumulonimbus tufts lazily floating into and out of view as they were obscured by balconies overhead. The place looked like the Trinity College Library and the Royal Portuguese Reading Room had a love child, and it was absolutely beautiful. If you're not a book nerd or an antiquarian like me, you probably don't get those references. Just think book heaven. But if those eluded you …

"Holy SHIT," I breathed. "Welcome to fucking Hogwarts."

"Oh, I get that one! Harry Potter! Great series," said the

priest. "I'd totally be a Hufflepuff, I think."

"Of course you would," I said jovially. "I don't know … I've always thought I'd end up in Ravenclaw."

Sallow looked at us both as if trying to decide whether or not to kill us on the spot. (Acting like a total Slytherin, by the way.) The magnificence of the view won him over as well, though, and he returned his gaze to the thousands of books, hundreds of reading nooks, and artfully filled alcoves.

"Why have I never been here?" I asked, mostly to myself. "I mean, I had no idea. I have seen the name on blueprints and such over the years, but I had no idea something so boring sounding could be so … can a library be erotic? Because this is totally book porn to me. This deserves a much better name than 'Administrative Branch.' This is absolute nirvana … a librarian utopia, which is the best kind of utopia as far as I am concerned."

"This IS nice," Sallow said. "You can get with your travel agent and start planning your return trip when this is all over, but for now, we should probably find THE book."

"Huh. Travel agent. That's a pretty obscure reference for someone of your limited intellect," I smirked at Sallow. "Nice. Still, though, you're not wrong. Padre? Thoughts? You mentioned super-secret sublevels and stuff. Think the circulation desk would have a map or a record of the book?"

"I don't know, Daniel," he said. "The forbidden tomes and confiscated properties are probably not for the general public's consumption, so I doubt they'd be listed there. They are probably catalogued locally within the restricted area, if I had to guess. There might be a map to the restricted areas, though."

Barmy though he might be, the priest made an excellent point. We walked over to and around the massive circulation desk to an opening that allowed us ingress. The three of us shuffled around for a bit, digging through drawers and stacks of books and papers. I tapped a key on a dusty keyboard in the center of the desk and a monitor screen projection blossomed into life, presenting a menu that included a catalogue and branch information.

I scrolled through the menu options. I had an epiphany as I did so, and reached back into one of the drawers I had previously searched and drew a memory stick out of a huge bowl overflowing with them. I plopped it down underneath the projection, and a small window opened, offering me the option to download a digital copy of the catalogue. I figured it was probably standard procedure back in the day for students or visitors to receive one so that they could navigate the labyrinthine stacks and not bother the librarians overmuch.

I downloaded the catalogue in its entirety in case I decided to return on a shopping trip in the future, and I placed the memory stick in my sling bag. Then, all business, I dug through the menus until I found a complete sitemap.

"Bingo," I said to my companions.

"What the hell does that mean?" Sallow asked with his characteristic charm and social aplomb.

"Ugh. Insert theatrical eye roll here. It means I found the map." I reached up and dragged my fingers through the projected map, tilting and panning and zooming until it showed the restricted area reserved for books. There was also a restricted area for artifacts, which I would definitely have to check out later.

"Here it is. Basement Level Four. A short walk from the elevator or the stairs. Probably locked up tight, though."

I rummaged around in the drawers nearby until I found a keycard on a lanyard. It was blank except for a stylized cross on one side and a magnetic strip on the other. I stuck it under the projection and a red-rimmed message window opened that read: "Keycard inserted. Coded for: General Access Only. Reformat? Y/N?"

I poked my finger through the Y. The message changed to: "Authorization required: _ _ _ _ _"

"Ok," I said. "Five characters. Surely it isn't ..."

I keyed in 12345.

"Access denied. Authorization required: _ _ _ _ _. Three

attempts left."

I cynically tried 00000.

"Access denied. Authorization required: _ _ _ _ _. Two attempts left."

The priest walked over and pulled open the drawer underneath the keyboard, nudging me out of the way slightly. He fumbled through the contents until he came up with a black notebook with a small yellow note taped to the front. He flipped the notebook around to show it to us.

"The password is JESUS, all caps," he sighed.

"Of fucking course it is," I replied, keying in the correct code.

"Jesus is The Light and The Way," Sallow said. I didn't know him well enough to tell is he was being ironic/sarcastic or not, but my guess was ... probably. I still hadn't figured out if his order was cool with half-alien Jesus or not.

"Access granted. Reformat keycard for Restricted Access/All Access? Y/N?"

I poked the Y again. The terminal beeped at me and the window turned green. "Reformat Successful. Please take keycard."

I did.

"This entire orbital was long overdue for a security audit before things went to hell," I noted. "But don't get me wrong. Gift horses and mouths, et cetera. Let's head down."

I stood and gestured for my companions to follow as I walked toward the back of the gargantuan book palace toward a hallway that the maps had indicated housed the stairs and elevators. As we were indoors and probably about to be in more confined areas, I again slung the Excalibur on my back and drew my Narcoject. Sallow drew his sidearm. Not to be outdone, the priest looked at us both and then walked back over to the desk. He ripped the cutting arm off a paper trimmer with a grunt and a pop of cracking plastic. Hefting it by the handle like a broadsword, he swished it in the air in front of him, and then returned to us with a slightly evil grin on his face.

"Great. Just what we need. Onan the Librarian," I quipped.

"I believe it was Conan the ... OHHH," Bishop flushed. "Never mind."

"No worries, Padre," I said. "We all have needs. Judgment free zone. Let's go. Stairs?"

We headed into the hallway. The door to the stairs was on the left hand side, directly across from the elevators. I pushed open the door to the stairwell and told Butch to zip on down to the fourth sublevel checking out the route as he went, and we followed suit.

Giant, glistening tentacles ripped up through the well hole between the flights and grabbed at our legs, sending us scrambling back into the lobby, screaming epithets and firing our weapons as we did so.

Ok. So, that didn't really happen. The trip down to Basement Level Four was completely uneventful. Boring, even. There was a horrible smell somewhere in the vicinity of sub level two, but that may have been the priest trying to surreptitiously relieve some gastrointestinal distress from the protein bar I gave him earlier. The rest of us politely ignored the crop dusting sonofabitch and suffered in silence. I may have heard Sundance give a little digital cough.

Once we reached Basement Level Four, we found Butch hovering outside a single, solitary door on the landing. According to the sitemap, it was located on the same wall that housed the entry to the hallway above and would open into a space three floors below the grand hall. It bore the legend "Restricted Archives A-B." The stairs continued downward. If dangerous books and artifacts were housed here, it made me wonder what manner of things could be found below even further from the general population. As long as they didn't slither up here after us, I figured that answer could also wait for a future visit.

I pulled the keycard and lanyard from the left pocket of my hoodie and swiped it on the smooth, blank panel to the right of the door. The door opened slightly with a metallic click. Inside, a tiny, nondescript foyer led to two more doors to the right and left: Restricted Archives A and B respectively. I swiped the card and opened the right-hand door to Archive B - as in Books - which may or may not have been intentional. Considering the horrible password security phrases we had discovered up to that point, I didn't credit the Canaanites overmuch for random acts of cleverness or forethought. Although, the subway tiles and the library interior had definitely exceeded my expectations. And Popemobile 2 was pretty swank. I shouldn't generalize. People can be just as amazing and clever as they can be lazy, and the two don't have to be mutually exclusive.

We stepped inside and found a gigantic warehouse of space, roughly half the size of the grand hall. It was just as austere and antiseptic as the room above had been warmly furnished and elaborately cozy; all whitewashed ferrocrete walls filled with overloaded plain metal shelving, and a rather claustrophobic one-story as opposed to ten. The area immediately inside the door lit up as we entered, but the rest of the enormous room stayed dark, obviously on a more localized and pragmatic sensor setting than the fancy showpiece upstairs.

Directly inside was a small, utilitarian metal desk that held a keyboard and a projection unit. Given its strategic location between the door and the shelves of forbidden goodies beyond, I assumed this had been home to an attendant/gatekeeper type. There were some books scattered on the floor between the aisles and near the door. There also appeared to be areas where entire shelves had been cleaned out. Seeing that gave me a sinking feeling in my gut, and I walked over to the nearest empty shelf to investigate. I found a small, red acrylic pyramid with a holographic image inside. Below a stylized exclamation mark, the image read as follows:

"Items 000056-000188. Contents of shelf transferred offsite 4/5/2465. Moved to A'aru Christian Archive, Diocese of New Cairo. Authorization: Elder Rev. Daryl Johns. Shipment No. 0000015876500-550. Classification: RED/THREAT LEVEL

ONE."

I handed the pyramid to the others, who looked it over.

"This is what I was telling you, Daniel," Bishop said, scratching at his enormous shock of white hair with one hand, the paper trimming arm dangling from the other at his side. "A lot of the confiscated items were moved off-orbital after the purge and before the Fall. I just hope our book wasn't among them."

"I'm not going to jinx it, but I'm not feeling terribly great about our odds, especially if the book gave off the heavy vibes you described," I said. "Still, we have to do our due diligence and see if we can pick up the trail if it's not here. How are you with computers? How about you dig and Sallow and I will walk the stacks and see what we can find. I'll leave Butch with you to download the forbidden catalogue if he can."

I handed him the keycard and instructed the tiny drone to assist. Sallow and I decided to take opposite ends of the room and meet in the middle, so we headed out among the stacks. Bishop talked to us (and maybe also to himself or Butch? Hard to say with him.) as he fired up the projection screen and began searching for our prize.

"Let's see ... I doubt they knew the book's proper name, although they might have grilled me about it when they took it," he said. "It's all been so long." I hear the soft clacking of mechanical keys.

"YES!" he shouted. "Here it is! The thugs were apparently thorough with me. Item No. 009874, Book of Raziel. Confiscated 2/1/2465 from keeping of Father Elias K. Bishop, Citizen No. 0587302 ... okaaaay ... had no idea I had a number ... pastor of Bridgeton Episcopalian Church, 113 Bridgeton Road. Classification: Red ... threat level one. Storage Location AJ-5K-201B."

Sallow and I came out of the stacks at the far end of the room at about the same time, both scanning the ends of the shelving units for markers that would lead us to the book's location. He spotted it first.

"AJ-5K," he said, pointing. "Middle unit right there."

We converged and headed down the aisle, Sallow in the lead.

"195, 196, 200, 201A ..." he intoned as he walked, reading labels from the left-hand shelf. "201B! Oh, bollocks!"

We reached a shelf about halfway down the stacks back toward the front desk and one from the bottom. A stupid red acrylic pyramid sat in the center of the shelf labeled 201B.

"Goddamnit!" I yelled. "I fucking KNEW it! Why does the universe hate me?"

"I can think of so many reasons," Sallow deadpanned.

"Now is NOT the time, Jonas," I growled. "My mellow is so harshed that it just caught a transport off this busted hulk, not unlike a certain scary-ass book of doom that we require to stop an apocalypse."

I picked up the red pyramid and studied it. The priest came to join us, trading his usual ambling gait for a quick trot. They both looked over my shoulders as I read.

"Items 009660-00760. Contents of shelf transferred offsite 3/24/2465. Moved to Avalon Christian Archive, Diocese of Narthwych. Authorization: Elder Imam Muhammed Ahmad. Shipment No. 0000014676400-221. Classification: RED/ THREAT LEVEL ONE."

I scanned the pyramid with my smartwatch and then tossed it back onto the shelf.

"Well, hell," I groused. "At least that's a direction? There should be a digital trail now, starting with the harbormaster's office here and, hopefully, ending in the town of Narthwych on Avalon. Either of you ever been? To the town or the orbital?"

They both shook their heads and replied in the negative.

"Ok, I've been to Avalon tons of times. I'm pretty comfortable there and might even have a bit of a rep. A few contacts and friends there as well. Never been to Narthwych, though. If I remember my geography, it's an outer rim town? That should make it a bit easier ... probably less interference from orbital police. Reeves, I believe they are called there. Anyway, let's get the hell out of here and we can talk plans on the way. Nothing else here that can't wait for a return trip."

The others agreed, and we made our way back up to the library's grand hall and down the street to the Elders' private subway station without incident. As we descended below street level and approached the subway's tracks, I noted that the Popemobile 2 had changed direction and was now pointed toward the outer rim. I looked down and noticed a railyard-style turntable under the train car that I had not noticed before. I used the Elder ring to unlock the car, and the three of us piled inside with the drones in tow.

The trip back to Bishop's neighborhood took about the same amount of time as the trip spindleward. The animated tiles on the subway tunnel roof did indeed change for our return, telling the same story as before. Sir Sallow the Unpleasant seemed at least marginally entertained by it, but I was too concerned with the upcoming trip to Avalon to pay it much attention.

I was especially torn on the subject of the priest. He had been helpful so far, and his knowledge of the book - such as it was - might prove invaluable. On the other hand, there was likely to be violence in our near future, and he was certainly a non-combatant by nature and ability, his deftness with a paper trimmer arm notwithstanding. I liked the guy, for what it was worth, and didn't want to see him carved up like human charcuterie if things went poorly on Avalon ... or beyond if the book's trail didn't terminate there. He deserved a chance at a new and better life after what he had been through.

But, then again, if Sallow's crazy story was to be believed, we might not have the luxury of letting him go as we needed every tool at our disposal to prevent whatever Archer (and Ponyboy, Derry, Azathoth, and Azrael) and who- and whatever else was a part of the stupidly-named Outsiders might have planned for the remnants of humanity. As we pulled in to Station Five at the outer rim, I decided to table the thought and discuss it with the members of the party once we were safely enjoying the relative luxury of the Shaggin' Wagon and leaving this shithole behind. I had definite plans to return and raid that swank library in the near future, though. Might even back the SW up to those double doors and fill it with as many books and artifacts as it could comfortably carry.

We bid the Popemobile 2 farewell and headed toward the street. Our short walk to retrieve Bishop's goodie bags from the postbox was again illuminated by what few streetlights had not been broken out by the douchebag denizens of the mostly defunct orbital. I re-jimmied the door that I had wedged shut, dug out both bags and handed them to Bishop. He slung the anime bag on his back and shouldered the other with his left hand, still clinging to the paper trimmer. He seemed incredibly relieved to have his small cache of belongings back. He smiled at me gratefully.

"Well, it looks like we didn't have to leave here in a bullet storm with our hair on fire, Daniel," he said.

"Why would you do that?" I looked at him, pained, glancing around the square.

"Do what?" Bishop asked, a look of confusion wiping away his happy grin.

"Invite the universe to fuck with us," I said, just as Sallow replied "Jinx it, you moron."

"But there's no one around, the Templars are no longer a threat, and you killed almost all of the evil men who were keeping me prisoner," Bishop said.

"What do you mean 'almost all,' Padre?" I asked. "How many were there? I killed seven."

"Oh, well, um, that means there are only, let's see ... five or so left? Unless ..."

"Unless ..." I made a rolling motion with my finger, encouraging him to go on.

"Unless they approach another tribe for help," he finished.

"Is that fucking likely?" I really didn't like where this was heading. "Also, let's walk and talk. Follow me." I hailed the drones. "Overwatch, boys! 100-yard perimeter. Lethal loads, 'Dance."

I ushered Sallow and the priest back the way I had come. I heard Sundance's drum magazines click and the whir of his barrels spinning up on a test run, much like an old ink jet printer aligning itself for a job in a classic office serial. We made it about a block and a half before the ugly and twisted hand (job) of fate caught up with us.

CHAPTER TEN

Shots rang out overhead. We ducked instinctively - as one does under unexpected fire, no matter where it is coming from. Butch's alarms went off as he sent info to my left optic. The three of us scrambled for cover. Luckily, the sad, red trolley was about 15 feet in front of us, still bisecting the four-way intersection, so we bolted for it, Sallow running right and the priest and I going left. More shots hit the pseudo-asphalt around us and plinked into the trolley, shattering a few already broken panes of glass.

Both Sallow and I had our sniper rifles at the ready. Bishop was still gamely holding onto his paper trimmer, holding it next to his face as he breathed in and out rapidly, bordering on hyperventilation.

"Elias," I said as casually as I could muster, reaching out with my left hand to clasp his shoulder. "Calm down ... slow your breathing. Relax. We're gonna get you out of this."

"I ... I've never been shot at before meeting you, Daniel," he wheezed. "And now ... twice in one day."

"Ok, well, I get that can be a bit disconcerting," I allowed. "But, hey ... think on the bright side. Silver lining is that if we get out of here alive, we'll be headed somewhere without guns."

"Will people be trying to chop, slash or stab us?" he asked, calming somewhat.

"Most likely," I grinned. "And they have bows there, too. And crossbows. To, you know, stab us at a distance. And big fucking quarter-staves ... probably halberds ... "

"You are shit at pep talks, my son." He choked on a laugh and gave me a small grateful grin.

"So I have been told. Hang tight." I raised the Excalibur and spun around Bishop to line up a shot around the end of the trolley car.

Butch had lit up a group of unfriendlies near the old church - some in the square headed toward the street we were on, a few on the rooftop of the building next door - all showing up in my left optic. I lined up the right with my scope. The two synced and a crosshair appeared in my line of vision on the magnified face of a nasty-looking fellow in a gimp mask, hunched over the roof's rampart with a rifle of his own. The reticle would still be there if I peered around the scope, now that my HUD specs and smart guns had done their magic linky thing, but I didn't need to look away. I breathed in, held it, exhaled, and parked a .308 round in the gimp's forehead. He didn't take kindly to it. In fact, he kind of lost his head over it.

I'm sorry. That was probably unnecessary. I could tell you that the back of his black mask blew out in a burst of shredded leather, skull fragments and pink mist and he collapsed in a heap, but that's just overkill, pardon the pun. Anyway, the dude was fucking DRT, or Dead Right There as one of my old shift-mates in law enforcement used to say. An X appeared over his number, which was 12.

I gave the other unfriendly icons a glance as I lined up my next shot. Looked like 17 total, minus the one I had just taken out. A couple of shots issued from the other end of the trolley, and two more icons gained the X courtesy of Sallow.

"Twenty points to Slytherin!" I yelled at him.

"What?" He glanced back over his shoulder.

"Never mind! Keep it up! You're doing GREAT!" I gave him a thumbs up. I have found positive encouragement often works wonders during firefights.

Sundance had already taken out several as well, it looked like. More gunfire rang out from the square. We were causing some damage, but I noticed a few more icons lighting up as more cultists approached from the west. The new total looked to be 36, give or take. I definitely saw a 36 icon, but I didn't have to keep looking as that was plenty.

"More assholes incoming," I yelled at the priest and the knight. "There's WAY too fucking many of them. We need to get out of here NOW!"

"Right," said Sallow, firing one last shot before turning from his work and placing his back to the trolley again. "Don't want to end up dinner!"

"We need to head straight down this street and hang a left in two blocks," I barked. "Stay centered and keep the trolley behind you as cover for about 20 feet, then race for the left sidewalk. Stay low. Run like hell on my mark, and the Hellion will provide covering fire. Butch, head for the lobby where we came up, double-time. Sundance, follow us on my mark and light up as many of them as you can. Three ... two ... one ... MARK!"

We bolted, running as hard as we could. Stray shots rounded the trolley and flew over it, some incredibly close to us. I counted us lucky that these guys probably didn't spend a lot of time on the range. Behind us, I heard Sundance kick into high gear as he neared the trolley, his little silenced barrels pushing out armor-piercing rounds as fast as his mechanisms could feed them. Butch zipped past us as we ran. I imagined I could hear a little digital "hah-hah" as he did so, but that was all in my head. I seriously needed to get that AI upgrade, though. My drones giving me shit as we run/fly from danger is just the kind of motivation I need in my life. We cut over to the sidewalk and kept up our feverish pace, rounding the corner away from the fire two blocks up as planned.

"Just a little farther," I called to them, breathing heavily with the exertion. "Just past the barber shop and the general store to the right. The glass lobby that looks like a therapist's waiting room! Follow Butch!"

We ran after the little drone, who reached the glass door of the lobby seconds later. He hovered there patiently, unable to pull on the door and open it himself. I reached the door next and yanked it open, ushering the others inside. Bishop ran in, followed by Sallow. Butch brought up the rear.

"Go!" I yelled at them. "Head down. I'm waiting for Sundance. He's right behind us."

They stumbled downstairs at my direction, the little drone flying over the edge and down the center of the stairwell. Sundance was only about 10 meters behind us, and flew in a moment later. I slammed the door behind us, and hit the stairs myself, flying down them three at a time or as fast as I could safely go. I yelled for Sundance to hover over the stairwell facing the door to cover us until the first wave of cultists hit, then drop like a rock for the bottom after hitting them with everything he could muster. As I ran down flights, I asked him to update my optic with his remaining ammo count. He showed me that he had about 50/100 armor-piercing rounds and 180/200 Narcoject spines. I figured that would be enough to give us a massive head start, providing no one had heavy explosives or RPGs they could launch or yeet down the stairwell after us.

And so, we ran down stairs, with me wishing all the while that a well-greased, 40-story fire station pole would appear out of the gloom of the stairwell that had accidentally gone unnoticed on my trip up.

Note to self, I thought as I ran. *Invest in a jetpack or a tiny parachute or a really long bungie cord and grappling hook.*

About ten flights down, I heard Sundance go weapons free, glass shattering as he mowed down cultists trying to get through the door. I listened as he ripped through all 50 rounds in his drum magazine and spun up his Narcoject launcher. A rapid-fire series of *thwips* ensued, all blending into a sound that sounded like a drum roll being played lightly on a rubber tire with billy clubs. I heard him expend his last spine (Boy, that was going to cost me.) and cut his quad gravlifts. A moment later, as we passed the landing of Subfloor 25, he plummeted past us on his dive to the bottom. Again, I could *almost* hear derisive laughter, in a slightly lower pitch this time.

Above us, I heard the sound of tinkling glass as the remaining cultists clambered into the lobby, knocking shards loose as they entered and began slogging through bodies to reach the stairs. As we passed the landing for floor 23, I saw something that I really had not expected. Apparently, the cultists were either crazier than I had previously given them credit for – which was saying a lot as they were obviously religious nutbag cannibal necrophiles – or pissed off to a level that beggared belief.

As I passed the large number 23 stenciled on the wall beside me, the priest and the knight a few paces ahead, I caught a glance of something in my left periphery: a falling body. I only glimpsed it for a nanosecond before a giant BOOM went off. We jumped and froze as the wall behind us was peppered with buckshot, and the cultist dropped out of sight. We were incredibly lucky that he hadn't known our exact position and hadn't had time to properly aim at us before falling past on his way to terminal velocity and a big, wet thump … both of which he would achieve at about the same time, if my math was correct. So, he had that going for him, which was nice.

I heard a few more BOOMS on his way down. I figured he was either firing them off as a last angry salute, or he was smart enough to sprinkle the landings below with double-ought buck as he fell, which could possibly force us to slow down to avoid slipping on the hot, little spheres and breaking an ankle or worse. If he was REALLY smart, he'd save the last shot for himself as people have been known to survive really long falls by lucking into a relatively soft landing into snowdrifts and the like. Survival isn't always the best outcome in those cases, though. I hadn't noticed a giant pile of snow or hay or mattresses (or an Acme trampoline if we're going 100% Looney Tunes) at the bottom on my way up, but who knows? If it were me, I'd probably plummet 400 feet and land in a pile of fluffy coats, hitting just hard enough to break every major bone in my body and mildly perforate every organ, ensuring my extremely slow death would be painful as fuck.

We kept going. Seconds later, I saw another shape drop into view.

"Down!" I screamed, diving for the others.

The shotgun blast hit right in front of where we were standing as we piled up on the floor in a heap with me on top. I scrambled to my feet and pulled the others up as we heard several more blasts from below us. Someone had given these guys marching orders before they jumped. There was no way they were coming up with this plan on their own. Crazy and half-baked as it was, it had a certain last-ditch brilliance.

"Go!" I yelled, pushing Bishop and Sallow on. "Watch for buckshot on the floor! They're peppering the stairs beneath us!" They both huffed an affirmative as they set out running again.

Four more times, suicide shooters came extremely close to hitting us as we descended. Sallow was winged in the left arm by a shot. Luckily for him, it only grazed the skin and cut a bloody furrow across his bicep, as we found out later. We continued running down flights as fast as we could, occasionally having to slow somewhat to avoid tripping on spent buckshot. The sounds of pursuit still could be heard from overhead, and we had been treated to six wet, cracking splats from below, as if, you know, someone had been dropping angry 200-lb. sacks of blood, muscle and bone wrapped in bondage gear over the railings. About three flights from the bottom, I began dreading the sight we would see when we arrived.

As it turned out, despite the fact that hurrying down forty flights of stairs whilst dodging suicide shooters had taken its toll and we were not running anywhere near as fast as we had been minutes before, we were still running too hard and were too intent on our destination to look behind us at the carnage at the stairwell's center. I saw red in my periphery as we took the last corner and barreled through the door at the bottom, and there was a distinct smell of shit and offal, but neither I nor my companions took the time to etch that abhorrent pile of nastiness onto our permanent memory. We tore through the doors and into the hangar bay with the drones hot on our heels and stopped short for a second to get our bearings. I looked around for the shipping container I had hidden the Wagon behind, hoping to see its telltale outline in the dimly lit expanse of the hangar.

"There!" I shouted and began running toward the blurry van shape to our right at the outer edge of the cavernous room. My companions followed suit. I tapped my smartwatch and issued voice commands to the Shaggin' Wagon to open the side door, lower the ramp, and start its engines as we approached.

We rounded the container and started up and across the ramp into the van's interior. As I nudged the drones' neon orange case out of the way with my foot and started pulling the others in, I heard shouts across the bay and the crack of gunfire. The drones flew in behind us and I hit the button beside the open hatch to close the door. I had a quick thought and hit the button to begin dropping the hatch again, which caused the others to begin yelling at me in alarm and consternation. I ripped open a storage locker and pulled out a canvas sack roughly the size of a throw pillow or a child's backpack, and I chucked it out the door toward the oncoming cultists. I hit the button again and dove toward the driver's seat at the front of the Wagon, tossing the Excalibur into the co-pilot's seat as I went.

"Buckle up, folks!" I called over my shoulder. "It may get bumpy."

Bishop and Sallow fell into the overly plush captain's chairs in the middle of the cabin and began fastening buckles furiously. I hit reverse, fishtailed backwards around the shipping container and rocketed forward into the open sally port airlock that would lead us to the skies beyond. The door behind us began lowering slowly. Or at least it seemed extremely slow to me at the time, circumstances being what they were. I heard small arms fire plinking off the armored hide of the Wagon and the airlock's inner door, which I am sure was closing at a normal pace and not at all procrastinating to piss me off and heighten my anxiety.

As soon as the door closed with a hiss and a thump we felt physically, the outer door began to open, and our ears popped with the change in pressure. As soon as the opening became large enough for us to pass, grinning like a madman, I tapped my smartwatch and triggered the package of plastic explosive I had thrown out of the van and into the hangar bay moments before. A muffled explosion could be heard through the thick inner airlock door. I'm sure there was lots of screaming and cursing as well, but those melodious sounds didn't make it through the heavy plate steel. I punched the throttle, and a van load of extremely exhausted and grateful sons of bastards shot out into the night sky and into the starlight five miles over a mostly dead planet.

CHAPTER ELEVEN

I set the autopilot for Avalon, pulling up the travel data. Roughly in geosynchronous orbit over Munich, Germany, it was 4,920 miles away from our current location, which was speeding away from fucking Canaan at maximum speed. That would give us a journey of about 16.5 hours, give or take. I checked my smartwatch to find it was 12:45 AM. That meant we'd be rolling into Avalon just after midnight tomorrow night, what with the giant time zone difference.

I cut off the chameleon theme to save power and turned my chair around to face the others.

"Well, that was … something," I said. "Ok, so … we need to talk, but I vote we clean ourselves up, eat and drink something, and then we can gab like a bunch of schoolgirls at a sleepover for the next few hours and get some shuteye. We can talk about boys and paint each other's nails in a bit, but first – I dig you guys and mean no disrespect – y'all fucking stink. And I am no fresh-cut bouquet myself. Anyway, that's my vote, and because I'm the goddamned captain of this gorgeous vessel, you guys don't get one. 'K?"

I stood and walked over to the drones' orange transit case and told them to hop in and power down. And yes, I told them what good boys they both were. I'm not a monster. I removed my tactical ear buds and placed them in their charging case, which I then placed in the case with the drones before locking it up and shoving it into a storage locker.

Pulling some fresh clothes out of a locker for myself and some spares for my two shipmates, who were roughly my size or close enough, I headed into the van's tiny bathroom to shower away the grit, gunpowder and sweat of the last day or so. Had it only been a day, I thought? It seemed like so much more.

I scoured off the grime and enjoyed the hot water maybe a tiny bit more and longer than was socially acceptable. As I was starting to get hangry, that won over the delightful feel of the high pressure shower.

I dressed in some knock around clothes – a vintage repro Gojira t-shirt and athletic shorts – and rejoined the group, drying my hair with a towel as I did so.

"Who's next?" I said.

"The priest can go," Sallow said, leaning forward with his forehead in his hand. "I'm still pondering the day's events, and to be honest, he smells worse than I do. Not that it is not a close race."

"That's fair," the priest said amiably. I handed him some clothes and a towel.

"Just chunk your clothes in the recycler over there when you come out." I pointed to a squat, capped tube near the replicator. "I doubt they're salvageable. We'll have to get you two new threads when we get to Avalon, anyway."

Bishop headed into the bathroom, and I ambled over to the replicator.

"I know it's probably not polite to eat without him, but I haven't had anything since noon except for a protein bar, and I am starving. The two of us scraping up something isn't going to get him fed any faster. What do you want?"

"I could go for a shepherd's pie and a pint of bitter," Sallow said. It took a minute or two to program his order into the replicator and search the database for recipes, but about 30 seconds later, I handed him a small tray with his food and drink. The pie looked pretty amazing, and it smelled even better than it looked, so I ordered the same. We clinked glasses and then sat in companionable silence for a bit, devouring our meals.

I had just cleaned up and tossed our trays and containers in the recycler when Bishop came out of the bathroom. He was sporting a Melvin's tee with a cartoon devil on it – because I care – and a pair of athletic shorts. Poor fellow. He definitely looked like he had skipped a decade of leg days. He looked less the mad prophet as he had trimmed his beard down to something halfway manageable and decent; now more sea captain than rogue wizard. He had also managed to tame his wild locks into a close approximation of an actual human hairstyle.

"Well, don't you look sharp, Elias?" I said as he tossed his worn out clothing into the recycler, hanging on to the borrowed sneakers. "Can I whip you up something to eat? Sorry we didn't wait on you."

"Thank you, Daniel," he beamed. "It feels good to be around decent folk again, and to have washed the stink of my long imprisonment away. Truly, I feel like a new man." He thought for a moment. "Do you think I could have a giant bowl of home-style mac and cheese with smoked sausage in it? And some habanero hot sauce on the side? And a water. And also ... maybe a pint of dark beer? Dealer's choice. I'm not feeling picky."

I walked over to the replicator to get the priest fed and watered as Sallow headed into the bathroom with the clothes I had picked out for him. I made Sallow aware that there was a medkit in the locker under the sink if he wanted to treat his arm. Handing Bishop his giant trough of comfort food and a pint of schwarzbier, I grabbed a pint of the same for myself and sat down across from him at the small table between the mid-row captain's chairs.

"Glad you're feeling better, Padre, and I'm extremely glad we got you out of that shithole with those fucking monsters," I began. "I think once you get a decent rest, you'll really start feeling like your old self again. You're probably still riding the adrenaline high of being in a firefight and on the run, honestly."

He barely looked up from his mac and cheese, merely grunting his agreement and smiling around a mouthful of food.

"Good talk," I said, grinning. "I'll leave you to it." I patted him on the shoulder and stood, walking to the cockpit.

I sat in the pilot's seat, turning it around to face forward. Outside the windshield/forward canopy, the unpolluted view of the star field above us was breathtaking. I slid the seat back, tilted it, and put my bare feet up on the console, sipping my beer, taking in the light show. I could see the arm of the Milky Way clearly. I let my mind wander. I am not exactly sure whether I just zoned out to the max or accidentally dozed off, but I snapped back to full consciousness as Sallow climbed into the co-pilot's seat to my right. He had dressed in the Orbit Culture t-shirt I had provided along with black sweatpants. His hair was still wet and slicked back. He had brought a couple of tumblers of Scotch whisky from the replicator.

"Saw it in the 'Recents' list and figured you wouldn't mind," he said, handing me one of the glasses.

"If you keep this shit up, I might just revise my opinion of you," I said and nodded my thanks.

"You have a poor opinion of me?" he said, halfway between joking and serious.

"I mean, you tried to shoot me in the face, my dude," I replied, sipping the Scotch and narrowing my eyes at him. "You're lucky to not be a chunky wad of shredded gristle and broken bones in a pool of man-juice on the sidewalk of a dead orbital. And by man-juice, I mean mostly blood and shit. That came out wrong. Or ... *did it*?" I waggled my eyebrows at him lasciviously.

"You are a disgusting human being," he said. "But look at all we've been through since. That was AGES ago."

"I suppose," I admitted. "You are very fortunate I have eaten and that you have excellent taste in food, beer and Scotch. All of these things have worked together in perfect harmony to improve my mood and my attitude towards you."

"It's *your* taste in Scotch," he laughed. "I just don't disagree with it. What is this, anyway?"

"Bruichladdich Unpeated Islay Single Malt," I said, sighing deeply. "The Classic Laddie, or, as it's known in the Universal Food and Beverage Database, Alcoholic Beverage #1007589. There are over 135 distilleries represented in there and tons of products and variants from each."

"I'm quite aware, Davidson," he replied drily. "I am from British stock, you know. The accent's not just for show, mate." He sipped on his beverage and might've let a little sigh slip as well.

"Family from New Arcadia?" I asked.

"A generation or two back, sure," he said. "My parents immigrated to Elysia as they got tired of the old-school classist bullshit. Everyone's supposedly grown past all of that. Maybe on paper or whatever, but those old attitudes die hard. And someone always has to be the worker bees, yeah?"

"Is your temple ... your order ... based on Elysia?"

"It is," he said. "You'd think it'd be one of the ancient-themed ones, given our history, but logistically, it's a whole lot easier to communicate with the other branches if we don't have to write by quill or use fucking carrier pigeons. I mean, they all have hidden comms tech, otherwise we'd get fuck-all done, but still. Seems like a whole lot of trouble for the higher-ups to spend their time cosplaying, innit?"

He appeared to be becoming more British as the Scotch disappeared down his gullet.

"True enough," I said. "You don't seem to have a lot of patience for the cosplaying stuff. I mean, obviously on one hand it's nuttier than a squirrel turd to me, but there's a certain Utopian charm to it as well, right? Universal Basic Income, people being financially incentivized for more physically or emotionally grueling labor, people being able to live out their fantasies and/or histories unfettered by judgment or ... fuck, I dunno. The harsh light of reality or modernity? On some level, who can blame The Powers That Be for trying to give us better, more spiritually fulfilling lives than we had on Earth -That-Was?"

"You are cut off," he grinned. "I like you better as a foul-mouthed, batshite-crazy arsehat than as a drunken neo-Marxist hippie talking about spiritual fulfillment and the like."

"I am not a Marxist, I'll have you know. I am an ethical capitalist. Semi-ethical, anyway, as I do kill people on occasion." I winked at him and took a slug of Scotch. "But, hey. Those people always need killing."

"You're a regular saint," he offered. "I'll bet you love old people and puppies. Probably donate to orphanages and the like."

"Proudly do all three ... I mean, well, not DO all three," I grinned even bigger. "You know what I mean. And I'm a regular blood ... and sperm ... donor."

"Oh, fuck," he pantomimed terror, opening his eyes wide. "You mean there may be more of you out there?"

"Legions," I agreed. "The seed is strong. Great swimmers in my family. We all won our races."

"The motility of your, eh, swimmers is the absolute last goddamned thing I want to hear about."

"Fair enough," I agreed. "Your mom, though ... completely different story."

"Shut your mouth, Davidson," he growled through a mouthful of Scotch. "My mother is a saint."

"True," I said, and paused a beat. "The Patron Saint of Anal."

He exploded into laughter, almost choking on his Scotch. "That's fair," he chuckled. "Mum did always favor a good buggering."

"Bless her soul ... I mean holes," I intoned, seriously. "And her prices were ALWAYS reasonable."

He laughed again. "You are fucking crazy, you know that?" He threw back the last of his Scotch and stood. "But as pleasant as this filthy banter is, I am dead on my feet. Where should I ...?"

"Back row seat folds back into a bed," I said. "You take it. Pilot's chair reclines and will work for me. I'll grab you and the padre some blankets."

We made our way back toward the rear of the wagon. I had briefly wondered why Bishop had been so quiet during our conversation, and the answer to that question was apparent when we found Bishop leaned back in his captain's chair fast asleep, his empty bowl and Nonic pint glass still sitting on the table in front of him. I grabbed a few blankets from a storage locker, spread one gently over the priest, handed one to Sallow and took one for myself.

"Nighty-night, Knight." I waved over my shoulder as I headed back to the cockpit.

"Been holding on to that one, have you? Idiot." He breathed a laugh.

"Maaaaybe," I said as I plopped down in the pilot's seat and reclined, pulling the blanket over me. "Good night, Jonas. Good work. Sleep well. I'll most likely kill you in the morning."

"What's that ...?"

"Gah. Princess Bride, 1987. Fuck *off*. I'm surrounded by assholes." I snuggled deeper into my chair.

"Was that Spaceballs? Mum loves classic Mel Brooks."

"And anal. Not that I'm judging, because who doesn't? Yes. Also 1987. I take it back. There's hope for you yet. Now go the fuck to sleep."

CHAPTER TWELVE

We slept a solid ten hours straight. Lucky for us, I had remembered to darken the canopy before drifting off, otherwise the morning sun would've cut our slumber drastically short. I woke to the smell of coffee and eggs and bacon and all sorts of other breakfast goodness.

I spun my chair around with my foot, not removing my blanket, and stared bleary-eyed at the vista before me. Bishop and Sallow were loading the tiny table – overloading, I should say – with the makings of a full English breakfast: toast, eggs, bacon, several different kinds of sausages, tomatoes, mushrooms, and (always inexplicable to me) beans. There was a pot of coffee sitting on the counter. My stomach started rumbling almost painfully.

"What the fuck is all this gloriousness?" I asked, freezing them in their tracks. "Have I died and gone to Heaven? The old one, I mean. Before I found out it might be crawling with tentacular, two-headed beasties who want to kill us all."

"Just thought we could use a decent meal," Sallow said. "It's 4 PM local time, I believe, and we just flew over the Azores according to your van's computer, so ... English brunch? Or what's between lunch and supper? Lupper?"

"English Lupper it is," I said, throwing off my blanket and walking back to the cabin. I grabbed some coffee and a plate. There was nowhere to actually sit at the table, so I piled my plate high with everything except the beans and walked back to sit on the back row bench, which was still flattened into a bed. "Morn ... uh, afternoon, Padre. Sleep well?"

"Good morning, Daniel," he replied as he piled his own plate high. "The lack of neck support notwithstanding, yes, thank you."

We tucked in to our work and lapsed into friendly chit-chat as we destroyed almost every victual available. I think we were all verging on food comas as we threw the remnants into the recycler along with our cups, plates and cutlery. Much happier and maybe a pound or two heavier each thanks to giant food babies, we congregated around the now empty table.

"So, Avalon," I began. "You two have never been. What do you know about it?"

"The standard stuff, I guess," Sallow said. "Mostly agrarian, looks like Middle Earth and the English countryside had a baby. People playing dress up like peasants and lords and trolls and what-not, lots of swords and axes and things ... mostly for show, I think, and not a lot of real combat? Just tournies and the like. Father?"

"Yes, all of that," the priest nodded. "Churches of all sorts, almost all major religions represented, as well as some lesser known pagan ones. Actual physical monetary system, no credits. No tech at all, or well-hidden or disguised if it is. No firearms of any sort. And, sadly, I guess we will have to leave your drones behind, which is a real shame. And we'll all need new clothes and weapons."

"Ok, so you both have the general gist of it." I said. "I already have kit for Avalon and all the other Ancients, but yeah. We'll have to get you guys some new duds. I know it all seems silly, and it does to me, too, but they take it deadly seriously there. You don't have to talk like you're at a Ren Faire or anything, but we do have to dress and act the part. That part of the law is very strict. Dueling is legal there, though, and the rules are far more lax as far as killing and maiming each other. I figure it's part of the appeal and keeps the population manageable. Honor and insult are a big thing, so we'll all have to be at our most polite."

Sallow scoffed. "That's going to be a real treat for you, I'd imagine."

"Oh, I can do polite," I grinned. "AND respectful, even. As long as there's no problem with cursing or genteel tomfoolery.

I will have to refrain from 'Your Mom' jokes, though, unless I want to be dueling some motherfucker every forty paces or so. How are you guys with melee weapons? Combat sports?"

"Well, I'm a knight, so … I can hold my own," Sallow said. "We train with swords, axes, maces, polearms, quarter-staves and the like. It's part of our tradition."

"No weapons training in the clergy," Bishop said. "At least, the regular, non-militant clergy. Not a combat sport, but I played baseball for a few years in high school. Wasn't very good, I'm afraid."

"Ok, cool. I can work with that. We'll get you a big stick … something vaguely bat-like or bat-ish. Something bat-adjacent at the very least." I laughed. "It's better than nothing."

"So, how is this handled?" Sallow asked. "I assume all visitors come in some sort of modern transport, and in modern clothing."

"Correct," I said. "We'll call for clearance and dock in a hangar bay just like we would anywhere else. On all of the Ancients, there are shops that ring the lower decks where you can hire transport, rent or purchase clothing, weaponry, rations, et cetera. Changing rooms and all. It's a hodgepodge below decks as everyone is getting situated, but it's all 100% cosplay up top. There's a little orientation movie for newcomers that explains the legal system, money system, and the fines and other penalties for obvious tech or breaking character in other ways. Firearms will get you imprisoned or banned for life. Lesser infractions will just hit your pocketbook, or, um, money pouch where it hurts. Unwarranted violence or severe misdemeanors could get you some more medieval punishment like the stocks or public flogging."

"Seriously? That's barbaric!" Sallow looked incredulous.

"That's kind of the point," I said.

"Huh. Right."

"You're starting to get it," I said. "The people here and on the other Ancients made a choice to reject modernity and live in a fantasy land. Or, in some cases, a more technologically primitive one that aligns with the traditions of their racial or ethnic or national folk heritage from old Earth. We don't have to understand it necessarily, but we do have to respect it while we're here. Otherwise, we could wind up in jail, thrown out or even executed. But, again, who are we to judge? Just like the cybernaturals or people who have elected to change genders or what have you, these people are just trying to be their most authentic, happiest selves. And in the wake of a climatological apocalypse, the deaths of billions of people, and a forced exodus from our planet and into low orbit, why shouldn't people enjoy themselves and live their lives as they wish? Even if they take it to extremes we may not fathom."

"Huh. You're not as much of a prick as I initially thought," Sallow said. "Speaking of cybernaturals, what sort of presence do they have on Avalon? I mean, I've read about the place and we talked about it in school and all, but you've actually spent time there. What's not on the brochure or in the history books?"

"Good question," I said. "Ten points to Slytherin!"

"Please stop that."

"Ok, fine. So, yes. There are orcs and halflings and elves and dwarves just as you'd expect from a place that desperately wants to be Middle Earth," I said. "But there are also vampire and werewolf clans as well. Both groups that are large, organized, well-intentioned and fully integrated with society AND smaller, more cultish and criminal clans. There's also a thieves guild. It's a dangerous place. Not that all the orbitals aren't in their own ways."

"How, um, authentic are the cybernaturals? I confess, I have not had much dealings with them," Bishop said.

"Very authentic," I said. "In the case of the vampires, they've gone so far as to jack their reflexes and strength, have surgically implanted retractable fangs, and even alter their DNA to give themselves porphyria – which is basically sun sickness; garlic allergies, and a form of anemia that requires them to feed on blood. The werewolves also have jacked strength and speed as well as cybernetic implants that alter their bone structure to mimic that of a lycanthrope. Not full on transformation, mind you, but a slight lengthening of the snout, chitinous fingernail razors, wolf-like eyes and such. They have genetic tweaks to give themselves hypertrichosis – that's head-to-toe body hair; and an allergy to silver. And have the whole lot triggered involuntarily on a lunar schedule, but most can transform at will as well."

"Why the hell would they give themselves weaknesses intentionally?" Sallow asked, ever the soldier.

"EVERYTHING about them boils down to authenticity and wanting to be as close to the historical or literary version of their fantasy self as possible," I said. "But don't think any of it will kill them. It's part of the package, but I guess their authenticity only goes so far when it bumps up against their will to live. Sunlight or garlic will irritate a vampire something fierce - like poison oak times 10 - but they don't burst into flames. A silver blade or club will hurt a werewolf more than a regular one, but only to a point. A stake through the heart or being beheaded will kill most things, and so will being cut or bashed enough that you have more blood on the outside than inside. They're basically just a hell of a lot tougher than us."

"You sound as if you speak from experience," Sallow noted.

"I may have run afoul of one or two of them during past visits," I said. "I'm not particularly proud of it, but yeah. Sometimes people ... or vampires or werewolves ... give you no choice. Every group of humans or semi-humans throughout history has had its outliers and extremists. Some of them take the apex predator thing a little too seriously. Some of them have to be reminded that many of us don't take kindly to being prey. So, I've had to remind a few. In the most definitive, most permanent way possible."

"I will add, though," I continued. "Taking one of them out is no picnic. Unless, like, your preferred picnic spot is in a fucking war zone."

"It most decidedly is not," Sallow said. "So, what are the chances there is any … residual animosity over your past visits and the ensuing mayhem and homicide, justified though it may have been? Pack or coven members or whatever they call themselves, looking to even the score?"

"You want odds? I'd say …"

"Let me guess," Sallow groaned. "80/20. And we're not going to like which is which."

"Hah. That's a fair assessment. Also, I feel seen."

"I *wish* I could unsee you," Sallow said.

"MEAN. Why you gotta be that guy, mang? I'll have you know that TENS of people enjoy my company," I said, frowning. "Or at least they offer no verbal or physical resistance to it, so that's practically the same thing."

"I enjoy your company, Daniel!" Bishop chimed in, enthusiastically.

"You're *such* a fucking sweetheart, Elias," I said. "You're an absolute beauty. Never change. And I don't just say that to all the half-crazed, mad prophet types I pick up from defunct orbitals. You're special."

"I am going to throw up," Sallow rolled his eyes. "And not just, like, in my mouth."

"Hush. Just let it happen," I said with a grin. "So, yeah. I think we're all up to speed now. Any last questions?"

No one had any. By my reckoning, we were a good eight hours from docking at Avalon. We passed the time as adult males who are virtual strangers often do: shooting the shit, playing a hand or two of poker, drinking alcoholic things. I finally scratched the itch and wrangled us up all a round of Mai Tais, which were met with general approval. I forced them to watch The Princess Bride, which was met with universal approval, as it should be. More food was eaten, naps were had, and time passed rather quickly. Before long, the Shaggin' Wagon's proximity alarm was going off and I walked to the cockpit to see Avalon growing large enough to fill the entirety of the viewport. I hailed the harbormaster, who assigned us a berth in a nearby docking bay, and we proceeded to go about the business of parking the SW's beautiful bulk. Next stop: Middle Fucking Earth.

CHAPTER THIRTEEN

We sallied through the sally port and into our berth with little to no issues. I figured the locals would at least appreciate the Gandalf vs. Balrog theme the Wagon was currently sporting. I grabbed my kit and headed into the restroom to change. A few moments later, I emerged a new man. Gone was my metal band tee and athletic shorts. In their place was a double-belted, blood red Clan Turner tartan kilt and a blousy, brown, peasant-style lace-up shirt. A traditional Scots sporran hung from my waist as well. And, yeah. It's basically a black leather man purse worn over the groin ... a fanny pack for Highlanders. I wore high socks, each with their own sgian-dub, or Scottish dress dagger (pronounced skiene-doo, by the way, you fucking plebes). These were far more functional than fancy, though. I had mid-length, steel-toe boots on, and my chest was crisscrossed with leather straps, which held a centered quiver and twin scabbards that crossed in an X underneath on my back. Each of the scabbards held a thin, slightly-curved scimitar-style short sword, very similar to those wielded by Legolas Greenleaf in Tolkien's Lord of the Rings. Apparently, my pop culture references know no bounds.

The quiver itself held 32 arrows in two groups of 16: half were non-lethal arrows with Narcoject tips designed to prevent deep penetration (functionally similar to Sallow's dad), and half were normal broadheads. I wore studded leather bracers on each arm - the left containing a concealed smartwatch - and sported an eye patch over my left eye. Far from impeding my sight, however, it instead contained some amazing covert tech: a hidden HUD that supplied me with all sorts of combat-relevant data, including range/wind info if I were to find myself using a bow, which I just happened to have on hand. Functionally transparent due to a series of micro-cameras on its surface, the patch also had a zoom function, infrared, night vision and all the basic targeting ability of my HUD specs, linking with my smartbow through the subdermal implants in my palms.

My smartbow was a very special weapon indeed. It sported a veneer identical to woodgrain but it was actually constructed of shape-shifting nanobots. With the touch of a concealed button (and proximity to my disguised smartwatch), the bow would straighten and round out into a passable quarterstaff, the bowstring completely retractable and hidden inside. Hard as steel, but as light as graphite, it was a fantastic weapon in either mode. I may have to cosplay while on Avalon, but what the locals didn't know didn't hurt them. (Or could hurt them very badly.) At least I was compliant in spirit, and for most folks, that was close enough. That spirit also included my mostly transparent Second Skyn body armor underneath, which reached to mid-thigh. I stepped out of the restroom and did a short, manly runway walk for the boys.

"I mean, this is a side of you I was not prepared for," Sallow said. "You look a bit like a Scottish pirate, but it's not bad. I'll give you that. Not that you'll be gracing the covers of any romance serials anytime soon with that face."

"Aw, shucks," I batted my eyelashes at Sallow, despite the fact that he could only see one of them. "I'll bet you say that to all the boys. Let's disembark and get you guys suited up for Medieval Fun Land, too. Let the games begin!"

We stepped out into the hangar bay, which was relatively quiet at this late hour. We walked over to the nearest set of doors and passed into a rather huge concourse of shops, none of which seemed to be terribly busy at 12:30 AM. All the better for us. We sauntered over to the nearest shop, which was, according to the beautifully carved pub sign outside, called War Haüs.

We walked into the relatively empty shop, passing displays

of armor and weaponry that would make any 21st century SCA enthusiast or tabletop dungeon gamer rock hard at first glance, metaphorically speaking. Or maybe literally, geeks being what they are.

The three of us marched up to the counter and beheld a giant of a man sharpening a wicked-looking dagger on a rough whetstone. His dark brown skin was glistening with sweat from the exertion and quite possibly his shop's lack of air conditioning, which seemed odd and possibly intentional. He tossed back his voluminous mane of dreadlocks like a male model in a beauty products ad shot in slow motion ... I swear wind came from somewhere. Maybe he had a fan hidden under the counter? And I shit you NOT, I heard the funky, primal strains of Barry White's "Never, Never Gonna Give Ya Up" being performed by minstrels on lutes and harps and other period instruments. Must have speakers hidden in here, too. Maybe all of it rigged to a motion sensor.

"The fuck?" I stage-whispered out of the side of my mouth to my companions at the same time Bishop said, "This is making me somewhat uncomfortable." Sallow just grimaced, as was his way.

The man greeted us warmly, wiping the dagger's edge on his gigantic green tunic.

"Welcome to War Haüs," he boomed in a boisterous yet practiced cadence. "We've got all manner of wares for war and prices you can't beat with a flanged mace! What can I do ya for, travelers?"

"My companions require suitable, um, clothery and armory, good sir," I said, stumbling somewhat but also not caring overmuch. "And also weaponry. I would love to say that money is no object, but we're shooting for mid-range here. We're not fancy lads. Nor are we planning on all out warfare. Just self-defense if it comes to that."

"So, no siege engines then?" He laughed riotously at his own joke, which wasn't very funny, but his good-natured laughter was somewhat infectious. "You've come to the right place.

Name's Rhulgeistmakkar. How did you hear about us?"

"Gesundheit! You were literally the first shop we came to," I shrugged. "But, hey. Looks like you've done a lot with the place. Really radiates menace. Lots of pointy and edgy things. And tons of especially metallic-looking and butchy outfits." I reached out to feel a leather jerkin on a mannequin next to the counter. "Why do they call them 'jerkins', anyway? Sounds kind of naughty."

"Please don't finger my jerkins," he said, which caused both Sallow and myself to smirk. Bishop barely repressed a titter.

"I wouldn't dream of it," I nodded gravely, pulling my hand back. "So whatcha got for us in the 'Keeping Newbs Alive' department?"

"Oh! Newcomers! Why didn't you say so?" He walked out from behind the counter and led us to an area near the back of the store where retail racks held a variety of edged and blunt weaponry as well as light armor and period specific clothing that ranged from Dark Age barbarian to Renaissance dandy.

"I mean, I thought I just did?" I looked at Sallow and Bishop, who both shrugged.

"What are your classes?" When we looked confused, he added "Trades? Professions?"

"Oh, like D&D classes. Right. So, the grim looking fellow is a knight and the bearded stunner there is a priest," I said. "You silver fox," I added as an aside to Bishop. "And I'm not making that up. Those are their actual jobs."

"Uh huh," Rhulgeistmakkar looked skeptical. "You can be ANYthing you want to be on Avalon."

"But they really *are* a knight and a priest," I said. "And I'm not setting up a joke. If I were setting up a joke, I'd begin with: This horse walks into a bar. Bartender says 'Hey, buddy. Why the long face?'"

"Well?" The giant asked.

"Well, what?"

"What did the horse say?"

"Nothing. He shit in the floor and sauntered out. He's a

goddamned horse."

"Oh," Rhulgeistmakkar's face fell with disappointment. "I thought he might've been a talking horse."

"There's no such ... wait," I said. "You don't have talking horses here, do you? There weren't any last time I was here."

"Nah, mate," he replied. "Those are only in fairy tales. And actual FUNNY jokes."

"Everyone's a critic. Ok. Just making sure," I said. "Anyway, we're getting off topic. How about something monkish or clerical for beard boy and something in a paladin/fighter model for tall, dark and gloomy over there?"

Rhulgeistmakkar grunted his assent and started picking through racks of clothing and armor. "And what about you?"

"Oh, I'm basically dual class: bard and rogue. Bardic rogue? Roguish bard? Barrogue?" I snagged a monk's hooded robe and a knee-length mail hauberk out of the rack the owner was pilfering through and held them up to Bishop to eyeball the sizes. The hood was absolutely enormous and would likely swallow him whole.

"All bards have the hearts of rogues," he winked knowingly. "You don't have your instrument with you? What do you play?"

"Field drum, usually, but I sing as well. Do lots of stick tricks. I'm not planning on performing this trip, though. Here on other business."

"Good enough," he said. "How about this for your knight?" He hoisted a light mail shirt with an armored leather shoulder guard and a mail coif, handing them to Sallow. He then pulled a white, sleeveless tunic and leather breeches off the rack and handed them over, as well as padded undershirts for both men. "Changing rooms are over there." He jerked his head back and to the left.

Bishop and Sallow took the proffered outfits and went to change. I eyed the proprietor.

"Pardon me for saying so, but you're an enormous dude," I said. "Your biceps are like bowling balls, man. You a retired fighter or something? Quit adventuring and decided to open up shop to keep a toe in the game? Or you just jacked from being a blacksmith?"

"You'd think so," he smiled a little sadly. "I get that a lot. Actually, my passion has always been fine period clothing and haberdashery. Museum-quality antique fashion, you know? I just work out a lot. Kind of has to be that way as my other passion is fine cuisine. I fire up the grill and cook for my customers on Fridays. You guys should come back. I make some kafta and mushroom burgers that will make you do backflips. Some wild game sausages, too."

"Might take you up on that, friend," I said. "What day is it, anyway?"

"Wednesday, I think," he replied. "Wait ..." he flipped open a small flap on his left bracer and peeked at a hidden smartwatch. "Yeah. It's been Wednesday morning for about forty-five minutes or so. I lose track a lot when I'm on the graveyard shifts."

"That's legit. I've been keeping odd hours this week, myself," I commiserated. "Fleeing cannibal sex cults and stuff."

Rhulgeistmakkar gave me the side eye, but before he could reply, Bishop and Sallow returned, looking every inch the medieval cosplayers they were about to become.

"Looking good, guys," I complimented them. "Whattya think?"

"Not bad," Sallow said. "Pretty comfortable. This mail is actually ridiculously light. What the hell is it made out of?"

"Trade secret," Rhulgeistmakkar beamed with pride at the question. "Proprietary alloy. We source it locally from a smith in Narthwych. Next-gen materials, but it looks and sounds like the old stuff. Twice as strong, about 10% of the weight."

"Well, it's amazing," Sallow said. "Great freedom of movement, too. I hardly feel encumbered at all."

"That's the idea," the big man said. "And reasonably priced, too, so your money pouch won't be overly *un*-encumbered when you leave. How about you, good friar?"

"The same, kind sir," Bishop said. "The robe breathes well, and the mail is far more comfortable than I would have thought. You hardly *need* an undershirt."

"I am so glad you approve!" the giant shop-keep said. "We'll grab you some footwear and check out the weapons racks next."

With both of the boys in some rugged leather boots, low-rise brown for the priest and regular in black for our knight, we crossed the area to the gleaming racks of armaments.

Sallow picked out a long, sleek broadsword with a leather-bound handle, a black steel cross guard and pommel. It came with a matching dagger and both included scabbards of black wood and leather. He also grabbed a small buckler shield for his left arm. Bishop hefted a club slightly smaller than a baseball bat that was studded with steel knobs all along the business end and gave it a few practice swings.

"This will do, I think," he said, grinning. "Light but hefty enough to do some damage. And if they turn the other cheek, I can hit that one, too. BAM!" He swung the club like he was swatting a home run over the fences at Fenway Park of old.

"Easy, tiger," I laughed. "Save some for the brigands." To Rhulgeistmakkar, I added "So, hey … do you have any anti-vampire and anti-werewolf gear?"

"Not a lot," he said apologetically. "I've got a few sets of silver-laced throwing knives. Outside of that, I have some garlic oil and a colloidal silver suspension. You can smear them on blades or dab them on arrowheads to help boost your effectiveness against rogue cybernaturals. I can let three sets of the knives go for 200 gold, and I'll throw in the bottles as you've been such great customers."

"Toss in a giant Black Sabbathy cross to go around the priest's neck, and you've got yourself a deal," I said.

"We have a cold iron Celtic cross on a semi-heavy steel chain with a concealed dagger in the bottom?" Rhulgeistmakkar fetched it from a nearby jewelry case. I imagined I almost heard the strains of "Into the Void" begin playing when he placed it around Bishop's neck.

"MY MAN! You're the best. Let's do this!"

We walked over to the counter and Rhulgeistmakkar tallied up our haul. "That'll be 6,500 credits or 3,500 gold notes. If you haven't had time to visit a bank or money vendor yet to exchange your credits for local currency, I can accept credits and also do an additional exchange here if you'd like. Save you a trip. All exchanges have to be done below the surface. Everything up top is strictly cash."

I looked at the others. "Oh, hell. I guess this one's on me. I do have the expense account after all. For now." I flipped open my left bracer to reveal the hidden smartwatch and paid the man, grabbing an additional 20K in gold notes. I folded them up and placed them in my money pouch and tucked that into my sporran. I am so glad they decided to do away with the heavy-ass coins a while back and embrace paper currency. The idea of several pounds of coins bouncing off my junk all day did not fill me with abject glee.

"Before we leave, big man," I said as we concluded our transaction. "You mentioned Narthwych. We may be headed that way. Anything useful you can tell us about it?"

"Well, other than being home to Avalon's best smith, it's a coastal town of the outer rim." He picked up his dagger and started sharpening it again as he talked. "The entire orbital is ringed by a mile-wide waterway, if you were unaware, and the land is crisscrossed with narrow canals, so we have a pretty good 'sea' trade. Of course, just like on all the other orbitals, it's all fresh water as we can't afford to take up space with water we can't drink, and the fish that aren't freshies have been genetically modified to survive in it. The town is home to a lot of fishermen and boat wrights and other tradesmen who make their living doing sea things. There's a pretty large merchant population due to the trade, and as a result a very active branch of the Thieves Guild, so watch your purses. Other than that, just your average small town."

We politely said our thanks and goodbyes to

Rhulgeistmakkar, promising to return for burgers and sausages if we were able, and headed toward the elevators that would take us to the surface. None of us were in the mood to take the stairs.

CHAPTER FOURTEEN

The elevators ferried us up 39 flights and opened on what could best be described as a giant welcome center and gift shop one deck below topside. I had no idea how many of these things they had here, but this one was either the same one I had passed through on earlier visits or it was completely identical. At this hour, it was virtually empty of travelers and manned by a skeleton crew of less-than-exuberant workers in bright yellow tunics sporting embroidered red smiley faces, all of whom looked like they were over my bullshit before I had even started to deliver said bullshit. To be fair, it is not a reaction I am in any way unused to receiving.

We approached the nearest staff member, a tall, thin elf with long blonde hair who looked particularly put-upon and unhappy to be there.

"Pardon me, your elfship," I began, waving in what I hoped was a friendly and non-threatening manner. "We've just arrived, and my companions are first-timers. We've geared up, and I think we're ready to head topside. Is there anything else we need to do before we go?"

The elf sighed heavily and began reciting a well-rehearsed speech in a flat monotone, devoid of the musicality one would expect from one so ethereal in appearance.

"Welcome to Avalon, travelers. We hope that your stay here is a pleasant one. May the cobbled roads of our fine orbital rise to meet your feet, and may its gentle, spring-like breezes caress your ..."

"Hey, that's ok ... um ... " I stretched to peek at the elf's name, which was burned or branded into a small wooden placard pinned to his chest. "Bob. Really? That's, um ... not what I expected. Not that Bob isn't a perfectly lovely name."

The elf sighed again and actually rolled his eyes. "It's short for Robbarthynn. My boss figured it would be easier for newbs to pronounce."

"I get it. Bosses, amirite? Anywho," I changed the subject quickly before triggering another of his deep sighs, which were rather epic in proportion and were heavy enough to possibly cause blunt trauma damage. "I'll save you the trouble of the welcome speech, as it's probably not your favorite thing to do nor mine to hear. We need anything other than clothes and weaponry to travel from here to Narthwych? I assume we can hire a cart or carriage or something up top if it's going to be far? I REALLY don't want to have to ride horses."

"You're in luck. It's really not far. Only a few hours' walk or so. Doubt you could get a carriage this time of the night, anyway," Bob the elf said, stifling a yawn. "You can always book a room at an inn topside and walk over in the morning. There are a few good ones to the right once you go upstairs."

"Well, shit, Bob," I frowned. "We just woke up a little while ago, and we're kind of ready to be on our way. The reeves won't take issue with us strolling along in that direction at this hour, will they?"

"Nah. They're used to it. Just don't look suspicious or anything and you should be okay."

I gave our little party the once-over: a chain-mailed Templar knight, a monk with a studded club that looked like he just stepped off a doom metal album cover, and my Scottish-pirate-looking ass.

"What exactly constitutes suspicious looking around here?" I asked.

"Oh, I dunno," he pondered, scratching his baby-smooth, alabaster cheek with his exquisitely manicured hand absently. "Just don't lurk in the shadows and look stealthy, I guess? Maybe walk down the center of the road, all well-lit and stuff, whistling a tune and looking carefree? Try really hard not to look larcenous or felonious, I suppose."

"I mean, isn't that what we'd do if we WERE up to something? To try and throw them off the scent?" I looked at him quizzically.

"I suppose," he allowed. "Just try to look sincere while you're doing it? Shit, man. I have no idea. I'm here as community service, okay? Got busted with a repro CD Walkman. It's my last night shift. I am beyond caring and over this goddamned place at this point. I just want to go home, have an ale or two, smoke some Longbottom Leaf and go the fuck to bed."

"Fuck yeah, my dude," I grinned at him. "Henceforth you shall be known as Robbarthynn the Painfully Honest, Legendary Oversharer, and Smoker of Bowls. We'll leave you be. I think we can figure it out. Maps and snacks?"

He pointed to a circular wooden rack nearby that held folded and laminated paper maps. There was a quick pick table of impulse buy snacks nearby as well.

"Thanks, Bob. Have a better night, man," I smiled at him. "What was the CD, by the way?"

He visibly perked up a bit. "Judas Priest: Unleashed in the East. 2469 Anniversary Reissue."

"Fucking choice! Victim of Changes is AMAZING on that record." I raised my hand for a fist bump and Bob actually smiled a little as he raised his hand to bump mine.

"We blowin' it up?" I grinned, still holding my fist out.

"Nah. I'm good," Bob said, his smile widening a bit, though.

"Fine. At least you didn't leave me hanging." I lowered my hand. "Later on, Robbarthynn. I may give you a shout later if we need bail money."

I actually heard him give a little laugh as we walked off. Best part of the job, really. I'm a beacon of fucking joy, I tell ya … leaving love and laughter in my wake everywhere I go. Ok, yeah. And sometimes dead bodies and burned out buildings, but no one's perfect.

We cosplayed over to the map rack and I snagged several: one labeled "Outer Rim Territories" and one specific to Narthwych. I also grabbed a couple of small leather pouches of spicy pork skins, a wineskin and a waterskin. Sallow and Bishop did likewise. Bishop also grabbed a bag of something called wolf jerky. I raised my eyebrows at this and he just shrugged. We paid and followed a series of bright green stylized arrows painted on the floor that seemed to be headed for the wide, single flight of stairs upward.

"I'm so over fucking stairs," Sallow grumped, taking a small shot from his wineskin. We all murmured agreement and began the trek upward to the surface.

CHAPTER FIFTEEN

At some point soon, I said to myself as we surfaced into the wide open air of Avalon proper with its smells of fish, grass, wood smoke and freshly turned earth, I am going to visit a fucking orbital during the daylight hours. The stairs ended at ground level in a square stone-lined opening and spilled us into a giant lean-to with a thatched roof and rough-hewn wooden logs for walls. Once we stepped out and looked around, it appeared we were on a small island near the outer edge of the mile-wide orbital-spanning waterway that Rhulgeistmakkar had mentioned, one that I was familiar with from previous visits. Surely it has a name, I thought. I can't just keep referring to it as The Waterway. I figured I would check the map later.

All of the welcome centers were located on the very edge of the outer rim, so to travel upward would naturally put one actually IN the river. Each exit point led to a small island little more than 100 meters wide and half as deep. The islands held more shops, carriage stands, and a small inn or two and were done in a style decidedly more medieval in appearance than the ones below decks: thatched roofs, timber frames, stone and roughly carved bricks. Little chimneys poked out everywhere, and diamond-pane windows, and it was all just so fucking quaint.

At each end of the island, there were small docks where travelers could book passage on small ships that would carry them to other destinations or where trade barges would berth to unload goods and staples for the shops. Central to each island was a wide pedestrian bridge made of stone and floored with wooden planks that traversed the waterway and would allow foot traffic or small carriages to head spindleward toward the central land mass that made up the bulk of Avalon. Each had a rather tall arch at its midpoint that would allow small sailing ships – the only kind needed on the orbital as the journeys were all brief and not transatlantic voyages on heavy seas - to pass through unmolested. Luckily for walkers and for the poor draft horses using the mile-long bridges, both the upward and downward grade of the arches were extremely elongated and very gradual. There also looked to be enough space between the rear of the island and the river's outer edge to allow most ships to pass as well.

As there were currently no boats tethered to the docks, we set out on foot via the bridge. Streetlamps lined its span, pleasantly symmetrical arcs of wrought-iron placed every 50 feet or so that curved inward toward each other like the upturned tusks of a giant beast, with candle-lit lanterns at their tips. I would hate to be the guy or guys responsible for lighting and extinguishing these at dawn and dusk each day, I thought to myself, not for the first time. Heeding Bob the elf's advice, we strolled as casually as we could under the lamps, chatting merrily amongst ourselves as I can't fucking whistle and that part was exceedingly dumb anyway and Bob was dumb for suggesting it.

Bishop pulled up his humungous hood against the slight chill in the air and was quickly lost from view entirely.

"This place is actually really nice," he said from somewhere underneath the gigantic hood, his voice slightly muffled. "The atmosphere and aesthetics are top notch. Very pastoral. I feel like I'm actually in the past. Far worse things to be doing than taking a long walk on a beautiful bridge with friends."

"Damnit, but I love your enthusiasm, Elias," I said. "Have you always been this positive? Also, can you even see out of that thing?"

"I tried to be positive, mostly, but often failed," the priest said with the hint of a sad smile in his voice. "I often let life's little failures get me down. But, then I spent a decade in a basement chained to a cinderblock and surrounded by cannibalistic necrophiles. Really puts things in perspective."

"Doesn't it just?" I agreed.

"Less feces than I imagined," Sallow said, agreeing in his somewhat sour way. "The water is sort of pretty."

"That's it, Jonas," I grinned. "When we get to the end of this road, maybe the kindly wizard will give you a heart! Or is it a brain?"

"Hah fucking hah," he said. "There was no real wizard, though. He was a used car salesman or something. Just rode off in his sodding balloon with an 'Oi! Get fucked!'"

"That's kind of close," I said. "There's not going to be a wizard at the end of this journey, either, though. Hopefully just a long-lost book and some sort of answers as to how we save the world and survive fucking over a race of eons-old, bat-winged horrors masquerading as fluffy-winged white dudes. And, you, know, maybe also an alien god responsible for creating our universe. And his half-alien son. And their ghost bro or whatever. All of whom probably have vast super-scientific powers beyond our pitiful human understanding. Depending on whose side they are on and all."

"When you put it like that ... sounds easy-peasy!" Sallow kicked a small rock off the side of the bridge.

"It doesn't matter," Bishop said. "I didn't have anything better to do, anyway."

"That's the spirit," I clapped him on the back with my left hand as I was currently using my smartbow/staff as a walking stick. Given our surroundings, I felt a bit like a wizard myself. "Ever the optimist, our Elias."

A group of people that appeared to be a family of four walked toward us on the opposite side of the bridge, the two fathers with an arm around each other and their opposite hands on the shoulders of a little boy and girl who looked to be somewhere around 10 years of age. They all looked muddy and exhausted, their breeches caked with nastiness and their cloaks tattered. Their posture and gaits radiated defeat.

"Hola, familia," I cheerily greeted them with a wave as they approached. "A bit late for traveling, isn't it?"

"You're traveling," the little boy said, a bit snarkily in the way kids can be that lacks malice. The man with his hand on the boy's shoulder tightened his grip.

"True enough," I agreed. "But we're not a family of four with little ones in tow. We're not brigands or thieves or anything," I added hastily as the fathers drew the kids closer to them. "We don't want anything from you. Just being friendly. Don't mind the guy in the huge hood. He's far less mysterious than he looks."

"That's good," the man with his hand on the little girl's shoulder said with a gasping sigh. "I'm not sure we can take any more. We've been robbed, chased, and had axes thrown at us. An inn burned down around us, our daughter has the worst rash I have ever seen, and Joel wound up with dysentery from our very first meal here, and this has literally been THE period WORST period VACATION period EVER exclamation mark!" Yes. He actually verbalized the punctuation.

"Damn, man," I said. "That's rough. I'm so sorry." I turned to the others. "Why do I feel like they're about to offer us a side-quest?"

"I'm not sure what that means," the other man said. "But we don't want anything from you either. We just want to get off this stupid orbital. And I want to stop SHITTING MYSELF TO DEATH. Um, sorry, kids. And thanks *so* much for bringing that up to a bunch of total strangers, Frederick."

"You must be Joel," Sallow said. "Sorry for your troubles, mate."

"Thank you. You seem like nice people, but we really must be going," Joel said, and he and his partner pushed the kids forward and began walking again.

"Hey," I said, stopping them. I dug my money pouch out of my sporran and peeled off a couple of 1000-gold notes. "I know you didn't ask, but maybe this will help you guys get home ... maybe buy you and the kids a decent meal or two to help put this behind you. I pulled out a digital business card with a hologram of my face and Mary Ann's on it and put it with the folded notes and handed them all to Joel. "You guys are ever on the outer rim of Elysia, stop by my shop for a pint and we'll find something special for the kids. On the house. If I'm not there, talk to the giant, scary, gorgeous green lady named Mary Ann and tell her Double D said you have the run of the place until I get back."

Frederick looked like he was on the verge of tears. Joel reached out and took the proffered cash and the card. He looked at the card.

"Thank you, Mr. Davidson," he said softly. "I don't know what to say."

"You just said it," I grinned. "It's Daniel. Believe me, I have had some awful trips, too, and could have used an act of kindness. Now get these kids home. It should be a safe, short walk back to civilization. You want us to go with you? We're tougher than we look. Except for the guy in the giant hood."

"Hey, I *can* hear you, you know," said the giant hood.

Joel looked at the tiny island a few hundred well-lit yards away. "No, thank you. I think we can make that okay. Come on, kids." He smiled his thanks again, and his partner and kids waved and were on their way. I started walking, and Bishop followed. Sallow stayed put for a few moments, then started following us.

"Davidson," he began as he caught up.

"It's not a big deal. Don't make it a big deal," I said.

"You didn't have to do that, though," he said.

"Obviously," I agreed. "But I did. I've been in tons of tough scrapes, and like I told him, I've had some really bad days when the smallest act of kindness from a stranger would have pulled me back from the brink. So, I had a chance to be that guy, and I took it. Besides. It's not even my money, really. It's Archer's money or the bad angels' money. And what better use for the likely ill-gotten gains of a bunch of eldritch horrors than helping out a sweet little family that's been royally shit on by life?"

I stopped walking and looked at Sallow. "And if I can't do a little bit of good here and there amidst the blazing guns and the fucking cut throats, what's it all fucking for?"

"Ok," he said, relenting and holding up his hands in appeasement. "Fair enough. Fair-e-fucking-nuff. You're still a good bloke though, and I'm sorry I tried to kill ya."

"Don't start going soft on me, Sallow," I replied. "Or I'll have to tell you the story of how I cornholed your saintly mum and wiped my dick on her curtains. On your birthday. She fed me cake afterwards."

"I take it all back," he chuckled. "You are a complete bastard."

"That's more like it. Never forget it," I grinned my best sociopath's grin.

"I'm praying for the lot of you," Bishop's voice issued forth from underneath his hood.

"That may be the first religious thing I've heard you say," Sallow remarked.

"I'm more of a show-don't-tell kind of priest," Bishop said. "And don't make that dirty. I'm definitely not THAT kind of priest."

"You're a credit to your profession, Elias, and a credit to your faith," I said. "But what do I know? I'm an atheist. Although, apparently I can be persuaded to believe in interdimensional beings who have been worshipped as gods for millennia. I'm not sure where the line is, really."

"It's okay to not know, and you know more than you think you know, my son," Bishop said. "And many of the faithful could learn a lot from you."

"Mostly compound curse words and filthy innuendo," I noted. "And maybe some sex acts they've never heard of, but, thank you, and let's change the fucking subject."

We grew quiet for a while as we kept walking, eventually beginning the gradual upward incline of the midpoint bridge. It was so subtle at first we didn't notice, but by the time we neared the end of the first quarter of the climb, we were all feeling it in our calves and liberally bitched about it amongst ourselves. When we reached the apex, we took a moment to chill and admire the view. To be fair, it was still the view of a placid, still waterway at night without much going on, but we were a good 30 feet higher than we had been and it seemed a cause for mild celebration. Bishop dug around in his gargantuan robe sleeves, pulled out his pouch of wolf jerky and offered us some.

"Where the fuck did that come from?" I asked the dark space under the hood that I assumed still contained Bishop.

"This thing has pockets EVERYWHERE," he said, inserting a piece of jerky into the darkness at approximately mouth height. "Mmmm. *Shit*. That's pretty good. Who knew wolves were so tasty?"

"What's it taste like?" I asked, taking a piece from the open pouch Bishop was still holding towards us. "And if you say 'chicken,' I'm going to rummage around in there until I find an eye to poke."

"It's hard to describe," he said. "A little like a gamier Mongolian beef?"

I bit off a hunk and chewed, thoughtful. "That's a fair assessment. Definitely some ginger in there. A hint of chili flake."

"Goddamnit," Sallow said. "Give me some." He grabbed a couple of pieces and tossed them in his mouth. "Huh. That IS good. I'm not even really hungry." He reached back toward the bag, but Bishop smacked the top of his hand.

"Be not among drunkards or among gluttonous eaters of meat," the hood said sagely. "Proverbs 23:20." Bishop tossed another piece of jerky into the hungry darkness and chewing sounds ensued.

"But *you're* still eating it," Sallow said. "Why the fuck am I the gluttonous one?"

"Let he that is without sin among you, cast the first stone," Bishop said, and I know I could hear the grin in his voice this time. "Besides, my child, it's my fucking jerky. Get bent." He turned and started walking toward the downward slope.

"You've been spending entirely too much time around HIM," Sallow called after the priest as he turned to follow.

"You're literally the only two people I know," Bishop's voice trailed back. "He's my oldest friend."

"That's fair," Sallow said, shrugging. "And a little sad."

"In so many ways," I said, laughing, and we hurried to catch up.

CHAPTER SIXTEEN

The second half of the bridge walk was relatively uneventful. We reached the end of the bridge, consulted our outer rim map amidst a rimjob joke or two, and turned left. The path ended in a hard T, the little intersection featuring what looked to be an inn specializing in seafood and a few trinket shops. So, left it was, toward Narthwych and destiny. We followed the banks of the waterway, which the map had listed as Thee Watyrway, by the way. (I thought this fucking place was supposed to be imaginative, but whatever.) Another hour's walk down the quiet country lane had us approaching a small town, which according the map, should have been Narthwych.

As we approached the outskirts of the town, our peaceful journey's end was disturbed mightily by Elias crop-dusting us with wolf jerky farts and issuing vehement denials from the infinitely vast chasm of his hood when outed by Sallow and myself. To this day, he maintains we walked through a skunk's trail, but Jonas and I maintain he sits (and/or sharts) on a throne of lies.

As we approached the town, a guard shack painted in bright chevrons appeared out of the early morning fog.

"Halt!" Someone barked at us in an imperious voice. "Who goes there?"

"That is so fucking unoriginal," I muttered to my companions. However, in a clear, hopefully non-felonious sounding voice, I replied: "'Tis but a few humble travelers, sir. Seeking entrance into your fine town so that we may enjoy your fabled custom and hospitality."

"That's laying it on a bit fucking thick, innit?" Sallow opined in a low voice.

"Shut yer fucking trappeth, good sire," I growled back. "We musteth keepeth up appearances ... -eth."

"But we heard not the whistling of innocent men," the guard yelled back, stepping out of the mist and into view along with his partner. Both wore royal blue tunics over chainmail. The tunics sported a stylized griffin rampant in white over an Olde English-looking Blackletter N. Both had rather sharp looking spears in their hands and dweeby nose-guard helmets that shone in the moonlight.

"Methinks ye might be approaching our fair hamlet stealthily and with ill intent," Guard Number Two said, adjusting his grip on his spear.

"Yethinks bullshite, good sir," I replied. "For I ... goddamnit, this is stupid. I can't whistle, fellas. We're trying really hard to be cool here, walking in the light and tossing about cheerful banter and such. We have no wish for trouble. We're cool, though. Like three little Fonzies. And what's Fonzie like?"

"I know not of this Fonzie, knave," Guard Number One said. "But if ye have no ill intent, prove it."

"I ... um ... how the *fuck* do I prove non-ill intent, guys?" I queried my companions. "Pretty sure I know how to do the opposite, but I'm at a loss here."

"Hold out your hands and prove you're unarmed," Guard Number Two called out.

"It's Avalon!" I shouted back. "Everyone is armed!"

"He's got a point," Guard Number One said to the other guard.

The fucking enormous hood containing Bishop stepped forward.

"Know ye hence," a slightly muffled yet strangely commanding voice came from under the hood. "I am a Man of God here upon a godly mission demanded of me by Holy writ, charged with ... all things godly and good. Whosoever standeth in my way shall incur the wrath not only of Mother Church herself but of the Lord Thy God. May he have mercy upon your pitiful, pedestrian souls. Now, let us pass!"

We heard quiet conversation between the two guards, who bent their heads toward one another.

"You and your companions may pass, Holy One," Guard Number One said, straightening up. "May His light shine ever on your, um, endeavors."

"You don't have to rhyme, Rafe," Guard Number Two said to his colleague in a hiss. "They warned us about that in guard school, remember? Said it made us sound like we were trying too hard to be fancy."

"I know, TOBIAS," Guard Number One hissed back, leaning into the name. "Sometimes it just sodding happens. I wasn't *trying*."

"Go forth with His Blessing," Bishop bleated quickly, grabbing us both by the arms and practically dragging us forward and past the guards and their festively painted shack at a half-run.

"And henceforth, the two of you may refer to me as 'Holy One'," he said to us as we speedwalked, probably adopting an expression of piousness under his hood.

"Not bloody likely," Sallow replied.

We heard more grumbling and sniping behind us, but as the threat was no longer immediate, we relaxed a bit and slowed our gait from a hurried trot back to our default saunter.

"That was fucking brilliant, Elias," I gushed. "I had no idea you had it in you."

"Whereas I am certain your mother had it in HER, and often," Bishop said. "DAMNIT. Sallow is right. I have been spending entirely too much time around you." He threw off his hood with an exasperated sigh and no little effort.

"Whoa!" I said. "It's not like you've had an alternative. Plus, I mean, I kind of grow on you ... like a funnier and infinitely more handsome version of genital warts. Also, good to see your face, man. I thought we'd lost you."

Bishop laughed. "I suppose there are worse things than being like you, Daniel."

"Don't start going soft on me, priest, or I'll have to tell you the story about the time I cornholed Sallow's mum …" I began.

"Damnit," Sallow yelled. "I've just about had it up to here …"

"That's what your mom said when I …" I broke in.

"SHUT IT." Sallow barked back. "I get it. You fucked me mum's arse! Let's move on."

"Jesus," I whispered to Bishop. "He's SO sensitive."

"He's just hangry," Bishop whispered back. "He usually takes it like a man. Also, that's what SHE said?"

Sallow took a beat and exhaled. "Goddamnit. Okay. Let's find an inn. I'm starving, and the wolf jerky is long gone."

"Told you," Bishop said with a beatific smile.

So find an inn we did.

It was approaching daylight when we happened across a cozy little inn that butted up to the water's edge. In fact, it looked like the back patio was on stilts and was actually over the water. The colorful pub sign outside read "The Psychedelic Unicorn." The carven imagery completely embraced the letter and the spirit of the name, with a rainbow-colored unicorn sitting on a giant mushroom with what I assumed was a tiny bong. Both its horn and the lettering were wreathed in purple smoke. I pushed open the door, and our twisted fellowship stumbled in, already over just about everything medieval.

The pub's interior was well-lit, a giant fire roaring in a fireplace that could've held an entire rugby scrum. It was awfully crowded for this time of day, I thought, spotting all manner of fantasy folk – bearded dwarves hoisting tankards, a group of halflings playing a game of cards over coffee, a few elves looking imperious here and there. Most were sitting at tables enjoying heaping breakfasts that looked amazing: plates full of flaky biscuits, platters of roasted meats, and bowls of earthy vegetables in what was no doubt rich broth. The smells that issued forth from the room and the kitchen behind the bar were absolutely mouth-watering: smoked meats, exotic spices, baking bread. The view behind the bar was also staggering: cask upon cask of ales in every variety. An orc barkeep paused in his glass-polishing to greet us.

"Ho, travelers!" The green giant shouted around his mandibular tusks in a deep basso profondo. "Welcome to the Unicorn! We've stews and brews to please even the most discerning of palates! What can I get fer yas?"

"Does every retailer here have a catchphrase?" Sallow asked.

"One of everything, my good man!" I replied to the orc, collapsing into a seat close to the fire.

"Not, um, quite that, but can we see a menu?" Bishop asked.

"First time in?" The orc asked as he put the glass down and walked around the bar, crossing his massive arms over his apron-covered bulk and not inconsiderable belly.

"Yup," Sallow said.

"HOOOO! We've got UNI-VIRGINS HERE!" The orc shouted. He ran over to the bar and yanked on a thick rope, causing a ship's bell mounted above to begin clanging with an eardrum-piercing clamor.

The regulars all started groaning and protesting at this, with one in the back shouting: "GOOD GOD, PERCY! LET IT GO. IT'S TOO FECKING EARLY FOR THAT SHITE." Grumbles and murmurs of agreement rounded the room and at least one "Fer feck's sake!" came from the back room.

We all winced and covered our ears with our hands.

"I was over it all, then the food reeled me back in, and now I'm over it all again!" I shouted to Bishop and Sallow. The din finally came to an abrupt halt as the orc read the room a few beats too late and stopped yanking on the bell pull.

"Well, aren't you lot all a bunch of grumpy geese," he said to the room, grabbing a few menus from the bar top and walking over to place them in front of us.

"I think it's 'grumpy gusses'," came another voice from the back room.

"Pipe down, Nathaniel, or I'll haul you out on the patio and toss you in the drink!" The orc smiled at us as we perused the menus, baring his huge fangs in a completely nonthreatening way. Luckily, thanks to my long friendship with Mary Ann, I am relatively immune to such displays. "I'm Percival, by the way. Percy to my friends. What'll it be, folks, or do you need a minute?"

"How about a bowl of the venison stew, a coffee and a water?" Bishop said. "That come with bread?"

"Yep," Percy said, writing down the order with a quill on a small pad he pulled from his apron pocket. "What about you, Sir Knight?"

"Mutton lettuce and tomato on rye with mayo ... house made chips, salt and vinegar, please ... black coffee and a small pour of your barleywine," Sallow said, handing over his menu.

"Got it. What about you, Calico Jack?"

"Oh, yeah. The pirate thing," I said, smiling. "I'll take the chicken shawarma flatbread - hold the onions – side order of home fries with malt vinegar on the side. And a flagon of your old ale."

"Coming right up!" The orc walked over behind the bar and shouted some orders through the pass in incomprehensible kitchen-speak, ripping off the top sheet of the pad and smacking it down on the sill. He then grabbed some glassware and started pouring our drinks.

"This one's nae newcomer," I heard a lilting female voice say from behind me and I felt strong arms wrap around me, pinning my arms to my sides.

"Fuck!" I yelped as Bishop yanked his club from one of his oversized sleeves and Sallow half-stood, partially drawing his blade.

CHAPTER SEVENTEEN

I felt lips on my cheek and heard a giant wet smacking sound close to my ear as one of the hands released me to tousle my hair. Then, before I knew what was happening, a pleasantly rounded, leather-clad body launched itself into my lap and my face was completely smothered by a giant mane of golden locks as I felt the arms encircle me again like fleshy cables.

I sputtered, and issued a muffled shout from beneath the bounteous piles of flaxen hair.

"That you, Helly?" I knew the answer already, though, from the scent of lavender blossoming up around me and the mop of spun gold that was trying to bury me alive. There was no one like Helly anywhere.

I managed to push/pull her to arms' length but not before she landed another kiss on the other cheek and brayed musically with laughter.

"So, I guess we're not under attack?" Sallow said, slumping back into his chair and letting his sword fall back fully into its scabbard.

"I mean, sort of?" I managed, laughing out loud myself as I returned the Dwarven woman's embrace fully. "Ah, I've missed you, you beautiful, sawed-off little shit."

She bit my ear with a growl for my trouble, bounced up out of my lap with a giggle and punched me solidly in the bicep hard enough to leave a red mark. If my Second Skyn armor hadn't soaked up the vast majority of the impact, there would have been a deep, dark bruise. "I'll show you sawed off, longshanks! I'll take me axe to your todger and …"

"Whoa, now," I said. "Just because I joke about there being plenty to go around doesn't mean I have any to spare."

“That’s not what me mum says!” Helly howled, squeezing my face between her palms. “And she said tae tell ye she misses yer fat cock, even if you’re a … how did she put it … a two-pump chump?”

“Christ,” Sallow said. “Did she just do a ‘your mom’ joke in reverse?”

“I think that makes it a ‘my mom’ joke?” Bishop said. “But I’m not 100% sure of the protocols involved.”

“Fuck,” Sallow groaned. “Now there’s three of you.”

“I like to beat him to the punch,” Helly grinned at them, her short stature putting her delightful heart-shaped face in our direct eye line as we sat. She stalked over to a nearby table, grabbed a chair and spun it over to an empty spot between Sallow and me. She plopped down, her feet just shy of reaching the floor. She leaned forward over the table, grinning her wide, gap-toothed smile, her pale, freckled cheeks blooming pink. “Hiya, boys. I’m Helleena Boughbreaker, Shield-Maiden-For-Hire, but you can call me Helly.”

“Where’d her accent go?” Sallow asked me.

“It comes and goes,” I whispered loudly. “But it’s not polite to notice.”

“Don’t talk about me like I’m not here, Danny Boy,” the tiny terror said, reaching out to pat me on the arm. “You’re lucky I’ve missed you so goddamned much, or I’d put you over me knee.”

“Don’t threaten me with a good time, you little minx,” I said, mrrowing at her, sending her into gales of rolling laughter.

“She’s an easy mark,” I explained to the others. “She laughs at all of my jokes, no matter how stupid. It’s part of why we get along so well. Come to think of it, she laughs at just about everything. It really is so incredibly good to see you, Helly. I am so glad you’re here. I would’ve called, but …”

“I know,” she grinned. “You had no idea you were coming here until you did. It’s fine. Mary Ann called me and told me your tracker was headed this way and to look for you. Boy, she is PISSED you haven’t checked in. You might have more than a spanking waiting on you when you get home."

"Fucksticks," I grumbled. "I really should've. I'll have to sneak into the bushes soon and give her a call. So, how've you been? Where's Ariana? She coming?"

"She'll be here soon," Helly sighed. "She wants to see you, too, but she has a busy day. Probably can't stay but a few minutes."

"Gotcha," I said. "Oh, and I'm sorry, guys. I'm being rude. Helly, this is Father Elias Bishop, an absolute sweetheart of a guy who's been a prisoner of a cannibal cult on Canaan for the last decade or so. And this is Jonas Sallow, A.K.A. Nightstar, a Templar Knight who is helping me on a case. Fellas, Helly and I go WAY back. We met some years ago when I came to Avalon on another case and needed some local muscle. Needless to say we hit it off."

"Charmed," Bishop said, smiling.

"Pleasure to meet you, Helly," Sallow said.

"Yeah, Daniel and I might've saved each other's lives once or twice," Helly grinned. "And, well, he's hard not to like once you get past all the ..." She made a vague gesture that I took to encompass the totality of me.

"Ouch," I said.

Percy walked up with our drinks, handing them out and plopping down a giant flagon of beer in front of Helly that was bigger than her head.

"The usual, Helly, my love," the orc said, smiling. He nodded to us. "Food'll be out in a few."

"Thanks, Perce, you gorgeous green slab of throbbing manhood," Helly said to the orc as he walked off.

"Still not my type, Hell," he called back over his shoulder as he returned to the bar.

"What's his type?" Sallow asked.

"Fuck if I know," Helly said. "But apparently it's not buxom, blonde, omnisexual dwarves." She sighed. "Always a bridesmaid." She quaffed about half of her beer, belched loudly and pulled out a short dagger from somewhere and started cleaning underneath her fingernails.

"Fucking shame," I said. "You have so much to offer."

"Don't I just?" She laughed. "Chief among them this magical VAJEEN!" She dropped her dagger, made the universal double-hand motion crotch-ward and said the last in a big, boomy voice that caused several people to look our way. The table of halflings glanced over disapprovingly. She gave them the stink eye.

Bishop choked on his coffee, sputtering.

"No comment," I said.

"But you could ..." Helly grinned evilly, poking the tip of her tongue out of the hole where her leftmost incisor used to be. "Which reminds me ... do you still do that thing with your ..."

"GAH!" I took a big swallow of my ale. "Never happened. No idea what you're talking about. Change of subject. Business? How about business."

She laughed. "FINE. I regret nothing. Mary Ann said you're looking for a scary-ass magic book?"

"It's not MAGIC-magic, but yeah," I said. "Info we found on Canaan said it might be here in a Christian Archive in Narthwych. You know anything about the place?"

"Nah. I still live hours from here," she said. "Just planned on taking the morning off after Mary Ann called last night and caught a barge over a little while ago. I don't have much use for all of the churchy-stuff. Too much abstinence. And I think the last book I read was ... shit. I actually have no idea."

"It probably had lots of pictures and very few words," I quipped.

"Says the adult who still reads comics," Helly fired back.

"Touché," I shrugged.

"Douché," she stuck out her tongue and blew a raspberry at me.

Our meal arrived, which resulted in a brief respite from casual insults. About ten minutes in, I glanced up and saw the front door open to admit a tall, wispy female elf with Asian features. She tossed her long black hair back over her shoulder and scanned the room, her eyes adjusting to the relative darkness. I stood and waved, wiping the corner of my mouth with a napkin. The elf broke into a smile that positively lit up the room and glided over. She paused just out of reach to strike a silly ballerina-like pose for my benefit, absolutely radiant in a blood red pantsuit with golden leaves and Elven curlicues. The long, curved sword at her belt seemed somehow an extension of her lithe self.

"Ariana!" I smiled and laughed with joy. "You're as stunning as ever!" I embraced her tightly, and she lightly kissed my cheek and caressed the other warmly.

"Daniel!" She sniffed at my neck theatrically like a hound might and wrinkled up her button nose. "Ugh. You smell like dwarf and lavender."

"Hey," Helly belched. "I smell like a goddamned spring garden in Hobbiton, you willowy twat!"

Ariana floated over and kissed Helly on top of the head and yanked lightly at a random braid. Percy strode over with a chair, and Sallow scooted closer to Bishop to make room for the elf. Ariana gracefully sat, in that magical Elven way that makes every movement a little symphony. I'm not sure grace comes with the upgrade, but I'd venture to say that the type of people who want to be elves are typically rocking it pretty hard beforehand.

"You didn't bring ME a chair, you inconsiderate oaf," Helly chirped at the gigantic barman.

"That's because I mistook you for a hairy footstool," Percy chirped back, winking.

"FUCKER," Helly laughed and thumped beer foam at the orc and flipped him the bird as he walked away.

"Is everyone you know as filthy as you are, Davidson?" Sallow asked around a mouthful of MLT.

"I resent that, human," Ariana said, loftily. "I am the absolute picture of style, dignity, class and poise."

"Apologies, ma'am," the knight said, gulping down his bite and looking chastened.

"Goddamned right," Ariana said, then added in her classiest tone while looking around: "So, who do I have to blow to get a glass of wine up in this bitch?"

Sallow cackled. "I fucking knew it."

"Ariana Silverblade," the elf said, nodding at my companions in greeting. "Forensic accountant and sometime dance instructor. You are?"

"Jonas Sallow, knight," our resident surly Brit said.

"Elias Bishop, priest, former basement gimp," Bishop said, toasting the woman with his water glass.

"Wonderful to meet you both," the elf said. "So, what brings you here, Daniel? Something about a book? And have you called Mary Ann yet? She was furious with you on the com last night."

"Shit, no," I frowned. "I will as soon as we leave here, I promise."

"Good, you inconsiderate turd," she said as she raised her hand overhead to take the glass of red wine that Percy had brought over. "Thank you, darling orc."

I swear, Percy blushed a little as he turned and walked back over to the bar.

"I think we may have found his type," Bishop grinned.

"She's everyone's type," Helly said, making theatrical goo-goo eyes at Ariana and batting her considerable eyelashes rapidly.

"So, are you two …" Sallow began.

"Roommates and lifelong besties," Helly said, laughing. "Don't get me wrong, though, I'd bang her like a screen door if she'd let me. Just LOOK AT HER."

"You're so sweet," Ariana said. "Not that she wouldn't bang just about anything with a pulse. Or that was still warm, anyway. I'm actually ace, though, Jonas. But if I were interested in such mundane things as sex and romance, I'd buy this little strumpet dinner and plow her like a farmer seeding a fertile field. Him, too." She nodded her head toward me as I choked on my ale.

"STAHP. I'm going to slide right off this chair," Helly said, giggling. She crumpled up a napkin and threw it at Ariana, who smiled and swatted it away gracefully.

"Good lord," Sallow groaned. "Now there's four of you. It's like I'm in an asylum or something."

"Anyway, amusing trifles aside, Daniel," the elf shifted gears. "What are you doing on our charming little orbital? And can we help you in any way?"

I gave them a brief rundown of the situation, starting with Archer and my trip to Canaan. I tagged Sallow in to flesh out the bits about the Angelic Host and half-alien Jesus. Halfway through his description of the Outsiders, Helly called for another round for the table. We had all but finished the second round when I concluded the tale of our adventures to date.

"So, okay," Helly said, draining her flagon. "Lemme get this straight. You have to find this book so you can double-cross some scary angels who look like Lovecraftian nightmares but pretend to be Aryan wet dreams with wings, and maybe fight God and Jesus, who are interdimensional alien beings of near infinite power? All to prevent the apocalypse? That about sum it up?"

"You know Lovecraft?" Bishop asked.

"I said I hadn't read a book in a while, not that I was illiterate, Father," Helly said, sticking her tongue out at Bishop, who smiled and gleefully reciprocated, crossing his eyes. "And I even read books without pictures sometimes, DANIEL."

"Fine, you're a regular bibliophile in miniature," I said before adopting a condescendingly paternal tone. "And bibliophile means someone who reads a lot."

She tried to kick me under the table, but her legs wouldn't reach.

"I will be out of this chair and on you like a goddamn spider monkey," she warned, smiling. "And not in a fun way!"

"Simmer down, Short Round," I said. "So, look. I have no idea where this building is. Is there an office where we can access public records? I'm sure it's not the sort of place that would show up on a tourist map."

"Boy, are you in luck," Ariana said. "I happen to know right where it is, seeing as how I had to audit the books of a furniture maker right across the street from it a year or so ago. I wouldn't remember it at all except there is a little lunch place next door to it that I ate at daily for the two weeks I was in town. Walked by the sign every single day and wondered what the hell went on in there."

"And now you the hell know," I grinned. "That's amazing, though! Can you take us there?"

"Of course I can, love," Ariana smiled. "As long as you pick up our tab."

"Naturally," I said. "I was going to do that anyway."

I hit Percy up for the bill, paid our not inconsiderable tab, and threw in a huge tip, thanking him for the stellar service. As we headed out, Helly grabbed a double-headed axe that was almost as big as she was from the guest weapons rack to the right of the door and slung it across her broad back. As she started to walk out, she spun on her heels and gave the table of halflings the old double bird, waggling her upraised middle fingers side-to-side in time with her outstretched tongue.

CHAPTER EIGHTEEN

We hung a left out of the door of The Psychedelic Unicorn and walked deeper into town. The slumbering burg had awakened around us as we ate our meal and sipped our ales. Foot traffic had definitely picked up, with all manner of cybernatural species hustling to and fro: orc porters ferrying huge carts of goods toward the docks, Halfling messengers zipping past us with packages, Dwarven tradesmen and tradeswomen hawking metal goods and food at small street side stalls. A few carriages and horse drawn carts jockeyed for space on the cobbled streets. Small fishing vessels could be spotted at work out in ... sigh ... Thee Watyrway, hauling their catches up and tossing nets and traps overboard.

It really was a very picturesque village. Bookstores, coffee shops, bakeries, clothiers, and other purveyors of sundries lined the street across from the water, with proprietors sweeping their stoops or cheerfully yelling at friends or passersby. I certainly understood the appeal of visiting a place like this, and maybe even living there. Not that I don't still think cosplaying your life away is a little weird, but hey. I'm sure a lot of people think my interests and proclivities are weird, too. Again, whatever. Live and let live and don't be a dick.

We passed by a particularly neat little bookshop with a giant, corpulent orange tabby perched in the round window, and Ariana urged us to turn right onto a side street. I took a moment to wave at the chonky kitty as we passed. She yawned at me as if to say "Your tribute pleases me, mortal, but I tire of you. Be gone with you." So, I winked at her and went on my merry way. (What? Fuck off. I like animals.)

The elf turned left again as we neared the back of the building, and we followed. I took a moment again to admire everything about my lovely, elegant friend. Her feet hardly seemed to touch the stones below us, and she barely made a sound as she walked, as nimble on her 'hooker heels' (her words, not mine) as most people are in athletic shoes. She looked positively resplendent, which, to be fair, is her natural state.

"Are you staring at me, Daniel?" She asked without even turning her head toward me.

I heard the smile in her voice, though. This was an old game with us.

"Yes, ma'am," I laughed. "In my defense, it's hard not to. You're just … fucking AMAZING in every way possible. You know, platonically and stuff. Not that you're not blazingly hot, I mean, I would totally …"

She laughed, the sound like strange music that is at once completely alien but also instantly familiar. It wrapped around me like a favorite childhood blanket. "I know. Reel it in, sailor."

"Whatever, you fucking goddess," I fired back. "I love you, you know?"

"Of course you do," she purred. "What's not to love?"

"Not a goddamned thing," I agreed.

"Huh. What about ME, Daniel?" Helly popped up beside me out of nowhere and smacked me on the ass. "Do ya love me, ya silly fucking git?"

"Of course I do, you tiny tart!" I reached down and picked her up and hugged her to my chest – no easy task, that, as she is as solid as a fucking Clydesdale - and spun around in a circle, kissing her neck until she giggled uncontrollably and slapped me on the cheek. I put her down and we both laughed like absolute loons.

"There's something deeply wrong with the entire lot of you," Sallow said.

"I think it's kind of sweet," Bishop said.

"And that's why you're on my Christmas list and fucking

Jonas is getting a sock full of coal," I said. "His mom, though ..."

"Is getting this fat DIIIICCCKKK!" Helly howled, grabbing her crotch.

"Not you, too," Sallow looked at Helly, betrayed.

The dwarf shrugged and winked at him.

"I thought you had a magical vajeen," Bishop asked, innocent as you please.

"It's a metaphorical dick, Father," Helly said. "Although, if we're going to be friends, I suppose I could be persuaded to talk about the contents of my toy box ..."

"Stop right there, you incorrigible slut," I said. "I will not have you corrupting the mind of my innocent, childlike priest with your filth."

"Hypocrite," she laughed. "Like *you* are unfamiliar with the contents of my toy box!"

"Silence," I cried. "These events you speak of never happened. I deny any knowledge of ..."

"Whatever," she giggled. "Deny all you want, but I'll never forget the time you did that thing with your ..."

"Hush, you two!" Ariana scolded, but without much heat. I could hear the smile in her voice, like a mother reluctantly reprimanding wayward children whose antics amuse her. "We're here."

We complied, although it was hard. Heh.

I looked up and, as pretty as a picture, Ariana was standing next to the sign for the Avalon Christian Archive - Diocese of Narthwych, framing the placard with her hands like Vanna White showing off the solution to a puzzle. (Really? Wheel of Fortune? Come on. I know it was mainly for old people, but goddamn, Vanna White was something back in the day.) She dropped her hands and stuck her thumb in the air, pointing to the little Greek bodega next door.

"And, seriously. Best gyros in town. The baklava is INSANE." She hung her head. "And now, I'm fucking hungry. Let's get this over with, Daniel."

"Yup. On it. Are you sure you have time for this, by the way?"

I asked the elf. "Helly said you have a busy day planned."

"I do," she said, smiling. "Or at least I did. Friends – and stopping possible apocalypses – come first. I'll work a few extra hours over the weekend. It'll be fine."

I grinned and stepped up beside her, turning to address the party.

"Ok, folks. I have no idea what we're going to face in there. It could be just about any situation imaginable. We're looking for a book with the power to unmake Creation itself. It could be a cakewalk or a milk run. It could be a punch in the junk from the icy fist of the Universe. We might be dealing with heartless bureaucrats, or we could be fighting our way out of this place covering our nethers after a smash and grab. No fucking idea. The plan is to pop in and do a little reconnaissance and ask a few questions, but shit happens, so ... let's be ready for anything, yeah? Anyone have anything to add?"

"Your pep talks make me moist," Helly yelled, her hands on either side of her mouth as a makeshift megaphone.

"What fucking doesn't?" I laughed, giving her the finger. "If there is no actual feedback here, I say we hit the doors and see what's what."

Everyone stopped short of actually drawing weapons, but shoulders were rolled, cuffs were shot, and general murmurs of assent floated over to me. Ariana held up her hand and assessed her manicure, sighing. Helly grabbed each foot in turn, stretching her quads, and then twisted at the waist a few times. Bishop pulled up his gigantic fucking hood. Sallow grimaced, as was his way.

We were as ready as this merry band of assholes could be for whatever karmic comeuppance or celestial joke waited inside to pounce on us and teabag us into oblivion, metaphorically speaking. I turned on my heels and reached out, pulling on the door handle and stepping inside.

CHAPTER NINETEEN

The party followed suit, and we found ourselves standing in a comfortable waiting room that for all intents and purposes resembled that of a doctor's office. If that doctor had been from Middle Earth, anyway. Numerous wooden benches sat against the wall on both sides of the door, and small seating areas with chairs and tables were spread out across the narrow lobby, some of them holding books that I assumed were to occupy time as patrons waited for help. A large unoccupied wooden counter stood in front of us, running from wall to wall. Beyond, large stacks of bookshelves and utility shelves reached almost to the ceiling, and monks hurried to and fro with armloads of books and scrolls.

"Ok, guys. Hang back. I have an idea," I said. "Except you, Bishop. Come with me."

"Oh, shit," Sallow said. "Davidson has an idea."

"Right?" Helly said. "That always worries me."

Ignoring them, Bishop and I walked up to the counter. Christian pamphlets from several different local churches were fanned out decoratively, and there was a small hand bell with a sign that read *Ring for Service* in fancy blackletter print. So, I picked up the bell and rang it.

"HOOOO! We've got UNI-VIRGINS HERE!" I heard Helly exclaim in a stage whisper.

"Too fucking soon," Sallow said, nudging her in the shoulder with his elbow. "The bell's triggering my post-traumatic stress as it is."

A moment later, we spotted a young halfling in a black friar's robe climbing down from one of the taller stacks on a rolling ladder. He approached the front counter and climbed a small stepladder so that he could see over it and be somewhat close to our height. He self-consciously brushed at his tonsure with a hand, flattening down an errant tuft of brown hair.

"May I help you, sir ... and ...?" The monk asked, smiling, looking at Bishop buried beneath his hood.

"Yup, there's another sir under there somewhere. And, yes, Brother ..." I dropped off expectantly.

"Uriel," he said. "Brother Uriel."

"Ah, nice! Like the archangel," I said, dropping some religious knowledge like it was hot, no doubt building rapport with the tiny monk. "Very good. Well, Brother Uriel, we are here about a book. It originally belonged to my companion here, Father Elias K. Bishop, and it was wrongfully taken from him on Canaan. We have traced it here and wish to retrieve it. How do we go about doing that? I'm hoping that we can fill out some paperwork in triplicate, get it stamped by management, snag this man's property and be on our way without having to resort to, um, legal means."

"Legal means?" Brother Uriel pursed his lips and knitted his brow.

I gestured behind me with my thumb in the general direction of the snazzy lady elf, who looked every bit the professional she was. Even if she didn't actually belong to *that* particular profession.

"We brought our lawyer along, Ms. Silverblade ... of Silverblade, Whiteknuckle and Horntooth? Surely you've seen the advertisements." I turned and smiled at Ariana and she gave Brother Uriel a little wave.

"Yes," he nodded thoughtfully. "I believe I have. Hmmm. I can certainly look into this. Do you have a Lot Number or the book's proper name? Many of the books from Canaan wound up here, and I guess you can see we have quite a few books ..." He trailed off.

"Yeah. Sure thing. Give me just a sec." I turned around with my back to him and opened my left bracer to peek at my smartwatch. I projected the pic I had taken of the damnable red pyramid in the bowels of the Canaan library and checked the numbers. I read them off to Uriel with my back still turned so he wouldn't see my breach of tech etiquette.

"Items 009660-00760. Transferred to Avalon Christian Archive, Diocese of Narthwych. Authorized by Elder Imam Muhammed Ahmad. Shipment No. 0000014676400-221." I left off the threat level stuff in case it nixed our chances at retrieving the book. "It's called the Book of Raziel."

"Ok," he said, jotting down the info on a scrap of paper with a quill. "Let me go see what I can find out. Make yourselves comfortable. I hope to not be long."

We wandered back over to the group and filled them in.

"You know," Helly said. "For someone who came in here without a plan, that's not half bad."

"Did ... you just compliment me?" I smirked. "I may swoon ... someone, quick! Write down the date and time so I can remember this momentous occasion FOREVER."

"I compliment you all the time, dork," she giggled. "Besides, I think it's the least I can do considering I cornholed both your folks. On their anniversary. We had champagne after."

"AH, memories," I said. "I hope you showed them both a good time."

"Don't I always?" She winked.

"No comment." I winked back.

About this time, I heard the sound of springs, um, springing and Brother Uriel walked out of a small gate at the end of the counter, allowing it to swing closed on its mechanism in his wake. He padded toward us, barefoot, as is the Halfling way. We walked back toward the counter to meet him.

"I am afraid I come bearing some not so great news," Uriel said. "It would seem that we sold that lot at auction some months ago."

"You did WHAT?!" I think my eyes may have bugged out of my head a bit. "You SOLD IT?"

"Please, sir," Uriel said, placating, trying to wave my anger down with one hand while covering his mouth with the other.

"Try to keep your voice down. I understand you're upset."

"Upset?!" I squeezed my forehead between my thumb and fingers, seriously considering bonking Uriel on the head with my smartbow/staff. In a lower, more reasonable tone, I tried again.

"Yes, Uriel," I began through clenched teeth. "I AM upset. And horrified. Some of these books are classified as dangerous, are they not? I mean, certainly not THIS one. This one is perfectly fine and in no way dangerous. Like, at ALL. But, I mean, how can you just sell them to randos off the street?"

"Oh," he exclaimed, brightening. "It's not just random people, sir. They have to be extremely well vetted. They have to be a Friend of the Church, and they have to fill out all sorts of papers and applications for any lot that we auction off. No criminal record, et cetera. All sorts of criteria. And, they have to make a sizeable donation to the Church. Like six or seven figures sizeable. I know we probably seem like a pretty well-oiled machine to outside eyes, but we can't run a place like this on faith alone. Unfortunately, it also takes, well ... cash. Lots and lots of cash."

"Uh huh," I said. "And with all this vetting and filling out of papers and applying and bribing ... I mean *tithing* ... sorry. Freudian slip there. So, how hard would it be for us to get a look at that paperwork to get a name? My companion here might like to purchase HIS former property from the gentleman, gentlewoman or gentlefolk who purchased it ILLEGALLY after it was STOLEN from him by the Church."

"Um, I'm afraid we're not allowed to ..."

"OR," I said, leaning casually down toward the little man. "I suppose I could go have a word with the lovely and talented and legally DEADLY Ms. Silverblade over there, and we could figure out whether to contact the Shire Reeves about the matter, since we're now talking about the purchase of stolen goods. Although, now that I think about it, considering we're now talking about crimes on multiple orbitals, maybe it's a matter for a higher authority? Pretty sure Ms. Silverblade has contacts with IOBI. You're familiar with the Inter-Orbital Bureau of Investigation here in this bucolic little backwater? Huh. I wonder how many of the other books here might've been stolen? How long do you think they'd shut you down for an investigation? Could take YEARS, seeing as how you guys don't use computers and stuff. Thoughts? Suggestions?"

The halfling swallowed with a gulp. "Um, I think I *might* be able to make an exception in this one particular case. Be right back." He shuffled back through the gate and practically ran off into the stacks.

"See?" I nudged Bishop. "No bonking necessary."

"Wait … you were going to have sex with him?" I could feel his wide-eyed stare from somewhere beneath the hood.

"What? No! BONK, not BOINK," I chuckled. "Huge difference. I thought about *bonking* him on the head. Sorry. Sometimes I forget people can't hear my internal monologue. Although, for a halfling, he ain't half bad." I winked at Bishop. I have no idea whether he could see it or not.

"I almost never have any idea whether or not you are joking," the hood said.

"Eh. I'd say the chances are about 80/20."

"Which is which?"

"PSSSSSSTTTT," Helly hissed at us. "How's it going?"

I turned and gave her a double thumbs up. About that time, Brother Uriel came back. He ascended his stepladder and held out a small piece of parchment to me.

"Here you go," the little man said, frowning. "I do NOT feel good about this, but this is the name of the Friend of the Church who purchased the lot in question. But you did NOT obtain this information from me, okay? Especially if you are planning on, um, getting your book back by extra-legal means and end up caught. You heard about it through … I don't know … maybe you found a memo about it in the trash bin behind the building, or overheard some random monk talking about a million-gold sale at auction awhile back while he was drunk on mead at a bar. Got it? We've never even met."

"Copy that, Brother Michael!" I said, giving him a huge overly dramatic wink.

"Very good," the halfling smirked. "What about him?"

"I don't think he can even see out of that fucking thing, honestly," I said. "You good, Elias?"

"Brother who?" the hood replied. "Never heard of him. I do know it was a tall fellow, deep in his cups. Couldn't handle his mead. Wouldn't shut up about it."

"Okay," the halfling said. "I suppose that will have to do. Now ... if there's nothing else you can do today to try and get me fired ... could you please leave?"

"Yup!" I said, grabbing Bishop by the shoulder. "We're out. And ... Brother Michael?"

"What is it, now?" the halfling groaned.

"I'm sorry for how this went down and also for raising my voice to you," I said, smiling. "You're just a guy doing his fucking job, and if this weren't like a life-and-death, maybe end-of-the-world type situation, I wouldn't have involved you at all. So, yeah. Apologies. You won't be hearing from us again."

We turned to go, but I caught a weird expression on Brother Uriel/Michael's face as we did, as if I had said something so out of left field that he literally had no idea how to process it.

We rejoined the group and walked outside into the bright sunlight.

"You get what we came for, Daniel?" Ariana asked, raising one perfect eyebrow.

"I did. A name," I said, unrolling the little scrap of parchment. "Lord Brianan Trom-Laighe. Sounds Celtic. I guess we can search public records for him or something."

"Fuck," the elf said, squeezing her eyes shut and pinching the bridge of her nose.

"Fucking shit," Helly said, tilting back her head to stare upward.

"What? What the hell aren't you both saying?" I asked, confused. "You know this guy?"

"We know OF him," Ariana exhaled forcefully. "Everyone on

fucking Avalon knows of him."

"Well, spit it out!" I said.

"That's not what HE said," the hood added.

"Goddamnit," I smirked. "Not now, Elias."

"Laird Brianan Thomson, the self-styled Lord Trom-Laighe, which means Lord of Nightmares, by the fucking way," Ariana sighed and paused before continuing. "Well, he's one of the biggest crime lords on the orbital. And he's also ... drum roll please ... an extremely powerful vampire."

"And this is the guy who has our fucking book?" Sallow said. "Any chance we could just ask for it back? Or buy it back?"

"Yes to the first, hell fucking no to the second and third," Helly chimed in. "He has more money than just about anyone in NEOS, so whatever we could possibly offer him would be laughable. And, also, well, he is not a big fan of Daniel."

"He's not?" I asked, genuinely confused. "I have that effect on lots of people, but I've never even heard of him much less met him. What did I ever do to him?"

"Well, you know those two vamps you killed last time you were here?" Ariana asked. "He is their Sire. They were his children and liegemen."

Sometimes there is no other appropriate response.

I sighed deeply. "Well ... fuck."

CHAPTER TWENTY

"WHY are you just NOW telling me this?" I asked Ariana and Helly. "For fuck's sake. You really buried the lede here, ladies. I have SO many questions."

"Ok, first of all, DANIEL," Helly said, cocking one knee out and crossing her meaty arms. "You haven't called in quite a while. REALLY long time. Secondly, I called and left you a voicemail right after we found out, which was right after your last visit when you killed the two bloodsuckers. Thirdly, I haven't mentioned it since you've been back because we've been super busy and also I figured you already knew because of the voicemail. And I also kind of forgot. FOURTHLY, there are people who want you dead on EVERY SINGLE ORBITAL including the fucked up and busted one now, so I didn't think it was THAT big of a deal, ok?"

Her face was flushed with the effort, and also maybe a little embarrassment. And because our tiny terror has outsized emotions as big as her huge fucking axe, sometimes being furious makes her cry. And then she gets more furious with herself and embarrassed about crying, so that makes her madder and she cries extra hard. It's a vicious cycle. I could see maybe just a hint of a tear welling up in each eye. She also gets extra EXTRA furious at herself if she thinks she may have messed up.

"Daniel Erick Davidson," Ariana began, gritting her perfect little teeth. "If you make Helly cry, so help me half-alien Jesus, I will stick this sword so far up your ..."

I handed my smartbow/staff to Bishop and reached out and pulled Helly to me in a hug. I leaned down and buried my face in her golden mane and kissed her on the noggin. I took her by the shoulders and moved her back out to arms' length and looked her right in her big, beautiful hazel eyes.

"Ok, ok. First of all, HELLY, my wonderful, loyal, amazing shield maiden for life," I began. "I didn't mean to imply it was in any way either of your faults. I love you both beyond measure, and you're so right. I should call and visit more often, but we're all busy, and I in particular get wrapped up in my own bullshit. Secondly, you gorgeous oaf, I haven't checked my voice mail in five years. Even my outgoing message says 'Don't leave a message. I never fucking listen to my messages.' Because 95 percent of them are from my mom, saying 'Daniel, call your mother.' Which I have told her not to do as I call her EVERY time I see she has called. Anyway ... I digress. But, yes, you tried, and that's also my bad. If nothing else, I should have called you back, so that's on me. Addendum to secondly ... calling them bloodsuckers is kind of low-key racist."

"THEY SUCK BLOOD, DANIEL!" Helly said, frowning and starting to tear up again. "I am NOT racist."

"Ok, FINE," I agreed. "It's just that not all of them are bad. Most do it with consent and don't hurt anybody, and I hate them all to get lumped together. Anyway, moving on. Thirdly ... shit. We covered that with secondly. Fourthly, fuck. I mean, intellectually I know I have made enemies on all the orbitals, but hearing you say it like that is kind of depressing and makes me question things about myself. But, again, point taken. It's not that big of a deal. I apologize. Let's move on and start making some plans, ok?"

She sniffed and hugged my waist, burying her head in my chest. I heard a muffled "Mmm'kay."

Ariana winked at me and mouthed semi-silently, "Good save, asshat."

Sallow leaned over to her and asked, in a whisper "Davidson's mother is still alive?"

"Don't. Even. Think. About. Saying. It." I gave Sallow my best I Will Without A Shadow Of A Doubt Kill You And Take A Large Dump On Your Corpse's Chest look, staring at him over Helly's diminutive bulk, of which I had yet to let go. (I know. It's a very specific look. My ex used to call it my cop look, but I kind of resent that. I am pretty sure I had it long before I was in law enforcement.)

When he visibly blanched, I added "Just kidding. She's a dirty slut. Anywho … how about you lot traipse into that little Greek joint and order us a pot of coffee and a heaping plate of baklava? My treat. I'll be right there in a minute or two."

Ariana was through the door of the bodega before the last syllable left my lips. The others followed, but I had yet to let go of Helly. She started to pull away, and I yanked her close again and squeezed her tight.

"One more, okay?"

"Mmmph," she replied. I assumed that since she also embraced me tightly that was some form of affirmative. I let her go, and she looked up at me and smiled that irrepressible, infectious, gap-toothed grin before turning tail and zipping into the bodega after the others.

I spotted a small alleyway just across from the bodega, right next to the furniture maker that Ariana had spent some quality time auditing in between world-class gyros and souvlaki. I walked over and into the relative cool and dark, making sure there were no prying eyes around. I flipped open my left bracer and dialed Mary Ann. I set the smartwatch to video call and projected it in front of me at eye level.

"YOU!" The comely face of my orc BFF appeared floating in front of me, looking absolutely enraged.

"Mary Ann … before you …"

"I should charter a flight to Avalon just to stick my giant, green foot straight up your admittedly kind-of-cute-for-a-human ass, you inconsiderate, no calling, taint-licking, booger-eating, piss-headed, shit-stained, anal-polyp-having, cheap plastic bucket of FUCK!!!! If I could crawl through this video feed and bite off your nose and stick it under your scrote before I wad you up into a little ball and kick it off the edge of …"

"MARY, my dearest platonic love," I interjected. "You are 100% right. I am an inconsiderate asshole. I have been hella busy trying to save the world ..."

She interrupted me with a rather fierce-sounding growl, but I bullishly charged forward.

"HOWEVER, that is absolutely NO excuse for me not taking a few seconds of downtime in between being shot at and having to browbeat hapless halflings to call the person I care the most about in the entire universe, and I am so very sorry and love you, and I'm safe, and please don't be mad. I miss you. And you're literally the hottest person in all of NEOS."

I took a deep breath as I had forcefully ejected that apology as quickly as I could before she figured out a way to throttle me telepathically over a 4,000-mile-plus stretch of sky.

"Well," she breathed, visibly calming a bit. "You're certainly not wrong about that last bit. But, goddamnit, Daniel. I should not have to hunt you down via Helly and Ariana or anxiously wait for your tracking dot to move to know if you're alive or dead! I would've called, but I am always afraid of blowing your op in case you forgot to turn your stupid watch to silent. Tell them both hello, by the way and give them tons of smooches for me and tell them I miss them. You are NOT off the hook. But ... I love and miss you, too, I fucking guess. Shithead. So, tell me what's happened. The quick and dirty version."

"So, my ops may be the only thing in all of NEOS you ARE afraid of blowing, but, hey, no judgment," I quipped, then I launched into a condensed version of the last few days before she could fire back.

"Okay, so that sounds ... wow. Ok. That's a lot. Do you need me to charter a flight over? Maybe round up some of the crew? It sounds like you might be outgunned ... not that the ladies can't hold their own and make you look like a goddamned amateur, which you certainly are NOT ..."

"Fuck, I dunno. Maybe? Do me a favor and call Carlos and Johnny Boy and put them on standby. And you, too, you beefy slab of she-orc cake, you. Oh, and call Travis and Desireé about watching the shop if we have to go with the nuclear option. Let me get in here and see about hatching up a plan with these guys, and I'll get right back to you on that. I promise. I will NOT make you wait again." I smiled at her with what I hoped was my most reassuring, newly-considerate, thoughtful-BFF-who-wouldn't-fuck-up-again-soon smile. (It's also very specific.)

"Done, done and done," she added, popping her neck from side to side. "You think this is big enough to call in The Twins?"

"Not sure yet. Hope not. But, hey, if we have to go scorched earth … it is what it is. Better dust off your go-go boots." I grinned wolfishly.

"Been awhile since I've been in a brawl," she grinned back orcishly. "I'd best do some fucking stretches or something. But you definitely call me, ok? I don't like it when you make me feel like I'm Mother Henning you. I shouldn't have to. I'm not your goddamned mother, or your wife. I'm your best fucking friend, and I deserve your consideration."

"Yes, you do, love," I smiled. "You absolutely do. Speaking of which, could you call mom, too, and tell her I'm travelling for work and that I'm safe? I'd do it myself, but …"

"But you don't have two hours to spare with the apocalypse nigh?" She chuckled. "I'm on it."

"Thanks," I said. "Gotta run. Love you. Miss you. MEAN IT."

"Fuck off, ass," she grinned and hung up.

I snapped my bracer closed over the smartwatch display and crossed the street. I opened the door to the Greek bodega and spotted the crew gathered around two small tables in the window. I sauntered over and pulled up a chair between the ladies. There was a pot of coffee and cups on each table as well as the giant plate of fresh, steaming baklava as requested.

"Wow, that smells delicious. You guys are the best," I grinned, pouring myself a cup of coffee and grabbing a baklava wedge. I took a giant bite and chewed, thoughtfully. "Holy SHIT that is good. And Mary Ann says hello and sends smooches to you both." I nodded to Helly and Ariana, both of whom practically glowed at the long-distance love from our orc friend.

"I figured that was what you were doing," Ariana said. "And, also, RIGHT?" She grabbed a wedge and reached out to toast me with it. We bumped baklavas as if we were clinking glasses. Which of course, made me think that bumping baklavas sounded kind of dirty. I suppressed a laugh.

"You're making something dirty out of bumping baklavas, aren't you?" Helly giggled. Goddamnit. They ALL know me so well. How did all these amazing women in my life get my number so quickly? I mean, not that I'm THAT complex or anything. Probably easier to read than a pop-up book, which reminds me ... but I'll stop. I could literally do this all day. (Which IS what SHE said.)

"Ok, yes, but let's move on," I grinned at Helly. "So, Lard Brian Tom-whatever ..."

"Laird Brianan, Lord ..." Ariana began, sighing.

"Nope," I winked at her, shaking my head. "Don't tell me. It's funnier this way. He's Lard Brian-Tom from here on out. I am NOT giving this douchebag the satisfaction of calling him Lord Nightmare in any fucking language, to his face or otherwise. He wants my respect, he can earn it. Until then, he's a two-bit criminal with delusions of grandeur. Anyway ... if this guy is such a huge, well-known underworld mastermind or what have you, how did he get to be a 'Friend of the Church'? Brother Uriel/Michael specifically said they vetted these folks for criminal records."

"That's part of the problem," Ariana said, chewing baklava and sipping at her coffee. "Nothing has ever stuck to this guy. He throws money at it, makes witnesses disappear, et voilá ... he's a pillar of the community. He pays to be on numerous influential boards, he *obviously* bribed his way into being a Friend of the Church ... not that those guys have ever been great judges of character. Um, present company excluded, Father."

"No offense taken," Bishop said, his massive hood now down so he could drink coffee and eat baklava in peace. Not that it stopped him with the wolf jerky. "I mean, the Christian Church has not had the best history when it comes to, well, lots of things. And, just like the old saying goes ... no one hates a dirty priest more than a good priest."

"Fair enough," the elf smiled at him. Priest or no, I caught a hint of a blush on his cheeks at being the center of her attention. She really does have that effect on everyone.

It would be so easy to hate her for it, I suppose, if one were that type of person. Me, I'd rather love her along with everyone else. And maybe try to out-love them all, because she isn't just a beautiful, graceful exterior. Ariana Silverblade is one of the smartest, kindest, most loving, most giving, most honest, loyal and forthright people I have ever had the pleasure of knowing, and to reduce her gloriousness to anything based on mere looks would be a goddamned tragedy of epic proportions. That is but one of her many, many beautiful facets. But, hell. I'm only human. It's hard to look away sometimes.

And before you accuse me of putting my many beloved female friends and familia on a pedestal, I'm going to preemptively tell you to fuck off with all of that. They all have flaws. Just like me. Many, many flaws. Ariana loves mathematics and theory so much that sometimes she finds it difficult to relate to people that she is not close with. She can be quick to anger. Sometimes, she can be condescending and rude. Helly overdoes everything in her life and the word abstinence is, well, let's just say it's the one thing she doesn't overdo. Likewise, she can be quick to anger and prone to violence. Sometimes she is extremely hard on herself and she suffers from self-esteem issues, her gigantic personality aside. Mary Ann, well, she's not perfect, either. But you don't love people for their perfection. You love them for who they are, warts and all. So, if I choose to celebrate the things I love about them and overlook and ignore their failings, it is because I fully embrace their indomitable spirits and their huge hearts and their bodies of all sizes and their missing teeth and their shoe collection that could probably fund an entire orbital for a year if sold at auction. It's but a small fraction of the forgiveness and grace they extend to me on a daily basis. In short, don't tell me how to love, assholes.

Not you guys. You're good. I mean those other pricks who want to pick apart everything and everyone, maybe because they are flawed or broken or hurt in some way and it makes them feel better. Or bigger. I don't know. I'm no psychologist.

Besides, before anyone tries to label me a sexist, I feel the exact same way about my boys. You just haven't been lucky enough to meet many of them yet in all their non-toxic masculine glory. Bishop and Sallow, even in his own sour way, may someday be family, too. But we're still early in their story. And, I digress, as is sometimes my way. One flaw of many.

"Ok, so this guy has pulled the proverbial wool over everyone's eyes," I said, reining us all back on topic. "Can we use that? Can we get something on this guy and go public? Does he have any big enemies in the Avalon underworld we can approach about helping to take him down? Or am I aiming too high here?"

"We may not have time to dismantle an entire criminal enterprise, as tempting as that may be," Ariana said. "I mean, really, we just need the book."

"Yeah. Legit. That's an excellent point. I'm probably overthinking it. So, I guess we should be planning a heist?" I looked around the table. The faces that looked back ranged from excited to curious to anxious to bloodthirsty and maybe a bit pouty. You can probably figure out which was which. Or which was whom? Or whom was which? Bah. I always get that wrong.

"Does this mean I don't get to bash any skulls?" Helly asked, and I swear, she looked like someone had just run over her favorite puppy with an oxcart.

"Of course not, sweetie," Ariana said to Helly while giving me the side eye. "The only possible timeline in which that would occur would be one where a Daniel Davidson plan goes off smoothly and without a hitch. That timeline is, to my knowledge, non-existent."

"Hah!" Helly barked. "Good point. Suck it, Daniel!"

"Ouch. Et tu, elf?" I held my hand to my chest as if covering a stab wound, and gave her a look of profound betrayal. "But, you may have a point. Which is why it's not going to be MY plan. It's going to be OUR plan. But, even if we put our heads together, we still don't have enough. So, like ... what does one need to plan a good heist? Dramatic pause ... wait for it ... intelligence!"

"We may be shit out of luck in that department where you are concerned," Sallow chimed in.

"Oh, the grumpy one speaks?" I sniped, smirking. "Very funny. A+ for effort ... especially with your, you know ... *condition*." I whispered the last part. "But you know what I mean. We need to know more about this guy. Where he's keeping the book, what sort of defenses are in place, how many guards AND their schedules. We need a murder wall and maps and blueprints and timetables ... all of that fun stuff."

"What's a murder wall?" Bishop asked.

"Oh, you know," I said. "Like in police procedural vids, shows about IOBI and stuff. They always have a big whiteboard or video unit or plain wall with pictures on it and lines drawn between things in marker or with strings outlining connections. Lots of push pins and sticky notes and stuff."

"Yeah," he said. "I get it now. We're going to make one of those?"

"Are you fucking kidding?" I gaped at him. "I've been wanting and/or waiting to make one of those MY ENTIRE LIFE. Of course we are making a murder wall. Come to think of it, why have I never done it before? Maybe THAT'S why all my plans go awry."

"I'm SURE that's it," Ariana said drily.

"Pipe down, you," I grinned at her. "All right. We need a war room somewhere, and we need intel. How about we split up and regroup here ... or even better, somewhere with booze ... in three hours. Say, 2 PM local time? I think we should probably split up into two groups with at least one local in each. How about Ariana and Bishop hit up public records to see if we can find out anything about Lard's properties. Helly, how about you and Sallow see if you can find out anything about his security situation? I know you have a lot of contacts in the muscle-for-hire community. I'm going to hit up the local newspaper and also make a few calls. Might also grab some red string and office supplies."

"He's really very excited about his murder wall, isn't he?" Bishop asked Ariana.

"He gets like this sometimes. Usually only over classic movies, old books and records, good food and Scotch, though," the elf sighed. "This is a new one. I say we just go with it. If we don't, he'll never let us hear the end of it."

"I am RIGHT HERE, you know? I can hear every word," I said. "So, what else can I do? Think Percy has a spare room he can rent us? I can go talk to him. That work for everyone? Break and meet at the Unicorn around 2 of the clock?"

Everyone seemed on board. "Great! Ok, hands in the middle, on me." I stuck my hand out in the center of the tables.

"Fuck. Are we really doing this?" Sallow said.

"Shhh. You'll hurt his feelings," Helly said. "Just do it, you twat."

Everyone reached out their hands and stacked them on mine. Helly had to stand up in her chair to reach and placed her hand on top.

"One, two, three ... murder wall? 'K?" I said. Groans all around.

"One, two, three ... MURDER WALL!!!!!" Needless to say, my voice rang out the loudest. Pretty sure we scared the living shit out of the poor lady behind the counter. We broke for our intel runs, and I walked up to settle our tab.

"Sorry about that, madam," I said to the little woman, who looked like someone's tiny Greek granny. Yiayias, I think they are called. "Your food is absolutely delicious, by the way." I placed a few gold notes down on the counter, then added a few more. "Do you think I could have a box of baklava delivered to the archive next door this afternoon? Put a note on it that says 'To: Brother Uriel' ... only cross out Uriel and put 'Michael.' Thanks so much!"

I smiled to myself and headed out to secure us a room, plumb the archives of the local gossip rag, and snag whatever passes for office supplies in a pseudo-medieval town.

MUUUUUURDER WAAAAAAALLLLL!!!!!

CHAPTER TWENTY-ONE

By the time 2 PM rolled around, I had paid a trip to the archives of the local paper, The Narthwych Griffin Gazette (which is admittedly a bit unwieldy, but I am just giving up on the locals as far as them ever meeting or exceeding my rather low expectations where their creativity is concerned), and scanned numerous articles on Lard Brian-Tom with my smartwatch when no one was looking. I spent some time chatting up the mostly bored newsies, and maybe bribing them with a baklava or two that I went back and snagged from Yiayia. I also snuck in a call to Mary Ann, letting her and The Twins off the hook as we didn't expect an all-out war with the vamps. I did, however, task the green goddess with digging up whatever she could about Lard from the public net and also from an old contact or two of ours at the EOPD, which is, as you might assume, the Elysian Orbital Police Department, where both Mary Ann and I used to work briefly, and where we met.

I also stopped and bought office supplies at "Ye Oldÿn Statiönairy Shöppe", where I found tons of parchment, quills and pushpins. And while I certainly appreciate the rather metal additions of multiple umlauts, I am not quite sure they achieve the grammatical effect the owner desired. I had to stop at a weaver's cottage to snag some red yarn, as we could hardly hope to have a proper murder wall without it. Lastly, after tying my bags to my smartbow/staff and traipsing back to The Psychedelic Unicorn looking for all the world like a bindlestiff hobo with a harpoon on his shoulder, I booked a private back room from my man Percy, purchased a flagon of a dark Czech-style lager, and started constructing, well, you know.

I started by picking up a quill and ink and sketching out a crude cartoon vampire on a piece of parchment that kind of looked like the old cereal mascot Count Chocula, drawing devil horns and giant fangs on him and adding a cape, seeing as how our mark is both a vampire and a pretentious douche canoe. I wrote the name "Lard Brian-Tom" in the most frilly, fancy lad script I could muster, and pinned him to the top of our ... huh. I have no idea what they call the contents of a murder wall, really, but there's usually a bad guy on top. Let's go with murder pyramid. Yeah. That sounds pretty badass.

I sat down in a wooden chair and leaned back, propping my feet up on the table, sipping deeply of my delicious beverage and admiring my handiwork. About this time, the rabble showed up.

Ariana and Bishop rolled in first. Bishop was holding a meter-long capped tube that appeared to be made of something very close to cardboard. Not sure that's necessarily period specific, but I guess the locals might skimp on a few items. Right on their heels were Helly and Sallow, who were empty handed but seemed in okay spirits, which was a good sign? They joined me at the table. Everyone ordered a beverage. Everyone started talking at once, but we quickly quieted when Percy walked back in waaaay quicker than expected with our drink order.

"No need to hush on my account, folks," Percy smiled, handing out flagons and cups of assorted alcoholic fluids. "I am the very soul of discretion. Many a caper has been planned in this back room, the details of which you could not pry from me upon threat of death. Besides, what happens in the Unicorn's back room stays in the Unicorn's back room!"

"'Cept for the crabs and the herpes," Helly laughed. "They leave with the patrons. Hey, Daniel, what's the plural of herpes?"

"Should I be offended that you are asking ME?" I snorted,

taking a sip of my lager. "Also, herpes IS plural. I think. Can't really have just one herpe."

"But, like, if there is more than one case? Say, if Sallow's mom left here with herpes, and his uncle did, too ... that's like multiple herpes-es, right?"

"First of all, fuck off," Sallow said. "Second of all, why my uncle? Why not my dad?"

"Because your mum's a whore? AH-HA-HA-HAAAAAAA!" Helly nearly fell out of her chair, laughing and holding her gut.

"That was NOT that funny," Sallow said. "Besides, she always told ME she got them from a toilet seat."

"Look at you, Jonas," I smiled at the knight. "Playing along like a goddamned trooper. You must be well fed."

"Still full of baklava, honestly," he grinned. "Although this cranberry mead is hitting the spot."

Ariana knocked on the table with her own flagon. "Please, children. To task. I can feel myself aging, and for an elf, cybernatural or not, that is saying something."

"Legit," I said. "The gorgeous elf lady is correct. The doomsday clock is ticking, so ... I move we go with the French-inspired 'herpeaux' for now until we can do more research. That's h-e-r-p-e-a-u-x. I didn't do it just then, but make sure you leave off the H when you say it ... for authenticity."

"Urp-Oh?" Helly said.

"If I could hate you all to death right now, I would," Ariana said, putting her forearm across the table in front of her and resting her forehead on it.

"Lies! But, point taken," I said. "Since you're all fired up, sweet elf, lay it on me. What did you guys find out?"

She raised her head and motioned to Bishop, who sat down his mug of stout and uncapped the cardboard tube, pulling out a set of blueprints, which he unrolled and flattened on the table.

"The plans on file with the town's zoning commission for the Laird's ... shit ... for Lard Brian's country estate," Ariana said. "It's about a mile outside of Narthwych proper, spindleward. He built it about 10 years back, and there have been no permits pulled or filed since for additions or alterations, so this is probably the best we're going to get. He might've gotten up to some secretive stuff since, but since he tries so hard to keep his nose clean? I don't know. On the other hand, he's a master criminal, so the chances of him adding secret rooms and such are probably …"

"80/20?" I grinned.

"Precisely," Ariana laughed. "And you won't like which is which."

"Still, better than nothing and I agree, it's definitely the best we're gonna get and more than we could've hoped for," I told them. "Great work!"

Bishop smiled his thanks and nodded to me appreciatively, and Ariana half stood and did a little bow.

"What about you guys, Hell?" I asked the dwarf, who was currently holding her flagon upside down and staring into at it as if questioning where the contents had gone.

"Oh, well, good news and bad news," she said, putting down the empty vessel with a tiny burp. "Which you want first?"

"The bad news," I replied.

"Lard B-T keeps about 100 mercs on retainer, and they patrol day and night. Reputable company, too. Great work ethic, everyone highly vetted, no gamblers or degenerates we could squeeze. They choose shifts of 50 by lottery and completely randomize their rounds, and change the shift overlap daily, which is both super impressive and depressing as hell. Even if we surveilled the place for months, we'd have no better idea of what we'd be facing at any point in the future. Oh, and they're armed to the fucking teeth. And absolute pros. We're not gonna brute force our way in, and I'd not put odds on us sneaking in successfully, either. Shit. I also forgot to mention the guard dogs. And, to top it all off, every door and window is either barred, bolted, reinforced or all three. In short, it's literally as secure as you can make a place on an orbital without tech."

"Holy FUCK," I said. "What is the good news?"

She sighed. "There is no good news. I just didn't want to completely crush your spirit."

"Ugh. Thank you for the sentiment," I groaned. "But wow. Yeah. That fucking sucks."

"Big ol' donkey balls," she agreed.

"I don't know why I expected any less," I sighed. "What's the point of being a filthy rich crime lord if you can't have your own fortress? Still, bad news or not, it's great intel, and you guys fucking rock."

Helly blew me a kiss, and Sallow surprised me by doing the same. I barked laughter.

"Thought you could use the pick-me-up," Sallow said, grinning.

"Careful, Jonas," I warned, smiling. "Too much time around the inmates, too much time in the asylum and all. You're starting to fit in."

"Fuck off," he smirked.

"That's better," I said. "Don't go changin' just to please little ol' me."

Ariana sipped on whatever non-vinous substance was currently filling her flagon and looked at me, cocking her head slightly. "Well, Daniel? What now? We have old, possibly outdated plans to an absolutely impregnable estate, and ... what else? What did you come up with?"

"Mostly rumor and innuendo," I admitted, standing up to pace. "I found a couple of articles on the Lard in the Gazette, but none were terribly useful. Mostly crap to do with the boards he sits on and society page/who's who bullshit. The stuff in the opinion columns and more gossipy featurettes, though ... well, there was some fun stuff there if I am reading between the lines correctly. Confirmed bachelor, all sorts of implied trysts with local celebs of all genders and beyond, and most cybernatural species - except werewolves - but nothing crazy or untoward about that, I guess, unless some of us are total hypocrites ..."

"Why you looking at me?" Helly hid behind her enormous empty flagon and peered over it at me.

"I mean … you're really going to ask me that?" I grinned and stood on my tiptoes to better see over her beverage or lack thereof.

"I mean, no, I get it, and I own it," Helly said. "But you're little better, DANIEL … I mean you …"

"I know, I know," I waved her off. "Pot, kettle. I said some of us, ok? Including myself. ANYWAY … moving on. The point is, our boy is a pervert. No judgment here, glass houses and so forth, but it gave me some ideas. So I made some calls, or called Mary Ann and had her make a few as she's infinitely more likeable than me. Shush, Helly. Hopefully, I'll hear back on some of them soon."

"Anything else?" Ariana asked.

"Well, just scuttlebutt around the newsroom, but I chatted up a few of the reporters. I may have dipped back over to the bodega and brought some delicious, nutty pastry bribes back with me," I said. "That coupled with my *copious* charms … shush, Ariana … and I found out that some of the people tied to Lard … that have probably been tied UP by Lard at the very least … have gone missing. In fact, quite a few people have gone missing in this community. Locals, tourists, men, women, kids … you name it. And some of the newsies think Lard may be responsible. All circumstantial evidence, and certainly nothing that would hold up in court or even net a warrant, but compelling nonetheless."

"So, what are you thinking?" Ariana asked. "It sounds like he's definitely up to some fucked up stuff up there. Beyond the expected prostitution, gambling, larceny, and professional hits we've heard about over the years. You think he's gone full-on rogue vamp? Thrill-killing?"

"It certainly sounds that way, and if there is a sexual component, there may also be some ritualistic bullshit involved," I said. "Which means we may have a psycho-sexual serial-killer, serial-rapist vamp on our hands, which is a step beyond someone killing for fun just to drink their blood, which is bad the fuck enough."

"That is Fifty Shades of Fucked Up," Bishop added.

"Nice one, Elias!" I gave the priest a high five, and he beamed with pride.

"Soooo..." Sallow began. "He's a major creep who should probably be put down, but how can we use it? He's still holed up in a fortress of ... what's something that rhymes with solitude, only it means fucked up sex stuff?"

"I don't know, but nice effort, there, slugger," I grinned at him. "Half a point to Slytherin!"

"Stop," he warned.

"Fine." I exhaled, sighing. "The truth is, I don't know. But ... maybe this will help!"

I grabbed a quill and wrote "Impregnable fortress, tons of mercs" on one piece of parchment. I wrote "Possible rapist/ sex killer/rogue vamp" on another. I tacked them up under the crude demon vamp picture. I unwound and cut a few pieces of red yarn and linked the two items below to the drawing of Lard.

"That do anything for you guys?" I asked, beseechingly. I was met with silence.

"Fuck. Me neither." I slumped back in my chair and took a long pull of dark lager and belched. Helly gave me a sympathetic fist bump. "So, here we are. Maybe one of my calls will pan out."

We drank some more. And then some more. And ordered food. And ate. The fish and chips were outstanding. The tartar sauce was next level. So tangy! And we drank. And made many, many more crude jokes. And then, my left bracer vibrated.

"Holy shit!" I punched in the code to answer, then I took the bracer off and sat it on the table. The party all crowded around one side of the table, blocking the view from the other room. Mary Ann's face popped up, grinning very seductively. Not quite in a sexual sort of way, but more in the 'I know something you don't know' teasing way.

"Hey, handsome," she said. "I know something you don't know."

"Well, that explains the seductive grin," I laughed. "Spill it. But wait ... say hi everybody."

Everyone exclaimed some sort of greeting all at once, resulting in a completely unintelligible cacophony.

"Hah. Hi, guys! Hello, Helly, you gorgeous little slut! Hello, Ariana, you stunning and classy thing, you. I miss you both terribly! And, hello, Father Bishop and Jonas. I don't know you, but I am looking forward to meeting you both! And, hiya, yourself, Daniel, my ruggedly beautiful partner."

"PLEASE tell me you have something good," I said. "We're hitting rock bottom here."

"Awww," she teased. "Murder wall not solve everything for you?"

"Goddamnit, no," I groused. "Still looks kind of cool, though. I regret nothing. But quit stalling, woman! Tell us!"

"Sooooooooooooooooooo," she dragged it out as long as she could without taking a breath just to drive me nuts. "Your hunch may have panned out. And if I haven't mentioned it, you may be the luckiest son of a bitch on all the orbitals. I don't know how you do it."

"Told you," Sallow said. "It's your goddamned superpower."

"Yup." Mary Ann agreed. "Although he does this thing with his ..."

"RIGHT?!" Helly said.

"Every fucking one of you is killing me slowly right now," I groaned. "Please, for the love of half-alien Jesus, pretty please with fucking sugar on top tell me what I am lucky about."

"Well, for those pour souls that you have most likely not kept in the loop because you are an inconsiderate turd," she huffed, then continued. "You asked me to reach out to some of our old pals at EOPD and, um, maaaaaybe break a little teensie law or two and dig into Lard's financials and recent purchases."

"Oh my god YEEEESSSSSS," I said. "Go on ..."

"Not the first time I've heard those words come out of his

mouth," Helly said, nudging Sallow.

Mary Ann grinned bigger at Helly's comment. "Anywho … Mr. Lard has a rather large purchase coming in on Saturday from a website called Wish.com …"

"YESSSSSS!!!!" I exclaimed. "Don't stop!"

"This is REALLY bringing back memories," Helly said. "I'll be in my bunk."

"Firefly! 2002!" Bishop yelled.

"FUCK yes, Elias! 50 points to Hufflepuff!" I yelled back. "But, please, my lovely Orcish life partner, please say the words. Tell me! SAY IT!!!"

"It's sex furniture!" Mary Ann screamed with glee.

"GAAAAAAAH!!!! And I'm spent!" I fell backwards onto the floor.

The others just stared at me. I climbed to my feet. "Mary Ann, I don't have the fucking words. YOU are amazing. You are the answer to every prayer I haven't even had the balls to utter. Can you please send me the deets on the purchase, especially the dimensions, specs and all of that stuff? Color, height, weight, materials … no matter how small. I need it all."

"That's what she said?" Bishop offered.

"Man, you're *killing* it today," I told the silver fox. "I am *so* fucking proud of you right now."

"You got it, D," Mary Ann said. "You love me a little bit?"

"You … I … I can't even express how much," I said. "So much that I can't even joke about it at the moment."

"Daaaaaaaaamn," said literally my entire crew as one.

"Fuck you guys," I rallied. "Smooches, darling orc, but I gotta go. Planning to do. Talk soon, ok?"

Mary Ann blew us all a kiss and cut the call.

"So, Davidson," Sallow said. "You gonna clue us in to this brilliant hunch or whatever? You have a plan now?"

"Oh, yes, my grim friend," I smiled my wickedest smile. "I have a goddamned plan to end all plans. But, you're not going to like it. But first, Ariana …"

"Yes, love," the elf perked up. Her tastefully pointy ears may have twitched a bit.

"How badly did you ream that furniture maker when you audited him? Tell me it all worked out and that he owes you big time ..." I clasped my hands together as if in prayer.

"I *may* have saved his livelihood, safeguarding it for future generations," Ariana smiled a tad smugly. "He owes me nothing short of his life."

"Well, my friends," I said, grinning my grinniest of grins. "We're about to call in that fucking marker. Also, we need a moving company, stat. The bigger the better. Orcs if possible. Folks capable of moving HEAVY weight with little to no sweat whatsoever."

"No ..." Ariana was the first to catch on.

"You've got to be fucking kidding me," Sallow chimed in second.

"Oh, this is going to be fucking CLASSIC," Helly breathed heavily, her lively eyes lighting up like a child's on Christmas morn.

"What's sex furniture?" Bishop inquired.

CHAPTER TWENTY-TWO

"I cannot believe you intend for us to Trojan Horse our way into a goddamned fortress hidden in sex couches!" Sallow exclaimed, throwing his hands skyward in consternation.

"I agree. It's absolutely ludicrous," I allowed. "And I will abandon this nonsense the very moment someone else comes up with a viable plan to sneak us past 50 heavily armed mercs on a completely unpredictable patrol schedule and a kennel full of guard dogs. And past all manner of locks and bars and other bullshit."

Dead silence.

"Aaaaand there you have it. So, until something better comes along, let's get cracking. Ariana, can you pop over to your humble furniture guy's place shortly with the info that Mary Ann is sending? I can forward it to your smartwatch. I am assuming this guy has to have some mechanism to view patterns or download templates or something, so he probably won't freak out over a tiny breach of tech etiquette. I will gladly pay for his time and efforts, but if we can call in your favor to get a rush job, that'll be great. I'll even pay for him to call in help if he needs it, but we need a deliverable sex-tional couch ... see what I did there? ... and shipping crates by Friday morning at the latest. I figure the real deal won't arrive until Saturday, but if our guys show up the day before ... I mean, who doesn't love when a highly anticipated package shows up early?"

"There are SO many things I could say right now," Helly noted.

"I know. Notice my artful avoidance of the phrase 'comes early,'" I said. "Anyway, I figure we can have it delivered during the morning hours. Hopefully, being a hardcore vamp type, he and his cronies will be asleep and we might only have to deal with a steward."

"How are you planning on getting out of the place? We'll still have 50 guards surrounding us," Ariana asked. "Hmmm. How about we have the delivery scheduled for lunch, and have the orcs pack a meal. They can unload the furniture, then refuse to assemble it until they'd had their lunch break?"

"Because they are Union!" Helly said, laughing.

"Oh, that's good," I said. "They can pop outside or otherwise lure the steward or whomever away, because he naturally won't want a bunch of strangers creeping around in Lard's house."

"Which is when WE exit and creep around Lard's house," Bishop added.

"Correct!" I said. "That would give us roughly 30-45 minutes to do our thing, find the book, and then … maybe seal ourselves back in the packing crates and have the orcs ruck us out?"

Ariana rubbed her chin, deep in thought. "That's pretty good, but we need a Plan B. What if the steward doesn't go with them? What if we get discovered? We need a way to exfiltrate in case the box plan goes tits up."

"Well, we'll use the secret tunnels, obviously," Helly said.

"What?!" Ariana and I said at the same time.

"I'm with them," Sallow added. "What tunnels?"

"Think about it," Helly said. "Lard obviously has a secret way to get in and out of the place. He is ALSO surrounded by 50 well-trained, observant mercs at all times who work for a company that is pretty reputable. They might be able to overlook rumor and innuendo in the press, but if this guy is constantly bringing in tourists or locals and doing horrible things to them, they would either notice that the people are never coming back out or become suspicious of whatever method he is using to get the bodies out of there. Plus, rich criminal masterminds ALWAYS have an exit strategy."

"That's pretty sound logic," I agreed. "So, maybe we look for said exit if we have time. Or, I hate to even say it, but we could Scooby Doo it."

"What the fuck does that even mean?" Sallow asked, one eyebrow raised.

"You know," I said. "Shaggy, you and Scoob and Velma head up to the library and find the book, while Daphne and I check out this sex dungeon ... er, I mean, look for secret exit tunnels."

"Am I Daphne in this scenario?" Helly asked sweetly, batting her eyelashes.

"Not all of us are privy to your obscure 20th century pop culture references, Davidson," Sallow said. "But, still. I think I catch your meaning. We split up. Divide and conquer."

"Which always works in horror movies," Helly helpfully noted, grinning.

"Oh, Helly," I said. "Just because we are entering the dark castle lair of a vampire called Lord Nightmare who may also be a serial rapist and killer does NOT mean we're in a horror movie."

Silence.

"Ok," I relented. "So there are a few, *tiny* similarities with the plot of a horror movie. But, hey ... at least we're not helpless, hapless, unarmed teenagers having sex while high in the forest next to a haunted summer camp or anything."

"I haven't strictly ruled out the sex part," Helly added. "But, yeah. The rest *totally* doesn't apply."

My left bracer vibrated. It was a message from Mary Ann with the sex couch specs. I forwarded them to Ariana. She immediately reached into the left pocket of her pantsuit and pulled out an ornate golden pocket watch. She pressed the winding mechanism to pop open the cover and glanced inside. "Got 'em."

"Awesome. I'm going to give you a wad of cash that should buy at least two of these things," I said. "Or, hell, I could just come with you. Wanna head over now? Helly, do you and the boys mind popping out and scaring us up a moving company? Maybe we can reconvene here at 6 for dinner and an update? Then maybe break for the evening? Are you guys staying in town tonight?"

Ariana sighed. "I really need to get back and work on a few accounts before bed. It's been a tough day of eating, drinking, harassing hobbits, planning heists and insulting old friends."

"Yeah," Helly agreed. "I want to say something pithy and filthy about staying here, jumping your bones, and breaking some bedsprings, Danny Boy, but I'm worn the fuck out and kinda want to sleep in my own bed. Especially if we're going to fight vamps on Friday. Rain check, though?"

I laughed. "Sure thing, short stuff. Alright, let's get some shit done." I handed the tiny terror a wad of bills for the movers that she accepted with a kissy face and a MWAH sound and some snide remark about singles and strippers that hardly bears repeating.

We parted ways for the next hour and a half and change. Ariana and I hit up the furniture maker, who turned out to be a really decent guy with a nice little family business. He agreed to our project with no resistance whatsoever, chiefly because things were slow and he needed the work, but he also seemed eager to repay Ariana for saving his shop. I paid him double with a small bonus on top to cover the rush and another pair of helping hands for the week. He didn't even balk at the idea of including people-sized secret compartments inside ... whether because he was afraid to ask or was excited at the challenge, I had no clue. Either way worked for me.

We stuck around long enough to make sure every single spec could be met along with the Friday morning deadline, and then we headed back to the Unicorn. I'm not supposed to tell you that Ariana demanded a piggyback ride for a few blocks and allowed herself to be spun around until she almost puked as that would destroy your image of her as the picture of elegance and grace and maturity. She swore me to secrecy, so I won't mention it.

We walked into the war room to find Helly and the boys back at the table and Percy taking a drink and food order.

I ordered some chicken vindaloo and a flagon of India Pale Ale, and Ariana added some sort of seafood puff pastry thing that sounded amazing along with a glass of white wine.

"So, how'd it go?" I asked the others.

"Pretty great," Sallow said. "Helly secured the services of a reputable, discreet service named 'Ten Orcs and a Huge Fucking Cart' or some such nonsense."

Helly laughed. "Close enough. They'll be at the shop to pick us up - literally - at 9 AM. No questions asked, lunches packed, fully onboard with the Union ruse. What about you guys?"

Our drinks arrived to much celebration. Many kind words were thrown at our orc host.

"Yeah, fuck couches commissioned," I resumed once Percy had left, his legendary discretion notwithstanding. "They'll be ready to go by then. We'll arrive by 8, get sealed inside and crated up for our orc teamster friends to cart up and haul on our short trip to Castle Von Douchestein. We should probably meet here by 7 AM at the latest to gear up. Maybe rub down our blades with some garlic oil. Zip it, Helly." She stuck her tongue out at me and I made to grab it, sending her into a giggle fit.

"Unfortunately, I don't think there will be much to do tomorrow except wait," I said. "Jonas and I can probably run the Padre through some rudimentary combat basics, despite it being my express intent to keep him away from it at all costs. I'd leave him here if we didn't need him to identify the book. I may scrounge around town and see if I can score some more garlic oil ... maybe enough for some molotovs? I dunno. I have a few other errands to run that may take up most of the morning. Totally up to you guys whether you pop back over, but we definitely need to get an early start on Friday. Two hour trip for you guys?"

Both Ariana and Helly nodded. "I *absolutely* have to get some work done tomorrow," Ariana said. "I will run through some forms and limber up and knock the rust off in my downtime, though. Helly and I can hop a barge and meet you guys here for an early breakfast by 6 or 6:15 on Friday."

"Yeah," Helly agreed. "I have to check in on a few clients tomorrow, too, but nothing special. I definitely want to sleep in, though."

Our dinner arrived, and we spent the meal conversing amiably, chatting about nothing in particular. Helly told us about her recent jobs. Elias told us a bit of what Canaan was like before the fall. Sallow gave us a little glimpse into a day in the life of a Templar knight. Ariana was quiet, smiling a little here and there at a naughty joke, but mostly looking like she was miles away in her head. I caught her eye and motioned her toward the door that led to the back patio.

We stepped out, leaving the door open behind us. We walked over to the railing and looked out over the moonlit water. I reached over and pulled her into a side hug and she rested her head on my shoulder. "What's shaking your tree, chickadee?" I asked.

She groaned. "THAT was perfectly awful. Please do not ever say those words in that order ever again."

"Heh. Fair enough," I grinned. "But, really. You were awfully quiet in there. Something wrong?"

She stayed quiet for a few moments. "I'm not sure I can put it into words. I put on airs, but I'm all about the math. Words are your thing, Daniel," she said quietly.

"Dirty words, mostly," I said.

"Hush, ass. I'm being serious," she uncrossed her arms a bit and swatted at my chest with her right hand. "I fully expect you to live to a ripe old age, despite your every attempt at getting blown up or shot or stabbed in search of ... whatever it is you're looking for on these adventures. And I don't mean the physical objects. And in your dotage, I expect you to sit down in a comfy room, with a bottle of Scotch, bathed in sunlight, and write about ALL of these idiotic adventures we took and the times we spent together. But ..." she silenced me with a hand to my lips before I could speak. "In order to do that, you have to survive."

"Ari … you're spooking me a little bit, not gonna lie," I said in a hushed somber tone. "We've been in worse scrapes than this and come out smiling … and *mostly* intact."

"Math is MY thing, Daniel," she repeated. "I don't like these numbers, I don't like these odds. I don't like that there are so many unknown variables. I mean, that place could be crawling with vamps. We just don't know. I love you, you know that, and like, no offense, but this plan is shit."

I laughed. "All of my plans are shit," I said. "In fact, MOST plans are shit. What's the old saying? Almost no plan ever survives contact with the enemy? All we can do is the best we can with the intel we have, which is incomplete. I will try and get more. It is my plan to try and get out there tomorrow afternoon while Sallow is teaching Bishop how to crack skulls and surveil a little bit."

She turned to face me, shrugging off my arm. "Alone? Are you fucking NUTS?"

"I mean, I don't think that was ever in question," I grinned, reaching out to clasp her shoulders. "But I will be safe. No heroics. Not even getting close to the property line. I'll be good. Promise. Just getting eyes on. Maps and blueprints only tell you so much."

"Fine," she said, frowning. "That makes sense. Increases our odds, I suppose. Infinitesimally, maybe, but I'll allow it."

"Oh, you'll allow it, will you?" I adopted a stern impression. "You're not the boss of me, woman. Elf woman. Lady elf. Bossy lady elf woman." I stuck my tongue out at her.

She grinned against her will. "YOU have been spending too much time around Helly."

I pulled her into a hug and kissed her cheek, burying my head in her long, black hair that smelled faintly of honey and apple blossoms. "I never get enough time around either of you."

"Girl, same," she said, and I could feel her smiling behind my back as she embraced me tightly.

I let go, reluctantly. "Alright, then. Let's drop this sad sack shit, go in, finish our drinks amidst fun and fellowship, and get you guys headed back home."

And so we did. We walked back in and sat down, finishing our drinks and laughing when prompted by Helly being Helly or Bishop being Bishop. Sallow didn't generate much laughter in general, but he was already less of a stick in the mud than he had been a couple of days ago when he tried to kill me, and he does manage to sneak a zinger in there now and again. *It was only days, right?* I thought to myself. It had all been a blur. And it was getting blurrier by the minute by the time we broke off the meal.

"Guys ..." I started, standing up and stretching. "As much as I would love to stay up all night, we need to break." I looked around the room at all the faces of my friends and new colleagues, who were all looking a little worn out as well. I spun my chair around and raised my right leg, planting my foot in the seat and crossing my arms. "Let's get some rest, settle our business tomorrow, and on Friday, we're gonna take on that motherfucker right THERE."

I reached down and pulled out my right sock dagger (which is SO much easier to spell than sgian-dub), flipped it over in the air, caught it by the blade tip, and threw it at the murder wall ... all with the maximum speed my jacked reflexes could handle. So, it, too, was pretty much a blur to bystanders. The dagger speared the crudely drawn Lard right between his beady eyes and sank deeply into the wall.

"Fuuuuck," Helly said. "That was pretty badass, dude."

"Well yeah," I said, grinning. "It's easy to do things like that when you're writing down the story for posterity years later and can make yourself look as badass as you want."

Ok, so I didn't actually say that. Also, well, it helps if they are smart daggers and you have an eyepatch with a targeting reticle on its hidden HUD and a throwing knife app onboard with a little spinny dial thing that tells you precisely when to release. I mean, I do practice and all, but believe me. The tech helps a LOT. But don't tell them that. Just let them keep thinking I'm that fucking cool

What I actually said to Helly was …

"RIGHT? A bit theatrical, perhaps," I said. "But I wanted to drive the point home." I looked at each one of them in the eyes, lingering a moment at each.

"He's just another criminal, y'all," I said, smiling. "He's not the fucking boogey man. He's a dumb little shit who calls himself Lord Nightmare to sound scary. If he were a real badass, he'd call himself, I dunno, Lord Toby or Lord Timothy or something. Then you'd know that asshole doesn't have to *pretend* to impress anyone. I want you to all look around this room at each other right now, and know that you are surrounded by BADASSES. Some real-deal, hardcore, pipe-hitting, skull-breaking motherfuckers. The proverbial heartbreakers and life-takers. I think you all forget it sometimes about each other because we're huggy and lovey and throw jokes around like most people breathe. And maybe even about yourselves. But I'd trust any single one of you with my life, and, point of fact … I have and I am. Well, maybe not Elias …"

"I'm RIGHT here," Bishop said. "I can hear everything. Still, point taken. I'm the weak link."

I smiled. "Only when it comes to bashing heads, Father. Not your heart and spirit. And we can work on the rest."

"Anyway," I continued. "This group of badasses is going to take on that there wannabe master criminal rapist killer fuck, and we're going to beat him. We're going to get that stupid book right out from under his pointy nose, and we're going to get the hell out of there. And, if we get the chance and it doesn't fuck up our escape, I'm going to take him off the board for good. But the book and saving the goddamn universe comes first. Everyone cool with that, you fucking badasses?"

"I feel like you've said 'badass' a lot in the course of this speech," Sallow said, grinning. "But, I don't disagree."

Everyone else chimed their assent, and we broke for the

evening. As we left the room, Helly grabbed my arm and pulled me down to her level to whisper in my ear.

"Your pep talks still make me moist," she said and gnawed on my earlobe.

"Ow!" I laughed and whispered back. "No shocker there, but why are we whispering?"

"Because I didn't want to ruin your moment," she said.

"You're so very considerate," I replied.

"Fuckin' A," she agreed, and we went on our way, arm in arm.

We saw the ladies down the street to a small ferry that would take them home for the evening. Hugs and kisses and fist bumps were handed out, and the three of us waved as the boat carried them off into the mists.

"Alright, boys. To our rooms. We have a long day ahead of us tomorrow. Drink some fucking water and get some rest."

"You'll most likely kill us in the morning?" Sallow grinned.

"Nah. I'm starting to like having you both around," I said, turning to walk back to the inn. "But don't let it go to your heads. Plus, I need you both to help me outwit a crazy killer vamp mob boss and fuck over a gaggle of asshole angels. So, pretty please, head in, hydrate, crank one out, say some prayers to half-alien Jesus or whatever, and go the hell to sleep. Just don't tell Him what we're up to. I'm not sure yet whose side He's on."

CHAPTER TWENTY-THREE

The buzz of my smartwatch alarm woke me around daybreak. I rolled out of my bed, which was very comfortable and cozy – thanks, Percy! – and forced myself through a few rounds of sit-ups and pushups. I washed up in the small private bathroom, dressed and went to the rooms next door to wake the others, which both were super happy about. Maybe a tiny bit hung over, the poor bastards. I guess not everyone is lucky enough to have a built-in hangover filter.

We stumbled downstairs and launched into a fairly standard breakfast of fried eggs, bacon, sausage, and toast with a giant pot of coffee on the side. Luckily, no Uni-virgins came in to set off that particularly catastrophic reaction that Percy feels adds to his business somehow, despite his regulars' feelings to the contrary. As we finished up, I told the boys I was off to run errands. I engaged Sallow as we were leaving the table.

"You mind running Bishop through some combat basics? Just Combat 101: what to do, what not to do, how to crack skulls, how to avoid getting your skull cracked? Don't wear him out or anything, but just try to get some bare-bones knowledge in him," I said. "Just in case."

"Yeah, I can do that," the knight replied, smiling. "I've trained my share of knights, you know, so it's not the first time I will be dealing with an absolute newb."

"Ok, good deal," I said. "Not going to try and tell you how to do your job. Micro-managing really isn't my style. I'll probably be gone at least until lunch, so I hope to see you guys then."

"Safe travels, cockbite," he said.

"See? I told you that you'd fit right in," I laughed. I said goodbye to both of my companions and set out.

About five hours later, I returned to the inn and sat down with them both for a quick meal before setting out again. Both looked like they had worked up a sweat and put in the effort in my absence, which was great to see. Bishop noted he already felt much better about the possibility of dealing with an attacker. I left them to resume their activities while I headed out to Castle Von Dickhead.

I purchased a small pushcart nearby and tossed some snacks on top of various sundries in a large basket I had purchased earlier that morning and set out for the estate. I hoped that I looked like a local innocently running errands on a country lane, enjoying the benefits of the pastoral life. Too bad I can't fucking whistle, I thought to myself. Apparently that removes all suspicion in these parts.

The walk was pleasant and uneventful, the mildly blustery afternoon gifting me with a somewhat overcast sky occasionally lit up by visits from the sun and also a light breeze that put a song in my heart. If this were a musical, I'd launch into it right now, but it's fucking well not.

I gave the estate a wide berth when I arrived. I made several circuits of the property, keeping well out of sight of any guards, but zooming in with my eyepatch HUD when details struck me.

The castle proper was impressive as all hell, a Transylvanian wet dream ... or a nightmare depending on your perspective, I guess. If you were a prisoner there or the guy who has to dust all the myriad alcoves, nooks and crannies I guessed were inside, you probably wouldn't think too highly of the Lard for building this monstrosity.

The keep itself looked to be 10 stories high or more, the top ending in crenelated battlements with copper-colored spires and domes here and there. Huge swaths of stone spread out from there in every direction like craggy spider legs, windows and grated openings here and there breaking up the visual monotony. Catwalks connected the keep to smaller outbuildings. Smaller still were other attached structures I took to be stables and a smithy. The whole thing was perched on a low hill that was surrounded by a filthy looking moat traversed by a small bridge leading to huge oaken doors, banded in iron and stretching to maybe 20 feet in height. At least the pretentious bastard didn't opt for a portcullis, I thought. Otherwise, the fortress of Lard Brian-Tom could have come straight out of the Castles 'R Us Winter Catalog and Christmas Wish List. I was kind of surprised the property itself wasn't fenced, but I guess it hardly needed to be with all the vamps (presumably) inside and armed guards surrounding the property.

Speaking of which, I noticed a few mercs in gangs of two to five making rounds. As expected, the timing of the rounds themselves made little sense. I didn't bother making a record of them. Near the northern edge of the property, I noticed some tiny stone buildings or sheds with pitched roofs. I had seen something similar on the blueprints and survey map, but there had been no label or legend to explain their presence. Seeing them in person, they made total sense.

I observed them for a while from the tree line, which started just over the property line about 25 yards away from the small units. I stood leaning on my cart, munching on fried pork skins and sipping from my wineskin, watching for activity. That lasted just until I grew bored with my own inactivity and finished my pork skins. I decided I was done and that it was time to return to the inn. I smiled and chuckled to myself as I walked off, practically skipping merrily down the lane. I mean, I didn't actually skip, because that'd be kind of weird for a grown-ass man to do, but I might've jumped up and clicked my heels once like a fucking cartoon leprechaun. Don't judge. Just be happy and appreciate my boundless joy.

Twilight was approaching as I walked back into town and

saw the now familiar and welcoming sight of The Psychedelic Unicorn, tiny wisps of smoke floating skyward from its quaint little chimneys, warm yellow light spilling from its diamond-pane windows. I walked in, gave Percy a high five as I passed the bar and headed toward the war room. The orc called out after me for my drink order, and I requested an old ale, haggis, neeps and tatties as I traipsed jauntily into the back room where my companions had already gathered.

"You look awfully pleased with yourself," Sallow noted. Bishop waved silently as he was in the middle of quaffing some sort of beverage greedily.

"I am," I said simply. "Things went well. Had a couple of long walks, enjoyed nature and some pretty scenery. Scouted some. Had some pork skins and wine. It was a good day."

"I feel like there's more to the story," Bishop said, bringing his flagon down and sitting it on the table with a small burp.

"Oh, there usually is," I agreed, smiling. "But enough about little ol' me. What have you strapping young lads been up to? Is Bishop a well-oiled killing machine yet?"

Both laughed at this. "Um, not quite," Sallow said. "He's not bad, though. He *might* survive if attacked by a couple of toddlers with wiffle ball bats. Probably wouldn't come out on top, though."

"Ouch," Bishop said, taking another sip of his beer. "I thought I did a little better than that. I guarantee, Daniel, that I am now able to fight off at least 10 toddlers, provided I have my club and they are completely unarmed. And kind of runty. And maybe their shoelaces are tied together."

"Well, that's better than I could have ever hoped," I laughed. "You must have had a wonderful teacher."

"No, he was a complete dick," Bishop said. "But a dick full of useful knowledge, nonetheless."

"I'm RIGHT HERE," Sallow said, smacking Bishop lightly on the arm with the back of his hand.

"AAAHHHH," Bishop grabbed his arm and feigned mortal injury. "That smarts, heathen. That'll be three Hail Marys, three Our Fathers, and two Go Fuck Yourselfs. Selves? You know what I mean. Grammar was never my strong suit."

"Well, it sure as fuck wasn't physical education," Sallow said, chuckling heartily.

"Ah, male bonding," I said. "It's just so fucking precious!"

About this time, Percy popped over with a giant platter of food, which was most welcome. We ate in genial comradery, tossing about more playfully horrid insults and alluding to the questionable sexual practices of each other's parents as well as insinuating they might not have been actually wed at the times of our births. As was our way.

The food finished and our plates cleared, I ordered us a round of Scotch as a nightcap. Percy happened to have a bottle of Talisker 18-Year-Old he was saving for special occasions, but the promise of an extra heavy tip netted us three doubles. We retired to the patio and sat quietly in loungers, watching the moonlight glint off the small waves of ... heavy sigh ... Thee Watyrway, sipping the amber nectar as small barges, ferries and other colorful and interesting watercraft floated by.

"You guys ready for tomorrow?" I asked, swishing a sip of Scotch around my gums.

"I suppose," Sallow said, taking a drink of his own. "I mean, we still have little idea what we'll be facing once we get inside, but I think we're as ready as we can ever be under the circumstances with the time we've had."

"Well said, Jonas," Bishop nodded, sipping and sighing. "I'm scared shitless, myself."

"Hah. You'd be an idiot not to be," Sallow said. "I'm scared, too."

"It's perfectly normal to be anxious and even scared before something like this," I agreed. "I'd commiserate and tell you I am scared as well, but I've heard it's a leader's job to seem fearless and tough and rally spirits and all."

"Oh, half-alien Jesus H. Christ tap dancing on a fucking cracker, you're not about to give another speech are you?" Sallow groaned. "That meal and this Scotch are far too good to throw up. Also, who said you were our leader?"

"I mean, I am the one building murder walls and giving inspirational speeches, after all," I said.

"You're literally the only one who wanted a murder wall," the knight grunted. "And it didn't help for shit. And your speeches are shit."

"Wow, what a Negative Nancy," I said to Bishop. "I mean, he's like two Karens crossed with a Debbie Downer."

Bishop laughed and nodded. "He's like the proverbial turd in the punchbowl."

"I don't know what any of those things mean, but I am guessing they are not good and go fuck yourselves," Sallow smirked, taking a belt of Scotch.

"In what situation would a turd in a punchbowl EVER be good?" I asked, laughing.

"I don't know," Sallow replied, wincing. "Maybe if you really had to go and were in pain, and all the bathrooms were occupied, and there's this punchbowl sitting there - all cool and inviting - maybe with a single ray of light shining down on it like an invitation from Heaven ..."

"Well, that'd be a completely different story," I agreed. "How could you NOT shit in that punchbowl?"

"It'd be an affront to all that was holy not to purge your bowels in that fucking bowl," Bishop agreed, sagely.

We clinked glasses. "I'm glad that's settled," I added.

"May be the first time we all agreed on anything," Sallow offered.

"I'll drink to that," Bishop chimed in agreeably.

We finished up and said our goodnights and turned in early to be ready for the shitshow that Friday morning would most likely be bringing us. Or as ready as three such n'er do wells as ourselves could be.

CHAPTER TWENTY-FOUR

At around 6:30 Friday morning, Ariana and Helly walked through the door of The Unicorn and joined us in the war room, where Percy had laid out quite the spread. (Heh.) The tall elf had traded her red pantsuit for a skin-tight, black patent leather outfit and what appeared to be a lightly armored black motorcycle jacket. With the exception of sleek, thin matte black armor plates on the thighs and shins, the whole look reminded me of Kate Beckinsale's vampire character in Underworld. I guessed there was enough Kevlar IV and carbon fiber involved to outfit a small police force. Helly had likewise switched her wardrobe for hardcore battle, swapping her typical brown leather breeches and boots, sleeveless white top and forest green vest for a dark brown leather armor ensemble with a vest and bracers. Still sleeveless, though, as she liked to show off the guns. I think mostly, though, it was to allow her total freedom of movement to swing her enormous fucking axe in all directions.

I immediately felt disgusting and gross as Bishop, Sallow and I only had the clothes on our backs and had not been able to make a super impressive wardrobe change. At least Percy's staff (heh) had been kind enough to wash our stuff overnight and return it, so we didn't smell overly ripe.

Plates of pancakes, waffles, eggs benedict, hash browns, and bacon were piled up on the table, and the elf and dwarf breezed past, tousling hair, kissing cheeks and clapping shoulders. We all tucked in heartily as we had no idea when our next meal would be.

“I hope you ladies had a wonderful day and a restful evening,” I said in between mouthfuls. “You were both definitely missed, but we lesser forms managed to be productive and get some stuff done.”

“I knocked out a shit-ton of work,” Ariana said, pouring herself a mimosa from a pitcher. “Made up for the day off and then some. Actually got a little ahead.”

“I wish I had gotten a little head,” Helly frowned, sipping a freshly poured coffee. “I got some shit done, too, though. But I missed your smiling faces! And even your grimacing one, Sallow.” She winked at the knight.

“Fuck off,” he said, amiably. “I for one enjoyed the lack of impending sexual assault in the air.” He pointedly stuck his tongue out at Helly.

“HAH!” Helly roared. “I KNEW you had it in you!” She slapped the knight heartily on the shoulder.

“His mom’s had it in her,” I chimed in.

“And often,” Bishop said. “Maaaaybe even in the butt.”

“You are the worst priest *ever*,” Sallow said, flipping Bishop the finger.

We cleared the plates and took a few last passes at the blueprints, which Ariana, Helly and I all scanned into our covert smartwatches in case of emergency.

On our way out, I cleared our tab with Percy, paying for our rooms, meals, drinks and various incidentals from the last few days. Just in case. You never want to leave a friend high and dry if the unthinkable happens. He actually gave me a big, orc hug before we left, which affected me more than I expected. I think he had gleaned enough insight from overhearing snippets of our discussions and the goings-on in the war room to know that today was a big deal. That coupled with the fact that I paid us up before leaving AND left him an historic tip for the ages … well, the savvy innkeeper no doubt deduced that it was zero hour for shit going down.

Once outside, we briefly stepped off the path and rubbed

our weapons down with garlic oil. As one might imagine, rude hand gestures ensued. Knives, swords, arrowheads, axes, and even Bishop's club were given a thorough kneading with the stuff. By the time that we resumed our walk, we smelled absolutely delicious. Pungently so.

The party made our way to the furniture maker's shop and walked in through the side entrance next to the big double doors that allowed ingress and egress from his workshop for larger orders. Such as, you know, giant, sectional fuck couches.

"Hey, folks," said the friendly furniture fellow - whose name was Johann, by the way - as we entered. "Just finished your … 'Yoga Couches' … an hour or so ago." He made air quotes when he said 'yoga couches' and gave us an over-exaggerated wink. He nudged Ariana, who was standing beside him with her arms crossed. She gave him the side eye.

"We can seal you guys up, crate you, and in a few short hours, you guys can all be enjoying some … 'hot yoga' … on these here babies!" He slapped one of the sectionals on its fuzzy, red padded seat. "Namaste!"

I walked over and ran my hands along the faux mahogany lines of the nearest couch section. These were, as close as I could tell, absolutely identical to the pics and specs Mary Ann had sent.

"You do amazing work, Johann," I said, admiringly. "And I can't begin to thank you for the rush job you did on them. It couldn't have been easy."

"My son and I loved it," he grinned. "We're sort of in a slump, so it was a godsend to us, really. And to my out-of-work brother. Your generosity allowed me to hire him on semi-full time. Hopefully, we can get enough orders in soon that I can keep paying him!"

The craftsman looked down, a little embarrassed. "Normally, I would never be so indiscreet," he began. "But I have been dying to know this whole time … what are you *doing* hiding inside these compartments?"

"It's for, uh, a prank," I said. "On our 'hot yoga' teacher. Yeah, he's going to really lose it, man. He may just laugh himself to DEATH!" I fake laughed very hard and too loud. I might've slapped my knee.

Johann and the others just stared at me.

"Seriously, though, Johann," I stopped laughing and glared at him. "No kink-shaming allowed."

"No, no, none of that here," Johann smiled thinly. "It's an awful lot of money for a prank, though. Wouldn't you say?"

"Well, that's only part of it," I said. "The rest is, well, the ... 'yoga studio' ... is kind of crowded and space is at a premium, so it will be nice to have extra storage for our ... 'yoga implements' ..." I winked knowingly at him in an exaggerated fashion.

"OH, yes ... I get it," Johann nodded, smiling wickedly.

"You know," I kept on. "The rubber dicks, chains, whips, nipple clamps, pocket pussies, gimp masks, furry costumes, adult diapers, butt plugs, buckets of lube, fisting dildos, pony playtime stuff and realistic fuck dolls we use for ... 'YOGA.'" I winked at him again and nudged his arm a few times with an elbow. I looked at the others. "Am I doing this right?"

Johann looked absolutely mortified and glanced around to make sure his son was not within earshot.

"Well, that's enough chit-chat for the day," Ariana said, giving the furniture maker her most professional-looking smile. "How about we crawl inside these amazing pieces and lock ourselves in before the orcs show up?"

We all agreed and set about that task. The sex-tional couch was made up of four smaller couches that latched together, each made up of a strong wooden base and cushioned tops that rose and fell in all manner of peaks and troughs and valleys to support people as they ... you know ... performed various yoga poses and stuff.

Normally, the bases would have had support struts crisscrossing their insides, buttressing the foamier tops, but Johann had – per our instructions - made the bases completely open and roomy, even vaulting upward into the spaces that would have been all cushioned peaks and such. We had also thoughtfully added hidden air vents to the plans so that we wouldn't suffocate. Unfortunately, though, there were only four pieces and five of us. It was decided that Ariana and Helly would share the largest and roomiest couch as the two combined took up the least space. The rest of us lucky souls would each have our own fuck couch.

We all slithered into our secret compartments, most of us having to remove scabbards, quivers and huge giant axes from our persons and slide them in separately. I crawled into my couch after sliding in my short swords, quiver, and smartbow/staff, waving to the others as I backed into the space. I heard Ariana make some snide comment about dwarf farts before I closed the hatch and locked myself in.

Johann called for his son and his brother, and they set to work. I heard hammering and the creaking of wooden slats as the men began assembling the shipping crates around us. After a short wait, I heard the muffled sound of voices - several of them decidedly lower pitched and orc-like - and I assumed the movers had arrived. We were picked up and gently lowered onto what I figured was the huge fucking cart mentioned in the name of the company. I heard packing straps being unrolled and affixed to the crates, and I'm pretty sure I heard a twang of vibrating nylon and a muffled orc voice say "That ain't going nowhere." Then, we started rolling.

There's not much to tell about the journey we made in almost complete darkness. I took the opportunity to text Mary Ann on my smartwatch and give her an update on the operation. Then, since I had some time to spare, I called my mom and chatted with her for a little while. She told me about her plumbing issues and about what the neighbor's kids were up to. Not that I gave two shits, but it's the sort of stuff she shares, and it was good to hear her voice, anyway. One of the orcs hit my crate with the side of his fist, urging me to shut up, so I gave her my love and signed off quickly as we were no doubt approaching our destination.

We wheeled to a stop a few minutes later, and I heard raised voices and conversation that amounted to a lot of "state your business" and "special delivery for the Lard" and debate about timetables and what-not. Then we started rolling again. We rolled on for a bit, then stopped. I heard straps being removed and a moment later, my crate was being hoisted aloft. The ride was a little bumpy, with some ups and downs. I was tilted to and fro a bit and it felt like I lost gravity for a second or two as someone lost their grip on my chariot such as it was. Finally, after tilting and turning for a few solid minutes, I felt my crate being lowered and placed on a hard surface with a small thump.

Next came the sound of prybars going to work, nails whining and wood creaking as the crates were disassembled around us. Right on cue, I heard one of the orcs boom "Well, it's lunch time fellas. Time for a break." Tools were dropped, clanking to what sounded like a stone floor.

"Now, wait just a minute," I heard a new voice say. It sounded like an adult human male to me. I imagined a stuffy butler-type in a black suit, but I actually had no idea. "You've been paid to completely assemble this furniture and haul off the packaging. The Laird specifically added that on."

"And you'll *get* that," one of the orcs said. "Once we've eaten. Union rules, pal. We have to have breaks at certain times, especially after moving heavy items like these. You don't like it, take it up with the Local. Also, come *on*, man. Cut me some slack. We're big dudes, but these things weigh a ton and those stairs were an absolute bitch. Give us 20 to 25 to pop up on the lawn, rest our backs, choke down a sandwich or two, get some sun on our shoulders, and we'll head right back down here to put your furniture together, ok?"

The butler-type paused a moment. "FINE," he said. "As long as you are all through and out of here by 2 PM at the latest." He was met with grumbles of assent, and I heard the shuffling of many orc feet. A heavy door banged closed. I waited a minute or two to make sure no one was coming back, then I unlatched my couch's hatch and crawled out. I looked around and was met with a dimly lit room with stone walls and floor. Manacles lined the walls, and there were definitely other furnishings – X-frames, cages, seats with holes in them, inversion racks – that skirted the line between fun-dungeon and dungeon-dungeon. Racks of toys, whips, studded paddles and the like ringed the room. A few knives and other bladed instruments were also present. I shuddered and then crept over to the other couches and knocked quietly. The others emerged and stretched, strapping their weapons back on and taking in the room as they did so.

"Charming," Ariana said. "I'm guessing from the long spiral stairway we descended that this is the space marked 'playroom' on the blueprints?"

"Probably," I noted. "Which means there should be storerooms all around us and some unfinished space as well."

"Oh, it's probably been finished by now," Helly said. "Remains to be seen what it's been finished AS or WITH, though."

"Should I be worried that there is a drain in the middle of the floor?" Bishop asked, sort of hugging himself. "Is that normal in a …"

"Dungeon?" I replied, just as Helly said "Fungeon?"

"Hard to say," Ariana noted. "It's difficult to tell what's just kinky, what's vampy, and what's straight up serial killer."

"Legit," Sallow said. "Let's get out of here. It's creeping me the fuck out."

"Guys," Helly said. "I REALLY have to pee."

I grunted. "No idea where the nearest bathroom is. I mean … I guess …" I looked down at the drain near our feet.

"Ugh. FINE. All of you turn around, though," the dwarf said. "And no peeking."

We all turned our backs and Helly dropped trou. I will save you the description of the sounds that issued forth, but there may have been a small sigh of relief involved. I heard the rustling of leather breeches being raised and Helly gave us the ok to turn around.

"Fucking A, I feel better," she said. "Thanks."

"Awfully modest," I grinned at her.

"We've discussed this, DANIEL," she laughed quietly. "I'm not into water sports."

"Nor should you be," I said. "Eww. Not to kink shame, but ..."

"Clock's ticking, kids," Ariana said, pulling us back to task.

"Right. Come on." I walked over to the heavy wooden door, which was painted red on this side at least, and pulled the handle, opening the solid slab as quietly and slowly as possible.

I crept into the hallway, scanning both directions, and the others followed. The stone walkways were empty and dimly lit by torches every 15 feet or so. No furnishings to speak of, only a few doors here and there. I looked at one across the hall and walked over. I slowly opened the door and peeked in. I moved out of the way and pushed open the door to show the others.

"It's a bathroom," I sighed, hanging my head.

"Goddamnit," Helly said. "Of COURSE it is."

We moved on. We turned right toward the staircase and saw another door next to the fungeon. Ariana was closer, so she edged the door open and peered in. She gasped softly.

"Oh. Oh, Daniel. You need to see this," she whispered in a tone I couldn't quite nail down.

I walked over and stepped past her into the room and the others followed. It was another dimly lit stone room. There was a torch in a sconce by the door. In the flickering light, I saw pale, white flesh. And for a moment, I couldn't comprehend what I was seeing. It was like a scene from a splatterpunk movie had come to life in the most unbelievable way possible. My vision almost seemed to vibrate as I looked into what I can barely describe as anything but a chamber of horrors.

Twenty or so dismembered torsos hung suspended and inverted from the ceiling on a system of ropes and pulleys, the flesh and meat pierced by wickedly sharp looking black iron hooks. Underneath the remains was a large, rectangular funnel system with a drain in the middle and what looked like a faucet or tap underneath. Stainless steel gurneys and marble slabs lined the room's walls, partially melted candles at their corners. White pegboard installations held a range of edged instruments running the gamut from bone saws to huge bowie knives, hand drills, scalpels, hatchets and more. There were several implements that would have looked more at home in a logging camp than in any other setting I could imagine. There was also what looked like a bottling station similar to what one might find in a brewery.

There were streaks of brownish, rust-colored dried blood everywhere as well as some that looked more maroon and wet, like they were only spilled moments ago. There were frothy, fatty chunks of pink gristle here and there as well as what might've been pieces of bone and brain matter. It was an abattoir. It was a butcher shop. It was a slaughterhouse. It was beyond horrific.

It was soul-chilling, so much so that words fail me. Any attempt to describe it fully just seems futile and exploitative. It was Grand Guignol at its most base and repugnant. My eyes didn't even want to completely focus on what I was seeing. My lizard hind brain rebelled and screamed at me in the most primal way possible: *RUN*.

The worst ... the absolute worst thing about it was the sheer variety. The partial corpses were women. They were men. They were non-binary. They were orcs. They were dwarves. They were ...

They were children.

Every single corpse, adult or child, sported fang marks. The ragged cuts where their limbs were severed looked like some of them might've been made while the subjects were still alive and struggling.

I never understood the phrase 'I saw red' until that very instant. My vision went crimson for a moment. I closed my eyes tightly and starbursts went off behind my eyelids. I felt a hand reach out to my shoulder to steady me as I am sure I might've wobbled a bit. I heard a small voice saying "no no no no no no ..." I didn't even have the mental or emotional bandwidth to realize it was me saying it.

I feel dumb writing this, even years later. If you've ever watched a horror movie, or a vid serial, or read a horror novel, none of this will be shocking to you. None of the things I have described are ideas that haven't been dreamed up by hundreds of authors and presented in so many forms before. But, I will tell you this. Nothing prepares you for seeing it in person. I have lived many lives, it seems. And I am obviously a voracious consumer of media in all forms, if all the random pop culture bullshit didn't clue you in. I even sell tons of it as the proprietor of a shop. I peddle it. But that's all fucking make-believe.

Until you have seen a dismembered corpse in front of you, seen the pale blue tracery of veins beneath the once-vibrant living skin ... skin that was once bathed, and caressed lovingly, that felt goosebumps at the kiss of that first hint of winter in the breeze ... you just don't have a goddamned clue.

And ... fuck me. The kids. That got me. *They* got me. Like a sledgehammer to the gut and a live wire stabbed straight into my cranium. It short-circuited me. Those sweet children, who once ran on their tiny legs and giggled and played innocently with total abandon. Who cried themselves to sleep at night, afraid of the dark until some loving parent crawled into bed with them and smooched their little noggins, and brushed back their baby-fine moppet hair from their foreheads for a peck and booped their button noses. Who asked endless questions, curious about the world around them, thirsting for ALL the knowledge at once. Who imagined. Who laughed and acted silly and goofy. Who trusted. Who BELIEVED that someone would take care of them. Would protect them.

And ... we failed them. All of us. Every goddamned adult who told them that monsters weren't real. That their closets and the spaces under their beds were empty of threat. That it was safe. That THEY were safe.

Monsters are fucking real, my friends. They are hiding in the shadows. They live in the spaces in between the stars, and in the deep, uncharted waters. They live in the abandoned houses and asylums, and in the cute little house down the street from you with the well-manicured lawn. Sometimes they live in pretentious, wannabe Transylvanian castles on fairy tale orbitals.

I felt the hand on my shoulder slip up to my face and I felt a lithe arm surround me and another pair of thicker, meatier arms grab my waist and I felt a cute little dwarf face nestle into my abdomen and felt wetness there. I heard Ariana's musical voice whisper in my ear.

"I know. I know. Daniel. I know," I could hear her voice break up with emotion. "But we have to go. We have to get the book or a lot more people are going to die. A lot more children, Daniel. Everyone. We have to go NOW."

I fought the lump in my throat, and I kissed the side of my sweet lady elf's face, and I hugged my beloved dwarf tightly. Then I let go. I wiped tears from my face with the back of my hand.

"OK," I struggled to say. "We go. We'll go."

I turned to look at them, and whatever they saw in my face was something completely unexpected. They didn't quite step back, but they both leaned a little further away unconsciously and instinctively, their eyes wider than they had been.

You see, I've found that people tend to forget.

Even people close to you forget. Maybe *especially* those close to you. Because they see your love, and you share your light with them and you make them laugh. Because that's primarily who you are at your core ... someone who wants to share beauty and fun and good times and leave nothing behind you but love and fond memories when you go.

And you're a joker and a merry prankster, and so, they fucking forget. Because you'd never in a million years or lifetimes hurt *them*. They forget how dangerous you are.

I mean, all of us can be absolutely savage when the stars align and the right conditions are met. Because we're all fucking animals. Even the merry pranksters among us.

But some of us, well ... some of us are more motherfucking dangerous than the rest.

Sometimes I look in the mirror and I like what I see. And I see what I hope and pray my friends and family see ... someone who loves them beyond all measure and would do anything for them. Someone who is fundamentally decent and kind. Who cries at animated movies full of BIG ideas and big feelings. And who loves animals and sometimes spontaneously sings to dogs when no one else is around. Someone worthy of being held. And loved.

But sometimes I look into the mirror and see the broken boy whose spirit was *almost* crushed. Who only wanted to laugh and play and was beaten for it. The boy who locked the bathroom door and hid in the cabinet underneath the sink, crying, scared of the man screaming and pounding on the door. The man who had hit his mother, too, and dragged her around the kitchen by her long, beautiful hair because she had been too busy tidying up the apartment and didn't have dinner waiting on him when he returned from work. Or fucking someone else.

Because sometimes the monster lives with you.

I see the boy that was beaten in school, too, because nowhere was safe. Small for his age and bookish, put in physical education classes with giants six years his senior. Bullied constantly, he retreated to books and drawing and writing and learning everything he could about the world around him, trying to get smarter and gain more power over his circumstances. And he learned to escape through old movies and books and music from ages ago. And he learned to make people laugh and be the class clown, because maybe if you made them laugh, they wouldn't hurt you.

Because sometimes you're surrounded by monsters.

Sometimes I see that boy's face looking back at me, and I want to hug him and cry and tell him everything will be okay. But sometimes ... sometimes I see someone entirely different.

At those times, I see nothing but darkness staring back at

me, my usually bright and lively and laughing eyes devoid of anything nice or pleasant. Or sane. Or *safe*. And I am always reminded at those times of that classic quote from the early 20th century film star Lon Chaney, Jr., who said, simply … "Clowns aren't funny in the moonlight."

Because sometimes, you are the monster.

I looked at two people I loved more than anything in the world – beloved, yes, but dangerous people in their own right - and what they saw in my eyes and in my face chilled them. I spoke to them in a low, soft tone.

"We'll go right now. And we'll find that book and save the goddamned world. And ALL the kids. But that motherfucker dies. HE *fucking* dies, and whoever is with him *fucking* dies. THEY. ALL. FUCKING. DIE."

CHAPTER TWENTY-FIVE

As we walked toward the staircase, I did my best to shake off the warring emotions and internal mechanisms vying for my attention: shock, sadness, fear, anxiety, and rage. Oh, was there *ever* rage. Rage like I have never felt in all of my years. But, you learn quickly in this life - or any sort of life where you might have to strap on a gun or a knife or a club to defend your life and that of others – that strong emotions will fuck you up, making you sloppy and getting you or others killed. DRT as my old homey on the force used to say. Dead Right There. The guy was practically a backwoods Yoda. So, I tamped it all down to manageable levels. You might say I put a leash on it all. It wasn't gone, though. It was all just waiting patiently and silently for that moment when the lead gets dropped.

We decided to split up ... very, very reluctantly. Helly and Sallow were going to explore the basement further and facilitate our escape plan by looking for the passage to the alleged secret tunnel. Which wasn't allegedly secret, but allegedly a tunnel, I guess. It allegedly existed. Or logically. Anyway, tiny terror and knighty-knight were tasked with finding the goddamn thing. Ariana, Bishop and I were tasked with finding the stupid allegedly world-ending book.

The three of us crept up the stairs and found ourselves in a large hallway with a deep red carpeted runner. Probably hides bloodstains well, I thought. Wooden chests and tables lined the walls as well as the completely expected and utterly cliché (presumably) empty suits of armor. Huge paintings of angry, haunting, Victorian-looking folk looked down at us from on high, and bullshit tapestries hung from heavy rods, looking ancient and annoying.

The wall to our right was solid and unbroken, but arches and doorways abounded to our left. To our immediate left was a large arch that lead to what looked like a formal living room or salon for entertaining, with deep couches and oval-backed chairs and tiny tables barely large enough to hold an oil lamp and a single tumbler of whisky. It was blessedly empty, thanks be to half-alien Jesus. We crept on to the next opening, which was a wide doorway that opened up into a billiard room.

Ariana nudged me. “We should probably pick up the pace, Daniel. Running short on time. Why don’t we creep over to that big old room the blueprints called a … library, was it? I hear they tend to keep books in those places.”

I whispered back, forcing a grin. “Yeah, ok. Seems like a logical place to start. Let’s do it.”

We soft-footed it down the hall as quickly and quietly as we could move. At the end of the long hall was a set of double doors. I turned the knob on the right-hand door and slid inside. The others followed.

The library, such as it was, was pretty fucking huge. It took up three stories, the walls lined with built-in bookshelves crammed with all manner of beautiful leather-bound tomes. Mostly for show, I would guess, as Lard didn’t strike me as much of a reader. It was an impressive sight, though. Huge ladders on rollers and affixed to brass rails were present on each wall to allow people to reach the upper stacks. I guess Lard hasn’t figured out how to pull off vampire flight yet. And no, that’s not a thing. As far as I know. But with cybernetics and prosthetics advancing at the rate they are, it may not be long.

Huge floor-to-ceiling windows separated the shelves, but all of them were covered with thick, velvety-looking blackout curtains. I would assume to protect the shitty pretend vamps from their own self-inflicted sun allergies during the day. So stupid. Anyway, the look was completed by a couple of huge fireplaces that currently lay dormant and unused and a number of deep leather couches surrounding them.

Over the largest of the fireplaces, there hung a giant oil painting of the head vamp himself: Laird Brianan Thomson, Lord Trom-Laighe. Count fucking Chocula himself. Of *course* he'd have a giant painting of himself commissioned at great expense so he could admire himself constantly. He wasn't a bad looking guy, I guess. If you were into murderous douchebag vampires and such. His jet black hair was slicked back and he sported a widow's peak. Probably had that created with hair plugs to get the full-on vamp look, the poser. He had a high-backed collar on his … you guessed it … full cape. It framed a narrow, regal looking face that was clean shaven except for a black, pointy, soap opera villain-style goatee. His sunken eyes had blood-red irises. In short, he was every inch the cartoon supervillain vampire that money could have made him. I hated him on sight. To be fair, I hated him already, and I REALLY fucking hated him once we found his handiwork in the basement. This was just the oh-so-creamy icing on the hate cake.

"Awful lot of books in here, boys," Ariana said to us, looking up and down the shelves. "Any idea where to start?"

"Um, there?" Bishop said, pointing to an alcove next to the door. There was a pulpit-style pedestal there with a closed black book sitting on it, plain, unadorned and completely unremarkable. Tasteful museum lighting shone down from above, spotlighting the artifact … not unlike Sallow's heavenly punchbowl awaiting the Turd of Providence, I thought, grinning in spite of myself.

"Oh, come *on*," I said. "It can't be that fucking easy. No safe? No cage hanging over it on a thin rope? No thick, blade- and bullet-proof museum glass cube over it? Just a priceless, beyond dangerous, potentially universe-killing artifact, sitting completely out in the open in an unguarded library, spotlighted for emphasis? It might as well have giant neon arrows pointing to it. Surely he's not this stupid or careless?"

We walked closer, looking everywhere for traps. I used my staff to gently poke the thick-piled carpeted rug leading up to the book's resting place. Ariana silently drew her sword – but not without a whiff of garlic, I might add - and did her best to canvas 360 degrees with her sharp Elven eyes. Bishop drew his well-herbed club out of his enormous sleeve of holding. We walked right up to the plinth without incident.

"Is this it, Padre?" I asked quietly. "Not a fake or a dummy book as far as you can tell?"

"Oh, yes, Daniel," he exhaled softly. "This is it. I'd know that book anywhere. Can you not feel it? The power literally thrumming in the air around us?"

"I mean, maybe?" I said. "To be honest, my emotions and senses are like maxed out at the moment, and I'm barely holding it together. I kind of feel something, though ... like when you stand too close to an electrical conduit or unshielded wiring hub?"

"YES," the priest said. "Exactly that! I am probably more attuned to it than most, even after all this time. Should we, um, grab it?"

I eyeballed the book from several different angles and saw no wires or any tell-tale signs of alarm systems. Just because that stuff probably shouldn't be here on the orbital didn't mean it wasn't.

I walked over to the nearest shelf and eyeballed the contents. I selected a book that looked to be similar in size, shape, color and thickness, and walked back over to the pedestal containing the Book of Raziel. The object of our heroes' journey. The point of our quest. Our MacGuffin.

I squatted down a bit to get on eye level with the book. I held the other book by its spine in my left hand and reached toward Raziel's book with the other. I breathed slowly in and out. I got the substitute book as close to the real thing as I possibly could. I took another breath and held it.

"OH," Elias said in a stage whisper, nudging Ariana. "Raiders of the Lost Ark! 1983!"

I exhaled without taking my eyes off the books or moving. "Very good, Elias," I whispered back. "But I'm kind of busy here. Only five points to Hufflepuff, though, because it was 1981. Now hush for a sec."

I breathed slowly in and out again. I inhaled, held it, and switched the books as quickly and seamlessly as I could, ramping my jacked reflexes up to about half as I didn't want to overdo anything.

Nothing happened. No alarm bells went off. No hidden wires were yanked by the movement of the book. No strobe lights started to flash. No huge, impossibly round boulder started rolling down a ramp towards us. I exhaled and stood up, holding the book in front of me as I turned toward the others.

"Seems like the coast is clear, as far as I can tell. Let's get the hell back to the basement. We've got to be right up against the clock." I moved toward the door and the others followed.

We crept quickly down the hall and heard voices approaching as we neared the spiral stairs. We spotted the steward and the orc movers coming into the salon through a French door just as we reached the entryway leading down. We zipped along as quickly as we could without clattering and stomping overmuch. When we exited the stairs into the basement proper, I flipped open my bracer and hit a key to message Helly. I simply sent her a question mark. The reply came back just as quick. "End of the hall. Last door on right."

We padded down and could just hear the booming voices laughing from above and echoing in the huge stairwell. I had no doubt the orcs were being extra loud to better warn us of their approach. Good dudes, those orcs. I would have to throw them a big bonus when we got the hell out of there.

The three of us bolted through the last door on the right and found Helly and Sallow waiting for us in what appeared to be a small, private study: more scary looking Victorian faces peering down at us from frames, a small rug in front of another fireplace, a small writing desk that seemed positively conservative compared to the rest of the place, and a narrow but tall bookshelf. Lit candles flickered warmly from mounting brackets and candelabras everywhere. It was honestly a wonder the dumb fucker hadn't burned the place down long before our visit, what with all the unattended torches, candles and gas lamps everywhere.

"You find it?" I asked Daphne and Fred ... I mean Helly and Sallow.

"Yup!" Helly grinned. "Check this shit out."

She walked over to the bookcase, which reached almost to the ceiling, and pulled on a mounted candle to the right. The bookcase swung open revealing a secret door.

"I mean, seriously?" I looked at the others. "This guy is just a fucking cliché. He's a cliché wrapped in a trope, swathed in idiocy and basic-ass bitchness."

"Yeeeah," Sallow agreed. "But you have to admit, secret passages are still pretty cool, cliché or no."

"Fair point," I smiled. "Let's boogie."

We all crowded into the narrow passage behind the bookcase and began walking forward. The tunnel was vaguely lit from above by some sort of recessed lighting that made the stone ceiling look a slightly lighter color than the surrounding walls. The bookcase creaked softly closed behind us, and we began to sprint.

We jogged for a while. Maybe three minutes or so. The passage doglegged slightly right once, but was otherwise a straight shot. About 30 seconds after the turn, we felt the floor beneath us start to angle upward in a gentle grade. The last few feet of the tunnel contained a short stone staircase that went upward. We bolted up, slowing down as we did, and found ourselves in a very dark, somewhat confined space that barely fit five intrepid adventurers. I couldn't make out much detail around us, but I felt cold, smoothly polished stone under my hands when I reached out. There was a thin, rectangular halo of light coming from a wall about ten feet away, and I headed toward it and pushed with both hands.

We stepped outside of the small structure and walked into a graveyard.

When the double doors ground open on their creaky hinges, it became clear to us that we were exiting a crypt, the bright sunlight pouring in to reveal slabs of brownish marble covering the walls all around us. No caskets or vaults, though, which was to be expected.

Exiting into the bright noonday sun, we blinked our eyes rapidly to adjust as we took in our surroundings. More squat crypts and single-user, above-ground tombs and raised vaults, statues of angels (of the traditional Caucasian pretty-boy variety), stone crosses at the heads of small mounds of earth. The usual.

"What the hell?" Sallow said. "He's got a pretend graveyard on his property? No one even buries people anymore. What an absolute wanker."

"Naturally," I grinned, looking around at the small buildings and ferrocrete crypts I had spotted and surveilled the day before while enjoying some tasty chicharrónes. "Why wouldn't a walking, talking vampire cliché have a fake graveyard? It's so painfully on-brand that I can't believe I didn't figure it out from the vague-ass blueprints days ago."

"Hey," Helly said. "As fucking precious as this little gothic slice of crypt-covered Halloweenland is, can we get the hell out of here and discuss it over beers?"

"I agree," Ariana said. "Let's not tempt fate."

"I can't believe we did it," Bishop laughed. "This was so incredibly easy. I am just shocked."

"Goddamnit!" Sallow and I said in stereo.

"What?" Bishop said, perplexed.

"You did it again, Elias," I said, sighing. "You summoned the great mystic handjob of Fate."

"I swear, I didn't," Bishop said. "Let's just go! Run for the trees over there."

"It's never that easy, Bishop," Sallow grimaced, as was his

way.

And then the lights went out.

CHAPTER TWENTY-SIX

In the blink of an eye, the noonday sun went dark and the ambient light surrounding us dropped to almost nil. It wasn't full night, but it was damned close to dusk. Surprised, I clicked the hidden button on my smartbow/staff, and within a second, the wood-like surface had shifted and reconfigured into a longbow, the bowstring zipping out to ready with a small *twang* as I shifted my thumb to allow its exit from the shaft.

Raucous, theatrical laughter issued from behind the crypt in front of us, and out walked the man, the vampire himself: Lard Brian-Tom, holding a small remote control in his hand.

"Did you fools really think it was going to be that easy to steal from ME? From the Lord of Nightmares?" He surveyed us coolly, looking pointedly down his patrician nose at us.

"No," Bishop sighed. "Not really. My bad, guys."

"Don't worry about it, Elias," I said. "This was always going to happen. We're just giving you shit."

"HEY," the vampire raised his voice, yelling at me. "I am talking to you!"

I ignored him and spoke to the group quietly, holding the book out to the priest. "I'm going to see if I can get him monologue-ing. Bishop, take this. Guard it with your life. Hide it up one of those gigantic sleeves. When shit goes down, run like hell for the tree line behind us. There's a cart back there. Crawl under it and hide and wait for us."

"He'll never monologue," Helly said. "That shit doesn't happen in real life, Daniel."

"Hello … cartoon supervillain? Pretentious, self-important vampire douche?" I smiled at her.

"Eh. Fair point," she grinned back, clenching and unclenching her fists in readiness.

"HEY!" the vampire said again, sliding the remote into a pocket and swishing his cape a little bit to catch the wind. "You are being addressed by the Lord of …"

"SHUT THE FUCK UP!" I barked, turning to look at the vampire. "I'll talk to you when I'm goddamned good and ready, you pretentious fuckwad. I have to hand it to you, though, turning the sun off was a nice trick. How'd you manage that, Lard Brian?"

"IT'S LAIRD BRI …" he began.

"Whatever," I dismissed him casually with a wave of my left hand. "Must be some impressive tech, though." I smirked appreciatively.

"Hah," he smiled and raised his hands to the side, cruciform-style. "They are called Portable Twilight Generators, you foolish child. I have spent millions developing them. They counteract the harmful UV radiation with a powerful blacklight attuned to a frequency of … shit. I really don't understand it all. BUT, I have them strategically placed over every inch of my property in order to protect myself and my coven when we are forced to hunt outdoors during the day."

"Huh," I noted. "Well, first of all, that may be the stupidest thing I have ever fucking heard. You spent millions of credits to build and emplace a system of high tech devices to protect you and your toadies from a disease you gave yourselves?" I turned to the others. "Sometimes I can't believe what we've let this world become, you know? It's just so dumb sometimes." They all nodded and murmured agreement.

"Secondly," I turned back to the vamp. "That is some highly illegal stuff to have on one of the Ancients, pal."

He smirked and raised his arms, pointing his outstretched thumbs at himself. "Criminal?"

"Fair point," I said. "And I don't really *care*, you murdering, raping, child-killing piece of shit. I'm about to park a broadhead right through your fucking eye so you never, ever have the chance to kill another soul. How about that, Count Chocula, you fucking fuck?" I spat at him viciously. "It's the least I can do considering you want me dead anyway."

"How's that?" he asked, looking genuinely confused. "I mean, yes, you have stolen something that belongs to me, and I plan on killing you. For revenge ... and sport ... and pure pleasure. But I don't even know who you are."

"Daniel Davidson," I said. "I killed two of your hellspawn the last time I was here. They tried to turn me into prey. I took that personally."

"Oh," he said, laughing his textbook villain laugh. "That was YOU? I had all but forgotten about them. Lives come and go. I just made two more!" He kept chuckling like a fucking goon. "And you thought you were ... what? Important to me somehow?"

I glanced at Helly and Ariana, who both shrugged. Oh, well.

"Doesn't matter," I said, casually switching my bow to my left hand and resting my right hand over my left wrist, stretching my neck from side to side as I did so. "Gonna fucking end you anyway."

More stupid muah-ha-hah-hah laughter. "And just how do you think you're going to do that? With a bow, an axe, and a few pointy knives against a master vampire?"

"Four on one, chump," I said, smiling. "And we're pretty good at what we do. Taken down much bigger threats than you. Sometimes before breakfast."

He stopped laughing, but grinned wickedly at me, his retractable fangs lengthening and his hands, now down by his sides, spreading fingers impossibly wide as his nails extended into chitinous, razor-sharp talons.

"That's cute that you think so," he rasped around his giant, enlarged canines. "But, my boy, you've walked into a trap. Motion sensors caught you the moment you crawled out of my dungeon! And ... *I'm not alone.*"

On cue, there was a rush of wind around us and a blur of motion in our periphery. Where Lard Douchebag once stood alone, there now stood some twenty additional vampires, some bare chested, some wearing ascot-laden evening wear ... all sporting shining rapiers in one hand and talons that matched their master's on the other. Fangs bared, they looked for all the world like what they so wanted desperately to be ... apex predators, confident in their superiority and ready for the kill. Hyper-violent, murderers all, with reflexes jacked far beyond mine and capable of speeds that boggled the mind and confused the senses.

Let this be a lesson to you, folks. Just because someone is an absolute douchecanoe and laughable on some levels, it doesn't mean that they are not genuinely dangerous. The overgrown moron in the Affliction shirt with the bedazzled jeans and wallet chain might not actually know MMA, but he might throw a hell of a country boy haymaker. But, I digress. As is sometimes my way.

I looked around at my companions, who looked tough as nails and ready for action, but also surprised and overwhelmed. I caught Ariana's eye, and her look spoke volumes. *I didn't want to be right, but I was, Daniel. The math was bad. There were too many variables. Now we're going to die. I love you. It's not your fault, but you've killed us.*

Those last few probably came from the voices inside my head.

"I know," I responded to her unspoken words, laughing bitterly. "I know, love. The odds are definitely against us."

"What do we do?" Sallow said. "I'm ready to die." He gripped the hilt of his sword.

"Don't wanna, though." Helly said, her hand on the haft of her axe.

"Girl, same," I said. "So ... I suppose ... we'll just have to cheat?"

With my hand still resting across my wrist and the open flap of my left bracer, I tapped my smartwatch once.

There was a whooshing, whining sound from the nearby forest and Sundance, my trusty Hellion hunter-killer drone, rocketed out of the trees like an avenging angel amped to the gills on crystal meth, inverting briefly in mid-flight to loose himself from the last of Bishop's t-shirts that I had piled on top of him to conceal him and his little brother in the huge, wicker basket. I glanced quickly upward and could just make out the tiny dot of Butch, hovering hundreds of meters above our heads where he had been since we arrived, scanning the potential battlefield and mapping out targeting solutions for his brother and myself.

"Illegal drones?" Baron Von Murdering Dipshit asked, frowning.

I pointed my thumbs toward myself. "Treasure hunting mercenary of dubious repute," I said, grinning. "'Dance? Light 'em the fuck up."

The high-speed, rotating tri-barrels I had installed on the drone the previous morning – switching them rather easily from his usual silenced twin single barrels in a matter of minutes – spun up and began firing Narcoject spines as fast as their reloading mechanisms could function as Sundance swooped forward, spraying the line of vamps from end to end. They scattered as fast as they could, which was absolutely blindingly fast, but they were no match for machine precision and the targeting info shared between the two drones' onboard micro-supercomputers, which allowed Sundance to lead the vampires and pincushion their stupid asses regardless of speed.

I had switched to the faster barrels and replaced the drum magazine of armor-piercing bullets with a backup drum of Narcoject spines and reloaded both, figuring that even the somewhat louder tri-barrels would still be far quieter than the silenced jacketed slugs. I wanted to avoid alerting and involving the 50-odd mercs who were patrolling the property, which was totally Alanis-level ironic as Lard had sent them all home at the first sight of us creeping his manor so he and his cronies could hunt us without being seen by prying eyes.

Non-lethal (or more accurately "less-than-lethal") or not, Narcoject spines can knock regular joes out with a single shot. Two can net you a longer, deeper sleep but come with catastrophic loss of bladder and bowel control. Three can induce complete catatonia and paralysis. Four or more can kill as well as a bullet. Of course, these vamps weren't regular people. But, hey. We were about to find out what 400 spines spread between 21 of the fuckers would do.

As soon as Sundance started firing and vamps starting scrambling, I whipped a broadhead arrow out of my quiver and nocked it, putting my targeting reticle on Lard's pretentious chest. I also screamed at Bishop. "RUN, ELIAS!!"

The others sprang into action before the syllables even left my mouth.

Ariana sprang forward, drawing her artfully curved blade with a cry as she did so. She ran three steps, launched herself sideways and took one step with her left foot on the side of a crypt and sprang upward and down into a group of vamps, slicing a deadly crescent through her chosen targets as she descended. Several of the other vamps had already collapsed, thinning their numbers somewhat, and the ones targeted by the graceful elf's deadly dance had already sprouted a host of Narcoject spines from their heads, shoulders and chests. They had not fallen, but they were certainly not capable of engaging super speed at the moment. Two vamps fell under her initial assault, their throats completely opened and necks almost completely severed before they could even raise their rapiers to defend, and she engaged a third immediately, thrusting, parrying and chopping like a whirling demi-goddess of death, a raging Valkyrie ripped from myth and dropped down in the midst of battle in answer to a pagan warrior's fervent prayers.

Sallow had drawn his longsword with his right hand and his dagger with his left. Charging forward, he bashed one pin-cushioned vamp in the face with his buckler and stabbed another through the chest, ripping the sword free at once and spinning on his heel to behead the vamp whose face he had just pummeled. He then lunged right, barely dodging the talons of another vampire that would have scarred him for life and likely removed an eye at the very least. He stabbed upward with his dagger as he moved, spearing the vamp under the chin and through the mouth and, hopefully, into his stupid walnut-sized brain. He yanked the blade free and surged forth into the tide of now spiky vampires, slashing horizontally before him like a scythe-wielding reaper mowing down tall wheat, workmanlike and solid, and completely devastating. He looked for all the world like a knight from the storybooks, an Avatar of the Light, bravely and selflessly stomping into battle, facing impossible odds and a demonic foe that threatened all that was holy and good in the world. Seeing him thusly made me very glad that he was on my side. But he's a tool, and he must never know that I said those words, lest he grow even more intolerable than he already is.

And my brave Helly. The tiny terror levered her huge axe off her back, screaming and thrusting it skyward, throwing herself bodily into the fight like a blonde wrecking ball fired from a cartoonishly gigantic cannon. Which, I suppose, would make her more like a blonde cannonball? That, like, wrecks stuff. Ridges of muscle stood out on her thick arms like steel cables under stress as she dove into the fray, spinning and twirling her axe in seemingly every direction at once, the deadly twin blades carving through vampire flesh on all sides. Blood spatter whipped thin crimson lines across her freckled face that was already flushed red with rage and exhilaration and the thrill and craziness and pants-shitting fear that can only be found in combat. She screamed again, the sound something between a laugh and a cry and a bestial growl of pleasure and horror. Heads literally rolled. So did arms and legs. There were some vampires that were almost cleaved wholly in twain under the punishing onslaught of Helly in full-on berserker mode.

My heart swelled with pride and love for all of them, but that was all I could catch of their initial attacks in the scant second or two between my yelling for Bishop to take cover and loosing an arrow toward Lard Brian-Tom, Lord of Shitheads. And, honestly, memory being what it is, I'm not sure how much of that I saw in those moments and how much I caught after and during the next few minutes. Stressful situations play hell with memory, and eyewitness accounts can often be less reliable than most think. I just remember thinking what wonderful, terrible, awesome people I am fortunate enough to know as they faced their own mortality and committed wholly to the slaughter of a gang of murdering, raping thugs with delusions of gothic grandeur who were likewise trying to kill us. And fuck those guys. I've said it before, and you'll likely hear me say it again. Some folks just need killing.

Vamps were falling like tenpins, and those that weren't killed outright were screaming holy terror from their garlic-filled wounds. Several had sprouted boils and bright, bumpy rashes on their too-perfect faces.

Unfortunately for me, another prickly vampire stepped in front of his Sire, the Lard, just in time to catch my arrow in his throat. I quickly grabbed another and fired again, but Lard was still moving pretty quickly, and I missed. I saw then only a small handful of spines had found him. Likely his shitty offspring had shielded him with their bodies, catching many of the tiny missiles meant for him. Sundance was still at it, though, panning around the battlefield in a circle, taking shot after shot at vampires who were clear of our party's flailing ministrations. Butch had also dropped significantly to better track the battle and process the data from a better vantage point, hovering only about 30 meters over our heads at that point.

I decided to try another tactic with a more global effect. I reached into my pocket and pulled out my left earbud and jammed it into my ear, tapping it and calling to my little drone.

"Butch, can you target the nozzles or dishes or whatever the fuck is generating that twilight effect? Lard said it was some form of blacklight on steroids?" I scanned the battlefield with my own eyes, trying to pick out discrepancies in the landscape and ignore the carnage and cacophony around me. The little drone beeped an affirmative in my ear, and seconds later, six inverted orange deltas appeared on my eyepatch HUD with helpful little blinking arrows overhead pointing down at them.

"SUCH a good boy!" I told the drone as I drew another arrow and targeted the closest emitter. The little drone beeped happily at me. Or in a way that my weird brain took to mean that he was happy. Fuck. I am totally getting that AI upgrade when we get out of this mess.

I fired an arrow, and thanks to my wonderful tech assist that placed a targeting reticle over the delta, it hit home. Bright, beautiful sunlight poured into the dome of dusk that had surrounded us since Lard had triggered his device, a cone of radiance shining down and lighting up a circular patch of grounds that I guessed to be about 15 feet in diameter. Two vamps that were unlucky enough to be standing underneath it as Helly wailed away at them like a pissed-off lumberjack started smoking with a hiss and cries of pain.

"Getcha summa that Vitamin D, bitches!" I yelled, taunting and laughing like a goddamned lunatic, spinning to target the next emitter.

"And the D stands for THIS DIIIIICK!!!" I heard Helly scream behind me.

I managed to take out two more emitters nearby, lightly searing some more vamps, before I heard footsteps rapidly closing on me. I spun, dropping my bow as I did so. I just had enough time to reach back and draw my Elven short swords before Lard was in my face, clawing at me and hissing like a snake.

"Is that Parseltongue?" I asked, raising my foot to kick him square in the chest and buy myself a bit of space to operate. "Sorry, Lard Voldemort, but I don't speak snake. Use your big boy words, you stupid fuck!"

"I don't know what that means," he croaked at me, swiping at me with his taloned hands, and deftly sidestepping the swings of my blade as I did my best to slice and dice him like a Benihana entrée. Both of us were spinning up our jacked reflexes as we fought, so I have no idea what the fight must have looked like to onlookers. Hopefully like some crazy cool badass Jedi shit.

He backed off his initial attack and retracted his claws. He reached behind him, under his cape, and drew two long, serpentine daggers, spinning them in his hands like a fencer warming up. Theatrical, yes, but it also let me know that he was no slouch in the bladed weaponry department. He slashed at me with his left hand first, feinting right.

"Even your cute little daggers are snakes," I laughed, dodging his attack and counterattacking by slashing inward with both swords toward his head. "You're totally a Slytherin! But, like, a Death Eater and stuff. Not like my pal Slughorn over there."

"SHUUUUT UP!" He yelled, raising his knives in unison to block my attack. He kicked out with his right foot, and I moved to block it with my left shin. "You're just speaking gibberish! Made-up words!"

"You'd like to think that, wouldn't you?" I grinned, taking the blow and backing up quickly, dropping my blades to point at his chest. "Or maybe you're just a culturally ignorant swine that spent a fuckton of money to make himself into a wannabe apex predator. But you're not a predator," I grunted and feinted right, slashing toward his gut.

"You're just a fucking bully. And I fucking hate bullies," I reversed my swing and cut upward backhanded, surprising him. I slashed open his shiny black shirt and the flesh underneath, and blood started pouring out.

"And you fucking kill innocent people," I exhaled forcefully, sidestepping and curving my stomach away from his dagger thrust. "Including CHILDREN!"

I turned my body back to face him. He leapt forward with

the speed of a jungle cat and slashed my face, cutting a bloody swath across my cheek. I felt a flap of skin peel down and dangle. While he was still within my guard, I brought the sleek, slightly pointy pommels of my short swords up and slammed them toward one another and his temples. I connected on both sides with a sickening crunch. I spat blood in his face and screamed. I raised my knee as hard as I could and rammed it into his crotch, and as he howled and fell backward, I drove my right sword deep into his side. I drew it out quickly, twisting slightly as I did so. And then, I rammed my left sword into the right side of his chest and yanked it free, the blade edge scraping awfully against bone on its way out.

He staggered backward, coughing and sputtering blood. He leaned forward, seemingly on the verge of collapse. His blades clattered to the ground. I leapt forward to deliver the killing blow.

And sometimes, no matter how savvy you are, no matter how practiced or how quick or well trained ... well, you get caught.

As I raced forward toward him with my swords at the ready, he leaned even further forward. Dumbass me, well, I thought he was falling. And then, he launched his arm upward and toward me so fucking fast that it was merely a thin, black-clad blur arcing at me with the speed of a bullet. Luckily for me, I guess, he didn't have time to extend his claws or even make a fist. He hit me open handed across the side of my face. He literally slapped me, like he was a 1970s pimp fresh out of an exploitation film, and I owed him money.

Quite simply, I had never been hit so hard or so fast in my entire life. He must have overclocked his augmented reflexes beyond their maximum range as he stared death in the face or some such shit. To be honest, I'm not even sure how one does it. But he connected. Solidly. And I went down, half-spinning and collapsing against the blood-spattered side of a crypt. Darkness started crowding the edges of my vision, the nearly dead vampire a hazy vignette as he picked up his stupid little snake blades and lumbered slowly toward me to no doubt bury them in my chest and finish me.

I fought it. I fought it so very hard. I tried to make my useless arms work. I tried to keep my head from lolling forward. I know I moaned pitifully like a sad zombie, my mouth not working right, either. I imagined my jaw was dislocated and probably very severely fractured. I felt teeth floating around in what felt like a sea of blood in my ruined mouth, dislodged completely from my gums, some probably broken at the root. I could feel it all slipping silently and wetly from my open mouth as my eyes drifted slowly closed.

As darkness and cold began to embrace me fully, I heard a sound the likes of which I had never heard before, and thankfully, I have never heard in the many, many years since.

It was a purely animalistic sound that somehow managed to convey rage and fear and anguish and loss all at once. It didn't sound human. It sounded like a creature caught in a trap, witnessing the death of its pups, at once whining and crying and loathing and hating with all of its heart.

It was my sweet Helly.

Her tortured, inhuman scream brought me back toward the light a bit, and my eyes creaked blearily open just in time to see our tiny terror barrel into the master vampire's side, her shoulder lowered like a football linebacker, her thick, tree-trunk thighs propelling her into him like a freckled freight train. She kept screaming as she hit him, and the incoherent, disjointed syllables coming from her ravaged throat began making sense, and one word fought its way out, stretched out into an elongated, mournful cry that was at once a lament and a threat and a warning and a promise.

"NO!!!!!!" My beautiful berserker screamed into the face of my would-be killer. She hefted her axe and swung it upward with terrible force, so hard that she propelled herself up on her tiptoes. And then, she brought it crashing down, deep into the chest of the Lord of Nightmares. And she did it again. And again. And again. And again. Until his chest was completely caved in, the ribs and sternum broken and shattered and the organs nothing but wet, scarlet pulp. I was still fading in and out, but my eyes blinked closed and were wrenched open as best I could as I clung to life and consciousness with all my might. With every fall of her axe, Helly screamed another word at the devastated corpse below her, the crushed remains of the child-killing fuck that the two of us had taken out of this world and ushered into whatever comes next, if anything.

"YOU!!!!!" *Thwack!*

"HURT!!!!!" *Thwack!*

"MY!!!!!" *Thwack!*

"DANIEL!!!!!" *Thwack!*

And my quickly fading gaze saw her fall to her knees in exhaustion next to the mess that was the vampire, utterly spent, her axe head on the ground, her clenched hand still clinging to the upraised haft the only thing holding her upright. She looked toward me then, to where I had fallen, her perfect, heart-shaped face still crisscrossed with blood and gore. Her bright eyes were dimmed and red and filled with tears, their tracks slowly etching pink lines downward through the bloody stripes that struck me in that moment as such a horrible affront to her smooth, pale skin.

Then … darkness.

CHAPTER TWENTY-SEVEN

I opened my eyes. Bright white light nearly blinded me, and I squeezed my eyes shut again, opening far more tentatively the second time around. I was looking at a white ceiling, I thought. Or maybe a white wall. I actually didn't know which. I shifted and realized I had no sense of direction whatsoever, nor of whether I was prone, which I had assumed, or standing up. There was a feeling very close to weightlessness. I tried to stand, or I told my brain to do that. I looked in the direction I thought was toward my feet, but the harsh ambient light made my eyes water. I thought I could make out my bare feet through the tears, but they seemed far more distant than they should have been.

I tried again, willing my stomach muscles to contract and crumple my body into an upright position. I thought it sort of worked? I kept blinking my eyes and eventually some sense of ... *being* happened.

As I sort of felt like I was now sitting up, I tried lowering one of my legs as if I were climbing out of a nonexistent bed. It seemed to stay there and be leg-like. I lowered the other and turned sideways, now sitting on the edge of the imaginary bed. *Fuck it,* I thought. *Let's see what happens.* I stood up.

I succeeded, or at least it seemed like I had. I turned and looked behind me, but there was only empty space where the imaginary bed should have been. I spun in a slow circle, looking in every direction. There was only bright, white light and, somehow beyond it, the impression of white walls, floor and ceiling … only at a vast distance. It clicked.

"Oh, no," I said, my voice echoing back from a great expanse as if I were standing at the very bottom of a monumentally huge cavern. "I finally did it, huh? I'm fucking dead."

I heard a sound in the distance, beyond the white, Gaussian blur of my surroundings. It sounded like *thwip, thwip, thwip, thwip, thwip*.

A shape began forming out of the imaginary white fog in front of me. It coalesced slowly, a brownish blob hovering above two smaller, elongated brownish blobs and further down still, two more tiny brownish blobs. *Thwip, thwip, thwip, thwip, thwip.*

The shapes formed into a smiling, bearded face with Middle Eastern features, two hairy arms, and two wide, hairy feet wearing flip flops. They were all connected by a pristine white robe. The figure approached me, stopped about ten feet away, and gave me a friendly little exuberant wave.

"L'chaim, my guy!" The man said, jubilantly. "I thought you'd never get here! I've been expecting you."

"Nooo," I said. "This … um … can't be happening." I looked around and gave the man the once over head-to-toe.

"This is," I began, struggling for words. "This is the most clichéd bullshit afterlife experience I could even imagine. This is almost as bad as the Transylvanian shitshow I left behind. I mean, what the actual fuck? And, I guess you're half-alien Jesus?" I laughed in spite of myself, but not maliciously. Just at the absurdity of it all.

"Eh. Jesus … Yeshua … Joshua … Josh … the Light, the Way … the Lamb of God," He grinned. "And before you even say it, yes. I'm a fan. And they were fucking *sick*."

I barked laughter, shaking my head. "And this is … is this Heaven?"

"Hah!" He laughed merrily. "No, Daniel. You don't actually think *you'd* wind up in Heaven do you?"

He paused a beat and looked at me seriously, a wicked grin on his face. I stared at him.

"Bwah!" He ripped into peals of laughter that were so genuine and heartfelt that I couldn't help but grin myself. "Oh, Daniel. I'm just fucking with you. But you should see the look on your face! Oh, that's rich. I *kill* me sometimes. But, hey, you've got a point. This place is kind of lousy."

He snapped his fingers, and instantly, we were on a beach, perched in wicker loungers underneath a giant green umbrella. He was wearing a gigantic sun hat and had a white smear of zinc oxide across his nose. His obnoxiously loud Hawaiian shirt sported little Alpha and Omega symbols in pastel colors. He raised a beverage in a coconut toward me, the little straw and umbrella spinning jauntily as he did so. I looked down at myself, likewise dressed in a Hawaiian shirt - with cartoon dicks drawn all over it, haha, funny guy - and white shorts. I saw a similar coconut drinking vessel in my right hand and beyond, our bare feet, the pounding surf of a gorgeous cerulean sea hitting the sugar-white sands with that particularly primal and pleasing music of unfettered nature at work. What the hell, I thought. I raised my coconut and clinked/thunked glasses with him.

"Oooh, we bumped nuts," he chuckled. "But don't worry ... it's only gay if you make eye contact."

"What is WRONG with you?" I laughed.

"Well, if that isn't quite possibly the most egregious example of the pot calling the kettle black I have seen in eons of existence." He waggled his eyebrows at me.

"Touché," I grinned, taking a sip of my beverage. Mai Tais, of course. And delicious ones at that.

"SO, no, Daniel," Jesus/Josh said. "This isn't Heaven, but before you lose your shit and think flames are about to erupt around us and I'm going to pull my face off and be a horrific red devil, it isn't Hell, either." He took a generous pull of his Mai Tai and burped softly, covering his mouth with his hand.

"Ok, so it's like purgatory? Limbo?" I took another sip, closing my eyes in pleasure. "'Cause if it is, Limbo got some drinks that are off the chain. Heaven must be fucking LIT."

He laughed, kind of sadly. "Actually, Daniel, this is just ... hmmm. I guess you could say it's kind of a way station. Like a really nice truck stop with super clean bathrooms and decent food."

"Holy shit," I laughed. "We're hanging out in some sort of celestial Bucc-ee's?"

Josh laughed in return. I had a hard time thinking of him as Jesus. He snapped his fingers again. A bowl of snacks appeared in my lap.

"Beaver nuggets?" I picked one up and tried it. "Sea salt and caramel. Fucking CHOICE, Josh. Well played."

He nodded his thanks and conjured a bowl of his own. "Didn't want to grope your crotch or anything," he said, raising a handful of snacks to his mouth and tossing them in.

"Ok, so we're hanging out at a truck stop, drinking Mai Tais ... and, like, cool ... but, why am I here? Not Heaven or Hell? Is it one of those unfinished business things? You're about to send me back to right some wrongs or something? Also cliché, but I'll fucking take it. Put me back in, coach."

"First of all, you have to disabuse yourself of such notions," He said, looking more serious than he had previously. "None of those places actually exist ... or, at least, I don't think they do? Not in the way many humans think of, anyway. If some form of them do exist, somewhere in the crazy, near-infinite universe, I've never seen or heard of them. Except in your storybooks."

"WHAT? I mean, ok. I've never been a believer or anything, as I'm sure you know," I said. "Or I think you do, if you're actually Him and stuff, or a half-alien version of the Jesus we've all heard about for 2,500 years or so ... but you seem kind of Jesus-like and nice, so I'm just rolling with it. But what happens when we die if those places don't exist? Not that I ever thought they did, except maybe when I was a kid, but ... fuck. I don't know what's going on here." I sipped my beverage aggressively, perplexed. Or perplexedly aggressive?

"No fucking clue," he said, staring out over the water and chewing on a giant mouthful of beaver nuggets.

"You ... YOU don't know what happens when humans die?" I stared at him, mouth agape.

"Nope," He said, turning slightly in his chair to face me. "Look, Daniel. Yes, I exist. No, I'm not exactly like the books say. Or The Book says. To be honest, 90% of that is just made up stories with a tiny grain of truth to them - well-intentioned though some of them might be - mostly written hundreds of years after the events took place and filtered through tons of translations and mistranslations and changes of cultural mores and what-not."

"As your friend Sallow mentioned, the Being you guys think of as capital-G God, is an interdimensional traveler ... one of gigantic proportions that beggar reality. In fact, one reason He *is* interdimensional is that one dimension isn't big enough to hold His presence and so he's sort of spread into other ones, including yours. This one was pretty empty when he got here, so he threw the proverbial magic lightning bolt or whatever to jumpstart life from the basic building blocks that did exist here. So it wouldn't be so empty. And he sort of watched you grow and then moved on. He left me behind to observe. That's it. I just watch you. And learn."

"You're just an observer? An intergalactic voyeur?" I chuckled, incredulous. "And that's it? No afterlife, and you don't sit in judgment of us all when we die? What about your dad? You say he moved on? He doesn't care about what happens here?"

"I get there's a lot to unpack," he said. "Come. Walk with me." He snapped his fingers and the loungers and snacks and drinks were gone. We were now standing next to the shore, the surf gently sliding up the wet sand to caress our feet.

"I *totally* wasn't done with that," I said.

"Oh. Sorry, man." Josh snapped his fingers and my Mai Tai reappeared in my now upraised hand, refilled to the brim.

"Thanks, bud," I grinned and sipped. He smiled, clasped his hands behind his back and turned, walking slowly down the shore. I followed.

"So, yes. I observe. But I'm not omniscient or anything. That's just nuts. I have a pretty wide band of awareness ... more a shotgun approach as opposed to your pitiful human pea-shooters ... but that's it. I watch, and learn. I don't usually affect events one way or another except in extremely small ways when it is needed. And, no, not in answer to prayers. I can't really *hear* them as such, unless I am already watching someone AS they pray. But, most people pray for the same things, anyway. And it gives them comfort, so it's not totally without merit." He bent down to pick up a small rock and skipped it across the water, perfectly. Which totally should not have worked in the waves, but I guess He can do whatever He wants at this here ephemeral travel stop. And maybe beyond.

"My Father is ... complicated. Our relationship is ... complicated, too. See, all that stuff about God being love is bullshit. God is a vast alien being that is barely capable of comprehending base human emotions such as they are. I think He gets the concept, but it's just not what He does. It's not His thing. Not everyone is cut out to be a father, Daniel. BUT, He gets enough of the concept to know it's good. And He's incapable, He truly is, but He doesn't want to be? Which is kind of sad? He created you all so that this little chunk of space wasn't so empty and lonely. That's what He does. He makes stuff and moves on. In this instance, though, He watched you long enough to learn something Himself. He felt enough of a kinship or a positive proto-feeling that He recognized it was something He lacked. Even He is not capable of creating the capacity to love in Himself, but He figured He COULD do something. He made ME."

"You see, that was His biggest problem, but it was one He managed to learn from. He made the angels in a neighboring dimension, and He did the best He could, in His hands-off way. But, they evolved without the capacity to love. Or laugh, really. They never developed a sense of humor. That's one of the reasons they hate you so much. Or some of them, anyway. Every time you crack a joke ... every time you fall in love

... every time you cry at a fucking commercial ... or hug your children ... you're spitting right in their eyes. But, He saw all that stuff. He saw you. Something in YOU made Him *want* to love. You ... humanity ... you were His favorite. In all your flawed magnificence. Your spirit, your creativity, your laughter, your love ... they made Him WANT something he didn't have ... couldn't have. I was the next best thing. Part of him that *could* love."

"He reached out in his clumsy, inexperienced way, and made contact with a human woman," He said, His smile turning a bit sad now. "My mom, Mary. She was thrilled at the chance to create life with Him. So was her husband, Joseph. It was all a lot less rapey than it sometimes sounds. It was more like a surrogate type thing. Don't even ask me how the conversations went, though. No idea. But, she had been barren, you see. Not a virgin like the tales tell. But, good ol' Dad fixed that right up, or at least allowed her body to ignore the reality of its condition just this once. And so I was born. Half unfeeling but needy alien god, half caring human. And, wow, Daniel. Do I CARE."

He stopped walking and turned to look at me. "You guys have created so much beauty. The stories you tell! The dreams you dream. And manifest! The jokes you tell! The food, the beverages, the movies, the shows, the art, the MUSIC! The love you have for each other and for LIFE. Not just the capital-Y you as in humanity, but you in particular. You and your friends."

I looked at him. "Us? You've been watching us in particular?"

"I mean, not when you're cranking one out or anything," He laughed. "Or doing any of that sex stuff. Which also seems pretty cool, but I don't care about that. I mean. It's kind of hot ..."

"I am not sure I want you to finish that line of thought," I laughed, reaching out to pat Him on the shoulder.

"Point taken," He said, grinning himself. "I'll drop it, but, just know that unlike what some people think, I don't give two shits about what one or two or more consenting adults do to themselves or each other. Or what gender you are or become.

Or what you wear. That's all human stuff, and I've always said 'live and let live, and don't be a dick.' Just don't be a raging douchebag, and we'll be fine."

"Hey," I said. "I say that, too."

"I know," He said with a smug grin, raising his arms and pointing his thumbs at himself. "Half-alien, semi-omniscient demigod observer."

"Gotcha," I grinned. "I totally deserved that."

"And more," Josh said, mysteriously. "But, really. I have been watching you and your friends for some time. Not just because your recent actions and the events surrounding them are leading up to a potential universe-shattering cataclysm. I mean, that, too, obviously. But you and your friends fascinate me."

"How so?" I asked, genuinely curious.

"You may be the most perfect examples of humanity I have encountered," He began. "And, no. Before you stupidly get the big head, none of you are perfect. Far from it. HUGE flaws, all of you."

"Ouch," I said. "That really stings more coming from you somehow. Even if I know you're not going to judge us when we die ... I mean, you're still kind of judgey."

"Touché," He said. "Look, no one is perfect. Even me, despite what the Book says. Perfection is a human concept. Along with all of the rest of your mythologies. But, I mean, one of you came pretty close. Fred Rogers, a minister and television ..."

"I fucking know who Mr. Rogers was, my dude," I laughed. "And yeah. He was probably the best of us."

"Flawed and human with all the inherent failings that entails," He said. "But, yes. I think so. You know why?"

"I mean, I can think of tons of reasons," I said.

"Yes," He agreed. "He was amazing. But mostly, it's because he was, at his very core, a teacher."

"People talk about me like I was a prophet, like I was a religious leader, a radical," He continued. "But I was not any of those things. At MY core, I was a *teacher*. I didn't have 12 followers or disciples ... I had 12 friends. Friends that I cared about more than anything in the universe. Friends I would have done anything for ... even died for. But, I never tried to start a religion. I tried to TEACH. And you know what makes teachers angry, Daniel?" I shook my head.

"WHEN YOU MISS THE ENTIRE POINT OF WHAT I WAS TEACHING," He raised his voice to a near shout, startling me a bit.

"Sorry," He said. "It gets me worked up, you know? So many people doing horrible things in my name ... spreading hate, hurting others, breaking up families because of borders, or sexuality, or religion itself. I don't give a shit whether you are religious or not, Daniel. I don't WANT to be worshiped! I just want to see people love each other, and laugh a lot and enjoy living their lives. Create! Dance! Sing! Eat! Drink! LOVE!"

"Are you basically telling me that the whole point of human existence is to 'Live, Laugh, Love'? Because half-alien demigod or not, I will punch you in the dick," I told him, grousing half-heartedly. "I mean, the goddamned Karens were right?"

He laughed merrily. "You would, wouldn't you, you stupid, ballsy sonofabitch? GOD, I love your spirit. But ... yeah. Kinda? I mean, I wouldn't etch it into a rustic board in a flowery script and hang it on my living room wall or anything, but yeah. That IS the point. Which brings me to MY point."

"You and your friends love more purely than just about anyone I know," Josh said. "You're dumb, you're silly, you're delightfully raunchy, you're witty, you're caring ... you LOVE each other wholeheartedly. You LAUGH so very much and so often. You LIVE like there is no tomorrow. You overlook each other's flaws, you celebrate the majestic and magical spirit in each and every one of you. You ..."

"You're SUCH a fucking hippie," I laughed. "I mean, I kind of expected that, but I mean, you're really laying it on thick. I may weep. If you pull a flower out of your ass or anything ..."

"STAHP," Josh said, grinning. "I get it. I'll stop. Just know that, whether or not I judge you when it's all said and done, I'm proud of you."

"I mean ..." I stumbled over my words. "That's wonderful and so very kind and all. It really means more than I can say, and stupid hippie or not, you're about to make me cry. But, I guess ... fuck. I dunno. Doesn't that let us off the hook? I mean, if no one is judging us? No one is judging ME? I have done SO many things I am not proud of, Jes ... Josh ... man. I kill people! I'm not proud of it, but sometimes, in the course of my work? Yeah. I have killed." I squeezed my eyes shut, and tears spilled out and my voice broke. "I'm a killer."

"Of course someone judges you at the end of all things, Daniel," He smiled, kindly. "It's just not who you think. It's YOU. ALL of you. You judge yourselves, you judge the merits of others' lives and how they lived. And history judges you all. You're not off the hook. Are you letting yourself off the hook, Daniel?"

"Stop saying my name in that beatific way, you turd," I sniffed, wiping my nose with the back of my hand. "But no, obviously. I remember every single one. And in some way, I regret them all. ALL the lives I have taken. Regardless of how bad they were, or whether or not they were trying to kill me at the time, or what they had done. I regret. I don't act like it, but I do. I'm glib and funny and I say tough guy shit, but I do. They all hurt me in some way. Deep down. In a way that never, ever goes away."

"See?" Josh said, smiling. "There you go. And did you enjoy killing those people?"

"What?" I asked. "No."

"Did taking them off the board, as you say, prevent them from harming others? From spreading darkness, from removing some love and light from this world? From harming innocents? And opposing and destroying innocence? I mean, we're not talking garden variety criminals, here. Or even politicians. People that had a bad day or made mistakes? No. We're talking about real monsters, Daniel, aren't we?"

"Yes," I said. "Undoubtedly."

"Then fuck 'em," He said.

"I can't believe I am hearing you say these words," I said, shaking my head.

"I'm not the guy from the Book, Daniel," He reminded me. "Although, have you even READ it? God kills a lot of folks in that thing, Daniel. A lot of them for far smaller and more arbitrary reasons than you have. Again though, most of it is just stories. I'm not saying it's okay to kill indiscriminately, which you don't. I am just saying that in some circumstances, it is far better than the alternative ... which is letting them live and spread their poison. In a way, it's kind of like you're sacrificing your innocence and humanity to protect that of others. Which, naturally, is right up my alley." He raised his arms to the side and hung his head, crossing his legs slightly.

"Ugh, don't do that," I laughed, covering my eyes in mock horror. "I'm not even religious and that seems blasphemous somehow."

"Fair enough," He grinned as he raised his head. "And, seriously. Why do my 'followers' wear crosses and use them for decoration? They fucking KILLED me on one of those things, dude. Do they think I'm gonna show up in a puff of heavenly smoke and be glad to see that shit? FUCK no."

"You say fuck a lot," I noted, smiling.

"I do," He laughed. "I *really* do. But they're just words, Daniel. All human constructs. None of them inherently bad or good. Except 'clafoutis.' I REALLY like that one. And 'gubernatorial' is fun."

"Oh, which brings me to the whole reason I brought you here," He laughed. "I tend to digress sometimes, but there was a lot to share. So, you have this problem. You have a book full of words that ... I'm not going to delve too deeply into the nature of the universe ... on a technical level, anyway. Plus, you're probably not smart enough to understand it."

"Again ... ouch," I said. "I'm right here. You are saying this to my face. But, eh, point taken."

"Ok, so there ARE words - sounds and symbols - that have

an effect on the fabric of the universe," He continued. I believe you called them the 'source code of the ethereal computer that runs everything,' or some such shit. That's pretty close. The Book of Raziel is written mostly in this language; we call it Angelic Script. You've been using that and Enochian script interchangeably, and that's not strictly true. Some of the appendices are in Enochian and were added later. Anyway, that's neither here nor there."

"The Angelic shit is what changes reality ... it's the dangerous stuff. It's the stuff the rogue angels are going to use to wipe out all of this magnificent reality that we BOTH love. And, seeing as how they're pretty much your superiors in every way, I figured you needed a hand to protect your dimension. Sadly, you have a whole book full of useful info, but your sad little human pea-brains can't comprehend it. And you can't translate something you can't comprehend. And even if you did, the translation wouldn't have the same effect. It wouldn't do shit as it's the combination of sound, symbol and intent that does the trick."

"You getting this so far, pea-brain?" He smiled at me and clasped my shoulder.

"Yes, dick," I said, laughing. "I think so. Go on."

"Ok, so I can't give you more intelligence," He said. "But, I CAN give you this." He reached in the pocket of his white shorts and pulled out a small scrap of parchment. "Don't open it yet, though. Wait until you are about to leave."

"Oh, I'm leaving? That's good news," I said. "What is it?"

"It's a weapon, Daniel," He said. "A most terrible weapon. It's called 'Angel Reaver.'"

"Ok, so that sounds extremely metal and VERY badass," I said. "But what IS it?"

"Doesn't it, though?" He laughed. "It's pretty fucking cool. It's a combination of three Angelic letters, the glyphs for 'Angel', 'Death', and 'Destruction.' It's a mashup, a sort of hellish amalgam that literally unmakes them. And, if you could say it, actually pronounce it with your human mouths ...

that would help. But, you can't. So you need to show it to them ... introduce them to it visually, physically ... whatever. And REALLY want them dead."

"No problem there," I said. "What about the sound component, though?"

"I can't help you there, but I know someone who can," He smiled. "You'll enjoy meeting him. He's um, a relative of mine. One who has a long history of fighting angels." He paused for dramatic emphasis, waiting.

"No," I said. "You can't be fucking serious."

"Yup!" He chuckled, "Got it in one. Look at your pea-brain GO! It's Satan, by the way." He winked in an exaggerated fashion, nudging me with his elbow. "Am I doing this right?"

"Hah. Nice callback," I allowed. "So, you just gonna transfer me over ..."

"Nope. I'm a half-alien demigod. He's a fallen angel. Different networks, shall we say? You have to go old school and summon him to your plane of existence." Josh clasped his hands in front of him. "I'll bet your quick little brain can probably figure out how, too. Sound, symbol, and intent, Daniel."

I thought for a moment. "Ok. I think I've got it. The sound, though. Would a song work? There are so many to choose from, though."

"Oh," He laughed. "He's a traditionalist. I'm sure you know the one."

"You've got to be kidding," I said. "Am I doomed to just surf through life, riding the wave of all these stupid hackneyed clichés you guys are throwing at me?"

"Perhaps," He said, smiling. "But go call him. We're almost done here. We're gonna fist bump, and you are going to open that folded note, and you're gonna wake up."

I looked back the way we had come and the sun was starting to set over the water, turning it a deep, burnt orange. I noticed that the wet sand only held one set of footprints.

"Hah," I said. "Nice touch, but don't you dare say the words.

But, seriously, Josh. One last question, though. Is any of this real? Or is this just some fucked up near-death experience, my rattled brain conjuring you up to tell me what I want to hear, drinking things I like, talking like I talk, acting like I act, and everything? It's almost too perfect a setup."

"Huh," He replied. "Interesting theory. I'd say the chances are about 80/20."

I laughed. "Naturally. Which is which?"

"Goodbye, Daniel and good luck," He raised His fist. "Don't leave me hanging."

I bumped his fist and held it. "We blowin' it up?"

"Goddamn right we are," He said, and we made the exploding fist gestures and sounds.

"Shalom, mothafucka," He said, waving goodbye.

"Really?" I said, laughing.

"I'm a Middle Eastern Jew, Daniel," He said. "What did you expect? Now, open it." He turned and walked off, his outline becoming faintly hazy as He did so.

I unfolded the parchment and a searing white light cut into my vision, a burning symbol blazing before my eyes. It grew until the light completely surrounded me.

And then ... darkness.

CHAPTER TWENTY-EIGHT

My eyes opened to a bright white light.

"God DAMNIT," I croaked. "Not again." I rolled over on my pillow, squinting and shielding my eyes with my arm.

"DANIEL!!!!" I heard a cry of joy from the foot of the bed that was slowly fading into view as my eyes adjusted. I looked down to see Helly, cleaned up and wearing a set of pink hospital scrubs. From the look of it, she had pulled a chair over to the edge of my bed, had been holding my leg, and passed out face first into the bed. She smiled a huge, gap-toothed smile of purest happiness, wiped the sleep from her eyes with the back of her hand, and scampered up to meet me.

Her eyes filled with tears as she gently put her arms around me and hugged. Not too tight, though, as she still seemed afraid I was fragile. I probably was. She pulled back a little and planted a kiss on my right cheek, then my left, then she kissed me full on the lips ... maybe lingering a moment too long for besties ... then she kissed my forehead and nose. And hugged me again, mumbling a muffled "MMMM THO GLD YR OK" into my pillow.

"Silly dwarf," I said into the mane of golden hair that was threatening to suffocate me yet again. "It's gonna take a lot more than a douche vampire or two to kill me. But, hey. For real. You saved my life, sweet girl. Yet again." I petted her head and snuggled close.

She pulled away, allowing me to mostly breathe again, and I spotted Bishop in another chair near the opposite end of the foot of my bed. He grinned and gave me a small wave.

"Welcome back, old friend," he said. "We thought we'd lost you."

Everything still looked weird and a bit fuzzy and I wondered if my vision had lingering effects from the giant pimp slap I had received. I greeted Bishop warmly as I took in our surroundings. It looked like an ultra-modern medical suite, with a rolling cart of flat screens next to the bed showing all manner of colorful visuals and info. It was connected to a tentacular mass of wires running under my bed covers, where I assumed they were attached to leads positioned strategically around my body. Intravenous fluid tubes ran from another machine overhead and to my left to a cuff on my left arm. I had not previously noticed the brown-skinned, heavily bearded dwarf standing in the corner of the room to my immediate right, sporting a white medical coat and tapping things on a digital clipboard with his finger.

"Where are we?" I asked Helly. "Are we on Elysia?"

"No, goofball," she laughed. "We're at a medical clinic in downtown Narthwych."

"But, like, there's high tech everywhere," I noted, confused.

The Dwarven doctor, sighed and shook his head. He didn't bother looking up from his clipboard. "Did you think we treated modern medical issues with leeches and drained off humours, Mr. Davidson? Practiced phrenology?" He finished tapping, clasped the clipboard to his chest and crossed his arms over it, looking at me like I was an absolute tourist and/or moron.

"Well, no, doc," I said. "I mean, I guess I never thought about it? All the times I've been here and I never wound up in the hospital. Just a little surprised is all."

He snorted. "I'm not Doc, I'm Sleepy." He stared at me for a moment, waiting, then sighed again.

"Dwarf humor," he deadpanned. "Anyway, moving on. In case you're wondering, you've been out for about 24 hours. We performed extensive reconstructive surgery on your face and finished up with a nanobot cycle for your brain bleed and cracked skull. We even managed to reconstruct your teeth and reinsert them. You were quite a mess, Mr. Davidson, but we fixed you up almost as good as new. There may be some residual tenderness in your jaw for a day or so, but MODERN MEDICINE is a *wonder*. Also, you were very lucky your friends got you here as quickly as they did after your 'carriage accident.' And, uh, thought to bring all your teeth."

"Which was really fucking gross," Helly helpfully added, smiling and crossing her arms. "I never knew a tongue looked like that when it ..."

"Please stop, love," I said, grimacing. "I don't want to think about that, and I'm, uh, very sorry you all had to see that side of me. And thank you, again."

She walked over and took my hand. "Eh. It was no problem. We'd do it all again in a heartbeat."

"I know," I smiled.

The doc coughed, obviously uncomfortable with sentiment. "So, all of that said, we have a little more paperwork to process, but you should be free to go shortly. One of the nurses will pop in and get you squared away, and you can get back to your *cosplay*."

He said the last with a fair amount of derision, and no small amount of hypocrisy considering he had at some point chosen to become a dwarf out of fantasy tales. I guess, from his standpoint, there was a fine line between manifesting one's authentic self and *mostly* giving up scientific advancements for swords and leather armor. I figured he'd probably switch orbitals after this rotation if he felt this strongly. He turned and walked out the door.

"Thanks again, doc," I called after him. "But your bedside manner is kind of hurtful."

I looked my companions up and down. "Are you all good? Anyone hurt? I'm so sorry I kind of abandoned you all back there," I said. "I tried to stay awake. I tried to keep going ..."

"Shush, you," Helly said, squeezing my hand tighter. "You

almost died, you freaking idiot. I think we'll give you a pass this time. And we're all fine. I mean, we looked like hell when we dragged in here yesterday ... we were all beaten, bloodied and bruised pretty badly. But Doc Sleepy back there and his crew managed to sew us up and fix our shit back the way it was, more or less."

"So, what happened after I blacked out?" I looked at Bishop. "You still have the book?"

Bishop adopted a look of sheer panic. He began fishing around in his enormous sleeves, looking at his body and patting himself down. "Oh, no, Daniel! I forgot all about the book in the heat of battle!"

I gave him the stink eye. "That was an absolutely horrible performance, Elias. Not that your distinguished looks alone wouldn't merit you a place on the stage, but your acting is for shit."

He laughed. "Fair point. I only had the one acting class, and it's been ages. The book is safely hidden away in a gigantic safe in the basement of The Unicorn awaiting our return. Percy was more than happy to help, as usual."

"Oh, that's fantastic! Tell me more. I am guessing you bolted for the cart as planned?" I asked.

"Yes. Everything went to shit pretty fast after you called out, so I ducked and ran. I know you had Sallow give me some pointers, Daniel, but there's no way I could have ..."

"Hey, buddy," I said, waving his words away with a hand. "No one expected you to, ok? That was pro-level stuff, and not for newly-christened amateurs. And, to be honest, most of that training was just to help you not panic. You protected the book. You got it out of harm's way. You did your job better than anyone could have hoped." He smiled at me gratefully.

"So, the rest of us pros trashed the remaining vamps after you dipped," Helly winked at me. "We dragged your heavy ass to the cart and bolted, Bishop and me, getting you back to the clinic as fast as we could. We dropped you off, then ran over to The Unicorn to stash the book. Ariana and Sallow stayed behind to, um, destroy evidence. They picked up every last one of your damned Narcoject spines, by the way. Ariana said they did their best to position all the bodies like there had been some sort of vamp coup and internal struggle or some bullshit. Probably wouldn't fool anyone TOO invested in figuring it all out, but I think a helpful anonymous tip about the slaughterhouse in the basement might've gone a long way toward making the Shire Reeves not give too much of a fuck."

"Smart thinking," I agreed. "Well fucking done! Where are they now?"

"They are over with the Shire Reeves in the back room of The Unicorn, probably going over the events of your 'carriage accident' for the third or fourth time," she said. "We took down the murder wall, by the way. They obviously couldn't come interview you, but you guys being outsiders and having been seen about town, well ... I guess the Reeves are dotting their eyes and crossing their tees. Or crossing their eyes? You're lucky you slept through it, though, as we all know what a rotten liar you are."

I flipped her a half-hearted bird, but agreed. "It's a fair point. I prefer to shock people with the truth."

"Ariana also had Butch and Sundance hop back in the basket and covered them up," she added. "Lucky she's still an authorized user. She and Sallow dragged their metal asses back. They are currently in Percy's basement as well."

"Sooo," she said. "That's pretty much it for us. My battle leathers are at the cleaners, so I'm dressed like the locals."

"Hellooooo, nurse," I said, waggling my eyebrows and causing her to giggle.

"What've YOU been up to? Other than lying here sleeping like the lazy shit you are?" she added, still laughing.

"I had the craziest dream," I said. "Or not. Maybe it was a vision. Or near-death brain trauma stuff. I don't know. It seemed important somehow. I met half-alien Jesus. We sipped Mai Tais on a beach at sunset."

"Sounds ... romantic?" Bishop said, grinning. "Did the two

of you ..."

"Gah. No, Elias. For fuck's sake, it wasn't that kind of dream," I laughed. "Although, he was kind of handsome as far as bearded half-alien demigods go. Great personality, too. Still ... not my type. But there was something he gave me ... something critical to our survival. It was a symbol, I could barely make it out ... it was SO bright that it burned my eyes ..." I trailed off. *Holy shit,* I thought. I closed my eyes tightly.

And there it was, hovering in the darkness behind my eyelids, burned into my retinas: Angel Reaver. Shimmering and simmering, bleeding blue light and blazing with power. Which naturally explained why my vision had been blurry. Sometimes I am not the quickest tool in the drawer, nor the sharpest knife in the shed. Or however it goes. I blame it on being happy to see my friends.

"Quick," I said, still squeezing my eyes quickly shut. "Grab me something to write with! Now!"

Helly bolted over to the bedside table, yanking open a drawer. "Fuck! Empty," she called out as she spun and ran for the door. She ran back in as fast as her short, thick legs could carry her, scrambling a bit to make the corner. She had an actual pen and a prescription pad in her hand, which she thrust toward me. "Here!"

I opened one eye and grabbed the pen and paper. I started scribbling with one eye open, still able to see the glowing sigil with the closed eye. I closed both intermittently as I sketched, trying my best to get every nuance. After a few minutes, I held the pad up and stared. As best as I can describe it, it looked like a simple circle divided by a cross hair, the vertical line of which descended further below the circle's edge to form an inverted cross with an arrowhead. An M was stamped over it, elongated horizontally to resemble outspread wings, the bottom v of the letter extended into an x. A downward curved bar sat just beneath the crosshair's horizontal axis. It looked so simple, but the combination radiated menace and barely contained power, the sigil almost vibrating on the page. I could FEEL that it was right. I closed my eyes and the sigil burned there was gone.

Not taking any chances whatsoever, I had Helly grab my smartwatch bracer out of the cabinet nearby where the clinic had stashed my now clean clothes. I scanned the symbol, saved it to memory, backed it up to the cloud, AND sent it to Mary Ann, Helly and Ariana. I paused for a moment, deep in thought, then I also forwarded it to the Twins and my armorer on Elysia. And my mechanic. I would get Sallow's info later and have him forward it to the Templars as well. Done, I handed the pad to Helly.

"Can you hang on to that until I get dressed?" She agreed, ripping off the top sheet that bore the symbol, folding it and placing it in the pocket of her scrubs.

We chatted among ourselves for a few minutes, then a tall, Elven nurse came in with a digital clipboard that bore my electronic discharge papers. She unhooked all my leads and my IV cuff, and we completed my paperwork. Once we were done, the others stepped out in the hall and I got dressed. I joined them moments later.

"What now?" Helly said. "Head over to The Unicorn for a bite and hook up with the others?"

"That sounds perfect," I said, grinning. "Then ... we have to summon the devil."

CHAPTER TWENTY-NINE

Helly and Bishop just stared at me in stunned silence. I waited.

"You know," I said. "Satan? Lucifer, Ol' Scratch, Ol' Nick, Ol' Splitfoot, the Morning Star, Son of the Morning, Son of Perdition, the Prince of Lies, the Prince of Darkness, Lord of Hell, that mean Ol' Debil Man... and my personal favorite, from the Scots ... Ol' Clootie?"

"Doc?!" Helly yelled. "I think there's still something wrong with his brain! Like, more than usual!"

I laughed. "Nah. It's just that my pal Josh – A.K.A. half-alien Jesus - told me we'd have to get in touch with a certain rogue angel that has spent a few millennia fighting other angels. He'll have some tips for us."

"So, Satan isn't bad?" Bishop said, looking confused. "But he IS a rogue angel, just not one of the REALLY bad rogue angels that wants us dead?"

"Well, to be fair," I said. "Josh didn't say anything about him being GOOD per se, or even not BAD. Just that he'd be able and willing to help. Maybe it's an enemy of my enemy thing? I guess we'll see."

I ran down the rest of the salient points of my vision, such as it was. They seemed to take all the metaphysical stuff pretty well, all things considered. They probably thought I was bat-shit crazy and dreamed it all up, and, honestly, if it weren't for the Angel Reaver burned into my sight, I'd have agreed.

We left the clinic and walked back through town to The

Psychedelic Unicorn. Ariana and Sallow were waiting for us in the back room, which was no longer private and no longer the war room. (Rest in peace, murder wall.)

Ariana leapt off her bench and threw her willowy self at me, wrapping me in a hug and kissing my cheek fondly. She pulled me back to arm's length and looked at me, her green eyes scanning my face up and down for any remaining sign of injury, then pulled me into another embrace.

"Damn you, Daniel," she whispered into my ear. "Don't you EVER do that to me again."

She pulled away and stood back, crossing her arms. She sort of looked mad, but there was a hint of a smile in the corners of her mouth. But, she also looked about a half second from crying. Sallow stepped up, clasped my hand warmly, and pulled me into a bro hug, slapping me on the back.

"You're looking fit, you lucky bastard," he said. "Pity they couldn't fix that face of yours and make you any prettier."

I laughed and slapped him on the back as well. "Aww, Jonas. Don't start going soft on me, or I'll ..."

He pulled away, smiling, and clapped me on the shoulder. "I know, I know. Mum sends her regards, by the way."

We sat, and Percy came in. The big, burly orc pulled me back to standing and enveloped me in a huge hug, then basically picked me up and sat me back down like one would a toddler. We ordered a late lunch and a round of drinks as it was nearing mid-afternoon, and I filled Ariana and Sallow in on my dream meeting with Josh and the significance of the symbol I had sent to the elf.

I also got Sallow's smartwatch address and sent it to him, although his watch was currently sitting in the Shaggin' Wagon as it had been too modern to bring along. He gave me the address of someone in his order, and I sent the symbol to him with a brief message from Sallow.

I updated the elf and the knight with all the information about my vision with Josh and the need to call up Ol' Scratch, which is also a pretty fun nickname now that I think about it.

Still not as great as Ol' Clootie, though.

Like the others, they also looked at me a bit sideways, but considering all the other stuff we had going on with rogue angels out to kill us and a pseudo-magical book of doom, we all sort of reluctantly fell in line with the idea that it was hardly weirder than the rest of our bullshit. And there was literally no denying the power of the Angel Reaver glyph. Just looking at a sketch of the damned thing on an Rx pad made the hair on your arms stand up.

"So ... sound, symbol and intent, huh?" Ariana noted as our food arrived. "I guess that makes sense. Every story or myth you hear about angels usually involves sound or music ... harps, trumpets, songs of praise and worship. Most church services involve musical instruments or choirs. You think maybe it's because these beings are sensitive to sound? Like particular frequencies? I mean, sound is all about vibration, and that symbol, well ..."

"Huh," I said, picking up my MLT with bacon and taking a bite. "That's a really interesting take. I hadn't thought about it, but that all makes sense. And any time you hear about ANY sort of mystic or occult ritual, it involves sound, symbol and intent. Cryptic markings, alchemical symbols, singing or chanting. Maybe the beings from this other dimension are affected by sound more so than we are. Maybe it thins the veil or something or alters or disturbs the frequency they exist on. Fuck if I know."

"Maybe music also affects them on a visceral or physical level because they don't have any of their own?" Bishop said. "I mean, if you can't love, you can't create art. Music is like the perfect marriage of art and mathematics, right? But it's also like passion personified ... making music is nothing short of altering reality. You sort of wish sounds into existence and paint the contents of your heart onto time itself, filling the void of silence with beauty. It's the perfect act of creation."

We all stared at the priest.

"Dude," I said. "That was fucking profound. And beautiful.

Also, are you high? What sort of mushrooms are those, anyway?" I nodded toward his salad, grinning.

"Just portabellas, I think," he laughed. "But, no, Daniel. I just love music. It's a kind of magic."

"Yes, it is," I agreed. "And, also, that's the name of a song and album by the British rock band Queen. So, kudos for the super appropriate reference, even it was unintentional. Ten points to Hufflepuff!"

"Damnit," Sallow said, frowning. "I had hoped the doctors had cured you of that idiocy."

"Impossible," I said, laughing. "Can't be done. My idiocy runs too deep. It's integral to my very existence."

"So, you're even an idiot on a cellular level?" Helly chimed in, winking and taking a bite of her sandwich. "You're like a mitochondrial moron?"

"Hah hah," I said in a nasal, mocking voice. "But, also, probably."

"This is a shock to absolutely no one," Ariana said, smiling and sipping her wine. "So ... how do we summon the actual devil? And where and when do you plan on doing this?"

"Well, I was thinking of doing it here," I said. "I'll rent the room for the evening. OR ... maybe Percy won't mind us using the basement? A little more private. I can pop out and grab some supplies for the symbol part. I'm thinking maybe some chalk for the pentagram and some candles for ambiance? Josh said he was something of a traditionalist. And I can rig up Butch as a sound system. He has a pretty kicking external speaker. Although, I don't think the music needs to be loud, necessarily. Just present."

"Yeah," Ariana said. "Probably best to avoid waking anyone with our blatant use of illegal tech. The basement will definitely be better insulated and farther away from everyone, too."

"Absolutely," I agreed. "And, I mean, basements are inherently creepy. Have you ever been in a non-creepy basement? Even daylight basements are kind of creepy. I would venture to say that probably 95% of demon and devil summoning takes place in basements. So, also in keeping with tradition, I'm thinking midnight? I will be glad to spring for a room for the evening as you guys will probably miss the last barge home."

"Shit," Helly said. "Are demons real, too?"

"I … huh," I said, puzzled. "I actually have no idea. It didn't come up with Josh. Sallow?"

"No fucking clue, mate," the knight said. "Never seen one."

"I guess we could ask Ol' Lucy," I said. "If we have time. If he doesn't try to smite us or something."

"Probably best not to call him 'Lucy', then," Ariana laughed, picking at her fish and chips. "You might even have to … insert theatrical gulp here … *behave* for once?"

"Where's the fun in that?" I replied, taking a sip of dark lager. "But, yes, Ari … point well-made and received. I'll do my best not to insult the devil."

We finished our lunch, and I meandered to the bar and rented a couple of rooms, one for the guys and one for the ladies. I looked at my rapidly dwindling pile of cash and thought to myself that we had better wrap this thing up quickly. I could probably only handle a few more meals and rounds of drinks along with the requisite summoning supplies before needing to travel below decks to exchange some more credits. Unfortunately, I had been in too much of a hurry on Thursday and too goal oriented to think to do that.

I grabbed Helly for company, and we set out for … sigh … Ye Oldÿn Statiönairy Shöppe. Ariana popped up to her room for a nap, and Bishop and Sallow set out to explore the town a bit while we were gone.

Many filthy jokes (and a quick stop to see YiaYia for some coffee and baklava) later we came back to The Unicorn with our haul just as dusk was settling in. We had snagged five fat, blood-red pillar candles, matches, and a bag of white chalk. The boys were still gone, and as Ariana was still sleeping in the room she and Helly were sharing, Helly came back to my room for a nap.

That's it. That's all that happened. I swear. 100% true story. Nothing happened. We slept together. I mean ... actually *slept*. Totally. Just slept. Just took a nap. Totally didn't bone or anything. Never happened. Nope. I mean, look, you don't have to believe me or anything. It's up to you. I'm just saying that we slept. And not, like, after some absolutely incredible, passionate, mind-blowing, post-near-death experience, bed-breaking, acrobatic monkey sex. That didn't happen. At ALL. Just sleeping. A little nappy nap. All curled up together like otters. Totally innocent and wholesome. No taking of the totally adorbs and beautifully curvaceous blonde thicc-ness to Pound Town. No bumping of uglies, no knocking of boots, no checking of the suspension, no tweaks to the undercarriage, no two-person pushups, no making of the beast with two backs, no playing hide the bratwurst, and certainly – under no circumstances – was there ANY hot yoga. Nope. Never happened.

I swear to Josh.

So, later on, after our super-refreshing, non-coital and completely wholesome besties nap that totally wasn't a besties-with-benefits nap (And quite frankly, I resent the implication, you perverts.), we cleaned ourselves up a bit ... from our NAP ... and headed downstairs with our sack of summoning supplies.

The others were sitting in our usual spot and greeted us as we walked up and plopped down. It was getting close to last call, so Percy hooked us all up with a final round.

"Soooo ..." Ariana began. "How was your ... *nap*?" She gave an exaggerated wink to the both of us.

"Great," Helly said, grinning. "Thanks for asking! Best *sleep* I've had in ages. I feel so ... *refreshed*. I mean, napping by yourself is always great, but napping *with* someone is always SO much better. Especially when they are such a good ... *napper*."

"I mean, you're pretty much a champion sleeper there

yourself," I grinned. "I don't know that I've ever *slept* so hard."

"SO HARD," Helly agreed. "I mean, we really napped the ever-loving shit out of each other. That may have been one of my all-time greatest naps. EVER. Like top five."

"Only top five?" I frowned. "Man, I thought that was literally like a top two nap for me. Maybe even better than our last nap. Neck and neck. And, seriously, THAT was a nap for the ages. Fucking epic sleeping was done that day."

"Are you two talking about sex?" Bishop asked innocently, sipping his whiskey.

"Nope," I said. "Not even remotely. SO ... now that we have all that amusing innuendo out of the way ..."

"In YOUR endo," Helly chirped.

"Maybe, but you'll have to buy me dinner first," I fired back, laughing. "ANYWAY ... fuck ... back to business. We grabbed all the stuff we needed from that place with the awful name. Henceforth, I shall refer to it as The Umlaut Shop. So, it's last call on Sunday, right? Today is Sunday? So, 11:15ish? We should probably finish our drinks and head down to the basement. Percy said he was fine with us using it for whatever ... I didn't go into details ... as long as we clean up after ourselves."

"Hopefully we will just be wiping up chalk and candlewax and not cleaning up our own blood and entrails," Sallow said.

"Well, that's just horrific," I said. "Thanks for that, as always, Debbie Downer."

"Punchbowl shitter," Bishop added, chuckling into his drink.

"Fuck you both," Sallow replied, taking a swig of his pint.

We chatted a few more minutes and finished our drinks, then we left a tip for Percy on the table and headed into the main room. We walked past the bar and kitchen and into the back hall, where a creaky wooden stairway led down to the creepy-ass basement.

At the bottom of the stairs was a heavy wooden door bound in black iron. I lifted the latch and pushed the door open. We found ourselves in a dimly lit room, maybe 20 feet by 25, with walls made of unpainted stone block. Moonlight poured in through a few small transom windows. The room was fairly empty except for a few crates of produce, some old wooden boxes, and some blocky shapes covered with sheets. There were a few shelves filled with various bottles of liquor on one wall. A large black metal safe sat in the far corner. There were a few bracketed torches spread strategically around the room. I struck a match and lit a couple of them, and we got to work.

Ariana took a nail and some of the leftover red yarn from my murder wall and used it like a compass or surveying tool to draw a near-perfect chalk circle on the floor. She then marked the circle with five equidistant dots. Helly and Sallow grabbed the yarn, and Ariana had them stretch it between dots so she could use the material as a kind of ruler. In a few short minutes, we had an absolutely amazing pentagram thanks to the elf's keen mathematical mind and perfectionist tendencies. Sallow took the five pillar candles and placed one of them at each point of the star, lighting them one by one when the circle was complete.

Bishop had politely begged off actively participating in the ritual prep as it just didn't feel right for him as a priest to be involved in summoning Satan, whether or not he was the actual biblical bad guy or not. Which we all understood, naturally. I mean, we'd already pushed the poor guy out of his comfort zone in so many ways.

I put in my tactical earbud and activated Butch, who fired up his gravlifts quietly and hovered out of the wicker basket, tilting briefly to throw off one of Bishop's t-shirts.

"Everybody ready?" I asked the party, who all murmured agreement. "Ok. Here we fucking go. Symbol done. Intent is next. Everybody look at the center of the pentagram and focus your intent on inviting Ol' Scratch to pop in for a visit. Butch, dial up my media list, please, and play The Rolling Stones' Sympathy for the Devil, volume level two."

Butch did as I asked, and a second later, the low

sound of congas and shakers filled the basement along with Mick Jagger's assorted 'ows' and 'uhs.' Then, of course, the hauntingly soft piano keys and Jagger's classic lyrics. You know the ones. The song played quietly for a few verses, until it reached the part about guessing the narrator of the song's name. Then all the candles and torches went out and Butch's speaker fell silent.

CHAPTER THIRTY

Our eyes struggled to adjust to the rapid absence of light, and as they acclimated to the dim moonlight still shining through the small windows, we could see a white shape in the center of the pentagram come into focus: a seated figure, dressed in white.

Just as soon as we were able to see in the murky basement again, the torches and candles re-lit, the pillar candles' flames blazing three feet high or more before subsiding to their regular size.

Aside from being creepy as all hell, it kind of hurt. It was, however, undeniably badass and one *hell* of an entrance, if you'll pardon the pun.

The tall, thin man at the pentagram's center wore an immaculately tailored three-piece suit of white linen. A gold pocket watch chain stretched across his stomach to a vest pocket. A white fedora shielded most of his face from view as he was looking down, his elbows on his knees and his hands clasped in front of him, fingers intertwined. He sat on a simple, white metal folding chair of the type that could probably have been found by the hundreds at old-fashioned tent revivals of the 20th century.

He looked up slowly, cocking his head slightly to one side as he did so, revealing a handsome face with an olive complexion and a well-groomed short beard of salt and pepper. His eyes were jet black obsidian with no visible iris. He spoke to us in a raspy voice that sounded like it was being filtered through a throat full of coffin nails.

"Why have you ssssummoned me, mortalssss?" he croaked. "And you have failed to pay the blood sssacrifice ... I ssssshall have to make one of you pay ... with their life!"

We stared at him in horror, stunned into silence.

He unclasped his hands, raised the left next to his face, and snapped his fingers.

His solid black eyes disappeared instantly and were replaced by normal, human-looking brown eyes twinkling with merriment. He put his fist over his mouth, coughed into it, and then spoke to us in a perfectly pleasant baritone, accented with just a hint of the Mediterranean.

"Oh, my," he laughed. "That was fucking brilliant! You should have seen your faces. Absolute pants-shitting terror! I couldn't tell if you were all about to draw weapons, run screaming or just die of fright. So sorry ... but totally worth it."

"Damn, man," I said, exhaling the breath I hadn't known I was holding. "That was just fucking *mean*."

He raised his arms and gestured to himself with both thumbs. "Devil." He shrugged and laughed musically.

"Valid," Bishop said.

"So, I mean, you've got tons of names," I began. "Lucifer, Satan ... the list goes on. What should we call you? Can I call you ... Ol' Clootie?"

"I'd rather you didn't," he grinned. "Lou is fine. No need for formality." He leaned back in the chair and crossed his legs, sticking his hands in his pants pockets.

"Ok, so ... Lou," I frowned, trying to wrap my head around the nickname. With Jesus it had seemed easier. Maybe it was the suit. "I thought angels didn't have a sense of humor."

"They don't," he said. "But, I'm an archangel. We're *better*. Plus, I've always been a bit of an outlier and a rebel. It's kind of my thing."

"Fair enough," I said. "And hey, we're sorry to bother you. You're probably a busy guy ... wait. Josh said there's no heaven or hell, so, like what DO you do if you're not Lord of Hell?"

"A little of this, a little of that," he said. "Mostly, I kill angels."

"Wow," I replied. "That's dark. For a hobby and all. You ever think of taking up stamp collecting? Macramé?"

"Well, they're kind of dicks," he smiled grimly. "Especially the rogue angels who want to destroy your entire dimension. I mean, this is literally the only dimension that has pizza, tacos and beer. What the HELL are they thinking?"

"I know, right?" I agreed, laughing. "Also, why DO they want to wipe us all out?"

"Jealousy, mostly," Lou said. "And hate. And revenge. You see, you were Jehovah's favorites. He thought they were a bunch of knobs, which they are. Not that many of you aren't as well, but at least you're amusing knobs. Your world is the closest one to our dimension, and the rogues have always had designs on it. It's a lot prettier than where we are from. Or it was, until you lot trashed it beyond repair. I am pretty sure they were waiting on you all to kill each other off, but they never expected you to kill the whole planet. So, they're a little pissed off about that, too."

"How many of them are there?" Sallow asked. "I know some have visited, but why have they not just come over and wiped us out previously?"

"Oh, only about 100 or so. There used to be a lot more, but I've been hunting and killing them for a while now. They are vastly outnumbered by angels who don't want anything to happen to what's left of humanity in deference to their Father's wishes, and Joshua's," Lou said, pulling one hand out of his pocket and looking at his nails. "Plus, it's hard for them to visit, especially in large numbers. Something about the frequencies of this dimension being slightly out of phase. They're weaker here, too, but they are still no pushovers. I think they basically want to kill you all and use Raziel's book to try and remake their own Earth over there. It will just take them SO much longer. They were going to try and get it previously and use it to make your planet more habitable for them and facilitate their passage. Or some such garbage. I don't really know. I don't really ask them many questions. I am not interested in interrogation, only extermination."

"Sooo, slightly off topic," Bishop raised his hand as if he were a school kid. "If you're not Lord of Hell, and you don't punish the wicked when they die, do you still tempt people to do bad things? Are you still the Lord of Lies? If you're not the bad guy of the Bible, how have you gotten such a bad reputation?"

"Oh, I'm most definitely a bad guy," Lou smiled wickedly. "I don't JUST kill rogue angels. I kill them all. I hunt them for sport and pleasure because I hate them. To most angels, I am like a terrorist and a serial killer wrapped up in one smartly dressed package. In our world, in our dimension, I am like the love child of Hannibal Lector and Osama Bin Laden, raised with Joseph Stalin as my au pair." He stood and stretched, moving his neck from side to side and shooting his cuffs.

"But I'm not the LORD of anything in particular," he added. "And I have no reason to lie to anyone."

"So, that previous bit was not at all worrisome or creepy. How about all of that stuff about people making deals with you and trading their souls for fame and fortune and guitar skills and such ... that's all just made up, too, right?" I asked Lou.

"Hah. No, that's actually true," he laughed. "Or sort of. I love being summoned here. I can come on my own, but it's so much easier if I am invited. I usually manage to squeeze in a few good meals and a few rounds of drinks. People have conjured me up throughout history to try and bargain with me for their heart's desire. So, I play along and promise them whatever they ask for in return for their immortal soul. They sign a contract, I disappear in a theatrical puff of smoke with a tiny whiff of brimstone after telling them I'll take their souls when they die. And of course, I do no such thing. They usually improve skills on their own while striving for greatness. The placebo effect is rather amazing."

"But, other than fucking with people mildly and eating your food and drinking your beer and whiskey, I have absolutely no interest in humanity. I have never hurt a single hair on a human's head. Nor have I inspired any of you to do anything whatsoever. Humans have never needed my help to be horrible to each other or commit horrible acts."

"Why do you hate angels so much?" Ariana asked.

"My reasons are my own, and I have no wish to discuss them with you," Lou said. "Respectfully, it's none of your fucking business. No offense."

"None taken," Ariana said in a small voice, swallowing hard. "Sorry to pry. There's just so much we don't understand."

"That, I am afraid, has always been and will always be a part of the human condition," Ol' Clootie said. (Sorry, Lou. I just couldn't help myself.)

"So, you guys seem just *great*," Lou added, turning the chair around backwards and straddling it, leaning his arms on its back. "But I have a date with the nearest all-night pizza joint, so let's get down to the reason you called ... shall we?"

"Cool, cool. Right. So, Josh gave us Angel Reaver," I said. "And that covers the symbol part, right? He said you might be able to help us with the sound component."

"Oh, *yes*," he said, rather sensuously, as if he were savoring every moment of what would come next, like a predator about to enjoy a long session of fucking with the mind of its prey before consuming it whole.

"I can certainly help you with that," he said, continuing. "Are any of you familiar with something called The Devil's Chord? Sometimes called The Devil's Tritone?"

"Is that like The Brown Note?" Helly asked.

"Hmmm. Oddly, sort of?" Lou replied, quirking his lips to one side in a contemplative fashion.

"It's a particular chord that The Church banned for centuries because it sounded so evil," Bishop said. "No music was allowed to include it."

"Very good, priest," Lou said, smiling. "And, honestly, even though I didn't create it, I have to admit, I am a fan. It is so ominous and fraught with inherent menace that it was not used in popular music until the late 1960s and early 1970s. I am sure you've already figured out that certain vibrations, especially sound, *especially* music can affect celestials in a positive or negative way?"

"We had actually been discussing that very thing not long before we rang you up," I said.

"Good. That gives me *slightly* more faith in you. So, in a sense, The Church was right to ban it, at least for their purposes. And those of the cabal of angelic sympathizers that has ever been a part of Mother Ecclesia. The Devil's Chord hurts garden-variety angels ... wounds them deeply ... the frequencies wreaking havoc with the very fiber of their being and their already tenuous grip on this reality when they are here. When coupled with Angel Reaver, the results are devastating. And deadly."

"So, what's a good example of The Devil's Chord that we can get our hands on, Lou? Are there any bands or musicians that used it a lot?" I asked Ol' Splitfoot, er, Lou.

He smiled an extremely wicked grin. The sort of grin that made me think that maybe he had been the guy that invented evil grins way back in the day when the universe was young. "There are a few. And, oh, Daniel. From what Joshua has told me of you, you are going to just LOVE this."

He told us. He was right. I laughed non-stop for like a minute or two ... deep, down belly laughs ... long enough that the others were looking at me and probably thinking about my recent brain injuries again.

I would totally table my worry and anxiety over Jesus and Satan discussing me privately until another time, perhaps a moment where there was a bathroom in close proximity.

Our business concluded, we thanked Ol' Nick and wished him the best of luck in finding some pizza and beer in the near future. He stood and the chair disappeared.

"Before I go, though, Daniel ..." Lou said, adjusting his tie. "There is one more thing."

He summoned the evilest of grins again and looked me dead in the eye. The effect was beyond chilling.

"The Prince of Darkness? That one's pretty close." He winked and disappeared. I might've peed a little.

The lights went out again, and all around us, in the dim,

creepy-ass basement, we heard Lou's deep, baritone laughter surrounding us, seemingly coming from everywhere at once.

"Holy SHIT," Helly said, shivering. "That guy knows how to make a fucking exit, too."

CHAPTER THIRTY-ONE

We cleaned up from the summoning, which luckily only involved chalk and candlewax. (In your stupid face, Sallow.) The party was pretty drained emotionally and physically, despite some of us getting in a fan-fucking-tastic NAP earlier (Seriously. You may have trust issues.), so we all wished each other a good night and headed upstairs to our rooms to bed down for the evening.

In the morning, we came down for a quick breakfast, then saw Ariana and Helly off on the barge toward the little hamlet they call home with many hugs, kisses, fist bumps and the like. Ariana gave both Bishop and Sallow a peck on the cheek, causing both of them to blush and me to stock that little experience away for future insults. We had made plans to talk over the next few days once Bishop, Sallow and I returned to Elysia. I had some calls and visits to make as well as a meeting and showdown with Archer - and hopefully his masters – to set up. I had some ideas as to how we could pull this off, but I'd have to let them germinate and gel over the next few days. Some of the calls I could make from the Shaggin' Wagon on the way home, as the subsequent measures fired up and set in motion by the recipients would involve some lead time.

Bishop, Sallow and I said our good-byes and see-you-soons to Percy and thanked him for his excellent service. And paid him well for said service and consideration with the last of my gold notes, of course. Naturally, prior to that, we followed the huge orc back down to his creepy-ass basement to obtain one extra-special, angel-written, black-leather-bound literary nuke. Percy, ever the soul of discretion, didn't ask one single question about the book when he handed it back wrapped in a thick, brown canvas swaddling, save to raise his eyebrows in an "are you fucking morons sure you know what you're doing" sort of way. It was a *very* specific look.

Helly and Bishop had parked my pushcart to the side of The Unicorn, so we put the basket containing my drones and Bishop's laundry on it, tossing the book inside as well, and headed out of town back toward the hangar bay where we had parked the Shaggin' Wagon. Leaving Narthwych was bittersweet, I have to admit. We had only been in the tiny town for a short time, but it had been an extremely eventful and fateful one.

I mean, we squeezed a lot of life experiences into the space of five days ... reunions, meeting new friends, lots of great food and booze, planning and executing a heist, a near-fatal fight with a shit-ton of vampires (For me, anyway. For them, fatal as FUCK.), riding country roads hidden in sex furniture, discovering a mass murder (and avenging that shit), meeting Jesus *and* Satan, AND having one of the best naps of my life with an old friend. And I built my first – but certainly not my last – murder wall. Frankly, I was worn the absolute fuck out, as were my companions. We didn't quite meander back to the van, but we sure as shit didn't get in a hurry. The walk was pleasant, relatively quiet, and blissfully uneventful.

I will note that the mid-point bridge over ... fucking enormous heavy sigh ... Thee Watyrway was a bit more of a pain as we now had to shove a pushcart up one side at great effort and then slowly and deliberately pull against it as we rolled down the other side so as to not lose control and send the cart careening, possibly dumping the contents in the water (watyr?).

We arrived back at my beautiful ride at around 9:30 AM local time. The three of us stowed our weaponry and the drones (Who are SUCH good boys. Yes they ARE!) and then changed out of our Medieval Fun Time wear back into casual, comfy athletic wear and naturally, very, very cool repro band t-shirts, courtesy of your friendly neighborhood purveyor of cool shit.

I set the autopilot for Elysia and the hangar bay closest to the shop, then settled in with Sallow and Bishop to discuss plans. We had roughly 16.5 hours of real-time journey, but we would gain 7 hours on the trip, putting us home around 6:45 or 7 or so, if my mental math was correct. Not that math was ever my strong suit.

We sat down around the Wagon's small back table with a pot of coffee and some protein cookies (What? Don't judge. You spend some quality time fighting modern, cyber-enhanced vampires and get back to me with your nutritional needs.) to discuss our plans upon arrival at Elysia, my home orbital as well as Sallow's ... and soon to be Bishop's, most likely.

"So, I assume you've got something in mind as far as an endgame goes?" Sallow started off, sipping his coffee and munching on a healthy-ass cookie, which can also be delicious, so don't be so fucking judgey.

"I have some ideas knocking around in my head," I replied, eating my TASTY AF cookie. "I put in a call to my armorer, and she's going to be waiting on us when we get back. I'm going to have ALL of my bladed weapons inscribed with Angel Reaver, and I've already put in an order for ammunition in various calibers that will have a tiny version of the glyph carved into them as well, including broadhead arrows. I'm not taking any chances. Even beyond this meeting."

"That's fucking smart," Sallow said, grudgingly. "Especially for someone with your ... *condition*." He whispered the last.

"Wait 'til I get going!" I said, in my best Wallace Shawn voice.

"Well played, sir," Bishop said. "10 points to Ravenclaw!" I gave Bishop a high-five.

"Goddamnit," Sallow said. "Not you, too. Anyway, moving on to less idiotic pastures, I will call the Temple armorer after our conversation and have him do the same to everything we own. Won't be quick or cheap, but hell, we're paying the guy a salary whether he's in the forge or not, so he might as well earn his keep."

"How many of your brothers and sisters do you think we can count on helping us?" I asked the knight.

"I'd say as many as we can scrounge up on our limited time schedule, so I dunno, really," he replied. "My best guestimate is about 25 or so?"

"How many of you are there in total?" Bishop asked.

"I'm actually not allowed to talk about that, even to allies," Sallow said, frowning. "Let's just say quite a few more than 25 and leave it at that."

"But our little potentially universe-destroying situation doesn't merit more assistance?" I asked, a little snarky but also genuinely confused as I finished my cookie. Also, damn, I thought, these cookies are delicious as well as nutritious. (So there. Nyah.)

"I mean, I'd love to say yes," he said, shrugging. "But, to be honest, the Order is typically handling more than one potentially apocalyptic event at a time, Davidson. Lots of balls in the air that we are juggling constantly, you know?"

I grinned. "So, you handle a lot of balls. Probably gets that from his mum," I added as an aside to Bishop, who chortled and almost spit coffee out his nose.

"Damnit, I KNEW as soon as it came out of my mouth that I was in trouble," Sallow said, placing his palm over his forehead.

"That's what *she* said!" Bishop said, reaching out and giving me a fist bump, which we exploded. Loudly.

"If I could hate you both to death ..." the knight began. "But, anyway, yes. Fuck off. Lots of things going on."

"Ok," I said, reluctantly. "I get it. I have a few more heavy hitters I'm calling in. Also have a call in to my mechanic to make some tweaks to the Shaggin' Wagon that may come in handy. Speaking of which, does your order have any weapons that you currently use against interdimensional threats? Anything that would work on rogue angels? Surely you haven't all been stumbling around completely in the dark since the Order was decimated?"

"Oh, we have a few things," he offered. "None as potentially devastating as the Angel Reaver sigil, but a few that would definitely help put a hurt on them. Especially if coupled with all the rest. My favorite is called Unholy Water."

"That sounds metal as fuck," I noted. "Tell me more, good knight."

"Good night to you, too," Sallow said, grinning.

"Sigh. A for effort, but they can't all be comedy gold, Jonas," I grinned. "Still ... hit me with some deets on this magical liquid."

"Fine. Everyone's a fucking critic," he said. "It's this red liquid we have formulated, mostly based on trial and error. I'm not sure what's in it, honestly, as that's above my pay grade and I'm just one of the dumbass grunts who gets to use it in battle. But it causes them a lot of pain."

"What sort of delivery system do you use?" I inquired.

"You're going to laugh, but high-pressure water guns," Sallow replied. "They look like the Super Soaker 5Ks that the kids use, only with all metal and carbon fiber components. We also have rigged up some smoke grenades that use it. They also work well."

"So, it works well in an atomized form through an air-delivery system and as a pressurized liquid?" I asked thoughtfully. "That gives me some ideas."

"So, are you actually going to hand over the book during the meet and then try to recover it?" Bishop asked. "That seems kind of risky. Couldn't they just disappear or teleport away or whatever they do? Then, like 10 minutes later, we blink out of existence without any chance whatsoever to stop them?"

"Yeah," I said. "That's a great question. I've been thinking on that one. I can't just hand them the book. I could try and pawn off a duplicate, but I think they'd know. They might've not seen it in person, though, or if they have, it was probably millennia ago. I might have something in mind that could fool them. I will put in a call to this lady I know. She is a professional booksmith that specializes in restoration and reproduction. She helps me out a lot with some of the antique printed material I find that has been damaged by water or fire or the ravages of time. I think I could have her make up a bang-up copy."

"Won't that still contain all the language they need to fuck us ... and everything else ... up?" Sallow said. "All they need is an accurate representation of the symbols, not necessarily the original."

"That's the way I see it, too, unfortunately," I agreed. "But I may have a way around that. She uses AI assist to help her recreate text sometimes, and her scanner can literally run through an entire book, page by page, in a few hours' time. I figure we can ask her to program the AI so that it distorts or warps or modifies and otherwise renders enough characters useless that it will ruin the inherent power. Maybe every other glyph or every three or something? Close enough to the real thing to fool someone at a glance, even someone who speaks the language, but nowhere near enough to pass a thorough inspection. Which means we'll have to handle the transaction and then basically make sure none of them ever has enough time to sit down with the book to work some destruction and realize we fucked them over."

"By killing them," Sallow said. "You're talking about killing them, correct?"

"I mean, absolutely," I replied with a grim smile. "Every last one of the motherfuckers we can get. Otherwise, they'll keep trying and trying until they get the book or find another means to wipe us and the remainder of humanity out of low orbit and into oblivion."

"You think you can get them all there? Won't that be suspicious?" the knight asked, taking a gulp of his coffee.

"Probably," I said, shrugging. "I mean, it'd set off alarm bells with me, for sure. But, we kind of have the power and hold all the cards here. We have the book. We could just tie Bishop's old cinderblock to it and drop it in some deep part of the ocean where they will never find it. God's not around to retrieve it this time, and even if Ol' Yahweh were here, I doubt he'd be so inclined."

"True enough," Sallow said. "Still, risky."

"What exactly have we done so far that wasn't a risk?" I asked, smiling.

"Fair," he allowed.

"Daniel," Bishop began. "I have a question. If you change half or most of the symbols, won't it change the, um, frequency of the thing? Or whatever makes it radiate power the way it does? They might not have ever read it, but I'm sure some of them have been around it … even if it was ages ago. I mean, I could tell it was the genuine article after almost a decade of not having it around, and I'm just a man."

"That is an excellent question, Elias, and one of the first stumbling blocks I thought of," I said. "But, I have an idea. Let's do a little experiment and see if it works. Can you, as a sensitive, I guess, tell the difference in the book and Angel Reaver? Is it like apples and oranges?"

I retrieved the book, took it out of its canvas wrapping and then grabbed the prescription pad sheet with my original drawing of the angel-killing glyph out of my pocket. I placed them side by side on the small table between us.

"Close your eyes and really concentrate," I said. "Hold your hands out and I will switch the two up a few times. I'll place one under each hand, and we'll see if you can tell which is which and if their energies are similar or not."

"I hate when you do stuff that makes you sound clever," Sallow said with his trademark grimace. "I far prefer to think of you as the dipshit jester who says 'fuck' too much."

"Even when I am cleverly saving our asses and those of everyone we know … and don't know?" I asked, grinning.

"Fair point, smart-arse," he capitulated with a half-smile.

Bishop closed his eyes and I placed the book and the glyph a few inches under his outstretched hands. I then moved them back and forth randomly like a street magician playing a cup game. "Ok, Padre," I said when I was satisfied the switcheroo had been sufficiently confusing to a man whose eyes were closed. "Tell us what you feel."

Bishop squinted his already closed eyes hard in concentration and was silent for a moment or two.

"I mean, there's no comparison as far as the *amount* of energy I feel," the priest said. "The book is underneath my left and the glyph is under my right. It's like comparing the heat of a candle to a raging inferno that has enveloped a whole city block. But, like, as far as the types of energy go, they seem really close. Like, they are still both heat ... an apple to an orchard full of apples, I guess?"

"That is fucking fantastic," I said to Bishop. "You can open your eyes. Well done! That is VERY good news. Now, let's try another experiment."

I walked over to a drawer and rummaged around for a few items. I kept my back to the other two and scribbled something without them being able to see what was going on. I stuck the remaining items in my pocket. Then, I turned, quickly putting my hands behind my back as I did so.

"Ok, this time, both of you stretch out your hands over the table and close your eyes," I said. They complied, and I walked over and placed the Angel Reaver sigil under one set of hands and a sheet of paper with a crudely drawn cartoon under the other.

"Now, tell me what you feel," I said. "Bishop first, then I want your opinion, Sallow."

"Ok," Bishop said with his eyes completely shut. "These feel ... pretty damned close, maybe even identical. Definitely two candles. Two apples."

"Sallow?" I asked, clasping my hands together expectantly in anxious anticipation.

"I concur," the knight said. "The hair is standing on both my arms, and it feels like there's a live, unshielded electrical wire under both of my palms. Energy matching energy as far as I can tell."

"Fucking AWESOME," I laughed with glee. "You two chuckleheads open your eyes."

They did and looked down. Under Bishop's left and Sallow's right, there was a new drawing of Angel Reaver on a plain, white sheet of paper. Under Sallow's left and Bishop's right, there was another plain, white sheet of paper on which I had drawn a cartoon penis with hairy testicles and a smile.

Both laughed lightly, with Sallow's being part groan, and looked to me somewhat incredulously for an explanation.

"This is fucking impossible," Sallow said. "And, really, your drawing skills are for shit."

"It was quick and dirty," I said, laughing. "Very dirty. But it got my point across."

"But … how, Daniel?" Bishop asked, staring at me as if I had just pulled a rabbit the size of a 1972 Buick out of a tiny top hat.

"Check this shit out," I said. I brought two of the three other objects I had dug up out of my pocket. I placed a small candle stub on the table and lit it with a match. I picked up the hastily scrawled dick pic and held it a few inches over the flame. When I did so, the heat from the candle created a reaction on the paper, and slowly, a drawing of Angel Reaver appeared behind the cartoon penis, looking as if it had been written in semi-transparent brown ink.

"What the actual hell?" Sallow said, his eyes wide. "How did you … no. You're joking."

"I mean, usually, but not this time," I grinned, throwing the paper with the newly revealed glyph on it down on top of the other drawing and snuffing the candle. I pulled the third object from my pocket and tossed it on top of the sketches.

Bishop picked up the small, capped yellow marker and read the words printed on the side in festive red ink.

"ACME Joke Shop, Elysia. Why laugh at the rest when you could buy the best? ACME Invisible Ink." He looked up at me. "Seriously, Daniel? A children's toy from a joke shop?"

"Yup!" I said, laughing. "And why not? Actual spies used

to use this stuff back in the day on Earth That Was. It's lemon-juice based. Reacts with heat and becomes visible. But, apparently, the glyph has power whether you can see it or not, which is amazing news and far better than I could have hoped for. I'm practically shitting myself with joy over here."

"Please don't," Sallow pleaded. "So, what's your plan? I think I have an idea, but I want to hear you say it."

"I have my booksmith friend print Angel Reaver on every single page of the fake book in invisible ink. The fake book will, of course, be bound identically," I said. "She and her pet AI will then cover each page with a close approximation of the symbols ... her printing process is cold, by the way, and won't affect the symbols underneath as long as they have dried. They'll look real enough to pass a casual inspection by an angel that has never seen the book or that hasn't seen it since before the dawn of time. Then, we pay her well, snatch the fake book, hand it off to Archer and his pals, who will feel its power and buy it hook, line and sinker. We get paid handsomely, then double-cross and murder the sons of bitches who want to destroy our world and everything and everyone we love. Sound good? Also ... I said 'snatch.'"

They both just stared at me. I get that reaction a lot.

"Fucking A," Sallow said. "I take back every bad thing I ever said about you being a dipshit. That is a pretty solid fucking plan, Davidson."

"Wow," Bishop said. "I mean, just wow."

"I'll take that as an agreement, you handsome piece of clerical man flesh, you," I said to the priest. "Ok, so we have a plan. Let's make some calls and put this shit into action, ok?"

And, well, we did just that.

CHAPTER THIRTY-TWO

Sallow called his order and put things in motion with them, providing for the alteration of weapons and some additional trigger fingers and sword arms. We had set a tentative meeting date seven days hence among ourselves, so we had a lot to do in a short amount of time.

I placed a call to a friend of mine that works at the Repat Center in my neighborhood to try and get some paperwork started for Bishop. Repatriation Centers sort of work like departments of immigration, human resources, housing, employment, and mental health all in one, handling not only survivors from Canaan – of which there are far fewer a decade later, obviously – that are in need of psychological evaluation and treatment, but also others seeking to move from one orbital to another. Canaan survivors are required to be registered and to undergo an extensive battery of tests prior to resettlement to ensure they are fit to be among the general population.

It was my hope that Bishop had managed to re-acclimate to "polite" society somewhat over the course of our recent adventures. Not that my friends and I are polite by any stretch of the imagination, but in our defense, we are extremely loving and supportive. So, he could've done a lot worse. To me, the priest seemed far more normal after leaving Avalon than he did when I found him in the church basement, and to be honest, he wasn't that bad off then. Certainly more stable than many would have been after being held captive for so long. Of course, I am probably a poor judge of normal.

My next move was to reach out to Mary Ann to fill her in on the latest, and honestly, just to hear her voice, which I missed terribly. We chatted for a few minutes, and she showed appropriate concern regarding my injuries at the hands of the master vampire, which I of course downplayed. I told her our estimated time of arrival and she promised to close early and stick around the shop until we showed. I also had her invite the Twins over as well, so I could give them the lowdown and engage their services for the meeting with Archer and his angelic posse.

Bishop, Sallow and I spent the time playing cards and insulting each other. We enjoyed a decent lunch, primarily of dishes that were less rustic and more exotic than Percy's cuisine had been. Not that the food provided by Percy and his kitchen staff was not amazing in every way, but we were definitely all ready for a change. The replicator food was never as good as meals cooked with love and craft, whether from replicated ingredients or fresh, but it was pretty damned good, nonetheless. Largely, though, the trip was uneventful, which was extremely refreshing after the week we had all experienced.

Around 7:30 PM, the Shaggin' Wagon arrived in Elysian airspace and was granted permission to dock. Inside the hangar bay, we took a vehicle elevator to the surface and drove the few blocks to my shop. I parked in the garage and unloaded all of my gear as quickly as possible so that I could usher the guys upstairs to meet Mary Ann. I dumped everything next to my soda machine armory and shooed everyone past the billiard table, multicade and pinball machine and upstairs, where we exited at the back of the shop.

We had barely crested the stairs and opened the door into the shop proper when I heard Mary Ann's musical bellow from the bar up front.

"Daniel Davidson!" my lovely orc partner yelled, shaking the windows a bit. "Get your sweet ass up here and give me hugs!"

I mean, what's a guy to do when a hot she-orc that can bench press you and three friends and the sofa you are sitting on gives you an order like that? You fucking get up there and give her hugs, that's what. We serpentined and slalomed our way through the stacks, with both Bishop and Sallow stopping briefly along the way to gawk at some of the albums or curiosities on the shelves.

I was only within arm's reach for a split second when Mary Ann reached out and threw her arms around me, picking me up off the floor and embracing me tightly. So tightly in fact that it bordered on uncomfortable. She kissed my cheek and held me close for a moment. I didn't mind one bit. I hugged her back as hard as a pitiful human can and kissed her cheek as well.

"Missed you, partner," I said. "I am so sorry I didn't call more. And I'm sorry I left you minding the shop. And thank you so much for everything. I know you probably felt like a glorified secretary running interference for me and stuff."

"It's fine, D," she said, placing me back on the ground but still holding onto my shoulders. "But next time, I go with. We have employees for a reason, and my needs aren't confined to the sexual realm. Sometimes, I need to be out there with you, pulling off heists and kicking asses and crushing skulls."

"I see you, Ms. Maguire," I said, smiling. "Honestly, though, it's probably better that you weren't with us. There's not a sex couch known to humankind that will fit you inside." I stammered and caught myself quickly at her glare. "That would fit your enormous but beautifully proportioned bulk that is perfect in every way and that doesn't have an ounce of fat on it and is the object of many, many fantasies orbital wide."

"Nice save, dick," she laughed. "So, rudeness personified, introduce me to your new friends."

"Oh, yeah," I said. "Apologies, boys. Please give it up for the lovely and talented Ms. Mary Ann Maguire, barkeep, bouncer, best friend, bookkeeper, and badass. My business and mostly platonic life partner."

Mary Ann gave a small, rather comical curtsey, pulling out the hems of an imaginary skirt.

"Mary Ann, I would like to introduce Father Elias K. Bishop ... what does the K stand for, anyway? Kevin? Kelvin? Keef? Kweef?" I said. "Anyway, Episcopalian priest, former basement gimp, fellow lover of obscure pop culture bullshit, admirer of Mr. Rogers, and totally stand-up guy. He's a fucking beauty, he is."

Bishop took a little bow and stepped forward, taking one of Mary Ann's giant hands in both of his.

"I am so very pleased to meet you, Mary Ann," he said, literally oozing that humble sincerity he is so fucking good at. "Daniel has become quite dear to me in the past few days, and as he holds you in such high esteem, I am beyond elated to make your acquaintance and look forward to getting to know you." He kissed her hand, then. If anyone else had done it, it would have been either cheesy or creepy, but Elias is the kind of guy that sells you on himself immediately, without even trying.

"You fucking smoothie," I noted. "You almost made her blush, which is the ... hell. I've never seen it. 10 points to Hufflepuff, you erudite bastard, you."

He laughed and let go of her hand, but still maintained eye contact with the orc, who probably had at little over a foot on him in height, smiling all the time and radiating peace and happiness ... the giant dork.

"And last but certainly least is Templar Knight Sir Jonas Sallow," I said, clapping the grim-faced asshole on the shoulder. "Don't tell him I said so, but he's a fucking beauty, too, and a hell of a fighter. I'd let him be my wingman any time. Despite his obviously sour disposition and homely looks."

Sallow grimaced, as is his way. But he reached out and took Mary Ann's hand and shook it firmly.

"Pleasure, Ms. Maguire," the knight said formally. "You partner is a dick, but he's competent and good in a pinch, and despite his idiocy, I might trust him to watch my back. On occasion. If there were no actual tough guys available."

"Oooh, he's snarky," Mary Ann said to me, still grasping Sallow's hand. "I like it. Can we keep him?"

"Oh, I suppose," I said. "He's a little weird around strangers and pisses himself often, but he's sort of cute in a weird, British way. He really puts the cock in Cockney. I guess we can let him hang around until we find a decent substitute."

Introductions done, we walked over to the bar and sat down. Mary Ann offered to pour us some libations, and we gratefully accepted. She poured each of us a double of Talisker 10-year and handed them out. I nodded my thanks, as did the others. She reached up and grabbed herself a bottle of vanilla vodka and poured some over ice with a splash of coconut rum. I would have made some comment about girly drinks, but I valued my life. Also, I don't judge. I will drink the shit out of fruity beverages with umbrellas in them.

About this time, the front door buzzer sounded, and we looked up to see the Twins standing outside on the sidewalk, waiting to be granted entry. Mary Ann reached under the counter and pressed a button, and the two men opened the door and stepped inside. They walked over to the bar and greeted us.

"Hola, motherfuckers," said the gigantic black-skinned, bald man that made up one-half of my own personal wrecking crew. Carlos Henderson was one of the largest, non-augmented human beings I knew. He stood almost seven feet tall, almost eye-to-eye with Mary Ann, who still had at least two inches of height on him. Almost as wide as he was tall, Carlos' massive muscular frame threatened to rip out of whatever ensemble he was currently wearing, which was a bright yellow hoodie and jeans at the moment. The hoodie sported the same grinning anime character as Bishop's backpack. I can't think of her name at the moment. He placed a dinner plate sized hand on my shoulder, and I stood to embrace him.

"Holy SHIT, it is good to see you, pal," I said. He hugged me tightly and patted me on the back hard enough to almost make me dot my drawers.

"Good to see you, Danny," he replied, reaching up to affectionately pat the back of my head.

"What the fuck am I? Chopped liver? The red-headed step-child?" The other man asked, moving in and prying us apart.

John Bryant Cox, A.K.A. Johnny Boy, pulled me into a hug of his own. No less humongous than my brother Henderson, his closely cropped brownish hair barely covered his round thumb-like head. He and his ridiculously outsized musculature embraced me, his pale, freckled skin blushing pink as he did so.

"Fucking been a minute," Johnny Boy said, releasing me. "Hate the apocalyptic circumstances, but it's so good to see you, man."

Mary Ann ran around the bar and embraced both of the giants in turn, both of whom greeted and embraced her warmly.

"The fuck are you still doing hanging around this loser?" Carlos said to her, grinning ear-to-ear as he matched her hug, petting her back lovingly. "You could have any gig you want, you fucking rock star."

Mary Ann laughed. "I know. But, I feel sorry for him. He has this sad puppy quality that I just can't seem to leave behind. And he makes me laugh. That goes a long way."

Johnny Boy stepped up and joined in and they shared a group hug.

"You're as beautiful as ever, Mary Ann," he said in his slow, southern drawl. "Any time you decide you want to settle down, you just give me a call. I'll make an honest orc woman out of ya."

Mary Ann laughed and slapped him lightly on the cheek. "As if I could ever decide between the two of you!"

"Who says you have to?" Carlos said, pulling back and waggling his eyebrows. "I'd totally cross the fence for you, darlin'. The redneck is a bit annoying with his well-then-there bullshit, but I reckon if anyone can make it worth my time to hang out with his dumb ass, it's you. I promise, we'll be perfect gentlemen and take turns."

"Where's the fun in that?" Mary Ann laughed and walked back behind the bar, where she poured a double of Black Jack for Johnny and a double of Patron for Carlos.

"Boys," I said to Bishop and Sallow. "These are the Twins, Carlos Henderson and John Bryant 'Johnny Boy' Cox. Two of the finest fighters and drinking companions one could find on all of the orbitals. My Blaxican brother Carlos is a heavy gunner, and my man Johnny is a demolitions expert. Not that you'd know from looking at him. You'd think his entire wheelhouse involved fucking his sister."

Johnny Boy feigned a cry of rage and pretended to punch me in the gut. I doubled over, and he pulled me upright, squeezing my shoulder. "I've missed you, you dumb sonofabitch. You know, you don't HAVE to wait until you're up to your gooch in world-ending bullshit to call us, right? We could just pop over for a drink sometime or go out for pizza? I'm almost insulted."

"Yeah, Danny," Carlos added, taking a sip of his tequila. "It's nice to be needed, but it's even better to be wanted."

"Aw, fellas," I began. ""Fuck. I know. I've been busy, but there's no excuse. I should reach out more often. I can order a pizza right fucking now, if it'll make you two little bitches stop whining." I grinned.

"Then do it, you pussy," Johnny Boy said, laughing. "Chicago deep dish if you please. Pepperoni, Italian sausage, mushrooms, pepperoncinis and black olives."

"Done and done," I said, tapping on my smartwatch and keying in the order. "But only because you asked so nicely."

"If the two of you are done sucking each other's' dicks, how about you fill us in on whatever the fuck is going on?" Carlos said. "Also, make mine a New York style, same toppings. I'm not down with no fucking casserole."

"You're killing me," Johnny Boy said to him, backhanding him lightly on the chest. "But whatever. You get down with your little thin-ass crust bullshit. So, yeah, Danny. Fill us in."

I did. I started with Archer's commission, recounted the tale of meeting Bishop and Sallow, described our adventures on Avalon in detail, and told them of our plan to defeat and double-cross the rogue angels. They sat silently, sipping their drinks and listening until I had finished. At that time, as if right on cue, our pizzas arrived. I had doubled up on both so that Bishop, Sallow and Mary Ann and I could also enjoy the savory goodness. I mean, you can't smell pizza and not want pizza.

As we tore through our food, the Twins expressed their incredulity at pretty much everything we had experienced. They got a huge kick out of us Trojan Horsing a sectional fuck couch, as I knew they would. Both were skeptical of my meeting with Josh and our summoning of Ol' Splitfoot.

"If it were anyone but you telling me this absolutely bug-fuck crazy story, Daniel, I'd be out the door already," Carlos said. "But it IS you, so ... it's still fucking weird, but I'll buy it. What do you need from us?"

"I sent you both Angel Reaver from the hospital," I said, tapping on my smartwatch for emphasis. "I'd recommend putting it on all your weapons and ammo. If you don't have an armorer who will do it, let me know. Mine will, but we have to be quick about it. I already feel like I am overwhelming her. But, the plan is to go big. Scorched earth, no survivors. It's literally what you beautiful bastards are best at. Providing we can secure the payment promised by delivery of the book, we'll all be golden. If not, well, we'll probably be dead anyway."

"Now who's the fucking Debbie Downer?" Sallow said.

"Pipe down, you," I said, taking a bite of pizza. "I'm just being a realist."

"Oh, so when I do it, I'm a 'punchbowl shitter,' and when you do it, it's realism?" Sallow said, sipping his Scotch. "I fucking see how it is."

"This guy shits in punchbowls?" Johnny Boy said.

"That's generally considered bad form, hermano," Carlos said. "No one likes a punchbowl shitter."

"Right?" Mary Ann chimed in. "Use the litter box like a civilized person."

"Far more hygienic," I offered. "Plus, it always blows the cat's fucking MIND."

"I've never actually ..." Sallow sputtered. "Good lord, this is like trying to plan an apocalypse avoidance event - or whatever the fuck this murderous con job is - with my sister's kids!"

"You have a sister?" Bishop said. "Huh."

"Is she hot?" Both Mary Ann and I asked at the same time.

"No, I don't have a sister! It's just a saying," Sallow exclaimed. "What the fuck is wrong with you people?"

"Just because she isn't real doesn't mean I won't crank one out to her," I replied, grinning.

"Girl, same," said Mary Ann, clinking glasses with me.

"Word," Johnny Boy said.

"Legit," said Carlos, finishing off his tequila. "I mean, women aren't my thing usually, but for your hot-ass imaginary sister, I'd make an exception."

Bishop shrugged amiably. "Even priests have needs, Jonas."

"I literally hate every goddamned one of you," Sallow said, laughing in spite of himself. "Even you giant bastards. And I barely know you."

"Once you *really* get to know us ..." Carlos started.

"We're even worse," Johnny Boy finished.

"It's true. Johnny Boy would gladly roger your mom roundly while Carlos takes your pops from behind in a manly fashion," I said. "They might even high five over their backs and make a London Bridge."

"Appropriate," Mary Ann chirped, taking a sip of her tropical monstrosity.

"I'll bet they both have that cute little accent, too," Johnny said. "That really cranks my tractor."

"Hell yeah," Carlos agreed. "I'd be all up on it, and he'd be all like 'Blimey, gov, but you're really giving me what for! Bully! Huzzah! Bloody hell, I'm arriving!"

"Like, instead of coming?" Johnny Boy said. "Nice! Because

he's fancy."

"Please stop," Sallow moaned, his head down on his arm where it rested on the bar top.

"That is DEFINITELY not what HE said," Carlos laughed.

"OR she," Johnny Boy fist bumped him.

"Ok, ok," I chuckled. "Let's give it ... and Sallow's parents ... a rest. Josh knows they'd need it after you two got through with them, you fucking reprobates."

Carlos turned to Johnny Boy. "He's using them big words again. Sorry, JB ... that means 'an unprincipled person or sinner.'"

"I know what it means, you shit-ass," Johnny said, winking. "Me talk good. Me use biiiig words, too. I reprobate often, in fact. One might call me a master reprobater."

And, so it went. Until the wee hours of the morning, when we saw the Twins off and Sallow headed home to meet with his order. Mary Ann cut the lights and headed home to her apartment, giving me another giantess hug before she departed. I set Bishop up on my couch downstairs with some blankets and a pillow before crashing myself.

Tomorrow would be a long day of errands and the true beginning of the prep work it would take for us to pull off this monumental con job and save what was left of the world ... and the orbitals floating above it ... and the millions of people that represent what's left of the human race. Those left behind. The shades of what used to be, orbiting a broken planet ... mere shadows over Earth -That-Was.

I'll bet you were wondering when I'd work that in, huh? Wait no longer. That was fucking it. Sometimes I wax poetic. Fuck off.

CHAPTER THIRTY-THREE

The next day, Tuesday morning, Bishop and I crawled out of our respective beds, cleaned up and scared up some breakfast in my small kitchen. After the monstrous meals we had eaten on Avalon, I was back to my normal routine of a protein shake and protein bar. Bishop noshed on a bagel with cream cheese. I think he was pretty nervous about his impending appointment at the Repat Center, which was completely understandable. I assured him he would do fine, and we quietly enjoyed our meal.

After, we popped next door and I cleaned out every single weapon from my soda machine armory and dumped them all in the back of the Shaggin' Wagon for delivery to my armorer. Well, almost every weapon. There was no need to bother getting any of my Narcoject models engraved as we would strictly be going lethal. I'm not even sure what a sleep spine would do to an otherworldly horror from another dimension. Probably just piss it off.

That done, the priest and I saddled up and drove a few blocks to a menswear shop, and I bought him a decent casual suit off the rack to wear to his interview and a modern smartwatch. I complimented him copiously over his new look, which he took with a small smile and nods of thanks, still nervous about how his day would shake out. We linked smartwatches so we could stay in touch and he could call me to hopefully pick him up later that afternoon.

We drove the few blocks to the Repat Center. I parked the

Wagon next to the loading dock as they didn't have an actual parking lot, and walked him inside. I had called ahead, and my buddy Sean met us at the front desk. A congenial sort with a head and face full of gray hair, dark brown skin, and a winning smile of the sort you see on 'zine covers or advertisements for dental offices, Sean walked up and shook my hand and then shook Bishop's. He assured us both that the process would be relatively painless and as quick as they could make it, depending on the outcomes of his initial battery of tests. He estimated the tests would take at least four hours and the subsequent committee meeting an additional hour. I told them to call me when they were done, clasped Bishop's shoulder in solidarity, wished him luck, and was on my way.

My next stop was to visit my armorer, who lived and worked one neighborhood over from mine. I took the scenic route and spent the 40-minute drive blasting a mixture of classic and late-era thrash metal including Metallica, Megadeth, Anthrax, Slayer, Sepultura, Exodus, Power Trip, Warbringer, Havok and Testament, which always improves my mood. Old school metal tends to help me get out of my own head. I was a little more apprehensive about Bishop's testing than I had let on to the man himself, to be perfectly honest.

The priest had come to mean the world to me in a short time, and I wanted him to have his freedom ... not only for his sake as he deserved a second chance at life, but also selfishly for my own sake as I didn't want to be deprived of his company. If the Repat Center's tests deemed that Bishop was not ready for repatriation, finding him to be a danger to himself or others, they'd lock him away in a facility for more intensive psychological treatment until he was deemed 'well-adjusted.' Whatever that means, really. Sean, old pal or no, could only do so much to sway the committee who would preside over my friend's fate. So, yeah. I was a bit nervous.

I pulled the Shaggin' Wagon up to a nondescript stone building with a small red awning over mirrored glass plate windows. It was situated at the end of a commercial block. The only sign was a tiny brass placard beside the door that read "Deep Mountain Defense – Professional Armorers." I pulled around the back of the building next to the loading dock and exited the van. I walked up a small metal staircase and pressed a button on a keypad/intercom combo to be buzzed inside. A digitized voice asked for my ID, and I held my smartwatch up to the scanner until it beeped, then smooshed my thumbprint on the scanner and waved at the camera above the reinforced steel door.

"Daniel Davidson for Nichelle Yoshida. I have an appointment." The door clicked open with a buzzing sound and I entered.

I walked into a richly appointed waiting room, all deep leather couches and overstuffed armchairs. The floor was hardwood, and the entire place was lit by small lamps on end tables, which all held tastefully designed weapons brochures and catalogs. The walls featured ornately framed paintings ... actual oil paintings, not prints ... of classic armaments such as the Maxim gun, the Colt Peacemaker, the Colt 1911, the Remington 870, and the M1 Garand. Except for the subject matter of said paintings, the place looked more like the waiting room of a high-end tailor than that of a (legal) arms dealer. One entire wall of the room was inch-thick bulletproof glass and looked out into a production bay where gunsmiths and armorers toiled over benches laden with gun parts ready for assembly and bladed weapons ready for the strop.

I barely had time to take in my surroundings before a door opened at the far side of the room, and my friend and associate Nichelle walked out, dressed to the nines in a bespoke charcoal gray pinstripe pantsuit. It was created by a master artisan, no doubt, as I could see no imprint or sign whatsoever of the huge semi-auto I knew she wore in a shoulder rig on her left side ... this despite it being extremely flattering. She stood tall and rather statuesque even without the six-inch heels, her hair abundant and currently upswept into afro puffs, which gave her a youthful look. The sole bit of color to her outfit was a gold

Egyptian ankh on a thin chain around her neck. Her café au lait skin radiated health, and her genuine smile of goodwill at my arrival tugged on my heartstrings.

"Hello, Daniel," she said, walking over to me, clasping my right bicep and air-kissing both cheeks. Ever the professional.

"How's it going, 'Chelle?" I said, taking her hand and giving it a squeeze. "How've you been? How's Haru? He still coding his life away for The Man?"

"Unfortunately," she said, frowning a little. "He's been working on his app in his spare time, but it's still months away from fruition. How have you been? How's Mary Ann?"

"She's well," I said. "She sends her love. Please give my best to your man, and tell him I would love to have you both over for drinks and some takeout when he's not buried up to his neck in code."

"I will," she said, smiling. "Life's pretty fucking busy at the moment, but we miss you guys. Let's make an effort to get together soon. Although ... from the look of your current order, there might not BE a soon. What gives, Danny? Are you in over your head? This is not your average ... anything. Frankly, I don't know WHAT this is."

"What THIS is ... well, it's a long story," I said, smiling ruefully. "And you probably wouldn't believe half of it."

"Try me," she said, crossing her arms and looking at me fiercely. And her fierce look is better than just about anyone's.

"Okay," I began. "But remember, I warned you. Here's the quick and dirty version: So, I was hired to get this old-ass religious book by a man representing a bunch of angels who look like horrors from another dimension, which is what they actually are. The book is written in Angelic language, which is pretty much the source code of ... um ... the universe and everything. They want to destroy our reality and everyone in it. Actual Templars tried to kill me, I made some new friends, we killed some rogue vamps, met half-alien Jesus and celestial serial killer Satan, and they gave me some pointers, one of which is the symbol that I sent you that needs to be engraved on every blade and gun I own and on a metric fuckton of bullets in various calibers. So I can kill a bunch of evil alien angels before they kill me, you, Haru, Mary Ann, and literally everyone else."

She stared at me blankly.

"Fucking told you," I said with a half-smile.

"You need to kill a bunch of evil alien angels," she repeated. "To save the world. And all of us."

"Yup," I said. "That pretty much sums it up."

She took in a breath, held it, exhaled and opened her mouth to say something but didn't. She raised the side of her fist to her mouth, looked up toward the ceiling, pursed her lips and tried again.

"Daniel," she said, then paused. "What the actual shit?"

"I know, right?" I shrugged. "It's been a fucking weird week. I don't know what else to tell you. If I hadn't lived through it, I wouldn't believe it myself."

She continued staring at me, looking into my eyes for any sign that I was pranking her or otherwise full of crap. Which, I mean, I am? But not about that.

"And when do you need all of this done?" Nichelle asked, steering us back to safer, less batshit ground.

"By Friday at the latest," I replied. "I haven't called the middleman to set up the date yet, but I'm going to do that today. Or first thing tomorrow. Five to seven days is probably the max I can drag this out without getting him suspicious or causing them to make a move on me first and catch me unprepared."

"The evil alien angels," she repeated.

"Yuppers," I said. "Still talking about them."

"Jesus Christ," she said, again raising her fist to her mouth, but this time propping her chin up with her thumb.

"He's actually pretty great," I said. "Curses a lot. Bit of a prankster. Goes by Josh."

"You mean Jesus," she said.

"Yes. Middle Eastern Jewish half-alien Jesus," I said

solemnly, holding in my grin as I was afraid she'd take it as a sign of me jerking her chain.

"Who you met," she said. "Along with the devil."

"Who is a deep-down scary motherfucker," I allowed. "But, he's definitely pro-human, pro-pizza and beer, and wants the evil angels dead as much as we do. Snazzy dresser, too. But absolutely terrifying."

"I am at a complete loss as to how to respond to this," Nichelle said, shaking her head slowly from side to side. "I've known you for a long, long time, Dan ... and I know you're a silly, often moronic jokester ..."

"Ouch," I said. "Right here. I can hear every word."

"But you'd ... I mean ... you wouldn't joke about something like this, would you?" She looked at me imploringly, practically begging me to tell her I was messing with her.

"Nichelle ... no," I said with all the seriousness and sincerity and solemnity and mortician-like gravitas I could scrape up from the roughly 10% of my conscious personality not devoted to innuendo, sarcasm, hilarity and filthy jokes. "I have never been more serious about anything. We're all going to die if I don't pull this off. Reality will just disappear. Everyone we know and love. Gone. In the blink of an eye. Not even a memory left. And I am terrified I am not going to pull this off. Like curl up in a crying fetal ball in the corner, shitting and pissing myself with fright kind of terrified."

She went silent again for a long moment. Maybe half a minute.

"Ok," she said. "Ok. I ... if this were anyone else ..."

"I know. I've been getting that a lot," I smiled.

"Fuck it. Two things," Nichelle said, crossing her arms again and setting her jaw. "First of all, I am deeply discounting this order. No labor, you just pay for materials, and ... no. You know what? It's on the motherfucking house," she said. "If you're right, and you pull this off, I'll ... we will ALL literally owe you everything. And if you don't, it won't matter and we'll be gone."

"And the second thing?" I asked.

She raised one exquisitely shaped eyebrow. "Do you need backup?"

CHAPTER THIRTY-FOUR

Nichelle had some of her guys come out and grab my giant pile of weapons and wheel them into the bay on a cart. She promised me they'd be ready by Friday and that she herself would be ready by Saturday. I thanked her, gave her a quick hug, and bolted for my next appointment.

I drove over to visit my friend the booksmith, Anya Smythe of Smythe and Co. Rare Books and Restoration, which was also located in Nichelle's neighborhood. She was likewise skeptical of the abbreviated version of the events I dropped on her, but she could feel the power of the book and the Angel Reaver sigil and didn't balk overmuch at the weirdness of my instructions and needs. As she reminded me constantly, her mother's family was from "The Old Country," so she grew up on stories of kikimora and rusalki and Baba Yaga. She believed that she and her AI assistant could knock out the job in a few scant days. I thanked her, paid her handsomely and was off.

I pointed the Shaggin' Wagon toward my mechanic's garage back in my own neck of the woods, taking a moment to dial up a realtor friend of mine, Jeff, who handles commercial properties. I went into absolutely zero detail with him, mostly because I didn't want him on the hook if something bad happened, but also I didn't need to give him reasonable cause to veto my rather odd and unconventional request. And, well, it worked. I rented a warehouse for 48 hours beginning Saturday morning. It was not cheap, nor was the safety/security/cleaning deposit I had to wire him that I one-hundred-percent *knew* I would be abandoning. But it met all of my needs. And come on ... who doesn't want to stage a climactic showdown in an abandoned warehouse at least once in their life?

My next call was to a couple of my old bandmates. More about them later, but I managed to borrow some essential pieces of sound and stagecraft from them that I would pick up later in the week after the SW was returned. As I still owned one quarter of it all, it wasn't that big of an ask.

I dropped off the SW and a shit-ton of digital cash for my mechanic, Fernando. Lucky for me, he isn't the sort to ask too many questions. My alterations did apparently warrant raised eyebrows, which for the extremely laid back and low-key Nando is kind of like yelling. Still though, he is used to weird requests from his high-end clientele. He promised me the Wagon would be done and ready by close of business on Thursday. I promised to meet him for beers and steaks one night next week ... an appointment I was really hoping to be able to keep.

As it was only a few blocks to the Repat Center from Nando's place, I walked that way, enjoying the gentle breeze and pleasantly sunshiny spring day, a bright blue sky visible beyond the lightly shimmering translucent haze of the orbital's dome.

I stopped in a coffee shop just down the street from the center to wait on Bishop. I snagged one of the rental e-readers from the rack by the counter and plopped down in a giant cushy chair to enjoy my cappuccino, a bagel sandwich, and a book from my cloud library for the hopefully brief hour or two until I heard from Sean or Bishop with news. Hopefully good news.

Around 2 PM, my smartwatch buzzed. I read a brief text from Sean asking me to come over. I checked my reader back in, chugged the last of my now room-temp coffee and headed out the door. I forced myself to keep a calm, rational walking pace and managed to refrain from breaking into an all-out sprint.

The two men were waiting in the lobby for me. They chatted like old friends as I walked across the room toward them, which I took to be a good sign. Bishop had not collapsed to the ground in tears yet, nor was he wearing a straightjacket and surrounded by tough-looking orderlies, so ... positive thoughts.

"Hey, guys," I said as I approached them. "Sooooo ... how did it go?"

Bishop looked at Sean to begin.

"Well, Daniel," the older man said. "Your friend Father Bishop is something of an anomaly, but in a very good way. I don't know that I have ever seen a Canaan refugee so well-adjusted and behaved and ... we strive not to use the word 'normal' in the mental health field ... but, yeah. It's as if he hadn't spent the last decade chained in a basement by himself drinking wine and reading."

"To be fair, of all the activities on the itinerary for that place these days, wine drinking and reading books are undoubtedly the most wholesome and fulfilling," I laughed. "And loneliness is probably preferable to the company of cannibal sex cultists. But that's good to hear. So, the tests went well?"

"He aced them," Sean said, returning my grin. "I didn't even have to pull any strings or step up to bat for him. He did it all on his own. Charmed the committee, too."

"Holy SHIT," I exclaimed. "You are amazing, Elias! Congrats, man!"

"Thank you, Daniel," he said, reaching out to clasp my shoulder. "I owe a lot of it to you. I mean, I wouldn't be here at all without you, but you and your friends really helped me."

"I think we can safely say they are now your friends, too," I clapped him on the back. "So, what happens now, Sean?"

"We'll monitor his whereabouts for the next six weeks via smartwatch," Sean said. "And he'll meet with one of our therapists twice a week for the next six months. We've got him a spot in our nearby transitional housing for that period, where he'll also be under supervision, but it's honestly pretty relaxed. Once his probationary period is up, we'll find him more permanent housing. And we have a part-time job set up for him so he can start earning some credits straight away. He starts Monday."

"It's only working at a replicator supply store, but it will do for now," Bishop said.

"And hey, if the world ends on Sunday, you won't even have to go in to work at all!" I said, laughing maybe a bit too loudly. Sean gave me a really weird look at that.

"Ahem. Anyway, Sean, thank you for all your help," I told the counselor. "I appreciate it so much. This guy means a lot to me. Come by the shop soon and have a pint with me. On the house. Any day but Sunday. We already have plans."

Bishop thanked Sean further, and he wished us both well. We left the center and walked out into the sunshine, both feeling nearly giddy with relief at the outcome, the sunshine feeling extra good on two unburdened sets of shoulders. Well, partially unburdened anyway. We were one hurdle down, and had a really good starting point for Bishop's new life at least. If any of us made it past the week, anyway. I again took the scenic route, and we explored a bit of the neighborhood on the way back to the shop, giving the priest a little walking tour and hitting the high points of his new home.

The shop was in full operation mode when we returned, bustling with business. Our arrival was met with a general murmur of low-key cheers from my regulars, and Mary Ann ran out from behind the bar expectantly. We told her the good news, and she hugged both of us in turn, picking Bishop up and spinning him around like a rag doll and planting a huge kiss on his cheek before putting him down, causing his carefully combed shock of white hair to poof back up to mad scientist status. She gave me a more reserved but deeper hug, and whispered in my ear.

"Thank you," she said, holding me tight.

"For what?" I whispered back.

"For being you," she smiled over my shoulder. "For being a

good and decent man. And helping out and befriending a lost soul."

I kissed her on the cheek. "Well, then ..." I thought of a million awful things to say, but I finally settled on: "Well, you're welcome, I guess? I AM pretty fucking awesome."

She laughed at that and let me go, smacking me lightly on the cheek.

"And there he is," she smiled. "Just had to ruin the moment, didn't ya?"

"It's what I'm best at," I grinned. "Well, that and being ruggedly handsome, charming and witty and ..."

"Imma stop you right there," she groaned, walking back behind the bar. "Can I get you two gentlemen a celebratory libation?"

"Sure thing," I said. "Two porters, please." She poured us both a pint, and I grabbed our drinks and bade Bishop follow me upstairs. I led him across the balcony to the window overlooking the little park with its sculpture garden and the tiny harbor, where my giant overstuffed armchair sat next to its faux mahogany table. The table still held the horror novel I had started a week or so ago before this adventure began, the bookmark still on the first page. I handed Bishop his beverage and sat down, offering him a seat on the small couch that sat on the other side of the table. We sat in silence for a minute or two, enjoying the view.

"This is one of my favorite spots," I said. "It's a place I come to relax and sort of meditate and let the stresses of the day melt away. And by meditate I mean drink and read, usually."

Bishop laughed. "Whatever works, my son."

"You haven't called me that in a while," I noted.

"You haven't called me Padre in a while, either," he said, taking a sip of his beer.

"True enough," I agreed. "You're definitely more of an Elias now. And how IS Elias? Are you okay? How are you feeling? I know today was pretty damned stressful for you."

He inhaled, puffing out his cheeks, and blew out a breath

looking contemplative.

"I mean, very relieved that the testing and committee meeting went the way they did," he said, scratching his beard. "And your friend Sean was tremendously supportive throughout the whole thing. I am also nervous and anxious. Elysia seems nice, but it's a lot busier and moves faster than I am used to. So, it's a little scary. But, again, it's a fun sort of excitement, too, as I'll be doing something new and moving *toward* something as opposed to just sitting in a basement marking the passage of time. Does that make sense?"

"Totally," I said. "All perfectly natural. I just ... I don't know ... I just wanted to check in on you. Your life has gone through some major upheavals in the last week or so. And I wanted to say that I hope you know Mary Ann and I will be here for you throughout all of it. And beyond. You're family now, so there's no getting rid of us."

He laughed and smiled. "I appreciate that more than you know, Daniel. Also, don't you start going soft on me ..."

"That's what SHE said?" I grinned, and he laughed and we clinked glasses.

"Much better!" Bishop exclaimed. "But, seriously. Thank you."

"You are most fucking welcome, Elias," I said.

We passed the next little bit in companionable discussion, which was interrupted once or twice by Mary Ann stopping by to drop off fresh drinks and ruffle Bishop's snowy white troll-doll hair. Sunset came and went, setting the sculpture garden and the water beyond ablaze and then fading into the dark blues of orbital night. Tonight was a late night for the shop, so we went down and I relieved Mary Ann behind the bar so she could sit and enjoy a drink and chat with Bishop. A few regulars came and went, checking in on me after my absence and talking collectibles and the like.

It grew late, and we shut down for the night and locked up. Both Mary Ann and I escorted Bishop over to the Repat Center's transitional housing block a half-mile or so from the store. We walked into the comfortably lit lobby and introduced Bishop to the night attendant, who sat behind a large desk gazing at an e-reader. We saw the priest off with hugs and back pats and well wishes and entreaties to call us if he needed anything. Then, we headed back, parting ways outside Mary Ann's apartment. I continued the walk back to my place, deep in thought.

Oddly, I kind of missed Sallow's grimacing mug. I decided to give him a call and see how progress was going on his end of things. I tapped my smartwatch and hit his number on speed dial, popping in an earbud from my pocket as I did so.

"What do you fucking want?" Sallow's annoyed voice asked in my ear. "I was just getting used to not having you around."

"Hah. Sounds like a miserable time to me, but whatever. You do you, Mr. Grumpy Pants," I grinned. "Just hadn't heard anything from you and wanted to check in and monitor your progress."

"Well, I've briefed the Order in full," the knight began. "The armorer is working on etching Angel Reaver into all of our weapons, melee and ranged, as well as ammunition for the team. I thought he'd be a dick about it, but he's actually a little bored and looking forward to the work. Of course, he's pawning off most of the unpleasant stuff to his apprentices, but I guess that's what they are for."

"That's good news," I said. "Do you think you and your team can be here by Saturday morning? I'm forwarding you the address of the meeting place. Also, how hard would it be for you to get me a few tanks of Unholy Water? Maybe a 25-gallon and a 5-gallon tank?"

"That's a fuckload, but I can get the quartermaster working on it now," he replied. "He can probably have it ready to leave with us Saturday."

As we talked, I walked by an alleyway and heard movement, causing me to look that way. I try not to walk too close to alleys in general, but I had been intent on my conversation and let my tactical awareness slip a bit. Two guys in cut up denim vests sporting bright gang insignia yelled at me from a few feet away. One had his hand on a pistol grip sticking out of his grubby-looking jeans and the other brandished a long, matte black knife.

"Hey, there, pal," the pistolero called to me. "We're gonna need you to come over here and empty your pockets. We're a little short on creds and were thinking you could help us out."

"Yeah," knife boy added. "How 'bout you spot us some creds, pretty boy?"

"Hold on a sec," I said to Sallow.

"Pretty boy? What the fuck guys?" I looked at the two wannabe toughs. "Did you come straight from central casting with that awful dialogue? I'm, like, handsome in an average, guy-next-door sort of way at best. Certainly not the kind of guy you'd label as a pretty boy. My jawline is *barely* chiseled. You can't see my abs. I mean, I even wear glasses. OOH, maybe I'm like the low-key hot girl who's a total nerd and a tomboy and idiotically no one realizes she's gorgeous until a popular girl gives her a makeover that consists of taking off her glasses, combing her hair and putting her in a dress? Of course, maybe beauty is relative? The two of you look like you were beaten with an ugly stick, after all. Or maybe each other's ugly dicks? Not that there's anything wrong with that. I don't kink shame. Never let it be said that I ..."

"What the fuck are you talking about?" Stupid Shit Number One said, gripping his pistol and partially drawing it from his waistband. "You talk too much. Shut the fuck up and give us your creds."

"Sorry. I tend to yammer on when I'm nervous. Like when I'm being robbed by such obviously tough and competent guys as yourselves. How much you need?" I asked. "I can probably spot you a few hundo, but that's about it until payday." I made a show of patting myself up and down for a credstick.

"All of it, asshole," Stupid Shit Number Two replied, pointing his knife at me and taking a step.

Of course, by this time, my theatrical self-pat-down had reached my chest, and I reached into my jacket and drew my

Narcoject from its shoulder rig with all the speed my jacked reflexes could muster. I shot them both in the throat before either could react. They crumpled to the ground.

"What the fuck was all that?" Sallow said in my ear. "And I agree. You're not very pretty. 5 out of 10 at best. Maybe a strong 6 when you're being clever."

"Eh. Just observing and, um, maybe hunting some of the local wildlife," I said, bending down to pluck my sleep spines from the necks of the would-be thieves. "Apparently I was fishing for assholes and was unaware. Lucky for them, I'm strictly catch-and-release."

I thought briefly about posing their unconscious bodies in a lewd fashion, but I discarded the idea as childish. (I know, right? It's like I am maturing before your very eyes.) I dragged them a little further into the alleyway one by one and leaned them both up against the side of the building. I patted them both down and found a few credsticks, which I took along with their weapons. I figured I could donate the creds to a local charity later tonight. I'm a civic-minded motherfucker, after all. I grabbed a couple of lens cleaning cloths from my sling bag to gently pick up the knife and the gun with care so as to not disturb existing fingerprints or leave my own behind. I should probably start carrying latex gloves. They come in awfully handy in a surprising number of situations. Picking up evidence, cleaning up surprise dog poop, random body cavity searches, guerilla proctology, etc.

I dropped the gun in one jacket pocket and managed to cram the knife in the other. Luckily, my "action jacket" has oversized pockets capable of holding a large trade paperback book. That will come as a surprise to absolutely no one who knows me. I thought for a moment, drew my Narcoject again and shot both of the assholes in the chest as they slept, causing their bowels and bladders to free their contents violently and loudly. I held my nose and leaned over to nick the spines, placing them in my sling bag. I gave the smelly gang bangers one last gleeful, evil grin, then I resumed my walk. Maturity is overrated.

"So, yeah. I'm back. Sorry about that," I told Sallow. "Two containers of Unholy Water, twenty or so knights, armed to the teeth with Angel Reaver, yada yada yada. Saturday morning. You guys have any thermal camo? I'd advise wearing it. And bring anything you'd need on a long stakeout or in a sniper's nest situation. Rations and the like. I'll handle the rest. Sound good? Oh, also, we're having a gathering at my shop on Friday night if you can manage to get away early."

"On it," he replied simply. "As far as Friday, I'll see what I can do. Need to run, though. Duty calls. See you soon." He cut the connection.

"So professional," I said to myself, chuckling and removing my earbud. I walked a few blocks out of my way on my return to the shop in order to pass by an EOPD substation. I tossed the confiscated weapons in the nighttime drop box. Maybe they could be tied to a few open cases, I thought to myself. I sauntered home with a spring in my step. If I were able to whistle, I might've whipped out a jaunty tune or two. But I can't. So I didn't. And whistling is stupid, no matter how innocent it makes you appear to certain idiotic yokels and stoner elves. So there.

CHAPTER THIRTY-FIVE

Wednesday morning, I got up and ran through my usual morning routine, which consisted of some time on the dreadmill, a few sets of pushups, situps and pullups, a quick shower and my protein bar and shake. Then I sat down on the couch in my living room with a tumbler of coffee, put in my ear buds and dialed up Archer, the creepy middleman extraordinaire.

"Morning, sunshine," I said when he picked up the audio-only call. "Anyone ever tell you look and sound like Major Arnold Toht, the Nazi Gestapo Agent from Raiders of the Lost Ark? I mean, it's uncanny, really. Can't believe it didn't hit me when we first met. I must be slipping."

"You have a most interesting way of saying hello, Mr. Davidson," Archer said drily. "And, no. It has not come up. Do you have the book?"

"I do. It wasn't easy, but, hey. You aren't paying me for easy."

"Excellent," he said, creepily, as was his way. "I will come and pick it up from you today."

"Can't do it today," I said. "Sorry. I have another job that will have me out of town until Sunday. We can meet up then."

"Your clients ... *our* clients will not be pleased about this delay," he said, with a hint of menace. "I *strongly* encourage you to reconsider."

"Can't. I'd love to, but I have a little old lady that has me searching for a priceless family heirloom, and, well, to be honest, she may not have much time left," I said, being anything *but* honest. I know Helly says I am a rotten liar, and I mostly am. Sometimes, though, inspiration strikes me. "Whereas, your clients ... well, they probably have all the time in the world, do they not? I mean, surely there's not something time sensitive they have in mind that requires a potentially deadly and dangerous artifact such as this?"

Silence.

He knew I knew. And now, I knew he knew I knew. Time to go all in.

"I want to meet your clients, Archer," I said, taking a gulp of coffee. "All of them. I want to look them in their eyes and hear from their mouths that they are not going to do anything dangerous with this book. It feels awfully powerful, Archer. I didn't believe you at first, but now, having seen it and felt it ... I do. I'm sold. So this is how it has to happen. I just can't take your word for it. That's not good enough."

"That will not be possible," Archer said. "They wish to remain anonymous."

"And I just wanted to pile up in my goddamned armchair, drink some Scotch and read a book, but here we are," I said, evenly and without malice. "Here we fucking are. Well ... I suppose I could just, I dunno, lose the book again. It's an awfully big world. And, you know what? I'm not even sure I would be limited to this world. I have friends in the space program, you know. Be a shame for it to wind up on a random asteroid somewhere. Or even at the bottom of Earth's ocean. Awfully big search grid there."

"They will kill us both, Davidson," he practically growled into the phone. "If you hide the book, they will kill me and you and everyone you hold dear."

"Oooh. That's the way to win me over, Sparky," I said, laughing without humor. "Threaten me and my loved ones. Look, there's no need for all that posturing. Tell them I want to meet them and look in their eyes and judge their intentions. Then, you'll get a book, I'll get some rent money, and we'll part as ... well, not friends, but ... yeah. I have no idea. But we'll both have what we came for."

"I'll take your offer to them," he grudgingly said through gritted teeth.

"Yup. You do that," I said. "Sunday night. 9 PM. I'll send the address the day of. Should I have refreshments waiting? I know a bang-up caterer. How many folks are we talking about?"

Long pause.

"About 75 to 100," he said. "This is insane. I still don't know why you ..."

"That sounds great," I said jovially. "Bring the whole family. We can play games in the yard and sip mint juleps and eat canapes. Maybe have a three-legged race. Ok, buddy. Gotta run. Old lady heirlooms to dig up and what-not. See ya soon!" I hung up. I exhaled a huge breath and flopped back on the couch.

There was no way this was going to work, I thought. They were going to try and double-cross me. Well, I supposed it was only fair. I was trying to double-cross them, after all. I guess we'd just have to see who was best at double crossing whom. Or whom was best at ... fuck. I always mix those up. Who or whomsoever was still alive after the smoke cleared at any rate.

Perhaps the most puzzling thing of all was that Archer had told the truth when I asked him how many of our "clients" would be attending. I could not think of a single reason he would've done that. He could've told me five and brought just enough to kick my ass and left the rest at home. He had no way of knowing I knew how many rogue angels there were. Maybe he was just caught off guard by the question? I doubted it, but there was nothing to be done for it except to plan for the worst.

The rest of the week was relatively uneventful. I picked up my guns and blades and the Shaggin' Wagon and the fake Book of Raziel. Anya had the book ready by Thursday, and she had done amazing work as expected. Nando had me pop over and grab the SW Thursday night. Everything was done to his usual high standards, which equaled perfection or damned close to it. Nichelle called Friday morning and I picked up my gear from her. Her crew had also knocked it out of the park.

Once I had the incredibly convincing fake book in my hands, I placed it in my gun safe and took the real one to my bank. I placed it in my safety deposit box with hard copies of my personal documents and locked it away until this mess was over with, at which time I figured I could come up with a plan for it without trying to do so while under the gun, so to speak.

I called Helly and Ariana to check in on them and let them know the plans. They said they would get their affairs in order and charter a trip to Elysia as soon as possible, shooting for a Friday arrival time. I checked in on Sallow again, and he gave me every indication that things were coming together satisfactorily with the Templars' preparations.

I ate nearly every meal with Mary Ann, and we went to visit Bishop several times, both taking him lunch and meeting him after we got off work for a bite and to check out his new digs. I called the Twins and made sure everything was a go for Saturday at the warehouse and Friday night at the shop. It was my plan to wait until at least noon on Sunday to let Archer know where to have the Outsiders meet us, so we could get our prep done before they showed up early, trying to ambush us before we could ambush them.

I also put in a call to a volunteer firefighter friend of mine from back in my days at EOPD. I got caught up with him and asked him if I could borrow a little of his time and expertise Saturday morning. I offered to pay him for his time, naturally, and he agreed to show up with the tools and gear I requested.

There were a few other small things I had to order to put my plan in place. I had a couple of deliveries scheduled for early Saturday morning at the warehouse.

I spent a little time cleaning up the drones. I switched out Sundance's Narcoject drums for 100-round armor piercing, which I filled with Angel Reaver ammo. I also switched his firing mechanisms and barrels over as well. That done, I loaded up my two Colt Heathens with Angel Reaver rounds as well, doing the same for a few battle and sniper rifles. And loaded spare mags for everything. Nichelle's crew had done an amazing job, engraving all of the guns on both sides with the sigil and producing custom grips for each weapon that bore the deadly marking as well. I set aside two heavy boxes of ammo that I had made for the Twins as well, and then I was as prepared as I could be.

And that was it. Nothing left to do but wait.

Ariana called Thursday night with an estimated time of arrival at the hangar bay nearest the shop, and Mary Ann and I were there waiting early Friday afternoon. We stood leaning on the SW, watching them disembark while Travis and Desireé ran the shop in our absence. The Wagon was currently sporting a custom Wagnerian theme that showed a Valkyrie swooping down from a storm-filled sky to rain hell on enemy combatants. It was a favorite of Helly's, naturally, shield maiden that she was.

Both of the ladies stepped down the ramp from their charter and looked around, spotting us. Helly gave a cry of joy and ran full-tilt toward us, her enormous travel bag and ax-case slung over her shoulder. She was wearing a slouchy, oversized blue hoodie and jeans. Ariana grinned widely, but walked toward us in a calmer, more collected manner. She carried a conservative rolling suitcase and had her sword slung on her back in a cylindrical transport tube. The elf was likewise dressed casually in jeans, a retro t-shirt of female punk band The Slits that she had gotten from my shop, and a gray hoodie vest with a smiley face pin on it. The little round, yellow face sported a bleeding bullet hole and was also from my shop.

Helly reached us first, naturally, dropping her burdens and launching herself into a hug/tackle of Mary Ann, who naturally bore up under the friendly attack like a champ, laughing uncontrollably the whole time. She swung the dwarf back and forth like a pendulum, hugging her all the while.

"Hiya, short stuff," the orc said, kissing Helly on the cheek several times. "Missed your sweet face!"

She placed Helly back on the deck, but the dwarf practically bounced back up, throwing herself at me. I am nowhere near as strong as my orc companion, so I didn't quite catch her, but I did wrap her in an embrace as she fell back toward the ground, staggering back a bit as I did so. She nuzzled my neck warmly and kissed it and then bit my ear.

"Ow, you little shit," I said, laughing. "You're lucky you are so damned cute. If you weren't as thicc as grandma's day-old oatmeal and didn't rock so fucking hard in general, I'd boot you right off this orbital."

"Would NOT," she said, pulling back and slapping my chest. "You LOVE me more than, well, some funny sexual metaphor I can't think of right now." She blew a raspberry at me. "Fuck off, it's been a long flight."

Ariana arrived seconds later and was completely enveloped in a Mary Ann hug. The orc didn't bodily pick her up, but leaned down and embraced her, kissing her cheek.

"Hello, gorgeous," Mary Ann said, smiling her toothsome smile. "You are a sight for sore eyes. I've missed you terribly."

Ariana pulled back and kissed Mary Ann's cheek, then backed out to arms' length, looking the green giantess up and down. "And you are every bit as beautiful as I remembered, you emerald goddess. And absolutely ripped, too. Why are you not on magazines and billboards?"

Mary Ann laughed. "I'm too antsy to stay still and pose for the camera. Plus, I have so much to offer the world of heavy drinkers and pop culture collectors. And, obviously, Daniel's professional and personal life would completely collapse if I were not around."

"Right HERE," I said, grinning with my arm around Helly. "Still NOT deaf."

Ariana laughed and came over to hug me as well. Both she and Helly raised their eyebrows at some of the more obvious work Nando had done for me, but more on that later.

"All right, kids," I said once I had embraced the elf thoroughly. "Now that hugs and handies have been passed out, let's head home, shall we?"

And we did. The first part of our reunion concluded, we grabbed our friends and their gear and piled in the Wagon, heading for the shop. Helly rode up front with me and commandeered the media server, blasting The Runaways the whole way. Which none of us minded in the least.

We pulled in the garage and headed inside. With the shop taken care of upstairs, we stowed the girls' gear in my spare bedroom, which sported two single beds for just such an occasion, and proceeded to grab some drinks and retire to the rec room. Mary Ann and Ariana started up a game of billiards, and I did NOT envy the orc. I hoped she wasn't naïve enough to bet money against the elf. Again. Ariana knew geometries better than Euclid himself. Helly and I hit the multicade and played a few rounds of Mortal Combat II, one of my personal favorites.

Around 5 PM, Bishop sauntered downstairs, still wearing his new suit. He was met with the celebratory cheers and pomp of a Roman General returning from a successful campaign. Helly gave him huge squeezes and jumped up to tousle his troll-hair. Ariana kissed his cheek and hugged him warmly, then proceeded to continue trouncing our orc friend mercilessly.

About 15 minutes later, the Twins showed up with Sallow in tow, who had obviously been able to wrangle the night off. We decided we were hungry, and after a brief discussion, we ordered Lebanese takeout. The eight of us piled up on the couches downstairs and gorged ourselves on delicious shawarma, kafta, shish tawook, and a pile of baklava that were almost as good as YiaYia's. Then we sacked out and watched The Fellowship of the Ring, which I projected on one of the bigger walls of the rec room. I was outvoted and we ended up watching the 2472 AI-assisted CGI reboot/remake, which admittedly is almost as good as the Peter Jackson version from 2001. The visuals are amazing, and it certainly fixes the mild issues I had with the forced perspective of the hobbits, but ... it's lacking a little in heart in my humble opinion.

I glanced around the room a few times, looking at the illuminated faces of my friends old and new as they watched the film, transfixed, laughing and crying at different times, a few of them clasping hands or leaning over on each other. My heart swelled with emotion at this simple gathering of people, who represented numerous races, different cybernatural species, different genders, a gamut of sexual orientations, and backgrounds as varied as could be. All strong, and tough and funny and warm and loving and caring and deadly. (Well, except Bishop. Unless you are a toddler with its shoes tied together. And he caught you by surprise.) Don't tell any of those wonderful motherfuckers, but I might've teared up a little and gotten a lump in my throat. A couple of them would never let me live it down.

This last night together before the buildup and the battle was both everything I had hoped for and simultaneously not nearly enough. But it had to be, for now. Hopefully there would be many, many more. But if not, there are no better people, no finer humans and human-adjacent folk I would rather spend my last days with and possibly die defending.

After the film, Mary Ann ran upstairs and came back with a bottle of Scotch and a bottle of Kentucky Bourbon. We grabbed some tumblers and ice and served ourselves. As we did so, the conversation naturally revolved toward the preparations and plans for the Sunday meet.

"You speak with Archer the creep?" Mary Ann asked from the depths of one of the couches, where she sat with Ariana's head leaned back on her shoulder. The elf was stretched lengthwise on the couch with her legs in Helly's lap, her drink perched on her stomach. Bishop sat between the Twins on the other couch and Sallow was practically lost in an overstuffed beanbag nearby. I leaned against the arcade cabinet across from them, one hand in my pocket and the other holding my tumbler of Scotch.

"Yup," I said, taking a sip of my beverage and crunching on a tiny pebble of ice. "I called him and told him I needed to look our clients in the eyes – ALL of them - and hear them tell me they didn't have anything nefarious planned with the leather bound atom bomb we are handing them. He seemed to buy it, but who knows. We'll just have to kill whoever the fuck shows up and hope for the best. Once we are paid, anyway."

"So," Sallow said. "What haven't you told us about your plan yet? I know we're going to show up and hand the fake book off, get paid and mow as many Outsiders down as we can. But I don't know anything else. I am guessing no one else does, either?" The others shook their heads.

I told them exactly what I had planned. Down to the smallest detail. The reactions ranged from worried to deeply apprehensive to contemplative to heartily amused to fucking psyched. You can probably guess who was who.

"That is ..." Sallow began.

"I know. You're going to say it's a bullshit plan," I smiled. "And you're not wrong. But, hey. At least it's not like the fate of our entire universe depends on it, right?"

Silent stares all around.

"Fine. Too soon," I said, laughing. "Fucking tough room. Anyway, I think it's as solid as we could hope for, considering we don't know how many angels will actually show. Nor can we foresee how they might try to double cross us. It really hinges on whether or not Archer buys the fake book. If he doesn't, well, we mow them the fuck down anyway and don't get paid. Which will suck, as rent is almost due, and I want you all to be compensated for your time away from your livelihoods as well. And, well, I plan on giving a substantial chunk of my take to the authorities on Avalon to disburse to the families of those people Lard Brian-Tom A.K.A. Baron Von Douchenstein murdered. After rent is paid, of course."

Sallow turned to stare at me with that fucking look on his face.

"It's not a big deal," I said. "Don't make it a big deal." He grinned and waved me off, not saying a word.

"I fucking love you, man," Carlos said, chuckling. "Never

stop being you, you fucking softie."

"Unless you can be Batman," Johnny Boy said. "Then always choose Batman. Or Dale Earnhardt. Which is practically the same thing."

Helly made heart hands at me and made a kissy face. I stuck out my tongue at her, making her giggle.

"Ok, so that's it," I said. "Any more questions, comments or suggestions? If so, fuck off. I'm tired. You motherfuckers get out of here so I can go to bed. We have a busy day ahead of us."

There was general laughter at this, and everyone stood one by one and started the process of saying good night with lots of hugs, kisses, backslaps, casual insults and love. Ariana and Helly went to the spare room to get ready for bed. The Twins and Mary Ann walked Bishop home before heading their separate ways. Sallow disappeared in a puff of Mephistophelean smoke.

Ok, fine. So he just walked up the stairs like a normal person, flipping me off over his shoulder as he did so. But the other would've been lots cooler. His banality disappoints me sometimes. Oh, well. You can't spell banal without 'anal.' Or so his mom pointed out to me once. Post-coitus.

I got ready for bed myself. I brushed my teeth and went to lay down at least. I stared at the ceiling for a long time before sleep finally took me. There's no anxiety quite like the kind you get knowing that all of your friends' lives, and everyone you've ever met and NOT met and, well, all of human history itself depends on your dumbass, half-baked plan being successful. *No fucking pressure at ALL, Daniel,* I thought as I drifted off. *None whatsoever. Sleep tight.*

CHAPTER THIRTY-SIX

I awoke half an hour before my alarm, which always pisses me off. My racing mind and my anxiety would not allow me to sleep any longer. Like Sallow's mom, I had a lot of balls in the air. Not that I judge. A lady has to make a living somehow, and sex work is real work. No shame in putting food on the table.

I fumbled my way out of bed and into the kitchen for a protein bar and shake. And lots of coffee. I ate standing up as I didn't think it was possible for me to relax long enough to sit, even for a few minutes. Helly and Ariana stumbled in, grumpy and slightly hung over. I greeted them, pointed their sleepy selves toward the fridge and replicator, then went and showered. I dressed in a pair of black jeans, a classic Mastodon tee and a black ball cap. I grabbed a few of my newly inscribed Angel Reaver rifles and sidearms with holsters for Helly and Ariana. I kitted out in my usual Narcoject shoulder rig and SOB-holstered Heathen and sat in the Shaggin' Wagon, waiting on the ladies, listening to some Corrosion of Conformity while I did so.

Looking somewhat refreshed, Ariana and Helly walked into the garage, finishing the last of their pastries and sipping on tumblers of coffee. We split and headed over a few blocks to grab a sleepy Bishop, the priest dressed in some athletic wear he must have brought in his bag from Canaan and drinking from a plastic jug of coffee larger than his head … minus the bushy white hair, naturally. That was the size of another plastic jug by itself. It reminded me a little bit of King Buzzo's hair from (The) Melvins circa 2022 or so when it was in its wild, untamed state. We greeted the priest in a low-key fashion appropriate for a group of decidedly NOT morning people.

We stopped to get Mary Ann, who was her usual charming morning self, and then we headed on to the warehouse where we would spend the day setting our trap and preparing for our final showdown with the Angelic Host and Archer, whoever or whatever that creepy motherfucker was.

I will spare you the monotonous details. It will be more fun that way. Suffice it to say that Sallow and his Templars, the Twins, and Nichelle all showed up, as did my two deliveries. My fireman pal came by and helped me with the job for which I had recruited him. Preparations were made as best we could make them. Imagine, if you will, a montage of activity similar to that of the villagers in Kurosawa's The Seven Samurai - hurried and flurried shots of people setting up traps for the raiders that would show up soon to rob, rape, pillage, and kill – only with more dick jokes. And, well, the villagers in this instance were FAR more dangerous, more akin to the samurai themselves. And better looking, if I do say so myself. And the montage had a much better soundtrack ranging from thrash to stoner to power to technical death metal. And jazz and blues. And old-school country. And there might've been some disco in there, too, because who doesn't like to dance a bit with their friends when the apocalypse is nigh? Basically, I just put the Shaggin' Wagon's media server on shuffle for the most mind-blowingly weird and random montage music one could imagine. Let's see them try to film THAT.

Food was ordered, bread was broken, and we tried not to frighten the Templars, A.K.A. the normies, too awfully much. I gave a clichéd but sincere semi-inspirational speech about humanity and friendship and fighting to the last that left every eye in the place damp, Sallow grimacing all the while, and Helly, well ... you know. Also damp. (Wink, wink, nudge, nudge. If you know what I mean.) Just imagine another montage with the music playing over me talking, only triumphant and strident and militant now, as the camera pans around to show slow nods and Templars misting up and my friends hugging each other and smiling through the tears, and then the camera lights on Sallow, who just looks annoyed, and then there's a slow-motion shot of everyone cheering and raising triumphant fists into the air, flipping the bird in the general direction of where we thought a dimension of shitty angels might be located.

And, yes. It's the sort of thing you *totally* see coming, and it's painfully overdone, but the sheer emotion of it sweeps you up and you can't help yourself and you start ugly-crying like Claire Danes in 2011's Homeland, and then you're wiping snot on your pajama sleeve and going to the kitchen and pouring yourself an entire bottle of wine into a giant goblet the size of a fishbowl and grabbing an entire carton of ice cream and a spoon.

Aaaaaand scene.

Of course, none of that actually happened, but it would've been cool if it did.

As the sun left the sky, we wound down and said our goodbyes. Bishop and I hopped in the Wagon and headed home. I dropped him off at the halfway house for wayward priests, and stopped off at the men's wear shop for a last minute bit of retail therapy. Of sorts. Or retail hilarity. But more about that soon.

I arrived home, readied myself for bed, and spent the next few hours staring at the ceiling. I might've sent a few sobby, maudlin texts, which I can't even blame on alcohol. Sleep again managed to find me, though, as hard as my spinning and careening mind ran screaming from it like a hysterical teenage girl in a slasher film. Eh. Not my best work, but you get the fucking picture.

I awoke the next morning, choked down some protein, showered and got dressed.

I called Archer and gave him the address of the warehouse where we would meet approximately 12 hours hence. He urged me to come alone, as they always do. I made a noncommittal sound and hung up. Then, I bummed around the shop aimlessly for most of the day, politely but distractedly engaging with the regulars and a few new faces. I popped out for Cuban food at lunch, but I mostly picked at my plate. Desireé and Travis closed up the shop around 7, and I trotted downstairs to gear up. I grabbed the fake Book of Raziel and put it in a canvas sack that advertised my shop, the screen-printed bear and sailor on it looking to be moments from actual conflict as always.

I called Bishop, and he walked the few blocks over and met me at the garage entrance. He was wearing his monk's robe, mail and cross from Avalon, looking slightly whack-a-doo amidst the gleaming neon cityscape of Elysia around us. Again, though, anything goes here. Most of us see far weirder before breakfast. He probably had his club up his sleeve somewhere. Who knows? He might've even managed to replicate some wolf jerky. We drove over to the next neighborhood and down to the orbital's edge where the warehouse was located. I had him drop me five blocks or so from our destination, and I set out on foot. As I approached, I checked my smartwatch. It was 8:50 PM. I sighed heavily ... a massive sigh that would've done Bob the Elf proud ... and stretched my neck, shot my cuffs and walked up to the small metal door next to the giant double steel doors of the warehouse. I turned the knob and walked inside.

CHAPTER THIRTY-SEVEN

I stepped inside the warehouse and was shrouded in darkness. There were industrial pendulum lights way up in the rafters that shot down cones of yellow-orange light to the warehouse floor. They were on, but a deep balcony ran around the entire room and the light had yet to hit me underneath it as I was. I stepped forward and looked around. The balcony was ringed with large, wooden crates: roughly six by six by six, old and greasy-looking, half covered with sheets and packing blankets.

The warehouse floor, which had been empty when I left it the night before, now sported a huge summoning circle, spray-painted in white. It was perhaps 75 feet in diameter, give or take. The symbol drawn within almost hurt my eyes. It seemed to reflect the ambient light in weird ways, appearing pearlescent and shifting slightly in the corner of your vision until you turned to try and catch the motion. As best I could make out, it resembled the elongated M-wings of the Angel Reaver with a smaller circle around the X. If I had to guess, it was the combined symbols for angel and world. They might be "higher beings" in a sense, but I don't think creativity is their strong suit. Of course, most symbolic, glyph-based alphabets tend to lean toward the intuitive. Maybe I'm being too hard on the motherfuckers. Was still going to kill 'em, though.

I waited, just feet from the edge of the light. Seconds went by, then I heard slow, deliberate footsteps. Archer stepped out of the darkness underneath the balcony about a third of the way across the floor, near the edge of the summoning circle closest to me. He turned to face me, still wearing his trench coat and fedora, the light hitting his glasses just so, reflecting and making them seem like opaque orange circles.

"Hello, Mr. Davidson," he said in his creepy, lightly accented voice.

I stepped into the light and held up the canvas sack from my shop. "Hiya, *Archer*. Got your book."

"Are you mocking me, sir?" The man sputtered, instantly angry and defensive.

I looked down at my newly-purchased trench coat, which was identical to his own, then angled my eyes upward to the brim of my new fedora, which also was a dead-ringer for Archer's. I was wearing my Wayfarer-style HUD specs, as usual, and while they were not identical to his little round frames, the sum total of the look got my point across.

"I have absolutely no idea what you are talking about," I said, grinning. "Isn't this appropriate attire for a clandestine meeting in an abandoned warehouse?" I held the book satchel to my chest and struck my best pulp magazine cover pose, simply oozing noir: a tough gumshoe frozen in the act of saving a gorgeous femme fatale from a group of bulldog-faced thugs in scally caps.

"You ... you are *insufferable*," he said coldly.

"Good thing we only have to suffer each other for a few more minutes, then," I said, laughing. "So, let's get this show on the road. Pay me, get your clients here, assuage my fears, and I'll hand over the book and you guys can fuck right off with it."

"First the book, then you meet my clients, then you get paid," Archer said through gritted teeth.

"Miles, where's the trust?" I asked. "Ok. Fine. I figured you'd say that. Tell you what. Call up your guys, have them pop in, and you and I will hand over the creds and the book at the same time while they watch. They can say a few words, and that'll be that. That work for you?"

He thought for a moment, then grunted his assent. Without

a word, he turned his back to me and began chanting in some other language that sounded like he was gargling mostly broken marbles. I'm not even going to try and reproduce it here. Just imagine it sounds like Sallow's mom when she's approaching orgasm, the poor dear. At least half of you probably know what that sounds like.

The lights began to flicker as he continued the chant, slowly raising his voice in volume and pitch. White shapes, tons of them, began to shimmer into being everywhere within the summoning circle. As Archer's dark song reached a fever pitch, he stopped, and the lights blinked out. A second later, they flashed back to life even brighter, completely illuminating the circle's occupants.

Around 100 extremely tall, dove-winged men stood around the circle, all facing me, their iridescent robes and pale white skin reflecting light painfully into my retinas. Their robes and feathers moved in an invisible breeze, as did their long, blonde hair. It was probably my imagination, but they all looked close to identical, to the point that it looked like the visual effects guy for my tale got bored and copy-pasted the same angelic dude into the room a hundred times or so. Their eyes, all pale glowing white, bored a hole into me.

Looking out onto a sea of eight-foot winged giants with glowing eyes, I tried not to piss myself. I succeeded, but it was a close thing. A drop or two might've eeked out.

"Well, Miles," I said, my voice trying not to crack. "You never told me you were working with a bunch of angels. I mean, wow. You REALLY don't seem the type to be on Heaven's payroll. No offense or anything."

"None taken," Archer said, stepping toward me. "Or not much, anyway. Enough small talk. Bring me the book."

I walked forward to meet him, taking the book out of its bag and tossing the satchel aside. "Creds," I said simply.

Archer reached into his coat pocket and pulled out a credstick. "260,000 credits, as promised."

I held the book out, and he likewise held the shiny, obsidian credstick toward me. He touched the book, and I grabbed one end of the credstick, but he didn't let go just yet. I saw the power of the book flow through him, and I imagined the hair on his arms was standing up under his coat. His eyes rolled upward slightly, and a soft moan escaped his lips. He let go of the credstick then, and I let go of the book.

I stepped back and tapped the credstick to my smartwatch and a tiny projection popped up showing the successful transfer of 260,000 credits to my account. I dropped the newly empty stick into my coat pocket. I made to look like I was casually grabbing my left wrist with my right hand and quickly tapped my smartwatch twice.

Archer held the book reverently with two hands, then he opened the cover, gazing quickly over the contents of the first page. He closed it, and held it tightly to his chest, closing both arms over it in an X.

"Our business is concluded," Archer said. "We ..."

I cut him off. "Hold up. Your friends haven't promised me that they'll do no harm with that bad boy."

"What good is a promise to one such as yourself," Archer said. "Are you a child? There is absolutely nothing you can do to enforce your will in this situation."

"Still," I said, smiling grimly. "Humor me. Pick one of them. Any one. Have him ... or they or whatever pronoun angels prefer ... step forward and tell me they mean humankind no harm with this book."

Archer stared at me for a beat, looked down at the book in his hand and visibly gave in. I sensed the invisible shrug. He couldn't figure out my angle, but he had the book, so fuck it. He turned and motioned to the nearest of the angels, who glided over, barely touching the ground with its bare feet. It stood about five feet from me. It turned to look at Archer.

"Tell him," Archer said impatiently. "Say it. He wants to hear the words." The angel turned back to me and I felt the weight of its glowing, otherworldly gaze.

"WE," it began in a voice that sounded like it was being

piped through a polyphonic octave pedal, at once projecting three separate voices and tones, totally creeping me the fuck out. “WE WILL NOT USE THE BOOK TO HARM HUMANKIND.”

I looked into that perfect pale face staring down at me blankly, that anthropomorphic image of perfection dreamed up by medieval theocrats, and I mustered all the courage I could and laughed.

“Eh. Fuck you, buddy,” I grinned. “I’m not buying it. Hit it, JB.”

A series of loud, sharp bangs issued from the balcony, like a string of firecrackers going off in sequence. It started to my left and rolled all the way around the room. Everyone looked up, including me. The front sides of the sixteen dirty, greasy, weather-worn crates had all fallen off with a loud crack from the tiny plastic explosive charges Johnny Boy had set to pop on my signal.

On the balcony to my left, Ariana, Helly, and Carlos stepped out from their thermal-blanket lined crates. Ariana was dressed in her battle leathers, her sword slung on her back. In her hands, she carried my Excalibur SR-2500. Helly, likewise covered in black leather, sported another of my guns, a Heckler & Koch HK 416K, a fine battle rifle. Not to mention the giant-ass axe on her back that was roughly the size of a Volkswagen Beetle. Carlos looked absolutely terrifying wearing his gyro-mounted, exoskeleton-supported GE BFG minigun, its Gatling-style barrels gleaming darkly in the reflected light.

To my right, Nichelle stepped up to the balcony’s edge dressed in sporty-looking red leathers (she’s such a fashionista) and carrying a huge next-gen battle rifle I didn’t recognize. Fucking show-off. JB was next in line, the big country boy sporting a bandolier of 12-gauge slugs and one of Unholy Water grenades courtesy of the Templars. In one giant, meaty paw, he held a semi-automatic shotgun with a gigantic 100-round drum magazine. In the other, a detonator. Mary Ann came next, my not-so-jolly green giantess friend sporting oversized motorcycle racing armor covered in matte black plates. The orc had a wicked, jagged sword slung on her back that was almost as big as a normal human and slightly larger than Helly. She held a .50-cal Orbital Eagle Defense pistol in each hand as she's never quite gotten the hang of long guns. (There's a joke in there somewhere that she would beat me for.)

The balcony directly across from me now held a group of twenty Templar knights in gleaming white Kevlar and ceramic plate armor, Sallow at their center. Each of them had a stylized red Templar cross painted across their chest and an M4-style rifle with a Templar Super Soaker on rails underneath.

Butch and Sundance hovered out from opposite corners of the back balcony as well, Butch flying high up in the rafters to help coordinate our attack, and Sundance floating out to fill the gap between the Templars and Mary Ann.

I took advantage of the distraction and threw off my trench coat and fedora. I was wearing black BDU fatigues with neck-to-toe Second Skyn armor underneath. I had a Colt Heathen slung in a drop holster on each hip, and an ultra-modern, tool-steel wakizashi with a flattened cross guard in an inverted sheath on my back so as to hide the grip under my coat. I reached behind me and swept forward the lovely FN SCAR-HX that was slung on my back, the battle rifle looking quite choice with its mottled gray digital camo furniture. If I do say so myself.

About this time, a creeping red fog began rolling out from all sides of the room, low to the floor. It had just started to reach the edges of the summoning circle, and some of the angels began to cough.

"And now, a little music, JB? Let's see what DJ Less-than-Lethal can spin for us." I said, looking up at Johnny Boy. He clicked his detonator once more and then placed it in his pocket.

Another couple of loud bangs rang out and the huge double steel doors fell forward behind me with a crash. Twin headlights backlit me briefly before I stepped aside to allow the Shaggin' Wagon to creep into the room next to me, a hooded Bishop behind the wheel. Giant loudspeakers had been strapped to the hardpoint ledges Nando had affixed to the sides on my request like little wings and a vertical speaker array had been bolted in a horizontal line in front of the spoiler. The Angel Reaver sigil had been painted on each of the four headlights, and the searing light burned into angels wherever it touched their flesh.

A wickedly sharp steel cowcatcher now welded across the van's front also sported one of the killer glyphs on each face. I had naturally loaded a new theme for the van for this special occasion: the insanely bright and garish yellow, red, and chrome of Judas Priest's Screaming for Vengeance album cover with its cybernetic raptor swooping down, talons outstretched, bringing swift death from above. I mean, come on. Could that even have BEEN more appropriate? If there's one thing I know a little about, it's fucking presentation.

Right on cue, there was a peal of church bells and thunder as the Shaggin' Wagon slowly, lovingly penetrated the room and the first haunting notes of Black Sabbath's title track from their eponymous 1970 debut album rang out into the huge space, amplified to window-shaking levels ... and there it was. The Devil's Chord. The Devil's Tritone. Diabolus in Musica.

The angels began to howl, some of them already doubled up in coughing fits from the Unholy Water fog I had flowing from my old band's smoke machines. They began to shimmer, their beautiful façades fading, dove wings turning charred black and sprouting eyes. Their robes faded and morphed into gristly gray bodies, their wet-looking flesh writhing with small tentacles everywhere. Their glowing eyes sank into dark pits that grew opaque, membranous covers. Screaming mouths grew impossibly wide and sprouted double-rows of shark-like teeth and twisting, grasping serpent-like tongues. Arms elongated and grew talons. Their agonized and furious howls were like the jarring grate and whine of metal grinding on metal.

I looked over and saw Bishop pick up the retro CB

microphone I used for the van's external speakers, which were now obviously being supplemented heavily. He held the mic to where his mouth was - hidden somewhere in that gigantic hood - flipped the bird towards the eldritch congregation before us, and pressed the talk button, a crackle of static popping out over the infernal guitar, the pounding of drums, and the punishing bass line of Sabbath at the birth of their legend.

"Tony Iommi sends his regards from beyond the grave, muthafuckas," the hood yelled gleefully.

I laughed and aimed my rifle at Archer, who immediately bolted for cover. The screaming horrors formerly known as Heaven's cover models took that moment to surge forward and I moved my aim toward them and started firing.

Once I had broken the seal, all of my friends started firing into the roiling sea of monster flesh as well. I heard the whine of Carlos' minigun barrels beginning to spin up, and the giant engine of destruction started raining down hellfire at about 2,000 rounds per minute, turning nightmares into instant pulp as he sprayed the gun back and forth like a suburban dad calmly watering his pristine lawn.

Nichelle's rifle was barking in three-round bursts, splattering ichor and offal everywhere her keen eye lighted. Helly was likewise mowing down rogue angels left and right, the massive grin on her face not a little bit scary to the average onlooker. Ariana was driving tacks, literally beheading interdimensional twatwaffles with every single shot. Mary Ann looked like an Old West gunslinger, dual-wielding her ginormous pistols to devastating effect, her thick arms taking the massive recoil in stride.

The Templars began their salvo by hosing down the angels with their Unholy Water guns, causing extra high pitched whines of pain everywhere the red liquid landed, then switching to fully automatic fire. Which reminded me ...

"Elias?" I yelled over the din as I fired into the crowd of screaming angels, my tactical earbuds picking up my voice and broadcasting it to the van's interior. "I think we need something a little more up tempo."

I could literally hear the smile in his voice. "You got it. DJ EKB-One at your service, um, yo."

"Needs work, but nice effort," I yelled. "Five points to Hufflepuff!"

The song abruptly changed, the murmur of rain behind the slow, droning riffs turning into a cataclysmic deluge, the peal of church bells growing louder as the primal devastation of Dave Lombardo pounding the skins hit us all like a three-punch combo from Ali in his prime.

One-two-three. The hiss of rain.

One-two-three. The whine of guitars creaking like rusty cemetery gates.

One-two-three. Sky-shattering thunder.

One-two-three. The twin axes of Jeff Hanneman and Kerry King gutting a hole in reality itself, their sinuous, harmonious riffplay twisting and intertwining like serpents mating on a grave.

One-two-three. Tom Araya's bassline pulsing like the angry heartbeat of Leviathan itself, causing tidal waves and abject destruction in its wake.

"Hit it, Helly." I said, firing my weapon dry, ejecting the empty magazine and slapping in a fresh one.

The dwarf turned from her grisly work and punched a giant, jolly, candy-like button on the wall behind her with the bottom of her fist.

Just as Slayer's exquisitely heavy masterpiece "Raining Blood" finished its intro and launched into a breakneck punk-like pace that would become one of the hallmarks of thrash metal, its pummeling and crushing tritones sending the Angelic Host into deeper fits of howling pain, the sprinklers far overhead began spraying red liquid down on everything and everyone.

My fireman pal had done his work and earned every penny. The Unholy Water reservoir we had tapped into the building's fire suppression system rapidly emptied itself, sending the Outsiders into an even higher level of screeching pain than they had likely thought possible and had probably never experienced in their eons of life.

Red rain poured down my cheeks as well as that of my friends as we continued our grim work, automatic fire and shotgun slugs and drone-based armor-piercing rounds cutting into angelic flesh from all sides. I'm not going to sugarcoat this. This was not a fight. It was not a battle. It was a shooting gallery. A heavily armed force cutting down the proverbial fish in a barrel, mercilessly and without regret. I *almost* felt a little sorry for them. Almost. The fuckers were going to wipe out our entire universe, after all. In the words of my Hawaiian-shirted half-alien demigod pal Josh … fuck 'em.

I heard a scream from the far side of the room. "Take out those speakers!" Archer yelled over the cacophony. So that asshole hadn't skipped dimensions yet, I thought to myself. Interesting.

The remaining angels, who looked to be about 30 or 35 in number at this point, started surging forward towards me and the van, black wings outstretched, razor-filled maws hanging wide and talons cutting the air.

"Hold your fire," I yelled to my assembled company as the Host approached me. Which was kind of redundant as they wouldn't have fired toward me anyway, being the pros they are. But, still. You have to say the words. I kept firing into the wall of creatures as they swarmed my way, taking them out in ones and twos, but not quickly enough. I heard my companions above start scrambling toward the metal stairs that led down to the warehouse floor. Ariana couldn't wait and somersaulted the railing to land next to me in a perfect three-point superhero landing. She drew her sword, grinning savagely like an aspect of Death herself.

"Hiya, sailor," she said to me, not taking her eyes off the rush of angels as they approached. (Rage of angels? What's the collective for angels? Rash of angels? An infection of angels?

An herpeaux of angels? No fucking clue.)

"You fucking goddess," I laughed, swinging the SCAR back behind me and drawing a Heathen with my right hand and unsheathing my wakizashi with my left. I spun it around to loosen my wrist and also to look badass in case anyone was watching.

The engines of the Shaggin' Wagon spun up to a higher pitch and Bishop punched the van forward past us, plowing into the oncoming angels, the sigil-bedecked cowcatcher cutting through them like a white-hot meat cleaver through sticks of warm butter. He zipped through them and hit the brakes, fishtailing around to the right, knocking a few more creatures off their clawed feet.

The soundtrack to our angelic massacre, which must've continued Lou's suggested tritone mix while Bishop was busy behind the wheel, launched into Judas Priest's "Painkiller", Scott Travis' brutal drums leading into another twin guitar assault courtesy of Glenn Tipton and K.K. Downing. Followed by, of course, the majestic screams of Rob Halford.

Ari and I ran forward, blades high. The rest of our group had reached the warehouse floor behind us and were drawing blades or guns better suited for close combat. Carlos had left his exoskeleton and minigun upstairs and had apparently borrowed a 12-gauge pump off of Johnny Boy. Mary Ann was still at her rootin' tootin'-est, only stopping to holster one gun and slam a fresh magazine home now and again.

Nichelle had traded her battle rifle for a next-gen Sig, her under-barrel green laser flashing through the red fog to land on fang-filled faces and giant wing-borne eyes, and she left each of them thoroughly ventilated. Johnny Boy was laughing like a madman, firing slugs into angels like a kid at a carnival trying to win an overstuffed animal prize, taking baseball-sized chunks of flesh out with every shot. Helly's axe left an absolute swath of destruction in its path, the resolute dwarf practically climbing the angels' bodies at a run to lop off heads and sever limbs. The Templars had drawn swords and were all doing their part, their white armor now smeared with black blood, gelatinous ichor and dark feathers.

Ari and I did our best to stab or sever everything we came into contact with, she doing it exponentially more gracefully that I. Watching her with a sword made me feel like the brawler and basher that I was compared to her, the elf clearly representing the next rung on the evolutionary ladder of martial prowess. She twirled and spun like a ballerina with a blade, dancing light-footed from angel to angel - vertical slices here, a quick thrust there, an upward cut – without so much as breathing heavily. And her hair looked AMAZING. I might as well have been an angry child with a machete, hacking my way through a bamboo thicket.

Before I knew it, we had slashed, shot, bashed, diced, chopped, maimed and killed every last creature standing. It happened so suddenly that we ended up in a confused, gore-covered wad in the center of the summoning circle, looking around for our next targets and finding none. The music stopped and Bishop stepped out of the van, his face still lost somewhere in the yawning cavern of his hood.

"Don't you fucking say it," Sallow yelled at him.

"Say what?" the huge-ass hood asked. "Oh! No. I'm good. I have learned my lesson. I will not say a single thing about how that went smoothly and easier than expect ..."

"FUCK," at least half of the assembly yelled, cutting Bishop off. The other half uttered some closely related curses or variants. I heard at least one "For fuck's sake," and a few exclamations of "Goddamnit!" and one, sad and resigned "What the hell, man?"

"That doesn't count, does it?" Bishop asked, lowering his hood. "I mean, I SAID I wasn't going to say it. Daniel does that all the time!"

"Only when he's insulting people, though," Helly said, leaning on her axe and crossing her arms. "If you say it in a jinx-context, you're literally taunting the universe; daring it to raw-dog you with no foreplay or lube whatsoever."

"Sorry, Bishop," Ariana said, smiling apologetically. "Thems the rules."

We heard a slow, rhythmic sound off to the side. We all turned to see Archer walking slowly out of the darkness nearby, holding the fake book to his chest with one arm as he mockingly slow-clapped.

"Bravo, intrepid adventurers," he sang out, smirking all the while. "Well done! Well done, indeed! You have laid waste to an entire host of angels. And barely a single scratch on you! I am so very impressed. Is this your vaunted 'Black Ops team', Mr. Davidson?"

"Part of it, sure," I said. "It's hard to get the whole crew together these days, you know? Kids, adult responsibilities, board meetings and the like. We're all so busy that it's rare we can get *everyone* to come out, even for a fun time like this."

"So droll, as always," he said, smiling his creeptastic smile.

"And if you don't mind me saying, you seem awfully chipper for a guy who just saw every one of his clients murdered in front of him," I replied, shrugging, still holding my short sword and pistol pointed at the floor.

"Oh," he said, laughing quietly. "I expected THAT. In fact, I was counting on it."

I leaned over to Helly. "This is where he starts monologuing," I said in a stage whisper.

"Nuh uh," Helly said, wiping some of the gore and red liquid from her face with her left hand and flinging it toward the ground. "Betcha he doesn't."

"What do you wanna bet?" I whispered.

"If he starts monologuing, I'll jump your bones later," she grinned. "If he doesn't, you can jump mine."

"I like it. Sounds like a win-win. Throw in dinner and you're on," I laughed.

"HEY," Archer said. "I'm right here. Talking. To you. You are being terribly rude."

"Whoops," I said. "My bad. Please continue."

"As I was saying," he began, and I looked at Helly and gave

her a knowing 'here it comes' smirk. "You double crossing the angels was part of my plan all along."

"Huh," I said. "I didn't expect that. How was it part of your plan? Go on."

"You can't encourage him, Daniel," Helly hissed at me. "That's, like, leading the witness or something."

Archer stopped and looked at us as if we were unruly school children disrupting his class.

"Sorry," Helly said. "Sorry. Just, you know, keep going ... if you'd like. Or not. As it pleases you."

Archer huffed. "I had fully intended for you to kill them all for me, as I myself couldn't do it, um, myself."

"Why's that?" I asked innocently.

Helly nudged me hard with her elbow. "You're still doing it!"

"Because of the politics involved," Archer said simply. "If I had taken direct involvement in their death, their people would have considered it an act of war against my people."

"Who are your people?" I asked.

"That sounds kind of low-key racist, Daniel," Mary Ann said.

"Shush, you. It's not racist. I said 'your people,' not 'you people.' He has a people. I'm not making a value judgment against them," I said, grinning. "I mean, he's an asshole, but the rest of them could be amazing. I don't know."

"Oh, that's not important right now," Archer said. "What is important is that they were my final obstacle to doing what I want, and you have delivered into my hands the very means to make obtaining my goal possible." He held the book out and waved his other hand in front of the cover like a book salesman showing off his wares.

"Well, fuck," Sallow said. "That doesn't sound good."

"Shhh," I said to him. "Let him keep going. He's just a few sentences short of a full monologue. I have an important bet riding on this."

"Oh, there's definitely going to be something riding on THAT," Helly said, giggling.

"You see," Archer said, finally having had his fill and

just ignoring us. "They wanted to destroy this world and everyone in it ... unmake all of you and everything you have accomplished throughout the whole of human history. They approached us about this as we can more fully operate within your dimension, and I was chosen to facilitate the genocide by obtaining the book for them. But I ... WE ... never had any intention of letting them kill you. You are too valuable to us. As are your works."

"Because we're so amazing and full of life?" Bishop asked.

"No, because you will make excellent slaves," Archer stated. "But also yes? Your capacity for love and imagination and creation makes enslaving you so very satisfying, and we feed off negative emotions: your dark thoughts and your crushed dreams. You are the only beings in the multiverse that I have found with the capacity for such despair and disillusionment, because you DO love, and dream, and hope and wish and create. And you prize freedom above all things. Taking those things from you creates the perfect vessel for everything we crave."

"I think that's it," I whispered to Helly. "That's TOTALLY enough for a monologue."

"Fuck," she said, hanging her head. "You're right. Heavy sigh. I guess you get to bone me. Or was it the other way around?"

"Eh," I said. "Tomato, toe-mah-toe."

"Are the two of you really making small talk and jokes while I am talking about enslaving your entire species?" Archer finally said, exasperated.

"I mean, kind of?" I offered. "We're just a little competitive. It was a high stakes bet. Anyway, so it's your plan to use us as despair batteries? Will you put us in stacked pods like in the Matrix trilogy or will you just subjugate us like Invasion of the Body Snatchers or something? Half and half? Do you guys have a dental plan or medical? How are you with preexisting conditions? You can't just take over an entire species and NOT take care of them."

"I don't know what any of that means," Archer began, frowning. "You fail to amuse me."

"It's not about you," Ariana said, her sword leaning on her shoulder. "He does it purely for his own amusement."

"Amen," Nichelle said. "He doesn't care if anyone finds it funny or not. And he'll just keep going, and going ..."

"Pipe down, you two," I said, grinning. "Also, ouch."

"ENOUGH," Archer yelled. "It is time for you to be silent and witness the birth of a New Age. The Age of Man has come to an end."

"That's a little low-key sexist," Nichelle said.

Archer ignored us and held the book out before him, opening it about mid-way. He flipped through a few pages looking for something.

"Wait ..." he said, a note of something like fear in his voice. "This ... is gibberish. I can't ... this ..." Archer slammed the book closed and threw it aside. "THIS IS A COPY. A FORGERY. A FAKE. WHAT HAVE YOU DONE? AND HOW? WHERE IS THE REAL BOOK?!" He was visibly shaking with rage by this point.

"You know," I said. "I could answer all of those point-by-point, but I'm kind of tired of your bullshit."

I looked around at my companions and smiled an evil grin worthy of Lou himself.

"Fuck you. You can't have us. Sincerely, Humankind," I said, raising my Heathen with all the speed my augmented reflexes could handle and pulling the trigger. I had placed my targeting reticle right between and slightly over his eyes. My gun barked once, and a perfectly round black hole appeared in his forehead.

Archer swayed backward, his fedora falling off along with his little round glasses. Before he fell completely, though, his body went rigid and swung back up to face us. The hole in his forehead began to knit itself closed, and he turned to look behind him, showing us a massive exit wound that appeared to be slowly doing the same.

He laughed then, a deep, rumbling chuckle that started

way down below and built until it became raucous, unhinged, hysterical braying.

"Oh, Mr. Davidson," he said, scratching the side of his nose with his middle finger and smiling. I think it was a coincidence. I doubt he was trying to flip me off. He pointed at me and shook his index finger, like an indulgent parent mildly admonishing a child. "You almost had me there, except for one small detail."

His eyes panned the assembled warriors around him, and he grinned like a creep, staring directly at me.

"I ..." he said in a cold, clear voice dripping with malice. "I am no angel."

CHAPTER THIRTY-EIGHT

Archer reached down and pulled his trench coat open, rolling his shoulders to shrug it off in one smooth motion. Underneath, he was bare-chested and thin, his stomach sunken and his ribs visible and prominent. His skin was mottled and gray in places and fish-belly white in others. There were *things* under his skin ... knobs and protuberances that moved furtively, as if seeking a way out. Two of these rose up to his armpits and began stretching out the skin until it burst with a wet squelch, spindly ropes of gristle and muscle vomiting out, growing thicker as they did so. In a moment, they had formed into a second, smaller set of vestigial arms, the exposed muscles red and raw.

His head snapped violently to his right with the cracking of vertebrae, the skin of his cheek and shoulder beginning to melt and reach toward each other, melding and meshing together, as his now-vertical smile grew impossibly wide ... rows and rows of jagged, razor-like teeth sprouting from his gums in a bloody torrent. His now blistered tongue lolled out of the abattoir of his mouth, lengthening and twisting upward, melting into his face as it went, stretching ever upward until it formed a long, smooth tentacle that draped down his back. His legs began to swell with muscle, ripping his trousers as they went. Likewise, his shoes split apart to make room for feet that had grown into large, lizard-like extremities that each held three toes with sharp-looking talons. A tail became visible between his legs, dropping down and splitting apart to form a third muscular proto-leg, pink and wet.

Thankfully, the landscape between his legs was a vacant lot and as smooth as a Ken doll's crotch, because I am not sure my sanity could have survived seeing his eldritch space junk.

What little body hair he had seemed to thicken and become stringy, rubbery flagella, the tiny tentacles waving and writhing all over the surface of his gray skin like a nest of baby vipers. His nipples split apart and blind, cataract-covered eyes bugged out in their place, bloodshot orbs sweeping left to right independent of each other as if in search of, well, anything.

The assembled crowd of erstwhile adventurers, myself included, stood stock still, watching completely transfixed and aghast as Archer transformed from creepy human into an absolutely inhuman horror show. I would venture to say that this experience was so outside any that we had ever witnessed that our minds might have short-circuited a bit, neurons misfiring and synapses failing to connect. I totally understood, then, why most of Lovecraft's protagonists ended up insane and had difficulty describing the cosmic horrors they had witnessed.

A deep, rumbling yet raspy voice that sounded like the Crypt Keeper on steroids (Oh, come on. Tales from the Crypt? 1989? Based on the successful horror comic series? Great score by Danny Elfman? Jeez, you guys are lame.) issued forth from somewhere on the creature and maybe also in our heads? It seemed to be broadcast directly into our craniums, but as I had never experienced telepathy before, it was hard to say. I know I heard it with my ears, but also, in other ways? I thought it at the same time in an alien voice that was not my own inner monologue. And my skin seemed to feel the words touching it as well. It is so hard to describe. It was a wholly new experience, and it 100% felt like a violation on every level.

"ANGELS ARE NOTHING COMPARED TO ME ... LESS THAN INSIGNIFICANT. I AM A CHILD OF HE WHO WALKS AMONG THE STARS, THE STEWARD AND MESSENGER OF THE OUTER GODS, THE CRAWLING CHAOS, THE BLACK PHAROAH, THE

GOD OF A THOUSAND FORMS, THE STALKER AMONG THE STARS, THE FACELESS GOD, THE HAUNTER OF THE DARK, THE WHISPERER IN THE DARKNESS. I AM SPAWN OF NYARLATHOTEP! GRANDSON OF AZATHOTH, THE BLIND IDIOT GOD, THE NUCLEAR CHAOS, THE DARK ONE, THE DAEMON SULTAN, THE COLD ONE, THE BLIND DREAMER, THE ..."

"Fuck me," I said, shaking my head and interrupting. "I know we're supposed to be all cowed and freaked out, and believe me, I am. I'm practically shitting my pantaloons here. But, like, do all these motherfuckers have like twenty names or more? If he's going to be much longer, I'm stepping out for a bite."

"I could eat," Sallow said, grinning.

"Anything but calamari," Ariana said, laughing. "Or octopus."

"Eww. And those growths along his ribs look kind of like roe," Helly added. "So, I think maybe sushi is out entirely. And caviar, too, now that I think about it."

"That thing in the back looks kind of like a raw frog's leg," Nichelle added. "Also, double EWW."

"Thank half-alien Jesus he doesn't have a dick," Carlos threw in. "Imagine what sort of food THAT would fuck up for us."

"Goddamnit, Carlos," Johnny Boy said. "Now I can't stop thinking about it. Pretty much any meat tube is out now ... kielbasa, knockwurst, bratwurst, good ol' American hot dogs, hot links ..."

"Let's just skip any phallic or phallus-adjacent snacks altogether," I noted. "Because his imaginary space junk could also look like kafta fingers, Armenian lula kebabs, egg rolls, Filipino lumpia, Thai spring rolls ... the ones with the translucent wrapping where you can sort of make out the insides?"

"His space dick would TOTALLY look like that," Helly said. "And goddamnit. I could've really gone for Thai."

"We still can," I noted, smiling. "Not a single thing on that monstrosity looks like pad thai."

"Huh. Valid point," Helly agreed. "Also tom kha kai soup. Fucking YUM."

"Right?!" I said. "I love that shit! So coconutty yet savory ... umami for days! With a touch of acid and that hint of lemongrass ..."

"WHAT IS WRONG WITH YOU PEOPLE?!!" the Archer thing screamed into our minds.

"YOU people?" Ariana said. "Racist."

"Right?" Nichelle said. "And not even low-key. Like, we should get him a pointy little white hood for his pointy little tentacle head."

"To be fair, though, we are kind of multicultural," Sallow said. "So, maybe he hates everyone?"

"We *are* quite diverse," Carlos said with pride. "We're like the cast of a CW show from the 2020s."

"I mean, fuck, man," Johnny Boy said. "You are half-black, half-Mexican and gay. You're like woke personified just by your damned self. You tick all the boxes."

"No one says 'woke' anymore, redneck," Carlos said, laughing. "That's your low breeding talking."

"Your mom likes to be woke up by this big ol' red dick," JB chirped. "Also, I used the word 'personified.' That's a big one for me. And you didn't even notice. It's like you don't even care anymore. Who ARE you?"

"STOP!!!" the Archer thing yelled. "I COMMAND YOU TO CEASE TALKING!!!"

"Or what?" Helly said. "You gonna gross us to death? Slimy-looking bastard."

"Maybe we can annoy him into another dimension?" I added helpfully.

"BRING ME THE BOOK OF RAZIEL!" it screeched into our minds, causing all of us to wince and grab our temples with free hands if we had them. I held the back of my hand that was still gripping my Heathen to my forehead. It didn't help.

"He REALLY has to stop doing that," I said. "I mean, fuck it.

Let's shut him up."

I raised the Heathen and started firing into the monstrous creature that used to be Archer. The others took the cue and raised their weapons and began firing as well, the entire giant semicircle of human and human-adjacent folk slinging as much copper-jacketed lead toward him as we could. And that was quite a bit.

The Archer thing, the spawn of Nyarlathotep, writhed and screamed as we fired upon it, bullets and slugs piercing every inch of its flesh. We were definitely hurting it and overwhelming it with our assault, but it appeared the bullet holes were knitting closed almost as quickly as we could make them.

And then it happened. We ran dry, hammers and other firing mechanisms falling on empty chambers, the contained explosions falling silent and turning into little staccato clicks all around.

"Well, fuck," I said. I had fired both of my Heathens empty and emptied my SCAR-HX as well after holstering my pistols and returning my wakizashi to its scabbard. All of my spare magazines were at my feet, empty as well. The others were in similar states.

Nyarlathotep's ugly fucking kid laughed in our heads, standing before us as pristine and whole as he/it had been before our attack. A bullet plunked down to the floor behind him, seemingly from under his vestigial third leg. Then a deluge of them followed, pouring down into a clinking pile like the worst casino jackpot EVER.

"Oh my Josh," Ariana said. "Where are all those coming from?"

"AHHH," Helly said. "It must have a butthole! A SPACE BUTTHOLE."

"He's literally shitting bullets," Sallow said, grimacing. As was his way.

"I mean, everything has a butthole?" Nichelle said. "Wasn't there even a children's book about that back in the day?"

"I think that was 'Everyone Poops'," a Templar named Mike chimed in, raising his hand.

"Can't poop without a butthole," Carlos noted.

"Sea sponges, sea anemones, and jellyfish don't have buttholes," Johnny Boy said. "They eat and poop from the same hole."

"Goddamnit," Sallow said. "I did NOT need to know that."

"Disgusting but impressive, my brother," Carlos said, fist-bumping JB. "I knew you had read a book or two."

"It was an audiobook," JB said, grinning, then sobbing theatrically. "I never learned to READ! Maw and Paw never taught me!"

"And the Oscar goes to …" Nichelle said, laughing. "Drum roll, please …"

"Speaking of doing many different things with the same hole," I began. "Sallow's mom …"

"SHUT IT!" Sallow said. "If I still had any bullets, I would shoot you right now."

The awful Star-Spawn of He With A Ton Of Stupid Names howled something unintelligible into our heads and started moving forward toward us, clawed hands grasping and vestigial limbs flopping about sickeningly.

We all drew our blades and prepared ourselves as best we could for the monster's attack.

"How can we kill it if it heals so fucking quickly?!" Sallow yelled at me, despite the fact that we were all wearing tactical earbuds tuned to the same channel.

"GAH. Simmer down, you," I said. "I don't know. I'm thinking!"

"Think quicker," Ariana said, stepping forward and raising her bright blade.

"That's not his strong suit," Helly said, drawing her huge axe. "He's more of a methodical planner. Half-assed but occasionally inspired. He's not the best at switching gears."

"I can hear you," I said. "I'm RIGHT here."

"I think I have something," Bishop said into our earbuds

from over by the wagon where he had stayed, semi-cowering during our one-way firefight with He Who Poops Bullets. "Can you guys distract him for a few minutes and then drive him toward me?"

"Toward YOU?" Sallow said. "You're the least competent combative we have on site. Fuck. That sounded mean, sorry. I just ... damnit. Don't want to see you hurt, that's all."

"Awww," Bishop said in our ears. "That's so sweet, Jonas. You're like a real boy, now. Your prayers have been answered. Praise be to Josh!"

"Worst. Priest. Ever!" Sallow grunted, swiping his longsword at one of the creature's arms that was currently reaching toward him.

"It's not always about hitting or slashing things, my Templar friend," Bishop said. "Sometimes, it's about what you know. Knowing is half the battle."

"G.I. Joe!!!" Ariana yelped, dodging Archer-Thing's head tentacle as it swished toward her face.

"NICE!" I said to the elf, hacking at The Former Bespectacled Creeper From The Neighborhood Playground. "Ten points to ... fuck. Did we ever assign you a house?"

"Ravenclaw, obviously," Ariana said, laughing. "Hello? Math nerd."

"That's fair," I said.

While this was going on, I took a peek around the creature to see Bishop – lost in his hood again - pulling the hidden dagger out of the giant Black Sabbath-meets-Favor Flav Celtic cross that was draped from his neck. He ran over to an open section of floor over to my far right, in front of the angelic summoning circle and closer to the warehouse entrance. He looked over at the creature, sizing it up, then he knelt and started duck walking in a large circle, holding the knife point as hard as he could against the ferrocrete floor of the building.

I had to pop back into the fight to dodge a few swipes from He Who Can't Take A Fucking Joke, but I had seen enough to know what Bishop was attempting.

"You are a goddamned genius, Elias," I said, grunting with the effort of dodging the creature's blows. Like 28 other armed motherfuckers in the room and the bastard had to keep swatting at ME. I guess he held me responsible for all of this? I suppose it was the least I deserved. "You know what you are doing?"

"Sort of," the priest said in our ears. "Pretty sure. We'll know in a minute or so."

"That'll have to do," I said, then continued quieter, hopefully loud enough to be picked up by my earbud and not loud enough for Archer Part 2: Electric Boogaloo to hear me. "Everyone, break left slowly and try to drive him toward Bishop. No hurry, just get him pointed that way."

The Templars off to my right peeled off one by one, running behind us to take a place at the other side of the line, instantly aiming our semicircle of hacking and slashing toward the priest. It wasn't easy engaging him as we were so many. He would approach a part of our line and people in front could manage to fight him off as a few tangential folks got in stabs, but big as he was, nearly thirty people fighting one big guy was awkward as hell.

We all threw everything we had at the thing, though, slicing nearly through limbs at some points and nearly severing his tentacle head completely. Finally, Mary Ann's gigantic orc sword swooped down like a celestial guillotine, her mighty blow actually taking off the creature's right arm entirely. The fucking thing used its fingers to crawl back over to him and up his body to get in the general vicinity of the stump where it came from and slithered out to reconnect itself with a wet slurp.

"Fuck," Nichelle said. "Did you guys see that?"

"Nah," Helly said. "I was zoning out and working on my grocery list for the weekend."

"Smartass dwarf," Nichelle laughed.

"It's part of her charm," Mary Ann said. "That and her rockin' little bod."

"Stahp!" Helly giggled. "I don't have time to think sexy things about giant orc women AND fight a … whatever the fuck this thing is."

"Well, that's a first," I said. "I figured at least one hemisphere of your little brain was always thinking of sexy things."

"Valid," Helly said, leaping back to avoid a swipe of talons. "Mmm. Big green boobs. Still, though, kinda busy!"

We pressed forward as hard as we safely could, driving the horror slowly back toward the hooded priest. It was exhausting work. I looked around the beast and saw Bishop scratching a few smaller symbols in the floor within the circle that was now about five feet from the creature's backside foot tail/leg thingy.

"Done!" the priest yelled.

"Out-fucking-standing," I yelled. "Now get the hell out of there!"

Bishop bolted toward the back of the building and then turned, now a good 15 feet away from his hastily scrawled circular sigil. It looked like two or three overlapping pentagrams and half-stars with connecting lines swooping away in spots. We hacked and slashed and continued driving Archer 2.0 until his back foot crossed the line of the circle, and then, finally, the entire creature stood within the outer ring.

"That's it! Back off guys, and surround the bastard," I said. Our group spread out and completely cut off the creature's escape. "Keep it in the circle! Whatever you're going to do, Bishop, fucking do it now!"

The priest raised one hand skyward, pointed the other at the creature with fingers splayed and began chanting in a guttural, liquid-sounding language similar to the one Archer had used when summoning the angels … all long vowels and sharp consonants broken up by grunts and choked sounds. The Archer-Thing screamed in our heads.

"NOOOOOO!!!!" it howled. "HOW CAN THIS BE?! YOU CAN'T … STOP … NOW! IT HURTS! YOU … PATHETIC ANIMALS!!! HOW?! I WILL KILL YOU ALL! EVERY LAST ONE …"

Bishop kept chanting, nonplussed.

"Everyone focus on that thing and want it the fuck GONE," I yelled at the others over Bishop's chant and the continuing litany of invectives, entreaties and threats from the monster. "Sound, symbol and intent!"

Like Archer before him, Bishop's incomprehensible sing-songy liturgy rose in pitch and volume until the priest was screaming at the top of his lungs one repetitive phrase, which, again, I will not even attempt to reproduce. I mean, I could, but it would go something like this:

"Blah-blah-BLAH-BLAH-NYARLATHOTEP-blah-blah-BLAHBLAHBLAH!" Bishop yelled, my inability to parse his vocalizations reminding me of the dog in the old Far Side cartoon by Gary Larson that could only pick her name out of the gibberish her human was speaking to her. (It was Ginger, by the way.)

After a number of repetitions ... I lost count as I was busy hating The Thing Formerly Known As Archer away ... the inhuman bag of gristle and sinew and tentacles drove one last mental screech into our heads, causing us all to drop our weapons and fall to our knees, covering our ears or grabbing our temples uselessly, and then ... it was gone. The creature merely popped out of being, leaving behind a smell like a boggy marsh on a hot day with a dash of sulfur and feces.

Silence.

"Holy SHIT," Helly said. "Did we, like, just win?"

"Well, we're not dead," Ariana said. "And the thing is gone. I'll take that W."

We all helped each other to our feet. Bishop slowly walked over to where I stood, pulling off his gigantic fucking hood as he did so. I reached out to pull him into a hug.

"What the hell, Elias?" I said, pulling him back out to arm's length. "That was incredible! How the FUCK did you pull that off? I mean, wow, man. I am so fucking proud of you right now. Fred Rogers would be SO very proud of you."

"Yeah," Sallow said, reaching out to grab Bishop's shoulder.

"That was ... I don't know what that was, but you fucking saved the day, mate."

"Well," Bishop said, grinning and maybe blushing a bit under the praise. "As you know, Daniel, my old basement had a copy of the Necronomicon ... not the original, mind you, but a very early edition. And, you know, I might've read it a few times over the years. Parts of it, well, maybe a few hundred? And I always liked to trace the symbols. I had entire notebooks filled with each of the Outer Gods sigils that I had copied thousands of times. This one, the symbol for Nyarlathotep, was always one of my favorites. In fact, it was even inscribed on the cover of the foul book itself."

"But, like, you're a Christian priest," Mary Ann said. "Why would you copy all of these pagan symbols over and over? And read an infernal book so many times that you apparently know a ritual of banishing from memory?"

"You make a good point," Bishop said. "I guess it was a combination of impulses. Part of it felt like, well, a know-thine-enemy sort of thing. Part of it was sheer boredom. Whether or not you believed all of the stuff in it, it was pretty fascinating. And the rituals, they kind of have a way of burning into your brain without you even trying to memorize them. Again, not that I hadn't read that particular one like a hundred times or more. And, last but not least, I had gone quite mad, you know. Totally barmy."

"Which came first, the madness or the Necronomicon?" Ariana asked.

"No idea," Bishop said. "Madness is a strange thing. It's a bit like having that alien monster's thoughts and voice in your head. You can hear it, but it sounds like you at first. And then, you realize it's not, but it also IS? I am not sure I am explaining this well at all."

"How the fuck did you know his father's sigil would work on him?" Helly inquired.

"I didn't," Bishop replied. "It was a total gamble. But, as Daniel says, it was the only plan I had, half-baked or no. I figured the odds of it working were about ... um ... 80/20?"

That definitely got a laugh from the folks that knew me well.

"Where did it send him? Where did you banish him TO?" Nichelle asked.

"I have no idea," Bishop said.

"Doesn't matter," I said. "Not HERE. He Who Can Go Eat A Bag Of Rotten Dicks is gone. For now. I doubt we've seen the last of him, though. But that is a problem for another day, my friends. I don't know about you, but I am fucking BEAT."

Murmurs of agreement made the rounds.

"Yeah," Helly agreed. "I slept like shit in that stupid box, Daniel." More, louder murmurs of agreement. "And if I never have to use a 5-gallon bucket as a toilet again, it will be too fucking soon."

"Come on, though," I said, laughing. "They're 'chemical toilets,' and I even sprang for the actual toilet seats for maximum comfort."

"Says the fucking guy who pissed in an actual toilet before sleeping in his own bed and not on an air mattress. And had an actual meal for dinner," Ariana groused. "And you *really* didn't have to send us pictures of it, Daniel. Dick move."

"It was only a salad. It was very pretty, but it wasn't *that* good," I grinned. "However, I am so very grateful for the sacrifice each and every one of you made, leaving your good night's rest, decent meals and ability to poop in private on the altar of saving the fucking universe. I knew as soon as I let Archer know where this place was, he'd start making preparations of his own. We couldn't risk him getting here first. And I have to say, walking into this place a little while ago with fresh eyes, it totally blew me away. We did a bang-up job aging those crates to look old as hell.

"Still have grease under my nails, thank you very much," Nichelle added. Lots of general moaning and bitching about that one ensued.

And so it went. The Templars gathered up all of their

empty magazines, retrieved their Unholy Water receptacles and unused grenades, and were on their way with many handshakes and clapping of backs. Sallow stuck behind for a few minutes after they left. I asked him to meet me at the shop later in the week where I would hand over the actual Book of Raziel to the Order for safekeeping.

"Well, Davidson," the grim knight said to me, barely suppressing a grin. "You fucking pulled it off. I had many, many doubts. I mean ... TONS of doubts. Soooo many doubts ..."

"Fuck off," I said, laughing. "I get the picture. Go on."

"And again, you may be the luckiest guy on all of the orbitals," he said. "But you did it. We all came out of this alive and managed to save the fucking world."

"It helps to know a shit-ton of amazing, talented people," I said. "I could not have pulled this off without each and every one of you." I looked around at my friends. "Thank you all so very much. I can't begin to express how much you all mean to me, and how thankful I am to know you."

"Such a fucking softie," Carlos said, grinning. "You're not wrong though. We are badass."

"Fuckin' A," Johnny Boy said. "But this does NOT let you off the hook for the salad pics. I was still looking at those at 3 AM, munching on a shitty protein bar the whole time and cursing your name."

"Noted," I laughed.

Mary Ann walked over and wrapped her arms around me and squeezed me tightly.

"Glad you're still alive, Daniel," she said into my ear.

"Same to you, pretty lady," I said, hugging her back. "Couldn't do ANY of this without you. Never EVER wanna try."

I let go of my orc BFF, and turned back to my small group of friends.

"Nope," Sallow said. Looking at the others. "He has that fucking look. He's going to give one of his half-assed inspirational speeches."

"I mean, come on," I said, laughing. "The tiny group of people in this room just saved all of humanity. We kept literally ALL of human history from being erased. We saved every last building on every orbital, and every man, woman, child, non-binary person, orc, elf, dwarf, halfling, vampire, and werewolf that lives, works and plays in them. Every creature in every warren, every bird in every tree. We saved every book, every film, every culinary tradition, every race, and every language EVER ... all from fucking extinction? And you don't think that merits a tiny little speech? One little heartfelt summary? One single soliloquy for the soul?"

"No fucking way," Sallow said.

"Not a chance," Ariana said.

"Nopers," Helly agreed. "Not even if they DO get me hot and bothered. Too fucking tired."

"Totally not in the mood," Nichelle said.

"Sorry, bud," Mary Ann said. "Maybe next time."

"Let's not and say we did," Carlos added.

"Let's go get a fucking hamburger," Johnny Boy said. "Mr. Talky-talk-talk over here can get himself another goddamned salad. I ain't had nothing to eat in 24 hours except stupid ration bars." Loud, raucous murmurs of agreement abounded.

I sighed and laughed, shaking my head. "Fuck you guys. Let's go eat."

EPILOGUE

I awoke the next morning feeling like someone had beaten me from head to toe with a ball peen hammer. I opened my eyes slowly and stared at the ceiling, groaning. A green hand reached into view and dragged an index finger languorously down my lips and neck and then my bare chest.

"Morning, tiger," Mary Ann said from next to me. I rolled over with a start, suddenly fully awake.

My beautiful orc friend was half covered by sheets and the comforter, one long green leg sticking out and resting comfortably over mine. Her bare shoulders peeked out from under the covers, and her voluminous red hair looked like it had been thoroughly manhandled, pardon the pun. She grinned her best predator's grin and licked her upper incisor.

"How did you sleep, lover?" she asked, stretching like a big, green cat. One of the large, dangerous ones. Not a domestic tabby. "I slept soooo good. I always do after a night like that. Half-alien JESUS, I had forgotten how good you are at the sex stuff. SO hot. And, wow, that thing you do with your ..."

"GAH!!!" I yelled, sitting bolt upright. "How ... I mean ... what the ... how could this have happened?"

"Well, Danny," she began, smiling. "When two people care for each other very much ... or they are very horny, or sometimes, blissfully, a combination of both ..."

"I know how SEX happens, you fiend!" I yelled clutching the covers to my chest. "I mean, how did we? I don't remember anything! And, I mean, I can't get drunk so ... HOW?"

"I don't know, sweetcheeks," she said, grinning evilly and reaching over to pull down my covers and tweak my nipple. "Maybe our lovemaking was so mind-blowing that it actually blew your mind? Certainly wasn't the only thing that was blown ..."

"FUCK!" I said. "I mean, shit. You know I love you ... and there was that one time, but this ... this complicates things."

"It's not THAT complicated," Helly said, stepping out of the master bathroom with a toothbrush in her mouth, wearing nothing but a pair of black panties and one of my concert shirts. It was a Lamb of God shirt sporting the eagle skeleton. She had rolled it up and tied it in front so it wouldn't be a dress on her. To be fair, it had never looked so good. Her massive blonde mane was wrapped up in a towel in such a way that she looked vaguely like a vizier or caliph of old.

The dwarf continued cleaning her teeth, talking around the brush. "I mean, both of you were fucking *amazing*. I had no idea it could even BE like that. Total top two for me. Hands down. Let me get cleaned up and we can go again!"

"What the fuck is going on?" I yelled, looking at the ceiling. "I'm still horrified, but also ... I mean, now I REALLY want to remember. How ... FUCK!" I threw myself backward into the bed and pulled the covers over my head.

Mary Ann started laughing uncontrollably and Helly joined in. I pulled the covers off my head and looked at them in turn. Both of them were sporting the proverbial shit-eating grin.

"Oh my GOD, did you see the look on his face?" Mary Ann said, howling. "It's too much! You are SUCH an easy mark." She threw off the covers and stood up. She was wearing shorts and a halter top. She stood and slipped into a pair of sandals, walked over to my dresser and started combing her hair in the mirror.

"He's certainly not very complex," Helly mumbled around a mouthful of toothpaste. "Pretty simple, really. Kind of cute, though."

"I suppose," Mary Ann said, turning to blow me a kiss. "Anyway, now that the charade is done, I've gotta go open the store. Get yourself cleaned up there, stallion, and come join me." She walked upstairs, laughing to herself.

"So, nothing happened?" I asked Helly as she returned from spitting out toothpaste and rinsing her brush. She had taken off her towel turban and was drying her hair with it.

"Jeez Louise, you catch on quick," she said, sticking out her tongue at me and crossing her eyes. "Me Daniel. Me smart. Me make plans and speeches and fight bad guys. Mur-mur-mur." She said all of that last part in a mocking voice. "But, no. Really. We raided an all-night burger joint, drank a few beers, and went our separate ways with hugs and smooches. Ari and I slept in the room next door. Thorry, thailor."

"Damn, you're mean first thing in the morning," I said, laughing. "And the two of you are fucking evil."

"Maybe just a little," she said, grinning. "But you love us anyway."

"I do," I said, smiling. "I really, really do."

"Good," she said, turning to walk back into the bathroom, wiggling her behind at me as she went. "Because, well ... a bet's a bet."

I sighed heavily.

"No way that you're gonna let me out of that one?" I asked.

"Are you telling me you're a welcher?" her voice rang out from the other room. "I always heard Daniel Davidson was a man of his word! 'Blah blah! My word is bond! I have a code! My word is something I will go to extreme lengths not to break! Hur dur durr!'"

"FINE, goddamnit," I said, groaning. "I said that. I did. FUCK. Ok. I'll do it. I mean you. Although ..."

"Yes?" she peeked out from the bathroom.

"I don't suppose I could interest you in a nap instead?" I said, grinning.

"Huh. Now that you mention it, I am still a little tired," she yawned theatrically, waving her hand over her mouth.

"Right? I'd love nothing more than to curl up with you and just SLEEP," I said, stretching. "Still SO worn out from the past week or so. And there's nothing better than napping with a good friend."

"A REALLY good friend," she agreed. "That is REALLY good at napping. Like fucking NEXT level good."

"Totally!" I laughed. "When two people that are really good at sleeping, you know, they're all wrapped around each other and stuff, just snoozing away ... I mean, there's nothing better."

"So true!" Helly laughed, walking toward me. "Goddamnit, I am going to nap with you SO HARD."

"SO FUCKING HARD," I agreed.

"I mean, I'm going to nap with you so vigorously that you're going to wake up begging for mercy," she continued, laughing. "You're gonna be like: 'Who the hell IS this tiny woman and how did she learn to sleep so well? Is she a professional sleeper or just a gifted amateur? I have NEVER napped so hard or so long or so thoroughly or to such a degree of satisfaction with anyone in my life.' You'll forget all those other naps and be begging me to nap with you again. You are going to be well rested AS FUCK."

"Wow," I said.

"Wow," she agreed.

"I'm sold," I said. "Let's get some fucking *sleep*."

Helly leaped at me, hugging me and giggling like a madwoman, burying me in her giant mane of flaxen hair.

And then, we napped.

That's it. We just slept. I swear. 100% true story. I don't know what you were expecting. We just curled up and went to sleep, two great friends, totally comfortable with each other, wrapped around each other in total companionable comfort, smiling and snoozing the day away. Totally innocent and wholesome. Like two rabbits in a burrow, snuggled together for warmth. There was absolutely no hot yoga. No coitus. No mating, no copulation, no fornication, no intercourse, no making love, no breeding, no rutting, no hanky panky, no gettin' down to bidness, no doing it, no getting to know one another in the biblical sense, and absolutely no sexual relations whatsoever. There certainly wasn't crazed, passionate, animalistic, gymnastic sport-fucking between besties-with-benefits that was so loud and raucous and destructive to property that a certain lovely elf friend of the couple that was trying to sleep in resorted to banging on the wall with the hilt of her sword and yelling at us to be quiet 'for Josh's sake'. That never fucking happened. Nope. I mean, believe what you want. It's up to you. We just slept. Let the sandman drag us to sleepy-time. Just napped. A little nappy-nap.

And, honestly, I'm kind of offended you think otherwise … you fucking perverts.

The Fucking End.

(For now.)

AFTERWORD

Daniel Davidson and his irreverent companions will return in *Happy Jack and the Wolves of New London.*

ACKNOWLEDGEMENT

A huge thanks to my alpha readers for their time and patience in wading through my manuscript and for their thoughtful notes and suggestions.

A giant pile of thanks to the wonderful teachers I have had in my lifetime - at every level from elementary to grad school - many of whom kindled in me an insatiable love of reading, writing, language, music and laughter. And very few of whom actively tried to crush my (often ebullient and sometimes disruptive) spirit.

Thanks to the Blountsville Public Library and former librarian Sue Cook for helping raise me and for not kicking me out when I spent entire days in the stacks reading weird fiction, horror, fantasy (and tons of books about shipwrecks) at a shockingly young age.

So much gratitude to the Fantasy Flight Book Club and Das Stahl Bierhaus for giving me a monthly place to nerd out over sci-fi and fantasy as an adult ... always surrounded by laughter and fellowship.

Likewise, thanks (and apologies) to the writers and creators who have inspired me throughout my lifetime, including but not limited to: J.K. Rowling, Stephen King, Richard Matheson, Christopher Moore, H.P. Lovecraft, Eric Powell, Jason Aaron,

Kurt Vonnegut Jr., Dashiell Hammett, Raymond Chandler, George Lucas, Steven Spielberg, Clive Barker, Mary Shelley, John Steakley, Bram Stoker, Arthur Conan Doyle, Edgar Allan Poe, Richard K. Morgan, William Gibson, J.R.R. Tolkien, Jonathan Maberry, Shirley Jackson, Alfred Hitchcock, George R.R. Martin, Neil Gaiman, Kim Harrison, Brandon Sanderson, Patrick Rothfuss, Jim Butcher, John Scalzi, Robert Heinlein, Robert E. Howard and hundreds more. There's a little bit of all of you in these stories and characters. I'm sorry.

Eternal gratitude to Fred McFeely Rogers and all of the other avatars of the Light who spend their lives leading by example and teaching kindness, love and acceptance above all things.

And, last but certainly not least, the deepest of thanks to my mother, Patricia Ann "Patsy" Russell. She made me who I am, so you can blame her for this. All joking aside, she taught me the true meaning of love from the moment I was born, and I am so very proud to be her son.

ABOUT THE AUTHOR

Rich Partain

Rich is currently a multimedia developer by trade, but he has also been a newspaper reporter and editor, a cop, a security guard, a sales manager for two craft breweries, a web and graphic designer, a bar manager, a grant writer and an IT professional. He is also the lead vocalist and drummer of a stoner metal band. Rich lives in Madison, AL, with his beloved wife, his two boys and one very needy but sweet-natured dog.

Made in the USA
Columbia, SC
26 June 2025

59682348R00224